Y0-BZC-426

THE LION AT BAY

Robert Low has been a journalist and writer since the age of seventeen in places as diverse as Vietnam, Sarajevo, Romania and Kosovo until common sense and the concerns of his wife and daughter prevailed.

To satisfy his craving for action, he took up re-enactment, joining The Vikings. He now spends his summers fighting furiously in helmet and mail in shieldwalls all over Britain and winters training hard. He lives in Largs, Scotland.

www.robert-low.com

Also by Robert Low

THE OATHSWORN SERIES
The Whale Road
The Wolf Sea
The White Raven
The Prow Beast

THE KINGDOM SERIES
The Lion Wakes

ROBERT LOW

The Lion at Bay

HarperCollins*Publishers*

HarperCollins*Publishers*
77–85 Fulham Palace Road,
Hammersmith, London W6 8JB

www.harpercollins.co.uk

Published by HarperCollins*Publishers* 2012
1

Copyright © Robert Low 2012

Map © John Gilkes

Robert Low asserts the moral right to
be identified as the author of this work

A catalogue record for this book
is available from the British Library

ISBN 978 0 00 743358 2

Set in Sabon by Palimpsest Book Production Limited,
Falkirk, Stirlingshire

Printed and bound in Great Britain by
Clays Ltd, St Ives plc

This novel is entirely a work of fiction.
The names, characters and incidents portrayed in it,
while in some cases based on historical figures, are
the work of the author's imagination.

All rights reserved. No part of this publication may be
reproduced, stored in a retrieval system, or transmitted,
in any form or by any means, electronic, mechanical,
photocopying, recording or otherwise, without the prior
written permission of the publishers.

MIX
Paper from
responsible sources
FSC
www.fsc.org   **FSC™ C007454**

FSC™ is a non-profit international organisation established to promote
the responsible management of the world's forests. Products carrying the
FSC label are independently certified to assure consumers that they come
from forests that are managed to meet the social, economic and
ecological needs of present and future generations,
and other controlled sources.

Find out more about HarperCollins and the environment at
www.harpercollins.co.uk/green

...UNTAINS ...LIBRARY

23. 7. 12   27-14

5216774060 4

LOW

To Monique and Simon, who gave me the best part of
Scotland – Lewis and Harris

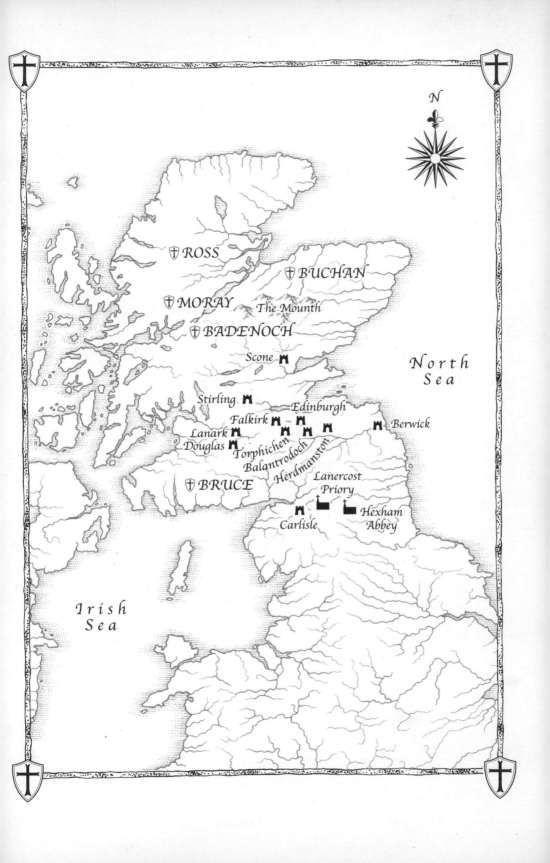

Being a chronicle of the Kingdom in the Years of Trouble, written at Greyfriars Priory on the octave of Septuagisma, in the year of Our Lord one thousand three hundred and twenty-nine, 23rd year of the reign of King Robert I, God save and keep him.

In the year of Our Lord one thousand two hundred and ninety-nine, our goodly king, then simply Sir Robert, Earl of Carrick, found he could no longer work together with his enemy and fellow Guardian of Scotland, Red John Comyn, Lord of Badenoch, who sought many and divers ways to undermine the good of the Kingdom.

Wherefore Sir Robert resigned, in order that Bishop Lamberton of St Andrews could become Guardian in his stead, hoping that, if Red John of Badenoch could find no favour in the Earl of Carrick, then surely he would not work against God. Meanwhile, Sir William Wallace, discredited after his failure to win at Falkirk, stayed in France, both for his safety and to seek the aid of King Philip IV for the good of the Kingdom.

The Kingdom was at war with itself and even with God – the Order of Poor Knights had incited the wrath of kings and popes by its pride and arrogance, so that they contrived

1

in bringing it to heel. The Pope wished to join it with that other Holy Order, the Knights Hospitaller. The king of France wished, through his greed and perfidy, to bring it down entire and sent out agents to conspire to that end.

At this same moment, Edward was persuaded to release the imprisoned John Balliol, the King in whose name Scotland still resisted, into the custody of the Pope. The Comyn and Balliol, with Wallace in France, seemed set to force King Edward of England to agree to return John Balliol to the throne.

It was this, the imminent return of a king already deposed, unsuited to a throne he did not want and unwelcomed by much of the community he had abandoned, which spurred Sir Robert to seek his own peace with Longshanks, sure that the community of the Kingdom had set foot on the wrong path. Others were of a similar mind – though some, scurrilous and cruel, claimed that good Sir Robert had sold himself for Longshanks' promise of the crown of Scotland and the hand of Elizabeth de Burgh, daughter of the powerful Red Earl of Ulster.

For all that, the deed was done and Sir Robert, new husband and newly returned to the king's peace, rode with King Edward the Plantagenet, the greying pard who had savaged Scotland summer after summer until the very earth groaned.

In the year of Our Gracious Lord thirteen hundred and four, the Kingdom was weary of war, the lords who fought it and the ruin they brought because of it. It seemed that even Longshanks grew tired of the ritual though he was determined to stamp his vengeful foot on the neck of the Kingdom, once and for all.

Uneasily, Sir Robert was forced to watch the last remnants of Scottish resistance crumble, as most of the nobility of Scotland scrambled to make their peace with Longshanks. Then, as the Kingdom's enemies gathered to witness the fall of Stirling, last bastion of the Scottish defence, God raised both His Hands and changed the world.

The first Hand hovered over the Lord of Annandale and

Robert Bruce's goodly father, who fell ill unto death. When God decided to take him into His Grace, it would invest the son not only with the lands and titles of all the Bruce holdings, but the claim to the Kingdom's crown. Sir Robert, aware of this sad and momentous event, was already laying the plans to bring about his kingship even as the last echoes of rebellion seemed to be fading.

The second of God's Hands raised The Wallace out of France and back to Scotland, so that, just as it seemed King Edward had crushed all before him, one talon of the lion remained unsheathed.

And was as much sharpened against Sir Robert Bruce as any English.

CHAPTER ONE

The moors of Happrew, near Peebles
Sunday of Candelmas, the Feast of the Purification of the
Virgin, February, 1304

Cold rain and Black John.

Not the recipe for a happy war at the best of times, Sir Hal
thought, but if you add to that the grim cliff of Bruce's face
these days, the endless march through February wet and the
wreck and ruin and smoulder they passed through, then the
gruel of it was all henbane and aloes.

The riders were dripping and miserable as old mud, the
horses standing with their heads down, hipshot in a sea of
tawny bracken and the clawed black roots of heather and
furze; only the moss splashed a dazzle of green into the mirr.

They were quiet, too, Hal saw. The knights and *serjeants*
were all concentrated concern over the well-being of their
expensive coddled wrapped and riderless warhorses. Wct and
sullen squires were set to checking hocks and hooves which
had already been inspected a dozen times. The rounceys the
owners actually rode were splattered with mud and weary, but
they were of no account next to the *destrier*, any one of which
could be sold for the price of a good manor in Lothian.

The Scots sat their shaggy, mud-raggled ponies uneasily, talking so softly that the suck of feathered garron hooves pulling from the soft ground, the clink and chink and tinkle of harness and blade sounded loud against their hush. Hal knew why they hunched and spoke in whispers and it had nothing to do with rain or the suspected presence of enemy.

This was Sheean Stank, which no-one cared for, a sudden knoll in a vast expanse of sucking bog and carse where the sheean folk – the *sidhean* – lived. No more than a score of feet higher than the land around, it seemed a great hill in the flat and everyone knew that this was where a man could be lifted out of this world and into the next, where the Faerie would keep him for what seemed a day, then release him, no older, into a world aged sixty or a hundred years.

Black John Segrave did not care for Faerie much. Cold iron, he had heard, did for those ungodly imps same as it did for Scotch rebels and it was probable that they were one and the same in a land whose features revealed the nature of it and the folk who lived in it – Foulbogskye, Slitrig, Wolf Rig, Bloody Bush. And Sheean Stank.

He glanced across at Bruce, Earl of Carrick and heir to Annandale, and tried to keep his face equable, for this was the new favourite of Longshanks, and the score of filthy Scotchmen surrounding him were supposedly experts in scouting this sort of terrain. Supposedly loyal to King Edward, too, though Segrave was beginning to doubt both claims – yet his king had tied them together with the one purpose, to rout out the last of the brigand rebels and bring their leaders to the leash. Particularly Wallace.

Yet he was being led by Scotch who could have been rebels themselves from their dress and manner. They were led by Sir Henry Sientcler of Herdmanston, whom everyone called Hal, even his own ragged-arsed scum of a *mesnie*, and captained by a grizzled hog of a man called Sim Craw, whom Segrave would have hanged at another time just for the insolence in him.

Segrave did not trust any of them and wished that Sir Robert Clifford's men had not become separated from him; there was a sudden sharp needle of fear at the last time he had split up a command, at Roslin the previous year. There had been ruin and death in it then – and a Sientcler involved, too, he recalled uneasily, another one of that arrogant breed, this time from Roslin itself; then, these two Sientclers had been enemies and now they were, ostensibly, friends.

He did not trust any of the Scots, even the most English of them – like the Earl of Carrick.

'What think you, my lord?' he demanded, his voice rheumed with damp. 'Is the enemy hereabouts? Is it Wallace?'

'So our intelligencers reported,' Bruce replied easily and Hal saw the smile force itself across the heavy face. There was a beard, black and close-cropped in a strange way that included the droop of a moustache and a nap on the chin beneath, leaving the cheeks bare. Hal knew this was because no hair would grow on Bruce's right cheek, so he had been forced to tailor his chin hair to suit, though it made him look, as Sim Craw had muttered, 'like a wee Frenchie bachle o' a music' maister.'

A curlew piped somewhere and then a horseman burst over the hill and down the slope in a flat-out, belly-to-the ground gallop that brought heads up.

It was Dog Boy on the blowing garron, gasping harder than his horse, his mouth working, silent as a fresh-caught fish, black fuzz of beard dripping and the dags of his hair plastered to his cheeks. No iron hat could keep that thatch in, Hal thought with a wry smile to himself; he marvelled at what the years had made of the skelf-thin kennel lad he had found at Douglas – when was it? The eve of Wallace's rebellion. Christ's Wounds – eight years ago . . .

'Take a breath,' Sim advised Dog Boy smoothly, 'afore ye try to speak.'

'Though it would be good to learn what has sent you to us

at the gallop,' Segrave added, 'before they come down on us.'

Hal saw Bruce's eyes flicker.

'No Roslin Glen here, my lord,' Bruce said, viciously gentle and Segrave jerked as if stung.

It was almost a year to the day, Hal was reminded since Segrave made such a slorach of a raid similar to this that the English forces had been scattered in a few hours by Red John Comyn, Sir Simon Fraser and Hal's Roslin kin and namesake, Sir Henry Sientcler.

Who had all then gone on to Herdmanston and burned it out. Hal grew sullen as old embers at the memory. Kin or not, the Sientclers of Roslin had been in the Scots camp then and Hal Sientcler of Herdmanston was in the Bruce camp. And Bruce was English. Again.

The price for following the Bruce was high – though not for Bruce himself, who had gained the daughter of the powerful Earl of Ulster as wife, new lands and the new favour of an old king who was wallowing in the winter of his years and had sired, so far, two wee bairns by his girlish French queen.

Now, of course, the Sientclers of Roslin had also bowed the knee, kissed the King's foot and received back their own lands by a gracious Edward trying some velvet on the iron gauntlet.

Hal saw Segrave unconsciously touch his side, where three ribs had been broken when he was tumbled from his horse into the grin of Sir Simon Fraser and the other Scots lords, shredding Segrave dignity as well as likely bankrupting his purse for a ransom.

Worse than that was the moment when Fraser had argued for killing all the prisoners, fat ransoms or not. Fraser had been persuaded otherwise, but the screaming, belly-loosening fear of that lived with Segrave still.

Now Sir Simon Fraser was the last hold-out of the Scots lords who had been at Roslin Glen that day and the closer Segrave got to him, the closer he was to ridding himself of the stain of it. Bruce, however seemed determined to keep the memory of it alive and Segrave's scowls grew blacker than his oil-boiled maille.

'What have you seen?' he spat, and Dog Boy, rain in his greasy new beard and streaking the filth on his face, finally managed to blurt out:

'Weemin, my lord. Ower yon hill.'

There was silence and the men uncovering their great cosseted warhorses paused, wondering if it would be necessary. The grimy Scots looked on wordlessly, gripping the hafts of their Jeddart staffs, those lance-long weapons which combined spear, cutting edge and hook.

'Women?' Segrave repeated, bewildered.

'How many, Dog Boy?' Hal asked, seeing the slow blink of Segrave's eyes counting down to explosive release.

'A shilling's worth,' the boy replied, his breathing regular and then, with all the worldly experience of his bare score of years, added: 'Fair quines too, in fine dresses.'

'What in the name of God are a dozen women doing out here?' Segrave snapped.

There came a low murmur from the men behind Bruce. The Earl smiled, bright and mild.

'My lads mention Faerie, my lord,' he explained. 'Perhaps these are they. Pechs. Bogles. The Silent Moving Folk. Sheean.'

At each word, the men behind Hal shifted and made warding signs, some with the cross, others with older symbols they tried to make quick and hidden.

'Christ be praised,' growled Sim.

'For ever and ever,' men muttered automatically. Hal sighed; he knew Bruce was provoking Segrave, but forgetting the effect it had on men who believed. Only Dog Boy had dared ride to the top of the hill in the first place and Hal was proud of the courage that had taken. More of it was needed now.

'Mair like a country event,' he said into the locked stare of Bruce and Segrave and, at last, had the latter turn his wet eyes on him.

9

'Country event?'

'Mayhaps a tait o' virgins,' Sim flung in cheerfully. 'Getting purified.'

The Dog Boy, still trying to control the trembling in his thighs at what he had done, was sure they were powrie women, for they were strange in their cavorting and one was almost certainly a bogle by the height and the raucous shouts. Still, he couldn't be entirely certain and did not want to appear like a fool in front of Lord Hal.

'They were dancin',' he ventured and wilted as all eyes clawed his face. 'In a ring.'

The thrilling horror of it spilled on them like bad honey, sweet and rotted. Women dancing by themselves would bring the wrath of the Church; only sinners, pagans and the De'il's own did such a thing. Dancing in a secret circle was proof of enough witchery to get all the women burned.

'Sheean,' growled Bangtail Hob from over Hal's shoulder and the men growled their fearful agreement.

'Christ be praised,' repeated Sim, but the muttered response was lost when a man shouted out from the pack behind Segrave, 'Faerie? Silent Folk? If you are afeared, my Scotch lords, then leave it to good, enlightened Christian Englishmen.'

Faces turned to stare at Sir Robert Malenfaunt, swarthy face darkened with rage and a scornful twist to his lips. Bruce merely smiled lightly, which was enough to crank Malenfaunt's rage up a notch; here were all the men who had once tricked him over the Countess Isabel of Buchan's ransom and, even if it had cost him nothing, Malenfaunt's pride was worth any price.

Hal only remembered Isabel, who had been the prisoner ransomed from Malenfaunt into his arms. Just weeks later, Falkirk's slaughter had ripped everything to shreds and forced her back to her husband. Hal had not seen her since and the dull ache of it was like cold iron in the heart of him.

Segrave regarded Malenfaunt with distaste, for he had

10

heard things about the Berwick knight that were unsavoury. Yet he was forced to agree with the man's sentiment here and was aware that others were already settling themselves into the high-cantled saddles of their powerful horses, placing domed bucket helms over their heads, taking lance and shield from hurrying squires.

He wanted to wait for Clifford, yet he wondered if the women were whores for the rebels; if so, they would have information . . .

'Fetch me some Faerie virgins,' Segrave said in French to Malenfaunt, 'and we will purify them here.'

'My lord,' Hal began warningly and then stopped as, with a whoop and a roar, the warhorses surged forward in a great spray of mud. Someone yelled '*til-est-hault*' as if it were a hunt.

But Segrave saw, for a fleeting moment, the spark of Hal's defiant anger from a face beaten to leather by wind and weather, fretted with white lines at the corners of his eyes. Segrave cocked one insouciant challenge of an eyebrow at the flare and saw the storm-grey eyes turn to flint-blue – 'Now we will see,' Segrave declared, throwing up one hand to ward off the gouts kicked up by the disappearing horsemen.

Then Bruce's voice cut through the tension.

'There's one of your Faerie women, my lord.'

They turned in time to see a fleeting swirl of disappearing skirts.

'I would not want that yin, my lord,' Sim Craw drawled and Segrave turned his wither on the white-streaked black beard and the broad, black-browed face it swamped. Unmoved, Sim nursed a powerful crossbow, wrapped against the rain, close to his great slab of body. 'I like my weemin with their chins shaved,' he noted casually.

There was a moment as the realization seeped in to Segrave, then he roared at a startled squire, 'Bring them back. Bring them back – God curse it . . .'

He turned to Bruce, but too late. He had missed that

man's silent flick of signal; all he found was the back of the chevronned jupon, trailing a tippet of riders behind him away to the west.

Treachery. The word sprang at Segrave and he felt anger and fear in equal measure. A trap, by God, with Clifford a good gallop behind and Bruce running away and leaving him with yet another Scotch battle against odds. The thought settled something slimed and cold in his belly and he turned to survey his last score of men as the first hundred breasted the ridge and vanished.

Malenfaunt had spotted the women at once, tucking up their skirts and running for the shelter of the woods beyond them like scattering ducks. He gave a whoop, peeled off the constricting great helm and flung it away, along with the lance to free up one hand, then set his horse flying at the runner, leaning sideways a little in the saddle to make it easier to reach out and grab.

Those immediately behind checked a little, mainly because his powerful warhorse kicked up a spray of muddy gobbets, while to right and left lances and helms went bouncing, carelessly dangerous, as the knights followed Sir Robert Malenfaunt's example and spurred on.

They saw Malenfaunt lean out as he slowed to a canter so as to better judge the snatch at the fleeing woman's wimpled head. They saw the woman turn, the wimple and barbette flying away to free a wild tangle of infested hair, the face a bearded snarl; Malenfaunt had time to realize the enormous horror of it before the man dropped to a crouch, brought round the two-handed axe he held hidden in his skirts and scythed out the legs of the *destrier*.

It was the saving of Malenfaunt. At the same time as he was reeling through the air in a tumble of moss and trees and sky, the edge of the wood spat a sleet of arrows from two points. Between them, moving ragged and relentless, came a clot of spearmen; the shrieking falsities in women's dresses raced to join them, their lure complete.

Segrave, down at the foot of the small hill, heard the whoops turn to shrieks, almost felt the blows that rang like bells on the shields of the unseen knights, audible even at this distance and through the muffle of the great iron bucket of his helm. He urged the huge warhorse forward, surging up the sodden slope, the handful of men behind him.

Ruin was beyond and Segrave saw it in a single glance when he breasted the rise. Horses were down, screaming and kicking, others cantering in aimless circles, the riders struggling to get up. Arrows sprouted from tussock and body, and a dark, bristling hedge of spearpoints – three hundred men in it if there was one – approaching. All the men who had ridden off with Malenfaunt were unhorsed, crawling like sheep, with horses scattering to every part, or kicking and dying.

He saw, too, the figure in black with surcoat and shield, the silver *cinquefoiles* bright as stars and his heart thundered up into his head in a howl of triumph – Fraser, who had all but ruined him in Roslin Glen. By God, Segrave swore, he will not do it again.

A flurry of arrows took the man next to him out of the saddle and set the great Frisian warhorse bolting, screaming from the pain of another two shafts in its chest, before it crashed to its knees and finally ploughed its proud Roman nose into a furrow of bog, kicking and snorting blood.

The men with him balked at charging a hedge of points backed by three-score of Selkirk archers, but Segrave had fire and rage shrieking in his head and was not about to stop.

Hal saw Segrave arrive, saw him charge, then Bruce, laughing out of his broad face with its music-master beard, pointed to the backs of the archers, took off his great helm and dropped it, then spurred his own warhorse forward.

He had led them in a perfect outflank and it was not a fight but a flat-out *chasse*. The archers heard the thunder of hooves just soon enough to let them turn their heads from the business of killing English to see a score or more of howling Scots on fast-moving little garrons come at their back.

Hal went through the wild scatter of them, trying to rein in the plunging horse and hack at a target, but he was sure he had hit no-one – the mount was no helpful *destrier*. He saw Bangtail Hob and others chasing running figures, circling in mad, short-legged gallops, for they were more used to fighting on foot than on horse, and he bawled at them, his voice deafening inside the full helm.

He pulled it up and off, pointed and flailed and roared until they all got the idea and started kicking their horses towards the clot of spearmen, who had started, frantically, to form a ring.

Too late, Hal thought, fighting the garron to a standstill, desperately trying to loop the helm into his belt – Segrave's knot of riders, trailing up in ones and twos, smacked into it, picking spots between spears, riding the men into the muddy grass; the spearmen suddenly seemed to vomit running men, like the black yolk of a rotten egg.

Blades clanged, bringing Hal's head round. He saw Bruce, perfect and poised on the powerful *destrier*, which baited under his firm rein, huge feet ploughing earth on the spot. Confronting Bruce, Hal saw, with a lurch that took his heart into his mouth, a familiar figure.

The autumn bracken hair was dulled and iron-streaked, the beard wild, untamed as it had been in the days when Hal had first seen him, before he'd had it neatly trimmed as befitted Scotland's sole Guardian. Yet he stood tall – Christ, he was even taller than Hal remembered – and the hand-and-a-half was twirled easy and light in one hand, the other holding a scarred shield with the memory of his heraldry on it, a white lion rampant on red.

Wallace took a step, feinted and struck, then sprang back. Bruce, light and easy as Wallace himself, parried and the blades rang; the warhorse, arch-necked, snorted and half-reared, wanting to strike out and held in by its rider.

14

'Get you gone, Will,' Bruce said coldly. 'Get back to France, if you are wise, but get you gone. The war is all but over and you are finished. Mark me'

'My wee lord of Carrick,' Wallace acknowledged lightly, a grin splitting his beard. 'Get ye to Hell, Englishman. And if ye care to step aff yon big beast ye ride, I will mark ye, certes.'

Bruce shook his head, almost wearily; someone called out and Hal saw the scuttling shape of a figure he knew well, a Wallace man – the loyal Fergus, his black boiled-leather carapace scarred and stained. Beetle, they called him and it was apt.

With Fergus and his broad-axe guarding his back, Wallace backed warily off. He was expecting Bruce to press, the surprise clear in his face when that did not happen. Hal saw Bangtail Hob and Ill-Made Jock circle, caught their eye and brought them to a halt; if this was to end in a fight, then it was Bruce's own, though he felt sick at the thought of it, sicker still at the idea of having ridden down men he might once have stood shoulder-to-shoulder with. This was what we are brought down to, he thought bitterly, to where even the best of us can only find it in their hearts to battle one another.

'Get you to France, Will,' Bruce repeated softly. 'If you remain, you are finished.'

'If I remain,' Wallace said in good French, sliding further into the dripping trees, 'you cannot get started.'

Then, like a wraith, he was gone. Hal heard Segrave calling out to the newly-arrived Clifford and bellowing curses because, somewhere in the trees and confusion, both Wallace and Sir Simon Fraser had vanished.

Hal turned to where Bruce, his face a slab of wet rock, broke his stare from the hole Wallace had left in the air and settled it bleakly on Hal.

'Not a word,' he said and turned away, leaving Hal wondering if he spoke of personal censure or admitting to Segrave that he had let Wallace go. Sim Craw came up in time to hear this and sniffed, then blew rain and snot from the side of his nose, making his own mind up.

'Good advice,' he declared, 'for if Black John hears that we had Will Wallace an' let him loup away like a running hound . . .'

He did not need to finish. The rain lisped down as the sun came out and curlews peeped as if horror and blood and dying had not visited the Sheean Stank.

'Faerie,' growled Dog Boy to Bangtail, half-ashamed as he stared at the dead in women's dresses.

Cambuskenneth Abbey, Stirling
Feast of St Ternan, confessor of the Picts, June, 1304.

'You missed your chance there, my lord earl.'

Bruce did not turn his head, merely flicked his eyes at the broad grinning face of Bishop Wishart, the shadows and planes of it made grotesque by the flickering tallow lights.

'There is one bishop too many in this game,' he growled, which made Wishart chuckle fruitily and Hal, frowning with concentration, realize his inadequacy with chess. He was sure he had blundered, surer still that Bruce had missed an *en passant*; had he done it by accident – the rule was new and not much used – or was it some cunning ploy to lure him into even worse trouble?

'Aye, well,' came the blade-rasp voice of Kirkpatrick, looming from the shadows. 'Here is yet another.'

A figure in simple brown robes and tonsure swept past him into the light, swift enough to cause the flames to flicker and set shadows dancing madly. He was, Hal saw, astoundingly young to be a senior prelate, his round face smooth and bland, yet his eyes black and shrewd, while the beginnings of a paunch were belied by slim, white, long-fingered hands, one of which he extended.

'Christ be praised,' the prelate said portentously.

'For ever and ever.'

Bruce rose, kissed the fingers with dutiful deference, then scowled.

'At last,' he said sullenly. 'We have been waiting, my lord bishop and my time is limited away from the King's side.'

'How is the good king of England?' Lamberton demanded cheerfully.

'Sickeningly well,' Bruce replied with a wry twist of grin. 'He sits at Stirling and plays with his great toys, while his wife and her women look on through an *oriole* he has made in their quarters. It is a great sport, it seems, for the ladies to watch huge stones being hurled at the walls while they stitch. His two new babes gurgle with delight.'

'I hear he has several great engines,' Lamberton declared, accepting wine from Wishart's hand and settling himself with a satisfied sigh. 'One called Segrave, I believe, which fires great heavy balls – now there is apt for you. I know this because of all the complaints I have had from wee abbots about the lead stripped from their roofs to make them.'

'You had better pray for fine weather, else we will all be dripping,' 'Bruce replied sourly. 'Cambuskenneth has also lost all the roofing, save from over the altar, so that God at least will not be offended. And Edward Plantagenet now has twelve war engines. One of them is my own, sent from Lochmaben – minus the throwing arm, mark you, which mysteriously took a wrong turn and will arrive too late to be of use.'

'He has Greek Fire, too, I hear,' Wishart added, with a disapproving shake of his head, 'and weapons that burst with the Hellish taint of brimstone.'

There was silence for a moment and Hal did not know what the others were thinking, but his mind was on the stunning sight and sound of those very weapons, great gouts of flame and blasts that hurled earth and stones into the air, fire that

17

ran like water and could not be quenched. Yet the walls of Stirling, pocked and scorched, still held.

'Aye, well,' Lamberton declared suddenly, rubbing his hands as if presenting them to a fire. 'Be of cheer – Stirling holds out yet, when all else has given in. Young Oliphant has done well there.'

'Young Oliphant holds out because Longshanks refused to accept his capitulation,' Bruce replied flatly. 'He offered it a week since. The King wants to see his newest engine in action, the great Warwolf. Fifty folk it takes to handle it and Edward is determined to have it fling stones at Oliphant's head before that man is allowed to come out.'

There was silence, broken only by the soft, slippering sound of hesitant feet. Then Lamberton sighed.

'Then all are finally given in,' he said. 'Save Wallace.'

Bruce shot the bishop a hard look; Lamberton owed his appointment to Wallace when he was Guardian and needing all the *gentilhomme* allies he could garner; Bruce wondered how deep the bishop's obligement went.

Other diehards, finally persuaded to give in, had also been initially excluded from Edward's conditions for submission. Yet even they had been forgiven in the end, by a Longshanks who had learned a little from all the previous attempts and was trying the kidskin glove as well as the maille mitten.

All forgiven – all but Wallace.

'That is one problem we are here to discuss,' Bruce began, then broke off as a new figure shuffled painfully into the light. Bent, with a face like a ravaged hawk and iron-grey hair straggling round his ears from under a conical felted hat, the man nodded and muttered thanks to Kirkpatrick as he was helped into a chair, then refused wine with a wave of one weary hand.

'John Duns,' Bishop Wishart announced and the man managed a smile out of a yellow face. Bruce knew the priest by reputation – a man with a mind like a steel trap – but was shocked by his appearance. The cleric was scarce forty.

'The new lord of Annandale,' said Duns, his voice wisped as silk, but his eyes steady on Bruce's own. 'Which title also brings you the claim to the throne of Scotland. Which brings you here.'

'I am here because the realm needs it,' Bruce replied. 'It needs a king.'

'Just so,' Wishart said smoothly, before anyone else could speak. 'Let us first offer prayers to God that each man here preserves the tone of this meeting, as it were, from the ears of those who do us harm. On pain of endless tortures in Hell – not to mention on earth.'

'And an agreed fine,' Lamberton added, just as smoothly, 'that would cripple a nation never mind a wee prelate in it. Was that necessary?'

'It was – but let us pray to Saint Giles,' Wishart responded with some steel, 'patron saint of cripples everywhere, that such a thing will never come to pass.'

The soft murmur of the bishops, moth-wings of holiness, brought the face of his father flickering across Bruce's mind. Prayers would still be being murmured for him, Bruce thought, circling round Holm Abbey like trapped birds. He tried to remember the old man in a better light than the one which usually lit his memory.

Saint-hagged, heavy-witted old man was what he recalled. Burned books and a splintered lute was what he recalled. Beatings, was what he recalled, for paying 'too much mind to that auld reprobate's teachings'.

The auld reprobate had been his grandfather, who had dinned into him the Bruce claims to kingship and pointedly scorned, as he did so, his own son's inadequacy in that regard. With some justice, Bruce thought to himself – grandda worked tirelessly to the end to further the kingship cause of the Bruces – God blind me, was he not called The Competitor for it – and my father, apart from one timid plea to Longshanks, did little.

Yet when he heard there was a last breathed message from

19

his father, brought by Kirkpatrick, for a moment Bruce's heart leaped at the promise of a final affection, for all the marring of their relationship by mutual stubbornness and temper. Then hope faltered, stumbled and fell for the last time.

Not before Longshanks is dead.

Simple and stark, his final advice, with all the love in it the elder Bruce was capable of bestowing. That was the legacy of the Bruces; that and the Curse of Malachy, Bruce added silently, as his fingertips brushed against the hairless cheek.

Hal saw the unconscious gesture and knew at once what Bruce was thinking.

So did Kirkpatrick and he and Hal exchanged a brief glance while the candles flickered, each man knowing just enough of the tale – something about a previous Annandale Bruce thwarting Malachy the holy man by promising to release a condemned felon and then hanging him in secret. The said priest was angered and cursed the Bruces, a curse made more powerful still when Malachy eventually became a saint.

It had hagged Bruce's father, who had dedicated a deal of Annandale rents to endowing the saint's last resting place at Clairveaux with perpetual candles and masses in an attempt to ease the burden of it.

Bruce fought against the fear of it more often than he would allow – Kirkpatrick knew it well enough never to admit that the man who had breathed his last fetid breath on to this Bruce's cheek years before had been named Malachy.

Kirkpatrick. Bland as gruel, with a face that could settle to any shape save pretty and was more than servant, less than friend to the Bruce. A dagger of a man and a ferret for Bruce, sent down the darkest holes to rout out the truths hidden there – especially about the stone-carver. Everyone else here thought he had been called Manon, a dying man Bruce was sure knew a secret and was taking it to the grave, so that he had bent close to him in the hope of hearing his last words. The carver had vomited out blood – and the last administered Host, a white wafer floating like a boat in a flood into the Bruce face.

Afterwards, Bruce's right cheek had flared with red pustules, but soon they had faded to dots of white – and now no beard would grow on it; Bruce already thought this little flaw a part of the curse – to know the full of it, Kirkpatrick thought, might cause no end of turmoil in the man's mind.

As if he had heard, Bruce's eyes flickered and he dropped his hand, dragged back to the dark room and the eldritch dancing shadows.

'I can count on your lordships' support,' he said, cutting into Wishart's final amen. 'I am sure of Atholl and Lennox and a great part of the lesser lords – Hay of Borthwick, Neil Campbell of Lochawe for some of the names.'

'You are assured of the bishoprics of St Andrews, Glasgow, Dunkeld and Scone,' Wishart declared with some pride and looked pointedly at Lamberton, who stroked his hairless chin and smiled.

'Moray, perhaps,' he said. 'Brechin more certainly. I have yet to sound out the abbot of Inchcolm, but I understand he esteems you well, my lord earl.'

'You may have the Abbot of Arbroath,' John Duns declared, 'provided he is my clerk, Bernard of Kilwinning. A good man, who knows all my thoughts and deserves such an appointment – Longshanks threw him out of Kilwinning Abbey for his loyalty to the Kingdom's cause.'

'You cannot crown pawns in this game,' Lamberton rebuked sternly. 'Only kings.'

Duns shrugged.

'No game of chess here, my lords. A horse fair, perhaps, though Bernard is scarcely equine, albeit he works as hard as one – and has the same appetite, that I can attest. He is, reluctant though I am to admit it, too fine to be my clerk and be taken off to Paris when I return.'

It was hard to take in, Hal thought. With the English king not a handful of miles away throwing stones at Stirling, last defended fortress of a failed rebellion, this wee room in the *campanile* of Cambuskenneth birled with fetid plans and trading in favours to make another, with Robert Bruce a defiant king.

Yet it was not enough, Hal thought. Two earls, a wheen of bishops and a rickle of wee lords was not enough when a man planned to make himself king. He did not even realize he had said as much until the silence and the still cold of the stares jerked his head up.

'Kirkpatrick I know,' John Duns said softly, looking steadily at Hal with his black gaze. 'This one is a stranger to me.'

'Hal – Sir Henry Sientcler,' Bruce declared brusquely. 'Of Herdmanston.'

The black eyes flared a little and John Duns nodded.

'Ah, yes – the one who cuckolded the Earl of Buchan. I understand his wife, Countess Isabel, is locked up like a prize heifer these days because of it. The pair of ye had little luck from that sin.'

Hal looked at him for a moment, a grey stare that Bruce did not like, for he had seen it on a calm sea not long before a storm broke.

'You will be John Duns, expelled from university in Paris,' Hal replied eventually. 'Hooring, I hear. Dying of the bad humours that has made in your body.'

It was softly vicious and Duns mouth went pursed – like a cat's arse, Bruce noted with some delight. Then Hal offered a bitter smile.

'I am sure there is more to each of our *haecceity* than these singular events,' he said and Duns blinked in surprise. His face lost the rising colour and the tight mouth slowly widened into a smile.

'You know my doctrine, then?' he demanded and Hal made an ambivalent gesture of one hand.

'He is a singular wee lord,' Bruce interrupted and clapped Hal on one shoulder, as if he was showing off one of his particularly clever dogs.

22

'You will know it yourself, of course,' Duns said wryly. 'I ken your brother does.'

Now Bruce's stare was sea-cold; young Alexander Bruce was the scholar of the family and reputedly the best Cambridge had. Bruce himself had arranged and paid for the obligatory feast that celebrated Alexander's acquisition of Master of Arts the year before – but the implication that the youth was the only educated one in the family rankled.

'I know of your *haecceity*, the "thisness" that supposedly makes each of us singular,' he replied, his voice a chill gimlet. 'I am less convinced by your arguments for the immaculate conception of Mary. I consider it sophistry – but that is not why we are here.'

'Ye have the right of it, my lord,' Hal interrupted, making Bruce's scowl deepen at the effrontery. 'I know why each of us is here – myself an' Kirkpatrick because the lord o' Annandale commands, the bishops because their advice and support is necessary. I dinna ken why this Master Duns is here.'

Kirkpatrick, his sharp hound's head swivelling backwards and forwards as he followed their exchange, bridled at the presumption of the wee lord from Herdmanston and, almost in the same thought, admired the courage that spoke up. He was sullen at Duns for his 'Kirkpatrick I know', the sort of dismissive phrase that was like the fondle of fingers behind a hound's ear. He was Bruce's sleuthhound, sure enough, but did not care to be reminded of it so callously.

He started his mouth working on the sharp retort it had taken him all this time to come up with – then caught Wishart's eye. The bishop's frown brought spider-leg brows down over his pouched eyes.

'Master Duns,' he said before Kirkpatrick could speak, his smiling rich voice soothing the ruffled waters, 'has a shrewd mind, which we will need for the essential task of squaring a circle.'

'Aye,' Bruce replied laconically. 'Trying to get the Comyn

to agree to my claims without actually telling them what we plan.'

'That is certainly one problem,' Wishart replied. 'There is another.'

Lamberton sighed and waved one languid hand.

'Let us not dance,' he declared flatly. 'We have to find a way to convince the Comyn that our cause is just and that the Earl of Annandale has claim to the crown. More than that, of course, we have to justify it to them and all the others.'

'Justify?'

Bruce's chin was thrust out truculently, but the sullen petted-lip pout of old was long gone and now he looked stern, like a *dominie* about to chastise a pupil.

'Ye are about to usurp a throne, my lord,' Lamberton declared wryly. 'It will take a cunning argument to convince Strathearn and Buchan and the Dunbar of March, among others, that you have the right to it.'

'Usurp a throne?' Bruce spat back and Wishart held up one hand, his voice steel.

'King John Balliol,' he declared and let the name perch there, a raven in the tree of their plans. Balliol, in whose name the rebellion had been raised and the reason Bruce had quit the rebels and sought his own peace with Edward two years ago.

Hal knew that was when the rumours of Balliol returning – handed over by the Pope back to Scotland – had first been mooted by a Longshanks desperately fending off the French and Scots at either ends of his kingdom. The arrival of an old king into the ambitions of Bruce was not something the Earl of Carrick could suffer – so he had accepted Longshanks' peace and rewards, in the hope of keeping his claims to kingship alive by persuading Edward that a Bruce was a better bet than a Balliol for a peaceful Kingdom.

Yet, not long after that, in a bitter twist of events, had come the Battle of the Golden Spurs, when the Flemings had crushed the flower of French chivalry at Courtrai. Common folk in great squares of spears, Hal had heard, had tumbled so many French knights in the mud that their gilded spurs had made a considerable mound.

It had forced the stunned French to make peace with Edward and freed Longshanks to descend on the north – the result sat outside the walls of Stirling, hurling balls of fire and holding victory tourneys that the newly pardoned Scots lords had to watch in grim, polite silence.

It had also ended any plans to bring Balliol back to his old throne – yet the Kingdom had fought in his name until now. And failed; Bruce was determined to change this.

'Balliol was stripped of his regalia,' Bruce reminded everyone roughly, though his growl was muted. 'By the same king who made him.'

'The lords of this realm made him by common consent,' Lamberton pointed out and had a dismissive wave of hand from Bruce.

'Nevertheless,' Lamberton persisted softly. 'Balliol is still king of this realm in the eyes of those who have consistently fought to preserve it. Wallace among them.'

'The community of this realm are finished with fighting,' Bruce snapped back angrily. 'Unless it is to be first in the queue for Edward's peace. Wallace is finished. No matter the harsh of it, that is the truth. This is no longer a Kingdom, my lords – in all the wee documents from Westminster it is writ as "land" and nothing more. Edward rules it now and his conditions for a return to his loving embrace include charging each lord of this "land" to seek out and capture Will Wallace. That man is not so well loved that such a command will go begging for long.'

'The matter of Balliol is simple,' John Duns said and all heads turned to him. His yellowed face was haughty, his fine fingers laced; Wishart felt a stab of annoyance at the infuriating arrogance of the man, tempered with respect for the intellect and steel will that went with it.

Duns had not been expelled from Paris for whoring, as Hal had declared, but for defying the Pope. And he was dying of some slow wasting disease that Wishart prayed to God to make slower still, since the loss of Duns would be a tragedy. Yet he was hard to suffer, all the same . . .

'We must remake the doctrine of the throne,' Duns went on. 'As a contract, between the King and community of the Kingdom, to the effect that the Kingdom itself reserves the right to remove an unfit king. Such an unfit king, of course, will be one who permits the freedom of this realm to be usurped by an invader, as John Balliol does, preferring gilded captivity to a struggle for freedom. Which, *gentilhommes*, is something no man gives up save with his life. As long as a hundred of us remain to defend it, we will do so.'

They stared at him and he sat, head tilted and preening just a little, for he knew he had slit the Gordian of it – even Kirkpatrick, blinking with the effort of understanding it, could see the breathtaking genius.

'That last is not my own,' Duns added lightly, 'but Bernard of Kilwinning's.'

Bruce cocked one warning eyebrow.

'That is the only part that is not mere elegant sophistry,' he countered levelly. 'Dangerous, too. The best defence for this kingdom has been the confusion and discord of England, thanks to Edward's own *nobiles* and their attempts to foist Ordinances on his power. Think ye this realm needs such curb on royal power?'

'There is only one ordinance in such a contract,' Duns replied calmly, 'and that is to defend the freedom of the Kingdom. Hardly a curb of royal power, to insist that a good king do that which he would anyway.'

Bruce nodded, reluctantly. John Balliol had defended the Kingdom and suffered for it – since then, of course, he had haunted the French court and the papal skirts defending nothing at all, so Duns' sophistry worked well enough.

Yet Bruce was English enough to see that the crown of this kingdom was not the same as any other. Kings in Scotland, he had long since discovered, differed from those anywhere else because they had long admitted that God alone did not have the final say in who ruled. The reality for a King of Scots was that his right to rule had long since been removed from God and handed, via the noble community of the realm, to the Kingdom's every burgher and minor landowner – aye, and even the cottars and drovers who lived there; it was a wise claimant who made his peace with that.

Not King of Scotland, but King of Scots and there was a wealth of subtle meaning in the difference.

Wishart saw Bruce acquiesce, slapped his meaty hands together and beamed. John Duns was clever, Hal thought, but his kenspeckled words were not enough to convince the Comyn Earl of Buchan, or the Comyn Lord of Badenoch, whose kin John Balliol was. The Lord of Badenoch had his own claim to the kingship and, even if everyone else allowed that John Balliol was too much empty cote to be endured, it was unlikely the Comyn would step aside for Bruce.

Hal did not even have to voice it, for Lamberton did and the arguments swirled like the greasy, tainted smoke of the tallow until Bruce held up one hand and silenced them all.

'Red John Comyn is a problem,' he declared, 'which we must address soon. Sooner still is the one called Wallace.'

He looked round the room of shadowed faces.

'He must be persuaded to quit the realm,' Bruce said. 'For his own safety and because nothing can proceed while he rants and ravages in the name of King John Balliol. That rebellion is ended, my lords, and will never be resurrected; the next time this kingdom wars against the invader will be under my banner. A royal one, lords – and against Edward the son, not the father.'

'If what you say is true,' Lamberton with a wry, fox smile, 'that might see you with grey hairs of your own. Is Longshanks

27

not in the finest of health, with a new young queen and two wee bairns tumbling like cubs?'

'Besides,' Wishart added mournfully, 'Wallace is unlikely to be moved by the argument that he stands in the way of your advancement, my lord Robert. Nor has he been much concerned over his own safety in the past.'

'Leave Wallace and Red John Comyn to me,' Bruce declared grimly and then shot a twisted smile at John Duns. 'God and time will take care of King Edward.'

'*Affectio Commodi*,' he added and John Duns acknowledged it with a tilt of his head.

Affectio Commodi, the Duns doctrine of morality, where happiness is assigned to 'affection for the advantage' and true morality to *affectio iustito*, an affection to justice.

Hal remembered the times the wee *dominie* his father had hired 'to pit poalish on the boy' had lectured on that, hands behind his back and eyes shut. Hal had struggled with it then and was more than relieved when the wee priest had given up and gone off to find more fertile pastures.

Justice or advantage. Hal did not need to look at Bruce to see the choice made and had it confirmed later, when he and Kirkpatrick, obedient to the summons, went to the Bruce's quarters.

In contrast to the roomful of plots, this blazed with light from fat beeswax candles and sconces, the flagged floor liberal with fresh rushes. Herbal posies were stuffed into wall crevices and looped round the crucifix which glared malevolently from the rough wall at the men who lolled carelessly beneath it.

They were young men, faces full of impudence and freckles, half-dressed in fine linen shirts, rich-dyed tunics and coloured hose, lounging in a welter of discarded jerkins and cloaks, baldrics, sheaths and ox-blood boots of Cordovan leather with fashionable high heels. A couple of gazehounds nosed the rushes, searching between jug and goblet for the remains of roast meats and chewed fruit.

28

One of these languid men was Edward Bruce, a warped portrait of his brother, big shouldered, large chested and with the same face, only as if it had been squeezed from forehead and chin. It made his eyes slitted and his grin wider – unlike his brother, he grinned all the time.

Hal saw Kirkpatrick stiffen a little and felt a slight, sudden stab of justified satisfaction; for years Kirkpatrick had been the only retainer Bruce had closeted with him, a shadowy ferreter of secrets – aye, and worse – at Bruce's beck and call. This was the reward for it – supplanted by those Bruce needed more.

Let him taste the bitter fruit of it, as I have, Hal thought savagely. My father dead, my home burned by my own kin after the battle at Roslin Glen, good friends dead in the mud of Stirling and Falkirk. Little reward for the middling folk who had ended up in the Bruce camp.

And Isabel. Her loss burned most of all. Gone back to the Earl of Buchan on the promise that her lover and his home would not be harmed. For six years Hal and she had kept to the bargain, though there was not a day he did not think of her and wondered if she still thought of him.

And for what? Buchan had found a way to burn Herdmanston to ruin anyway and would, Hal knew, seek a way to kill him. He will come at you sideways, like a cock on a dungheap – his father's bleak warning echoed down the years.

Now all that was left was shackled to the fortunes of Bruce. Kirkpatrick shared the chains of it, Hal saw, though he had not considered the man an unwilling supplicant until recently, when this fresh *mesnie* had grown around the new Lord of Annandale and Carrick.

Not great lords, either, but an earl's bachelor knights, fashionable, preened and coiffed. They stared at Hal and Kirkpatrick as if two aged wolves had stepped into the room, a mixture of sneer at what they considered to be old men out of touch with the new reality, the coming man that was Bruce, and envy that their lord and master treated so closely with such a pair.

Bruce showed the truth of it when he did not bother to announce Hal or Kirkpatrick and indicated that they should draw apart. Into the shadows, Hal saw with a sharp, bitter smile, where we belong.

'Wallace,' Bruce said in a voice so low it was more crouched than a sniffing rat. Neither Hal nor Kirkpatrick replied and Bruce, his eyes baleful in the dim, raked both their faces with an unsmiling gaze.

'Find him. Tell him he has my love – but he must quit Scotland before it is too late for him. If nothing else, he will end up making the name of his captors odious in Scotland, for they will be Scots men, mark me. That is part of Edward's scheme.'

Kirkpatrick, his eyes like faint lights in the cave of his face, nodded briefly and Hal jerked his head at the distant murmur and laughter at someone's poor attempts to play and sing in the Langue D'Oc of a troubadour.

'Finding him will be hard,' he said, more harshly than he had intended. 'He is a hunted man and unlikely to caw the craic, cheek for jowl, with any as declares they are friends.'

Bruce smiled. There had been a time when this would have been as incoherent as a dog's bark, but time and exposure had improved his ear.

'You speak their way,' he said to Hal in elegant French, 'and understand a decent tongue besides, so you can walk in both camps easily enough. Better yet – you have dealt with Wallace before this and the man knows you. Trusts you even. In case he does not, Kirkpatrick knows what to do when men come at you from the shadows.'

'A comforting thought,' Kirkpatrick answered in equally good French, though his burr added a vicious twist to the wry delivery. He jerked his head backwards at the coterie of quietly murmuring knights.

'Why not ask Crawford there? Is he not kin to Wallace?'

Bruce merely looked at him until Kirkpatrick dropped his eyes. Only the auld dugs would do for this, he thought. At least it means he trusts us, as he does no others.

Hal cleared his throat, a sign the other men knew meant he had something difficult to hoik up on the way. They waited.

'Wallace kens what is hid in Roslin,' Hal said flatly. Bruce said nothing, though the problem had nagged him. He had arranged for the Stone of Scone to be supplanted by a cuckoo and the real one carried off to Roslin. Murder had been involved in it and, in the end, Wallace had found out. He had done nothing then – Falkirk fixed that – and said nothing since; Bruce now wrestled with the problem of whether he would keep his silence.

The Earl eventually shrugged, as if it no longer mattered.

'Mak' siccar,' he said to Kirkpatrick and then turned away.

Later, in the cool breeze of a summer's night, Hal stood with Kirkpatrick and watched the flaring fire from Stirling, heard the sometime thump as the wind veered.

'Edward will be getting a lashin' from his young queen,' Kirkpatrick noted wryly, 'for keeping the royal bairns up wi' such racket.'

'He is not short of pith for an auld man,' Hal answered. 'I fear our earl will have to be doucelike patient if he waits for Longshanks to get kisted up afore he makes his move.'

'If Wallace remains it will be longer than that,' Kirkpatrick answered. 'So we had better be on the trail of it.'

'What did he mean,' Hal said, 'by his parting words?'

'Mak' siccar?' Kirkpatrick smiled sharply. 'Make sure. Make sure Wallace is found and given the message, of course. That he stands in the way.'

Hal watched Kirkpatrick slide into the shadows and wondered.

Stirling Castle
Vigil of Saint James the Apostle, July, 1304.

He knelt in the leprous sweat of full panoply, hearing the coughs and grunts of all the other penitents suffering in the heat – yet ahead of him, Bruce saw the straight back and brilliant white head of the King, rising up from the humble bow to look to where the prisoners knelt, humbler still; he could imagine the smile on Edward's face.

Oliphant's face was a grey mask, not all of it from the ashes dumped on his head; together with the hemp noose round his neck, it marked his contrition and the final humiliation of surrender. Behind him, as suitable a backdrop as a cross for Jesus, the great rearing throwing arms of the Berefray, the parson, Segrave and the notorious Warwolf leered triumphantly at the pocked and blackened walls of Stirling.

'O gracious God, we remember before thee this day thy servant and apostle James, first among the Twelve to suffer martyrdom for the Name of Jesus Christ . . .'

The Bishop of Ross was a pawky wee man with a matching voice, Hal thought, and then offered apology to God for the impiety, true though it was.

Still, he was also a prelate trusted by the English, more so than the ones he and Kirkpatrick and Bruce had quit only weeks before at Cambuskenneth. Better still, being full of his own self-importance, he had handled the entire affair of the surrender of Stirling fortress with suitable gravitas.

Just as well, for a single snigger would have undone the wonderful mummery of it – the stern, implacable Edward, ordering the gralloching of Oliphant and the other supplicants staggering out of Stirling with their hempen collars, draped in white serks and ashes. The lisping French of the beautiful young Queen, begging her imperious husband to relent and spare them, for the grace of God and on this day of days, the Vigil of St James the Martyr.

32

Three times she and her women, Bruce's Irish countess among them, had pleaded and twice Edward had loftily refused, perfectly coiffured silver head and rouged cheeks tilted defiantly skywards, while everyone watched and tried to remain suitably dignified.

And then, when the weeping and wailing had worked its inevitable magic and the rebels were spared, the collective sigh exhaled by everyone watching all but rippled the trampled grass.

'God be praised,' finished the bishop.

'For ever and ever.'

The reply from a host of murmured lips was like a covey of birds taking flight and the rest of the Augustinians went off into chant and slow march, swinging their censers; the acrid thread of incense caught Bruce by the throat and Hal heard the subtle little catch of breath next to him.

Head bowed, draped so that Bruce could only see the half-moon of eyelash on cheek, his wife was young and beautiful. Creamed flesh and black hair, a true Irish princess was Elizabeth and Bruce tried to think of her and not her powerful father, the de Burgh Earl of Ulster.

She was polite and deferential in public, a delight in private, so that love with Elizabeth de Burgh was no sweating work of grossness. He did what he wanted, feeling her writhe and knowing that she took pleasure in it, so that there was for him, too.

Yet, afterwards, there was always the memory of his first wife, Belle, his hand on her small, heaving bosom, feeling her life drain away, seeing the baby she left. Poor Marjorie, he thought with a sharp pang of guilt and regret, I have not done well by that child.

And before, with Belle, there had been times when he felt he could believe in the power of *sheean* magic, in that lazy hour of lying together when outlines hazed and a sunbeam slant, danced with golden motes.

In the day Elizabeth de Burgh was dutiful. In the night, she was wanton and that was workable – in the night, he thought, I lose my ability to see. But Belle was slim as a wand, with breasts like nuts. Elizabeth is as lush as the lands she brings to me, Bruce thought, so that even the dark cannot turn back time. The Curse of Malachy, he thought, to have the world and taste only ashes – would it be like this even when he was king?

Elizabeth rose, smoothing her dress, adjusting her wimple, smiling at him gently, making an expression of winsome regret as she began to move to the side of the equally young Queen, who smiled with bland eyes below a pale forehead and brows almost blonde. For all her youth, three faint lines already touched that brow, as if the age of her husband was leaching her youth.

Ashes. The taste drifted to his mouth, palpable, so that he turned in time to see a brown-hooded figure signing the cross at a man in white, neck-roped and clouded with flying ashes where he had shaken himself free of them. The ceremony over, Oliphant was smiling at the chance to wash and get back into decent clothes.

'*Ave Maria, gratia plena,*' intoned the monk. '*Ora pro nobis peccatoribus, nunc et in hora mortis nostrae . . .*'

Pray for us sinners, now and at the hour of our death. Not that Oliphant faced death now or anything near it, Bruce thought. He had won himself a deal of fame by holding out so long and even managed to avoid serious injury or penance; Bruce nodded acknowledgement to the man and had back a grin that bordered on sneer from the grey-smeared face.

Bruce felt movement at his elbow and turned into the curious stare of Hal, felt unnerved as he often did when he found the man looking at him. He did it more and more these days, as if silently accusing, though Bruce did not know for what – unless the Countess Buchan, of course, the poor wee man's lost light

34

of love, who had been Bruce's initiation into the serious arts of the bedchamber once.

Hardly that, for he has known of that since the beginning and made his peace with it. Herdmanston, then? Burned out, it needed rebuilding and I promised him aid in it, but God's Blood, the man was on wages for himself and thirty riders which took the rents of a couple of good manors. Surely he realized that rebuilding his wee rickle of stones in Lothian was no great priority when a throne was a stake?

Yet he smiled, at him and Kirkpatrick both; they were useful, though not the pillars to support a man who would be king. Still, he needed their questing-dog purpose even if, so far, it had come to nothing; he knew they smarted over their failure to find Wallace, knew also that they would not give up if only because of their rivalry in it. Bruce's smile widened; divide and conquer, the first rule of kings.

The monk and Bruce watched the prisoners stumble off, then the monk turned and Bruce gave a start, for he knew the face. So did Hal, coming up on his elbow and seeing the smeared smile of the little man, whom he remembered as one less than holy.

'*Benda ti istran plegrin: benda, marqueta, maidin. Benda, benda stringa da da agugeta colorada*,' the monk intoned with a grin as brown as his robe.

'Kirkpatrick,' Bruce called and the shadow was beside him instantly, scowling; Hal became aware of the rest of Bruce's *mesnie*, suspicious and sullen, closing in.

'Lamprecht,' Kirkpatrick said, as if the name was soiled fruit in his mouth. The man admitted his name with a bow and a quick flick of his head left and right, to see who was within earshot; he did not like the presence of so many armed men and said so, then repeated the phrase he had used before.

'*Andara, andara, o ti bastonara*,' Kirkpatrick growled in response, and Hal saw the looks that passed between Bruce's noblemen – but none asked what they all wanted to know, namely what tongue the man used.

Hal knew, from the last time he had met the little pardoner; it was *lingua franca*, the old crusader language, a patois of every tongue spoken along the Middle Sea, with more than a dash of heathen in it. Pilgrims used it and the last time Hal had seen this Lamprecht – at least six years ago – he had been claiming himself to be one, with shell badge in a wide-brimmed hat and a collection of relics and indulgences. The meeting had not been profitable for him, nor the ones he had been involved with and Kirkpatrick had, Hal recalled, threatened him with a knife. What had brought the skulking wee pardoner back here, of all places?

'What is he saying?' Bruce demanded and Kirkpatrick, who was the only one who spoke the tongue, revealed that the little man, his pouched face shrouded in rough brown wool, was begging alms. Kirkpatrick had told him to go or be beaten.

'*Peregrin taybo cristian, si querer andar Jordan, pilla per tis jornis pan que no trobar pan ne vin.*'

'Good Christian pilgrim, if you want to journey to the Jordan, take bread with you, for you will find no bread or wine,' Kirkpatrick translated it and someone laughed as the priest held out one grimy hand with half a chewed loaf in it.

'Is he trying to sell you bread?' demanded Edward Bruce, his voice rising with incredulity. 'Be off, priest,' he added though he did it politely, for there was no telling what powers a pilgrim friar had – or what such a one might become after death. The Curse of Malachy, Bruce thought wryly, seeing his brother's scowling fear.

Hal saw the gleam in Lamprecht's eyes, like animals in the dark of the cowl. He glanced at Bruce and saw he had seen the same. There was a moment – then Bruce reached out, took the bread and turned to Kirkpatrick.

'Give him a coin.'

Pilgrim Lamprecht, with obvious delight, took the coin

from under Kirkpatrick's scowl, frowned at how small it was, then made it disappear.

'Cambuskenneth,' he said, clear as new water, then he was gone, leaving bemused men looking at his scuttling back. Edward Bruce looked at the bread, then smiled his broad, slit-eyed grin, his cheeks knobbed as late apples.

'I would not eat that if I were you, brother.'

He went off, hooting, while the others trailed after him. Bruce looked at the half-loaf, rough maslin with a grey dough interior, indented as if someone had poked a finger in it. He scooped, found something hard and pulled it out; Kirkpatrick whistled, then looked right and left while Bruce closed his fist on the object and moved on, nodding and smiling as if it was the everyday thing for the powerful lord of Carrick and Annadale to be holding one half of a poor loaf.

But all of them had seen the red gleam of a ruby, big and round as a robin's egg and that itself would have been marvel enough. Bruce knew more, had known that ruby and its eleven cousins when they had been snugged up next to each other along the length and breadth of a reliquary cross last seen tucked under the arm of an English knight heading south to Westminster.

Inside the jewelled and gilded crucifix-casket, Bruce knew, had lain the Holy Black Rood of Scotland, the holiest relic of the Kingdom and, together with the Stone of Scone, as much the mark of a coronation as the crown itself.

CHAPTER TWO

Riccarton, Ayrshire
Transfiguration of Christ, August, 1304

Mattie Broon first caught sight of them as he plodded through the drizzle, his idiot son lumbering awkwardly at his side and jumping in puddles. Late in a wet August afternoon for Mattie to be heading out to his sheep, folk said later. Too long in Creishie Jean's alehouse, the knowing said. Too slow and indulgent with that daftie boy said those who knew better.

Mattie saw the cattle first, small black shapes with long, curved horns. Being a sheepman he did not care for cattle much and was surprised to see them, for this was no drover's road. The dogs came next, rough-coated slinkers moving the score or so stirks along the road.

First came long shadows, eldritch as Faerie, from men walking determinedly on foot, four of them – no five. One a priest, or a pilgrim lay brother – Mattie had never known such a thing before. His original thought, that they had stolen the beasts, was now thrown into confusion, for surely no priest would be party to cattle-lifting?

The cattle lumbered over the low ground, a seemingly disorganized mob of shaggy bodies and wickedly curving horns.

The topsman – Mattie presumed – lifted one hand in greeting and to show it was empty, that they meant no harm.

No harm, Mattie snorted to himself. It was clear they were circling the beasts, planning to make camp and he shifted away from them, ignoring the plaintive repeat of questions from his son. He moved off a little way and hunkered, hearing their rough laughter, the lowing of cattle and sharp barks of the dogs clamouring to be fed.

When the breeze brought the smell of onions and oatmeal with the whisper of grass Mattie rose up, chivvied his son from digging in the mud and moved off. His sheep would be untended, but he knew that this would have to be told to Heidsman. He would know what to do.

The drovers watched him go from under the loops of rough wool drawn up over their heads, eating stolidly from horn spoon and wooden bowl, save for the young, dark one who was making a fuss of the fawning hounds.

'Is he away?' asked Hal, who had his back to the man. Kirkpatrick flicked his eyes up and toed a loose brand back towards the fire.

'Heading away, fast,' he growled. 'Herding the boy like a coo. No right in the head, that boy.'

'Away to fetch the maister,' Sim Craw said and looked over at the Dog Boy. 'Leave the dugs, man. Sit and eat – nivver miss a meal, for ye dinna ken when the next will appear.'

Dog Boy gave a last friendly cuff to the fawning beasts and then went to the fire, taking his bowl and spoon from Sim and offering a wide grin in payment. Hal smiled with him – the Dog Boy was enjoying himself, even if it was only a couple of sleekit cattle dogs he worked with and the price for it was spending the last weeks looking at the shitty arses of a dozen scrubby kine. He was the only one with any joy of the affair.

'I said,' Kirkpatrick muttered, 'that this idea of pretending to be drovers was bad. We are nowheres close to a drove road, so any who spy us will think we stole the baists.'

'Which is for why we brought our own wee priest,' Sim replied, bowing his neck to Lamprecht and having back a brown sneer for it. 'No stolen kine here, wi' a wee friar in tow.'

It was one reason they had brought Lamprecht from Stirling weeks since and not the most important, Kirkpatrick thought. He caught himself staring at Sim, taking in the slab of a face, the span of shoulder, the grizzled beard. More iron than black in that beard, he thought and that monster crossbow he used to span constantly with a heave of those shoulders is now latched back with the belly hook and belt more and more these days. We are all getting old, he thought moodily.

Sim Craw felt the eyes on him and spared Kirkpatrick a brief flick of glance, which took in the sharp, long-nosed mummer's mask of a face, little knife points of dagged hair, wintered here and there, plastered wetly to hollowed cheeks. Bigod the wee man was ugly.

The only one uglier, Sim Craw agreed with himself, was yon murderous Malise Bellejambe, the Earl o' Buchan's man just as Kirkpatrick was Bruce's murderous wee man. It seemed to Sim that every highborn in the land needed a murderous wee man like a shadow and he was ruffled as a wet cat at the idea that he and Hal were somehow included in that *mesnie*.

'Farthing for that thought,' Hal offered, seeing Sim's familiar glazed scowl. The man blinked and grinned loosely.

'Malise Bellejambe,' he answered and saw the cloud darken Hal's face. He wished he had not answered so truthfully now, for Malise was dark and unfinished business, a man who, for sure, had killed Tod's Wattie and two prime deerhounds as well as a yielded English lord waiting for ransom. There were other killings that could be laid at his feet, though none of them could be proved – but the worst about Malise Bellejambe was that he was Isabel's keeper, the Earl of Buchan's snarling guard dog on his wife and one reason why Hal had kept away from her these past years.

Hal was spared the brooding of it by the arrival of the

40

Heidsman, with a bustle of curious and concerned locals at his back, one of them the local priest. In his pretend role of topsman of the drovers, Hal stood up and moved to greet him, being polite but not fawning.

'Christ be praised,' the priest announced.

'For ever and ever,' Hal responded and there was a slight ease of the tension now that it was established that the strange drovers were neither Faerie nor imps of Satan, who could never get such words past their lips. He saw the idiot boy laughing with the fawning dogs and Dog Boy grinning with him, the shared delight in hounds an instant bond.

After that, matters were established quickly enough – that this was an overnight camp only and that the cattle would not be allowed to stray into plots of beet, or the fields of uncut hay. The priest, Hal saw out of the corner of one eye, moved to greet his brother in Christ and Hal felt a momentary stab of concern.

'Whit where are ye drivin' the baists?'

The question took him by the chin and forced his head back into the frowning chap-cheeked concern of the Heidsman's face. He grinned without parting his lips.

'Here an' there. To those who might need the comfort of good beef.'

It was as clear as waving a saltire who the cattle were meant for and Hal had hopes that the Heidsman in Riccarton, a Wallace stronghold, would be sympathetic. He was not wrong, but a few idle questions later had determined that, supporters though they were, no-one in Riccarton knew where the Wallace was – or even his uncle Adam, who was also on the outlaw. Riccarton's wee keep was now garrisoned by English, which made it doubly unlikely that Wallace would be nearby.

The priest appeared puzzled.

'He speaks awfy strange, yon friar,' he said to the Heidsman and Hal forced his smile wide, a satchel of innocence.

'He is a pilgrim, from the Holy Land,' he replied and that

41

was enough, it seemed, not only to answer the puzzle of his strange way of speaking, but to gain Lamprecht a measure of spurious respect.

Dog Boy heard the boy's father call him and the daftie turned reluctantly away, then smiled, innocent as God himself, at the scowl that was Lamprecht.

'Shell,' he said and the pardoner waved him away like an annoying fly. Sulkily, the boy turned away, muttering about how he wanted the shell and was never given it.

The deputation moved away, satisfied; Hal returned to sit by the fire, where he told them that Wallace was not lurking around here.

'Aye well, it was a poor chance at best,' Sim sighed. 'Still – we have the other matter.'

The other matter felt the eyes on him and stopped, spoon halfway to his gums, food sliding on to the raggle of his beard. I take it back, Sim thought to himself, Lamprecht is uglier even than Malise Bellejambe.

Lamprecht saw the faces, knew what they were thinking and hoped they had not worked out that he was about to take himself off very soon; hoped, even more fervently, that they would not discover the truth of it all until it was too late and his revenge sprung. He remembered the time five years ago at least he and the lord and his retinue had met, in the lazar at Berwick. The one with Satan's face, the Kirkpatrick who spoke the *lingua*, had held a knife at his throat then.

The prick of it burned yet and it took all his will not to reach up one comforting hand to the spot, thus giving away his thoughts to the same Satan. Now the revenge was his. *Dar cinquecento diavoli, che portar tua malora . . .*

Five hundred devils made no appearance to take the curse that was Kirkpatrick, so Lamprecht finished the action of spoon and mouth, chewed, swallowed and grinned.

'*Non andar bonu?*'

'Speak a decent tongue, ye wee heathen,' growled Sim and Lamprecht scowled back at him.

'*Questo diavolo ignorante non consoce il merito*,' Lamprecht began, stopped, took a breath and began again, speaking deliberately to Hal, his English wavering like a sailor finding his land-legs. 'This devil does not know talent when he sees it. I am to help. I have the thing. You want the thing. *Capir?*'

He had the thing. Truth was, Hal thought, he had a portion of the thing, which he had brought out like a cradled bairn when Hal and Kirkpatrick had come with the Earl Bruce, chasing the promise of that single ruby.

Lamprecht had unwrapped the sacking lovingly in the amber light of wax candles and the dancing shadows of the pilgrim's cell he had claimed at Cambuskenneth.

Even half the thing took Hal's breath away and the whole, an ell length at least, must have been an ache on the eye.

Bruce had taken the gilded fragment, the lower end of a cross lid, badly hacked off. Five similar rubies studded it and the nest for the prised-out sixth revealed the depth of beaten gold. Bruce, slow with wonder, nestled the ruby Lamprecht had given him into it, watched the perfect fit for a moment, then removed it again.

'It is from the Westminster,' Lamprecht had said, his voice reverently low. 'From the *furfanta* – the swindler. Pardon . . . the robbery. Of the King's treasure.'

In the quiet of the cell no-one had spoken, for they had all heard of this, taken delight in it if truth was told. While Longshanks ravaged up and down Scotland, a nest of thieves – his own canons of the minster among them – had stolen the Crown treasure from Westminster. That had been almost a year ago and the howling rage that was Edward had not diminished, if the arrests and racks and beheadings were anything to go by.

Nor had it all been recovered. Pieces of it were turning up all over the country – and abroad, too, Bruce had heard. Yet this was singular. This was part of the reliquary of the Black Rood, taken from Scone on the day Longshanks stripped John Balliol of everything that made him a king and a man and the Kingdom of everything that made it a realm.

'*Si*,' Lamprecht had said, as if reading Bruce's thoughts. 'I have this from Pudlicote man. For . . . some small services.'

'Who is Pudlicote?' Kirkpatrick had demanded and Bruce, turning the rubied cross over in his fingers so that it flared bloody in the light, knew the answer.

'Baron of the thieves,' he had said darkly. 'Clever in the planning, stupid afterwards in spraying Crown jewels all over the county as if they were baubles. He paid the price for it – his flayed skin is nailed to the door of the Minster now.'

'*Si*,' Lamprecht had agreed. 'Pudlicote is discovered – all is lost. *Cosa bisogno cunciar? Pardone* – what am I to do?'

'What DID you do?' Kirkpatrick had asked.

'Ran,' Lamprecht had revealed. 'Ran with Jop. Jop had half, I have half. Six Apostles each and we go our way. Jop comes to the north.'

The rubies, all twelve, were known as the Apostles, said to contain the very blood of Christ – but even they were not as valuable as the sliver of dark wood they had decorated.

'And the Rood itself?' Bruce had demanded. Lamprecht, pausing, tried not to look sly. Failed. Then he had shrugged his rat-boned shoulders and offered a brown smile.

'Jop knows where relic is. Piece of Holy Cross which is of this land.'

He had then managed, at last, a sly, knowing look.

'Bishops of here will want it back. Jop, he will not tell me where it is – *cane. Cornudo.*'

'This Jop,' Bruce had said slowly. 'A small man. Bald.'

'He is not. Big. Fat belly. Much hairy. He is man who bears the standard. *Ti credir per mi, mi pudir assicurar per ti.*'

'I do believe you,' Bruce had answered grimly.

'*Ti star nobilé, è non star fabbola* – sorry, permit me. As you are noble, this is no fable. I have no money. For this piece and the information, I ask only a paltry. A twenty pound of silver.'

That had all but choked Kirkpatrick and made Hal blink. That price would keep Sim Craw for a year in England – six months longer if he stayed north of Berwick.

'Does Jop have the Rood?' Bruce had demanded.

'If not, he know where,' Lamprecht had replied. 'I cannot get in to him. You go to where he is – you know this place?'

'I do,' Bruce had answered, then handed the gilded prize back, which surprised Hal – but not Kirkpatrick, who knew that possession of such an artefact would result in punishments from Edward that Hell would balk at. He scowled, however, when he realized the sixth Apostle was staying with Bruce – but at least a single, flawless ruby of price was explainable in the purse of an earl.

'If Jop helps us, you shall have twice the price,' Bruce had declared and Lamprecht's grin was wide and foul. It did not waver when he was told that he would have to go along, for that had been taken into account in his planning – was the necessary risk in it.

There were more questions – the Kirkpatrick man especially was all lowered brow and suspicion, wanting to know why Lamprecht had come to Bruce at such risk when he had, clearly, riches enough. Lamprecht, scornfully, had pointed out that losing such a gem to the Earl of Carrick was no loss, when even attempting to sell one would have a pilgrim like him arrested, drawn and quartered.

'In an earl's purse, is to be expected,' he had sneered. 'In mine, not.'

Some of what Lamprecht had said was true – he could hardly sell what he had and hope to make money on the deal, or even escape. So he thought to profit from information with a man who would want to know about the Rood – though that fact brought its own unease. Bruce was, ostensibly, a loyal follower of King Edward so Lamprecht risked his neck bringing it to such a man – unless his loyalty was known differently. And if such as Lamprecht knew it, then Longshanks knew it; the thought brought a shiver up Hal's spine.

Kirkpatrick had subsided, glowering with unease, while Lamprecht kept the lie in the tale as a hugging secret close to the burning core of him, trying not to show a vengeful smile when he looked at the Lothian lord and Kirkpatrick.

It did not take long for Bruce to reveal who Jop was, for the only Jop of the description was Gilbert of Beverley, a sometime lay brother who had been paid by the abbey to carry its borrowed Holy Standard in Edward's army when he came north to fight Falkirk. A fine imposing sight Gilbert had made, too, having the height and width of shoulder for banner-bearing, which might have given the English something of a clue as to who he was.

They found out soon enough. Gilbert, known as Jop to all his Wallace relatives, had promptly scurried off and joined them in rebellion, only to quit that when matters grew warm. He had vanished shortly after and now they all knew where and why.

His arrival back in Scotland had come as no surprise to folk, who thought he had just lain low for a while. Now he was snugged up in Riccarton's chapel to Saint Mirin, having claimed 'the knowledge of Latin' to wriggle out from under Edward's harsh law into the court of the Church, who had some sympathy towards ex-rebels.

There would be no church or God, though, which would keep him from the wrath of Longshanks if he ever discovered Jop was one of the thieves of the Crown's treasure from the minster.

The fire sparked, little worm-embers snapping Hal from remembrance. That cloistered conversation had been a month ago and Lamprecht had grown no more easier to be with since. Neither him nor his tale, Hal thought.

'Jop,' he said and wanted to say more on this cousin of

the Wallace, who had none of the man's better qualities save height. He did not need to say more on it, all the same, for each man recognized the problem of Jop and, eventually, Sim voiced it.

'This Jop,' Sim said, breaking Hal's reverie. 'Is tight-fastened in a kirk. It will be as hard to crack open as Riccarton's Keep, I am thinking.'

'Less soldiery in the kirk,' Kirkpatrick declared. 'I hear the English have stuffed the keep wi' English, to mak' siccar The Ogre takes no rest there. They must be sleeping three to a cot in that wee place.'

'Aye, weel, they will be dressed soon enough if a wee priest hurls up crying that mad drovers are beatin' in his chapel door,' growled Sim and Kirkpatrick's laugh was low and mirthless.

'Ye should get abroad more, Sim Craw,' Kirkpatrick declared, his accent broadening, as it always did when he spoke with the likes of Sim. He could make it refined and French, too, when he chose and Hal realized this was part of the shifting shadow of the man.

'Whit why?' demanded Sim truculently.

'Ye would learn things. Like the time there was an auld priest o' Riccarton,' Kirkpatrick answered. 'Years since. Had the falling sickness, which laid him out as if he had died. He had such a fear o' what would happen that even a week's wake and a belled coffin was too little precaution for him – so he took steps to mak' siccar he would never be buried alive.'

He had them all now, locked tight in the shackles of his eyes and words.

'He had a lidless kist made and passage cut from the chapel crypt into the graveyard beyond,' Kirkpatrick went on, 'in case they tombed him up alive.'

'Did he ever have use o' it?' demanded the round-eyed Dog Boy and Kirkpatrick shook his head.

'Went on a pilgrimage to Rome, for relief o' his condition and sins. Drowned at sea.'

47

'Ah, bigod,' sighed Sim, shaking a rueful head. 'What is set on ye will no' go past ye, certes.'

'So the passage is there still?' demanded Hal and Kirkpatrick nodded, his grin catching the firelight in the dark.

'We will be in and out o' Saint Mirin's wee house, easy as beggary.'

He looked at where the sun was dying, seeping red into the horizon like blood from a flayed skin; insects hummed and wheeped in the iron-filing twilight.

'When it gets dark,' he said.

Sim grunted as he levered himself up. Tapping Dog Boy on the shoulder, he went out to check on the cattle and the dogs, followed by the boy. Dog Boy kept glancing behind them.

'Are yer sins hagging ye?' Sim demanded eventually and Dog Boy shook his head, then shrugged.

'Lamprecht,' he said and Sim nodded.

'There is something not right,' Dog Boy insisted.

'God's Hook, laddie, ye have said a true thing there – stop twitching in the dark and help me with these God-cursed stirks.'

Hal watched them go, hearing them mutter, while Lamprecht slithered off into a bower of leaves and branches, clutching his precious bundle to him and muttering morosely about the discomfort. Hal felt like telling him he was lucky it was summer still, for in winter the drovers made a bowl-shaped withy of sticks, then broke the ice on any stream or loch, dipped their cloaks and spread them out over the withy to freeze into a shelter.

'Sim Craw must favour one o' those cattle,' Kirkpatrick said with a lopsided smile, 'since he cares for them a deal, it seems.'

Hal did not reply; Sim Craw had bought bullocks and horse both from Stirk Davey in Biggar and had them cheap on the promise that Davey would buy them back if they were returned undamaged. It meant Sim and Hal would keep the money, which had come from Bruce for the purpose, and it would go into the trickle of silver that would, one day, become the pool to rebuild Herdmanston.

Instead, he wondered aloud his fears regarding Lamprecht and that it all might be a trap set by Longshanks himself to test Bruce loyalty.

'It might,' Kirkpatrick agreed laconically, 'though such subtle work is not the mark of that king. If he suspects our earl to that extent, he would be hauling in folk likely to speak of it under the Question. Confessions would be enough without all this mummery.'

Which was true enough to silence Hal to brooding on Kirkpatrick himself, until he finally voiced what had been on his mind for long enough regarding the man.

'Whit why do ye serve the Earl?'

The answering smile was bland, with some puzzle quirking the edge of it.

'Same as yersel',' he replied and saw Hal's laconic lip-curl, faint in the growing dim.

'Ill luck and circumstance then.'

'Circumstance, certes,' Kirkpatrick answered, the slow, considered words of it forged in a steel that did not pass Hal by. 'Ill luck? Hardly that for you, my lord. What have ye suffered?'

A lost wife and son to ague. A light of love to politics. A keep to fire and pillage, done by those he counted kin and friends.

'There is more,' he finished sarcastically and Kirkpatrick stirred a little, then poked the fire so that flames rose and embers flared away and died like little ruby hopes.

'Your wife and boy are a decade gone,' he replied sudden as a slap. 'Others have suffered loss o' dear yins, from ague, plague an' worse. Your light o' love is someone else's and you have been apart from her for five years at least, so the brooding is of your own making. Your wee keep was slighted a bit – it is lacking the timber floors and is blackened, but the folk still huddle around it, you still collect rents an' your kin in Roslin manage it and oversee the repairs. Yourself provides the siller, from the rents, the money the Earl pays you as retinue . . . and what you can skim.'

He stopped and turned his firelit blade of a face, challenging and grim, towards Hal.

'Where is the suffering in this?'

'You think you are worse?' Hal bridled and Kirkpatrick sighed.

'Ye have a dubbin' as knight, the arms to prove it and lands,' he answered, the wormwood of his voice a thickened gruel of bitterness, his face shrouded. 'Yer da, blessed wee man that he was, had no learnin' beyond weaponry and a wee bit tallying – but he made sure ye could read and write like a canting priest and provided other learning betimes.'

'I am a Kirkpatrick o' Closeburn, kin to the Bruces – my namesake holds the place from the Annandale Bruces, yet he has been more seen in the company o' those who are King Edward's men through an' through. My namesake is the lord, and I am the poor relation, who has no way with letters or writin', for who would bother hiring a wee *dominie* to teach the likes o' me that?'

Hal shifted uncomfortably, remembering his own teacher and how he had fretted against him; here was a man who was bitter that he never had the same.

'I speak the French, mind you,' he went on – breaking into that tongue and speaking as much to the fire and his own thoughts as to Hal. 'And some of the Gaelic learned from the Bruce. And a little Latin, for the responses. And the *lingua franca* yon little toad Lamprecht uses, learned while in France and . . . elsewhere.'

He stopped, paused, then continued in French, as if to prove his point.

'I have never been touched by sword on shoulder, nor handed a set of gilded spurs. I can bear the arms of Closeburn, but so tainted with lowly markings for my station that it is less shameful to bear none at all. I can use the weapons of a knight, but I have never sat a warhorse in my life, nor expect it.'

He broke off, bringing his stare back to fall on Hal's face. He shook off the French, like a dog coming from a stream.

'Yet the Bruce esteems me for the talents I have, which are considerable. I ken the hearts o' men and women both, ken when they lie and when they plot. I ken how to use a sword, my wee lord o' Herdmanston, but I ken best how to wield a dirk in the night.'

There was a chill after this that the flames could not dispel. Hal cleared his throat.

'You expect advantage from all this, from the Earl when he is king?'

'Weesht on that,' Kirkpatrick answered softly, then sighed.

'I did so,' he added flatly. 'Now I see that what an earl wants an' what a king requires are differing things.'

He was silent for a little while, leaving the fire to speak in pops and spits. Then he stirred.

'When I was barely toddlin',' he said, 'I got into the habit of makin' watter wherever I stood.'

He broke off at Hal's chuckle, his scowl softening, then vanishing entirely into a smile of his own.

'Aye, a rare vision, I daresay, but I was a bairn, for all that. My ma warned me never to piss in her herb garden, which were vegetables and did not benefit from such a waterin'. Being an obedient boy, I never did so, preferring to keep it in until I could spray the chickens, which was better fun entire. Until the day the rooster turned and pecked me on the pizzle.'

Hal's laugh was a sharp bark, quickly cut off lest he offend. Kirkpatrick's chuckle was reassuring.

'Jist so. A painful experience and it was so for a time. Peelin' scab and stickiness was the least o' it – but my mither soothed me with ministrations and good advice she thought a boy like me might remember. Chickens is vegetables, she says to me.'

He stirred the fire again so that sparks flew.

'Since then,' he added, 'I have been aware that nothin' is as it appears.'

'Nothin' is, certes,' Hal agreed morosely. 'I fought at the brig o' Stirlin' and at Callendar woods with Wallace – yet these last months I have been fighting against the same men whose shoulders I once rubbed.'

'So?'

The challenge made Hal bristle.

'So it is no way for a future king of Scots to behave, cleaving his own folk. They will not care for it, I am thinking.'

Kirkpatrick waved one hand, which had the added effect of scattering the midges.

'Sma' folk,' he growled and jerked his shadowed head at where Sim and Dog Boy sat, shadows against the last of the bloodstained sky. 'D'ye think they care who rules them? As long as they have their livelihood, the De'il could wear the crown. It is the *nobiles* of this kingdom Bruce will have to worry ower.'

Hal thought about it. He had seen the sma' folk, barefoot, shit-legged, trembling, yet determinedly hanging on to their long spears and immovable from the shoulders of the men next to them. Not noble, some not even landed, unable in many cases to understand the very speech of the man next to them and with the men from north and south of The Mounth suspicious of one another, they came together for one reason. They had cared enough to be angered.

Though it had been slow and long in the growing, a realization was sprouting in Hal that there was a kingdom here that the commonality marked enough to defend – more to the point, it was one where the bare-footed shitlegs considered they had as much say in who ruled them as any earl. He said as much to Kirkpatrick.

'Mayhap,' Kirkpatrick growled at this, trying to shrug the matter off and failing, for he was no longer as sure as he once had been.

Chickens is vegetables, he thought.

CHAPTER THREE

Balmullo, Fife
The same night

They brought him in the dark on a litter, a milling crowd of riders and footmen strangely silent save for a grunt here, a hissed warning there. They hefted the litter up the steep stairs and across the span of wooden walkway to the door of the stout stone house.

There were lights from torches that let the curious, peeping from the wattle buildings clustered around Balmullo, see who it was who had arrived, but not who they carried in. The Earl of Buchan, visiting his wife, they saw; one or two of the women, swaddled in shawls, added 'puir sowl' to that, for it was hard enough for the Countess of Buchan to have to endure the presence of the Earl's creature as her gaoler without The Man Himself descending on her for his rights.

The creature met the litter at the door, spider-black and hair-thin with a face somehow twisted out of true. The nose, speckled with the fade of old pox-marks, was bent and twisted and there was a permanent stain, like a birthmark or blood bruise, on one cheek where he had once been hit with an iron skillet. There was a chin on the man, but not much of one and

54

it made the teeth stick out like a rat from between damp lips limned by a wisped fringe of beard and moustache, greying now.

He was preparing, Isabel saw, to be scraping and deferential to his master, the Earl of Buchan, in the hope of preferment away from his duties at Balmullo. No more than a mastiff, she thought, set to watch as much as guard and knowing he is hated.

Yet the mastiff that was Malise Belljambe had to stand aside when the grunting men sweated through the yett and into the main hall with their burden, who said nothing beyond a muffled curse when they set him down too hard.

Malise did not want to tangle with the carriers, who stank of sweat, woodsmoke and old blood; the leader lay in the litter like the Devil at rest, but a lesser imp, in his black carapace of boiled leather, spat curses at the careless handlers in a tongue Malise knew to be the *Gaelic* used by those strange caterans north of The Mounth.

Buchan followed, peeling off his gloves and shifting to remove his cloak from over his head without unpinning it, seeing Malise scuttle to help him. He nodded only a brief recognition – Malise was a mammet, no more, useful for the scut work that was necessary in these savage times. Then the light from the sconce flared in the night breeze and lit up his wife.

He took a breath, for he had not seen her in some months and had managed to forget how she could look, fresh from bed. Her hair was still richly coppered and, even when he knew there was artifice involved in that, the knowledge did not spoil matters. She was beautiful still, the body hinting at slender promise even wrapped in nightclothes and a fur-trimmed gown. Her eyes, lapis in the torchlight, were hard and cold as those gems and he felt the old slither of resentment and anger, quickly beaten down, for he had not come to quarrel.

She saw the cat and dog of that chase itself across a face

heavier than before. He seemed weightier altogether, she thought, surprised at how six months could make such a difference. Then she saw that it was not fat – though there were colonies of that round his middle and chin – but a droop to the once-powerful shoulders, as if he carried too much across them.

His hair was pewter, his eyes glass and iron; for a moment Isabel wondered if he would wave imperiously to the bed-chamber and follow her in, as he usually did – though less this last year than ever, she noted.

Buchan thought of it, then dismissed it. He had almost done with grunting and sweating on her for no result – even the pleasure of it was licked away by her dignified detachment as she left him at the end of it, he spent and ashamed at his grossness.

No offspring came from it and, for a long time, he had wondered whether this was natural or contrived by her – but he had had other women since and in numbers, too, as if to make up for the lack she offered, and none had conceived. Buchan was beginning, with a nag of fear he could not dismiss, to realize that the problem lay with himself.

'Wife,' he grunted at her in the end and she acknowledged matters with a cool, curt bow and then brought forward a servant and a tray with wine and food on it.

'Malise,' she declared, 'see to the care of the others and the stabling of their horses. Find room for them all where you can – but be polite in the asking.'

Malise hovered malevolently for a moment, caught Buchan's eye and bowed obsequiously.

'My lord's visit?' Isabel asked and Buchan, goblet in hand, nodded to the litter, perched near the fire and surrounded by the grim-faced men.

'Wallace,' he growled. 'He is sick from a wound, so I brought him here. You have some skill with the medical and can be trusted not to blabber.'

She tried hard not to blink, to stay as stone, but it was difficult. Wallace was outlawed and harbouring him was as good as a death sentence to Buchan, only just returned to the favour of King Edward. Her skill with 'the medical' was one more perversion of her sex and station and she had thought that, if her husband had considered it all, it was to add it to the black sin of her.

Isabel looked her husband full in his fleshy, pouch-eyed face and had back a cool, wordless stare; she realized, suddenly, what the stooping weight he bore was and that there was steel in the man – more so than even she had thought, with his dogged persistence in carrying on resistance to the English, whether openly or covert.

'I will take to your chambers,' he gruffed, 'so that folk will spread the word that this was merely the Earl coming to take his rights of his wife. Happily for you, I need sleep more than your loins for the moment, so you need not fash over it.'

He did not wait, but barrelled off into the hall's dim, smoke from the torches fluttering like dark insinuation in his wake.

The men round the litter parted deferentially when she came up and the figure on it, half propped up on his elbow, gave her a grin from a familiar face, sheened and grey.

'Coontess. Good to greet ye, certes – though I am sorry to be trailin' trouble to yer hall.'

She had last seen him before the battle at Stirling and was shocked. The hunted years had leached the autumn bracken from his hair and streaked a grey turning to silver. The great size of him was the same, but there had never been much fat to start with, so that hunger had started in to wasting muscle that hard running was turning twisted and clenched like hawsers. The smell of him was rank, like the crew who surrounded him, overlayed with another, pungent stink that Isabel knew well.

She inspected the leg, seeing the green-black lump on it just below the knee, the fret of little red lines.

'Took a dunt some time back,' Wallace said cheerfully. 'At

Happrew. Cracked the bone in my shin, but it seemed to knit well enough. Then came this.'

'There is rot in it,' Isabel said flatly and Wallace chuckled harshly.

'I ken that, lady,' he replied. 'Pain, too – if ye as much as blaw on it, it hurts as bad as if ye had struck me.'

'We will needs do more than blow on it,' Isabel answered and Wallace's throat apple bobbed twice, then he nodded. The smile was gone.

'Ah spier ye, lady – fit's gan wrang?'

The voice was thick, the accent strange from the black-carapaced Fergus the Beetle. Isabel explained as best as she thought the man would understand and he nodded, blued bottom teeth sucking his top lip, brows lowered in a frown and eyes peering from the tangle of hair and beard, his face dark from sun and dirt, sheened with grease as protection against wind and rain.

'Ah howkit oot a daud o' muck frae it,' he told her. 'Black as the De'il's erse, beggin' the blissin' o' ye, lady. Wull he gan live yet?'

'Away with ye, Fergus,' Wallace said gently, hearing this. 'Leave the good wummin to her skill.'

She had water heated and brought, with cloths and a keen, sharp skewer; Wallace followed it with his eyes, then met hers. Isabel felt clammy at what she had to do to a wound that hurt with a breeze on it, but he swallowed once, then nodded.

'Hold him,' she ordered and his men went to shoulders and feet. She hovered the skewer over it and saw him brace – then she struck.

He howled, thrashed, vomited and fainted. The skewer went flying from her hand and skittered across the rushed flags; even as it did she knew she had failed.

It took ten minutes for him to recover. Slick with new sweat, he managed a wan grin from the whey of his face.

'I have the idea o' it, now, lady,' he said and held out his hand for the skewer. 'Ye have the strength o' purpose but no arm for the deed.'

She handed it to him and he wrapped all but the last fingerjoint length of it in a cloth while she watched, fascinated and appalled. Could she do this if it were her suffering?

He placed the tip of the skewer gently, just where she indicated and the blue-black mass seemed to Isabel to be pulsing now. Then he nodded to Fergus and the others, who came up and placed their hands on him in readiness.

'Bigod,' he said, lifted one great fist and hammered it down on the handle of the skewer.

When he came to his senses for the second time she had placed both fists on either side of the punctured wound and squeezed a festering, stinking mass of green-black pus until the blood flowed cleanly. Then she washed it in clean water and bound it in a warm bran poultice and made him a drink of henbane, knotgrass and yarrow.

He drank it obediently, made a face.

'What did ye lace into this?'

She told him.

'I stirred in some honey,' she added, 'which is what you do wi' wee boys.'

He grinned, though his face was still pale.

'I thought ye had poured in a pint o' my pish, rather than taste it yersel' to find what is sufferin' me.'

She tidied up stinking cloths and bowls, moving soft so that the men, Fergus among them, would not be woken, though she doubted a shrieking Devil could have stirred them.

'I have no need to lick your piss, or cast your astrology,' she told Wallace, smiling the while, 'for it would still come out the same – yon wound had black bile in it. If ye keep the cloths clean and take rest, ye will be none the worse in a few days.'

He experimented and grinned admiringly at her.

'Och, the pain is vanished entire already. I will sleep the night a bit an' be gone away by mornin'.'

'You need more rest than that,' she argued. 'Some decent meals would not go amiss either.'

He frowned and shook his infested tangle of hair.

'I have not far to go. Tam Halliday at Moffat is a safe place. We go there when all else has failed us.'

She looked sharply at him.

'You should not be tellin' me that, where other ears can hear. That said in a kitchen is told in a hall, sir.'

He shrugged and gave her back a lopsided smile.

'Yer husband kens fine I am headed for there. He is safe now – I am here, am I not, at his instruction?'

'Is he so safe, then?'

The words were out before she could stop them and he cocked his head on one side.

'Give yer tongue more Fair days than yer head, lady,' he replied, his smile robbing it of sting. 'He has good points, has yer husband.'

She flushed at his chiding and he sighed a little and waved one hand.

'Besides,' he added, 'the man is a lion in his own cause.'

'His cause is himself,' Isabel persisted warningly and Wallace nodded.

'Exactly so – and so it is that he has need o' me. His cause is the spoiling of Bruce, ever the Comyn way, which is why he needs me, to keep Bruce dangling on declaring a kingship that belongs to John Balliol.'

He paused and the smile grew broader.

'Mind, I would not be as sure o' the new wee Lord o' Badenoch, Comyn though he is.'

She nodded, knowing Red John Comyn, Lord of Badenoch since his father's death, had his own claims to the throne. A cousin to her husband and more important because of his lineage, that wee red-headed lord could be tempted – save that he was still currently imprisoned for his part in the rebellion. She had no doubt that he would wheedle his way out, as everyone else had.

She thought of Hal and wondered where he was.

'I will let you sleep, Sir William,' she answered, turning away with the light.

'Have ye seen ony o' yer man?' he asked, soft, gentle – and vicious as a slap. It made her turn and put one hand to her throat at the sudden rush of memories. All she could do was shake her head and he gave a long, slow series of nods in answer.

'A good man is Hal o' Herdmanston,' he went on, speaking low, his face almost vanished in the dim beyond her light.

'Not a name welcomed by some in this house,' she managed.

'Blue's beauty, red's all taken, green is grief and yellow forsaken,' he replied, half to himself and she heard his chuckle. 'I still have memory o' the words o' love, ye see, for all that it seems to have passed me by.'

'Leave,' she said suddenly, flooded with sadness for the man. 'Leave this land. Find a life elsewhere. Peace . . .'

The chuckle was dry, rasping as talons on a wall.

'Too late.'

His eyes glazed and she knew he was looking to a future that might have been.

'Is John Balliol worth this?' she asked bitterly. 'Is any king?'

Wallace snapped from his reverie.

'There speaks the Eden serpent's yin true friend,' he replied, though his grin took any venom from it. He leaned forward a little, his face set, his eyes hot.

'John Balliol is our liege-lord,' he said. 'To fight for anything else in this riven kingdom is simply to forge your own chains on behalf of some usurping tyrant.'

He leaned back on the pillow and managed a tired smile.

'And if that is too fine coming from the brigand likes of me, then settle for this – too many men would bid me to a roast an'

61

stick me with the spit these days. I have picked my road and will walk to the end o' it.'

She felt a wave of sorrow and, suddenly, his face formed in the sconce light as he rose up and thrust his stare at her, serious as a stabbing. For a moment she thought he had felt her pity and was ashamed of it – then realized that all the pity came from him.

'Your road, lady, is forked an' ye have stood at the cross for too long. *Birk will burn be it burn drawn; sauch will sab if it were simmer sawn.* Mark me.'

In the morning, he bid her farewell with thanks and a gift which she hid from Buchan. Then he and all his men were gone, leaving only the sour smell and the litter behind. Buchan, risen and breakfasted early, was able to take leave of his wife at the house door in daylight, as if only he and his entourage had arrived.

'Wife,' he said, grunting up on to the palfrey. He felt a sudden rush of utter sadness, for her as much as himself and for what might have been if matters had twisted differently. She was beautiful still, while the events of the night before and the reason for his coming at all showed the strength and skills of her. A fine countess she would have made.

Then the memories of all her stravaigin', her slights and breathtaking dishonours wrenched pity from him and he nodded over her head, to the spider-leg thin Malise at her back.

'Watch,' he said and turned the horse's head.

She stood as if dutifully mourning his going, but her mind turned Wallace's words over and over. *Wood will burn even if drawn through water and the willow will droop if sown out of season.*

Five years she had resisted her natural inclinations, shackled by the knowledge that, if she stuck to the bargain, Hal would remain safe from Buchan's wrath.

Did he still hold feelings for her, after all these years?

Could she fortress herself against the promise of them for longer?

The tchik, tchik seemed like a forge hammer on an anvil in the chill dark of the place, bouncing off the hidden stones; the sparks seemed big as cartwheels. It did not seem possible for any one of them not to start a major conflagration, never mind smoulder some firestarter charcoal into embered life.

'There are dead folk here,' Sim Craw intoned. Lamprecht snorted; he heard the fear in the man's voice and it pleased him to see this great beast rendered trembling by the dark and the dead. Neither of them held any fears for Lamprecht.

'That is the usual purpose o' a crypt,' Kirkpatrick said dryly and his face was suddenly looming out of the dark, reddened as an imp's in the fires of Hell, cheeks puffed as he blew the spark into a tiny blossom of flame, fed the nub end of a candle to it and then the candle to the lantern.

Light bloomed, making them blink and look away even as they crept closer to it. For all his insouciant airs, Hal thought, Kirkpatrick is as ruffled as the rest of us; he had heard the lantern's loose horn panels rattle in the tremble of the man's hand. Then he looked at the red-dyed devil face of Lamprecht and corrected himself. All ruffled save this, he thought.

Four stone kists glowered in the flickering shadows and Hal saw that every wall of the place was niched with small, square holes. The common folk are turfed up in the chapel yard but this place is reserved for the priests, Hal thought, with the stone tombs for the start of it then, when only the bones are left, they are stuffed in a hole in the wall. Cloistered in death as in life.

'Is this the very kist, then?' Sim hissed and Hal saw the only one without a heavy cover.

'Aye,' Kirkpatrick grunted, moving to the door at the top of three worn stone steps. It led to the inside of the chapel and

Hal hoped it would be an easier opening than the one that had led to this place.

Choked with weeds and disuse, it had to be dug out and each grunt and thump of it panicking them with discovery. They had brought three of the steers with them, to pretend they were gathering them up from grazing among the dead, but it was not much of an excuse. Dog Boy had been left at the entrance, as much for the trinity of kine as a guard for the backs of the ones in the crypt.

'Ach – it is empty.'

Sim's voice was still a hissed whisper, but disappointment had robbed him of his fear, so that it was loud and seemed louder still in the echo of the place.

'Weesht.'

Kirkpatrick's scowl was matched by a notched eyebrow of Sim's own.

'I only thought there might be someone in it,' he protested. Loudly.

'I have no care if Christ's very bones are in it,' Kirkpatrick spat back. 'I should have handed ye a horn and had ye announce us.'

'Open the bliddy door,' Sim responded in a low mutter and Kirkpatrick drew out his dagger, the four sides of it winking malevolently. Hal and Sim waited, half-crouched as if the niches of the place would erupt shrieking demons, but there was only the smell of stone and old must. Yet the square holes of the place seemed like accusing black eyes on Hal's back.

The rending creak was a rasp along all their nerves, so that Kirkpatrick stopped at once and everyone froze.

'No horn needed,' Sim growled bitterly and Hal silenced him, deciding that matters had gone far enough between him and Kirkpatrick. The latter put away his four-sided dirk and heaved the door open, heedless of the shrieking grate of it.

'Who is in here anyway?' he demanded into their wincing. 'A rickle of old bones, yon wee priest and Jop himself, too huddled in a hole to be a bother.'

Jop was not cowering, for they found him after creeping, mouse-quiet, through the chapel, a place as simple as a barn, no transepts, with a second-storey *campanile* and beams just visible in the light.

Vine leaves painted an eye-watering green adorned the corbels and capitals of pillars built into the half-stone walls and lurid, flaming scenes from the scriptures jumped out from rough white plaster on every side; Hell burned more fiery in the glimmer of Kirkpatrick's lantern.

There was a font near the door, no more than a large bowl on a plinth and, apart from an altar on a dais, nothing else but a worn flagged floor. Above the altar was a painting of Saint Christopher bearing the Christ Child, who scowled disapprovingly at the unlit sanctuary lamp.

There was no sign of the priest they had seen earlier – but Jop was up and fiercely challenging when they came through the door to his room, up some stairs of the wooden *campanile* and one level below the belfry itself.

'Who's this – who the De'il are you?'

He was big, Hal admitted, seemingly bigger in the low-ceilinged room, already crowded with a truckle bed, a stout kist and a brazier of red coals. Copper hair, a fierce eye, big shoulders – for a moment they all three thought they had stumbled on The Wallace by accident.

Yet a second glance told the truth of it – the face was the same, but as if someone had stuck bellows in the mouth and puffed it up. The eye was fierce, but the heart behind it was not. The height was the same, but the shoulders were fatty and the belly an ale cask.

'Jop,' Kirkpatrick declared and hauled out the four-sided dirk, so that the big man backed away, collided with the truckle and sat so hard Hal heard it splinter.

'Who sent ye?' the man hoarsed out and Kirkpatrick chuckled.

'Nobody in London, if that is what ye think,' he replied. 'Though ye will speak of that place afore we are through.'

'No English neither,' Hal added. 'Though Longshanks will be anxious to ask you aboot the cross ye have snugged up somewheres.'

Jop blinked and sagged, which brought a vicious chuckle from Kirkpatrick.

'Aye, we ken of it. Ye will tell us where we can find it.'

'It were only half the cross. Yon wee pardoner, Lamprecht, the coo shite, had half of it,' he offered to Kirkpatrick. 'We helped shift some loot from the back o' the minster where it had been hid, for Mabs in Sty Lane, though it was ower treacherous to try at that time, wi' Pudlicote's skin still wet on Westminster's door.'

'And did you take it to yer kin, The Wallace?' Hal asked.

'Him?'

Jop was scorning and wiped some sweat from his palm across dry lips, watching the wink of the knife.

'If ye see him, offer my blissin',' he said sourly. 'God be wi' The Wallace, for he ne'er took from a man but all he had.'

'Meaning?' demanded Hal, and Jop, his tongue like a lizard, spilled it all out like water from a spout.

He had sought out Wallace in the hope that his kin might shelter him and buy the gilded half-cross he had brought with him, for it was well known The Wallace had the hard cash of a dozen good raids.

Hal and Kirkpatrick shared brief glances.

'So Wallace knows all this?' demanded Kirkpatrick and Jop curled a lip.

'Aye, he does. Laughed. Then took the shine,' he said in a bitter whine. 'I had six and Lamprecht had six. Bliddy Wallace took mine, for The Cause he says.'

He spat into the coals of the brazier.

'Kin,' he added venomously.

'And the Rood?' demanded Hal.

Jop's face almost folded in half with the frown.

'The Rood? Lamprecht had that, coveted it above all else . . . here, did he send ye?'

Hal and Kirkpatrick shot savage, stunned glances at each other, for it was clear the pardoner had cozened them all and lured them here. As if their thoughts had summoned up the Devil, the clank of a poor-iron bell above their heads was a shattering explosion.

Jop reeled up and bellowed with the shock of it, so that Kirkpatrick reared back; Jop, seeing his chance, lashed out and the blow slammed Hal backwards into the wall with a crack. Sim sprang forward and he and Jop locked with each other like rutting rams.

In an instant, all was chaos and fury. Sim and Jop strained and staggered, knocking over the brazier with a clatter, spilling hot coals in a glowing mockery of rubies; Kirkpatrick, cursing, started forward, was hit by the struggling pair and knocked sideways and over the kist.

Hal hauled himself up, saw the smoulder of old rushes and started stamping on the bloom of flame. Sim and Jop finally crashed into the bed, fell on it, broke the poles and rolled on to the floor. There was a thump and a roar, then Sim rose up and staggered back a step or two.

'Ease up, Jop,' he bellowed. 'Doucely, man – we mean ye no harm.'

'Murderers. Thieves. Lamprecht . . .'

Kirkpatrick fought the panic in him – the noise of the fight, the shouting, Hal's mad stamping on flames was all fit to wake the dead in the crypt. Jop roared forward in a rush of fear and Sim, caught off balance, went sideways. Kirkpatrick, fast and unthinking as a hornet in a fist, whirled and struck.

Jop gave a coughing grunt, swayed a little with a look of amazement on his face as he stared at where Kirkpatrick had punched him . . . not a hard blow . . .

Then the dagger thrust to his heart felled him, and like a tree he crashed to the rushed floor, his head bouncing hard enough to let everyone know he was dead.

Hal's feet finally stopped stamping on the flames.

'Christ be praised,' he murmured, shocked.

'For ever and ever,' Kirkpatrick intoned reverently, then wiped the dagger clean on Jop's tunic, pinched out a coal smouldering in the man's hair and straightened.

'Murder was no part of this,' Hal accused.

'It is now,' Kirkpatrick answered, his sneer bloody in the light and there was no denying the logic of it, which made Hal click his teeth shut.

'We should be away,' Sim interrupted, then jerked as the bell boomed out again, loud as the doors of Hell opening.

'Christ's Bones . . .' hissed Kirkpatrick.

'Lamprecht,' Sim spat and Kirkpatrick's curse was pungent.

'We should be away from here,' Hal warned, but Kirkpatrick was already at the door and the others followed him. At the lintel, Kirkpatrick paused, turned and kicked the overturned brazier so that the last coals spilled out, the soft flaring chasing him out of the room.

They moved swiftly into the dim of the hall, where their shadows scored the walls in a mad dance. Someone loomed out of the dark, making Hal shout with surprise.

'Hold,' called a voice and Kirkpatrick whirled and struck, rat-swift and hard – save that his wrist was suddenly shackled. He gave a roar and a jerk, but Sim held the grip.

'Christ's Wounds,' he spat. 'Would ye kill a priest now?'

The wee priest, woken and brought to the body of the chapel by the noises, had fallen in his shock and sat looking up in horror at the glittering dagger and the gripped wrist that stopped it coming down on him. Sim let it go, moving swiftly to put himself between the dirk and the priest, whom he hauled up by the front of his robe, staring down into the little man's anguished twist of a face.

'Do ye ken me?' he demanded and had to repeat it before the priest blinked and focused on him.

'Ye are thieves an' violators o' the house o' God . . . oooff.'

The air was driven out of him by Sim's belly-blow and a second massive fist crashed behind his ear and sent him slamming to the ground.

'Good,' Sim said and Kirkpatrick moved to go round him. Hal caught the man's elbow and hauled him back.

'Mak' siccar,' Kirkpatrick hissed and Hal jerked roughly on the arm he held.

'No need. You heard the man – he does not ken who we are and so can tell them nothin'. Have you no' had killing enough?'

'He has lots he can spill . . .' Kirkpatrick hissed back, trying to tear himself free.

'Not blood this night,' answered Hal grimly and locked his stare with a hard one of his own.

The boom of the pounded door opening racked them from the moment; Kirkpatrick cursed and they were off like hares for the crypt door, scurrying through as smoke spilled out of Jop's room behind them, stumbling down the crypt stairs and between the kists, then out into the rain-washed night, where they sucked in air and a mirr of rain soft as the lick of a fawning dog.

There was no moon, no stars, just the wet of the grass beneath their feet; then behind, flames flicked and Hal realized that Kirkpatrick had tossed the lantern aside in the crypt. Beyond that, a dull glow showed where the church burned.

The guards had come up fast, for they had been waiting, night after night, in hourly expectation of capturing the creeping, sleekit Wallace, and the dull clanking of the church bell had spilled them out, ready armed. They were holding axe and sword – one had a spear – with heater shields, maille and helmets so they thought they had the edge on three men in drover's rags with no more than knives.

Hal cursed; the English garrison from Riccarton had not been part of their plan – though it was clear to Hal that it had been an integral part of Lamprecht's.

The guards closed in; there was a wild whirl of grunts and the belling of steel on steel. Sparks flew from the blades and a spear from the shadows, flung at Hal by a desperate hand and falling short to skitter madly along the rutted track.

Sim's roar was so close it made Hal's ear buzz and he jerked back as a sword came at him, managing to fend it off with the dirk, though the blow numbed his arm and all but ripped the weapon from his grasp.

He ducked, spun, slashed and felt the blade catch, heard a howl. A blade slithered at him and he only just managed to turn sideways so that it slid through his tunic, leaving a strange cold line under his ribs. The man behind it stumbled on, unable to stop and off balance so that Hal's knife thrusts, three quick viper strikes in his unprotected neck dumped the man onto the muddy track.

Kirkpatrick was snarling like a pit-fighting dog in a mad jig with two guards. More were coming up and the bobbing lights of their lanterns were clear; behind, Hal heard curses and the crypt door splinter, half turned to see the last flare of flame as more guards stamped out the fish-oil flames of the thrown lantern and freed the entrance into the chapel cemetery.

They were in deep trouble, Hal knew, as two men came at him. He stepped, half-turned and slammed a shoulder into the nearest, sending him reeling back and cutting him with a slash. Then something hit him on the back of the head and the world wobbled, a place of whirling dirt and muddy water.

He found himself on his hands and knees, forced himself to rear upright, slashing wildly, feeling the back of his head start to burn, hearing the roar of his own sucking breathing. His mouth was full of the salted metal tang of blood and he felt the sudden talon grasp of fingers on his shoulder; he wondered, almost idly, what had happened to the Dog Boy.

70

The hand wrenched him round and he swung weakly, felt his knife hand clamped and a voice hissed:

'It's me. Sim. Leave off that.'

Then, in the misted haze of his head, Hal heard the bawling of cattle and almost laughed. Sim, on the other hand, was cursing and dragging him sideways; the pair of them fell in the mud and rolled over as black shapes clattered past, bellowing their annoyance. A slim, dark shadow yelped and nipped at their heels.

Hal shook himself back to the road and the night and the mud, in time to see the little black cattle, horns like curved scimitars, stampeding off down the road in a scatter of mud and water and English garrison.

'Time to be away,' said a calm voice – Dog Boy – and they wraithed off into the night, Dog Boy calling up his cattle dogs as he went. By the time lack of breath forced them to stop, he was frowning, for one of the pair had not responded.

'I fear it is killed,' he growled. 'Good Beauchien,' he added, patting the other.

Beauchien, Hal thought and laughed, then winced at what that did to his head. Sim was fussing round his ribs and muttering, so that Hal realized, with a sudden shock, that he had been badly cut. Kirkpatrick nodded admiringly to the Dog Boy.

'Timely appearance,' he said. 'That trick wi' the kine saved our hides, certes.'

'I had the wit of Lamprecht's intent too late,' Dog Boy said mournfully apologetic. 'I am sorry.'

'What wit?' Sim demanded, peering at the dark stain along Hal's ribs and tutting disapproval.

'The daftie boy,' Dog Boy said. 'He wanted the shell from yon pardoner's hat but it was only later that I realized he had asked for it before and also been refused.'

He stopped and stared at the slowly comprehending faces.

'Lamprecht came here before and the daftie boy saw him. I

am betting sure the pardoner went to see Jop – and then went to find us and the Earl Robert. I dinna ken why, but I was sure no good was in it.'

A plaintive bawling snapped the silence and Sim cursed.

'Stirk Davey's coos are scattered,' he moaned. 'The Riccarton English will be sooking the juice off steaks afore the morn's done – and we are out by a pretty penny.'

Hal thought that a harsh judgement on a timely use of charging cattle, but his head hurt so much that he felt sick and could not speak for a long time. When he did, it was not cows that he spoke of.

Instead, his question fell on them like a crow on a dead eye, made them realize who was missing.

'Where's Lamprecht?'

CHAPTER FOUR

Lincoln
Nativity of Christ (Christ's Mass Day), 1304

Steam from horses and riders blended with the fine gruel of churned up mud and snow in a sluggish mist that was filled with shouts and grunts and clashes of steel so that the men behind Bruce shifted on their horses.

'Wait,' he commanded and he felt them settle – all but brother Edward, of course, who muttered and fretted on his right.

Bruce looked at the wild, swirling *mêlée*, men hammering one another with blunted weapons, howling with glee, breaking off to bring their blowing horses round in a tight circle and hurl themselves back into the mad knotted tangle of fighting.

'Now,' Edward growled impatiently. 'There he is . . .'

'Wait.'

Beyond the mud-frothed field loomed the great, dark snow-patched bulk of the castle, where the ladies of the court watched from the comfort of a high tower, surrounded by charcoal braziers, swaddled in comforting furs and gloved, so that their applause would sound like the pat of mouse feet.

'Now,' Edward repeated, his voice rising slightly.

'Wait.'

'Aaah.'

Bruce heard the long, frustrated growl, saw the surge of the powerful *destrier* and cursed his brother even as he signalled the others to follow the spray of kicked-up mud. With a great howl of release, Bruce's *mesnie* burst from the cover of the copse of trees and fell on the struggling mass.

Too soon, Bruce realized. Far too soon – the target saw Edward descend, the trail of riders behind him, and broke from the fight to face them, howling from underneath the bucket helm for his own men to help him. De Valence, he bellowed. De Valence.

Edward's light, unarmoured horse balked and swerved as de Valence's powerful warhorse reared and flailed with lethal hooves, the blue and white, mud-stained caparison flapping. Coming in on the other side, Bruce leaned and grabbed a handful of de Valence's surcoat, took a smashing blow on his mailed arm which numbed it, causing him to lose his grip.

De Valence, off balance on the plunging *destrier*, gave a sharp, muffled cry and fell sideways, raking one spur along the caparisoned back of the warhorse. It screamed and bolted; de Valence, his other foot caught, bounced off behind it, yelling once as he carved a rut through the mud and into the dangerous, prancing pack.

'Him,' yelled Edward and his brother screwed round in the saddle as a figure – the one who had hit him, he realized – tried to get away from the Bruce men. 'Rab – get him.'

Bruce reacted like a stoat on a rabbit, without thinking, seizing the man round the waist and hauling him bodily out of the saddle ignoring the curses and kicks and flails. He carried the man out of the maelstrom *mêlée* and dumped him like a sack of metal pots.

Malenfaunt, dazed and bruised, felt rough hands on him; someone tried to tear off the bucket helm, but it was laced

74

to his shoulders. Then a voice, rough as a badger's rear-end, bellowed into the breathing holes for him to yield. He waved one hand, sore and sick with the knowledge of what this might cost him – and at the hands of the Bruces, whom he already hated. Even the satisfaction of having saved de Valence from capture did not balm it much.

Bruce saw the man's device, knew the man for Malenfaunt and rounded on his grinning brother.

'We struck for an eagle,' he said bitterly, 'but ended with a chick.'

Edward scowled; the friendly scramble of tourney continued to whirl like the mad scrapping of dogs, to celebrate the birthday of Christ.

Abbey of Evesham, Worcester
The same night

Kirkpatrick slid to Hal's side.

'Gone to London,' he grunted softly out of the side of his mouth, rubbing his hands at the flames of the great fire and not looking at Hal. He hawked, then spat in the fire so that the sizzle made those nearest growl at his bad manners. Kirkpatrick's grin back at them – travellers and pilgrims all – was feral, as befitted his pose as a hireling soldier, rough as a forge-file and not to be trifled with.

'Had that from three of his kind, bone-hunting wee shites like himself. Heading for Compostella, says one o' them.'

'They ken it is him?' Hal demanded and Kirkpatrick nodded.

'Aye,' he said in a whisper. 'An ugly dung-drop who speaks strangely and is named Lamprecht? Not hard to find even if he keeps his name hidden. Besides, he was a known face to the wee priests here.'

Hal stared moodily at the fire, while the wind howled and battered. There was snow in that wind and the travel next day would be hard and slow – they would probably have to lead their horses for most of it, so there was another curse to lay at the door of the wee pardoner, whose cunning had robbed an earl and almost led Hal and Kirkpatrick and others to their death. Hal shifted and winced; the cut under his ribs was still scabbed and leaking.

'Should have watched him closer in the first place,' Kirkpatrick said, as if in answer. 'Should have dealt with him and Jop both in that night.'

Hal turned brooding eyes on him.

'Easy as that, is it? Killed then or killed soon,' he replied bitterly. 'Scarce makes a difference – murder is murder.'

'Weesht,' hissed Kirkpatrick, looking right and left. 'Keep that sort o' speech laced.'

He leaned forward, so that his lips were closer, his breath tickling the hair in Hal's ear.

'That bell did not ring itself and it was clear that was what wee by-blow Lamprecht came for, not any Rood or rubies. He rang it out and set us in the path o' the English garrison for revenge and now he has the power to do the Bruce a bad turn, for the Earl has revealed himself in his desire for the Rood, as plain as if he had nailed his claim to the crown to the door of St Giles. And if the Bruce suffers, we suffer.'

'Jop is beyond us. Lamprecht is a creishy wee fox,' Hal replied, 'who has contrived to get us killed and failed. He is running and will want to take his ill-gotten goods away. We should let him.'

Kirkpatrick made a head gesture to say perhaps, perhaps not. There was merit in the Herdmanston lord's appreciation of matters – the wee pardoner was certainly headed south, from monastery to abbey, priory to chapel, all places where he was sure of a free meal and a safe bed for the night. But the wee bastard had the Rood and Bruce, for all that pursuing it was a danger to him – and so all those round him - could not see it pass him by and do nothing.

Returning to London was certainly not safe for Lamprecht, Kirkpatrick thought, so it may be that Hal has it right and Lamprecht was planning to carry on to the coast and a ship to France. Back to the eastern Middle Sea, where his riches could be sold with no questions asked and where his way of speaking would not mark him.

'He was daft to try what he did,' Hal muttered. 'He must hold a hard hate for what we did to him that night in the leper house of Berwick.'

Kirkpatrick flapped a hand, keeping his voice low as he hissed a reply.

'We did nothing much – showed him a blade and slapped him once or twice. He was fortunate – for his partnering of that moudiwart bastard Malise Bellejambe he should have been throat-cut there and then.'

'Your answer to all,' Hal replied tersely and Kirkpatrick looked back at him from under lowered brows.

'That way we would not now be dealing with a nursed flame that will not be put out as easily as spit on a spark,' he said. 'Our saving grace is that the wee pardoner is stupid enough to try and play intrigue with the *nobiles*, whose lives entire are spent in makin' and breakin' plots and plans more cunning than any Lamprecht may devise.'

'Like Buchan?'

Kirkpatrick nodded grimly.

'Throw a Comyn in the air and ye discover a wee man thumbin' his neb at a Bruce when he lands. Buchan has sent yon Malise in pursuit of Lamprecht, to find out what he has that the Bruce chases.'

'Death for the wee pardoner, then,' Hal growled sullenly, 'no matter who reaches him first.'

Kirkpatrick, swaddling himself in cloak, surged with irritation.

'Christ, man, ye are a pot o' cold gruel,' he spat in a sibilant hiss. 'Make your mind to it – the wee pardoner is a killed man and ye had better buckle to the bit if it is yourself has to do it.

Else it will be us killed. As well that Jop is cold – as yon wee Riccarton priest should be betimes.'

'Yon priest kens nothin',' Hal muttered bitterly, 'though Jop might have explained what Lamprecht intended, had he been allowed to live a wee while longer.'

'Aye weel,' Kirkpatrick growled, aware that he had been hasty with the knife – but Christ's Bones, the man was coming at him. The wee priest, on the other hand, was neither here nor there. For certes, Kirkpatrick said to himself with grim humour, he will, by now, wish he is no longer here – and explained to Hal, patient as a mother, why it would have been better if he had died.

'The wee priest kens folk were spyin' Jop out. He kens the name Lamprecht, which was spoke out for all to hear,' he whispered, flat and cold. 'That name has already reached Comyn ears, which is why Malise is sent out. It will, for certes, be whispered in Longshanks' own by now.'

Hal said nothing, for the truth of it was a cold burn, like the wound along his ribs. Jop was better dead, if only for his own sake; the King's questioners would not have stinted on their store of agony – for all Edward Longshanks proudly pontificated about there being no torture in his realm – and the priest would be telling all he knew to anyone who would listen.

The more Hal thought on it, the more he wondered about what might have been inadvertently revealed that night. His dreams were cold-sweated with what the priest might be saying, but Hal knew he would have been hard put to kill the man for it. Nor was he sure he could kill Lamprecht as coldly.

Yet the nagging why of it was a skelf in the finger. Why had Lamprecht come back to the north in the first place, after all that had happened to him? Just to risk himself for the chance of revenge on those who had wronged him, as he saw it? It was possible, as Kirkpatrick put it, that he nursed a flame of hate. And Buchan would be interested because a Bruce was involved in it.

'Aye, weel,' Kirkpatrick said in answer to the last, a short chuckle saucing his bitter growl, 'as to that last, you underestimate the sour charm you exert on that earl – he might be spying the chance of vengeance on you himself. The bright shine on this is that Buchan, who can never resist the charms of seeing Bruce or yourself discomfited has sent Malise Bellejambe after Lamprecht and so he is let loose from being the chain-dog o' your light of love.'

'A perfect chance for me to rescue her,' Hal replied laconically, 'save that I am here.'

And five years lie between us like a moat, he added to himself; she may not even welcome a gallant knight's rescue, never mind a worn lover with blood on his hands.

'Besides,' he added, bitter with the memory, 'Buchan has already had vengeance on me. Why would he suddenly want more?'

Kirkpatrick, shuffling himself comfortable in the middle of a snoring, growling pack of other pilgrims, did not say what he thought – that perhaps, even now, the Earl's bold countess had mentioned Hal's hated name aloud. Worse yet, cried it out when her husband broke into her, as Kirkpatrick heard he was wont to do, like a drover earmarking a prize heifer.

It would be enough, he thought, to drive the Earl to visit some final judgement on the man who so cuckolded him. Christ's Bones, if it were mine I would be so driven.

Yet it was not only the lord of Herdmanston that Buchan pursued, but Bruce. The wee Lothian knight was simply a hurdle in the way of that, for the Comyn would do all they could to bring down a Bruce. And the same reversed.

Somewhere, the monks began a chanting singsong litany and a bell rang.

'No rest for any this night,' he muttered in French.

'It is the Christ Mass,' Hal answered him, with a chide in the tone of it.

'Aye, weel,' Kirkpatrick growled back, 'like most weans, He benefited from the peace o' silence in the cradle. A good observance for these times, I am thinking.'

'Yer a black sinner,' Hal replied, with a twist of smile robbing the poison of it.

'Ye are a dogged besom o' righteousness, Hal o' Herdmanston,' Kirkpatrick answered, 'but ye are mainly for sense, save ower that wummin.'

'Christ,' Hal growled back at him, 'enough hagging me with that. If you had a wummin you cared an ounce for yourself, man, you would know the sense in what I feel for Isabel of Mar.'

Kirkpatrick laughed, though there was little warmth in it.

'You once asked me as to what I wanted from serving the Bruce,' he said suddenly. 'So I ask you in return, Hal of Herdmanston – what is it keeps you here, if you carp at the work Bruce has for us? Siller? Your fortalice restored? Yon wee coontess?'

I miss Herdmanston, thought Hal. And Bangtail and Dog Boy, sent out to chase after Wallace and neither of them up to the task of it. And Sim, who oversees Herdmanston's rebuilding. And women to talk to rather than swive in a sweaty, meaningless rattle. And bairns laughing, with sticky faces. And men building rather than tearing apart. And an end of folk the likes of Malise – aye, and Kirkpatrick himself.

Above all, there was her and the music of laughing she had returned to his life, a music that had ended when his wife and son slipped out of the world. A music that, for five years, he had lived without, with no prospect of it in the black void that was today, would be tomorrow and would be still the next God-damned year. That's what he wanted back, what he hoped Bruce would somehow help him achieve.

'Music,' he said to Kirkpatrick and left the man arrowing frowns on his face.

Music?

In the end, sleep stole Kirkpatrick away from making sense of it.

Lincoln
The same night

Music flared loud as light, half-drowned by talk in the Great Hall, where banners wafted like sails and the sconces jigged in the rising haze. Sweating servants scurried in the sea of people, bright finery and roaring chatter while the musicians strummed and blew and rapped out *Douce Dame Jolie* as if Machaut himself were there to hear played what he had written.

Sir Aymer de Valence, limping and lush with glee, told the tale – yet again – of his daring escape from the clutches of Bruce by the mad expedient of hurling himself from his own horse into the middle of the *mêlée*. All the gilded coterie, the King's close friends and those who wanted to be, applauded, laughing – all save Malenfaunt, bruised and furious that the sacrifice he had made for de Valence was no part of the tale.

'Turned the German Method back on you,' de Valence yelled across and Bruce raised his goblet in smiling acknowledgement of the feat, all the while studying the ones around the bright-faced young heir to the earldom of Pembroke.

Had de Valence paid Malenfaunt's hefty ransom? Bruce pondered it; though his mother held the Pembroke lands, de Valence had the family holdings in France and so could well afford it.

If not him, then who? It was certes Malenfaunt himself did not have such coin, nor any call on someone rich enough, for all he was part of the *mesnie* of de Valence. Yet he had ransomed himself and his horse and his harness, which had not been cheap.

The music shrilled; dancers, circling in a sweaty *estampie*,

81

bobbed and weaved and laughed. The slow drumbeat thump-thump, insistent as nagging, finally silenced the players; one by one the last of the half-drunk dancers stopped stamping, blearily ashamed. Heads turned to where the Lincoln steward stood with his iron-tipped staff rapping a steady beat and, behind him, the King.

He looked every inch regal, too, Bruce thought. He stood with one mottled hand on a dagger hilt of narwhal ivory and jacinth, coiffed and silvered, prinked and rouged, brilliant in murreyed Samite and orphrey bands, but draped in a fine blue-wool cloak – no Provence perse here, of course, but good English wool; even in dress, Edward was politic.

He had good reason to look pleased with himself, too and the lavish Swan Feast was simply the statement of it, fit for the monarch of two realms. With the French king humbled to peace and with his Gascony lands secured, Edward straddled a sovereignty over the island nation that none before him had ever enjoyed.

He was sixty-six years old – less than half a year would take him past the point of being the longest-lived king England had known. Nor, Bruce added moodily to himself, was he showing any signs of ailing anytime soon – it was clear to everyone that his young queen was pregnant again.

The Plantagenet voice was equally firm and ringing loud when he spoke, of discordance made harmony, of lambs returned to the fold. Bruce watched some of the lambs – Buchan and the recently freed Lord of Badenoch for two, smiling wolves in fine wool clothing, watching him in return and offering their lying, polite nods across the rushed floor.

Then there was Wishart, wrapped in prelate purple as rich as his complexion, and Sir John Moubray with his lowered scorn of brow. My ox team, Bruce thought to himself, the three of us shackled to Longshanks to bring the Kingdom – no, the *land* – of the Scots to order for his nephew, John of Brittany, to rule as governor. That was a platform Bruce had a use for.

Yet even now the Comyn were exerting themselves, insidious as serpent coils, and Bruce could feel them undermining him with an inclusion of extra 'assistance' on this concordat of *nobiles*. Like mice, he thought, eating the cake from the inside out.

One by one, the summoned Scots lords came forward, knelt and swore their fealty in return for the favour of the silvered king and the restoration of their lands with only hefty fines as punishment. Bruce was last of all; once he would have bridled at this affront to his honour and dignity – he had once before, signing the Ragman Roll – but he had been younger and more foolish then.

Smiling, a beneficent old uncle, Longshanks raised him up pointedly, so others would see the favour – Bruce saw the silk and velvet Caernarvon scowl as Gaveston whispered something in his ear; Gaveston was a mistake, Bruce saw, and not the bettering influence Edward had hoped for his son.

The music returned, the talk, the bellowed laughter and the mingling. It was then that Edward sprang the steel trap, signalling Wishart and Moubray and Bruce close to the high seat. In front of him was a wrapped bundle, which he twitched open with a small flourish.

Bruce's heart faltered a beat, then started to run at the sight of the battered gilt. The rubies had been removed, but the Rood reliquary, blackened and charred still glowed with gilt; Jop's half, Bruce thought, trying to gather the wild scatter of his thoughts.

'Taken from Riccarton, my lords,' Edward growled, his drooping eye baleful, 'which was a Wallace holding in the lands of the Scotch.'

Behind him, the prince and others craned curiously to see better and it was a mark of things that Edward let them.

'Indeed?' Wishart replied, frowning, his voice innocent. 'That looks greatly like the cover for the Black Rood, which Your Grace took to the safety of the minster.'

'It is the same,' snapped Edward, then waved one hand dismissively. 'Removed by thieves last year. Now it seems likely your Scotch were responsible, my lords. A chapel was left in flames at Riccarton and a man murdered, a certain Gilbert of Beverley also known as Jop; a search of his belongings discovered this. A miracle it was not consumed by flame, my lords.'

'Christ be praised,' intoned Wishart.

'For ever and ever.'

'Gilbert of Beverley,' Moubray pointed out sourly, 'is an Englishman.'

The drooping eye raked him.

'Kin to the Wallace.'

The King presented the fact significantly, like a lawyer ending his case.

'Has Your Grace made enquiries?' Wishart asked blandly and the King's drooping eye twitched a little as he considered if the bishop's innocence was real. In the end, he made a small flicking gesture of dismissal.

'The local priest claimed only to be witness to the invasion and torching of the house of God. He might have said more than he did, save that God gathered him to His Bosom. His heart gave out.'

'Aye,' sighed Wishart with beatific sadness, 'the Question will do that to a man.'

The King looked hard at him.

'There is no torture permitted in this realm,' he declared. 'Only the rule of Law.'

No-one spoke and the lie hung there.

Bruce remained silent, trying not to let the relief that flooded him rise up and swamp his face, wondering wildly how long the priest's heart had lasted before it had stopped the mouth. What had the priest told Longshanks, Bruce wondered? Not enough, certes, or I would not be standing here, watching that eye droop like a closing shutter . . .

In the end, Edward was forced to continue.

84

'Find the rest of this reliquary and the relic that was in it,' he demanded. 'Find Wallace – mark this, my lords, the Scotch who wish to return fully to my grace, who wish remittance of their fines and full return of their lands, have until forty days from now to hand Wallace over. They will be watched to see how they do.'

'There are Scots loyal to you,' Wishart declared, which was stepping carefully with words, Bruce thought. Then a voice crashed in like a stone in a pool.

'All Scotch are thieves.'

Eyes turned and Malenfaunt, leaning through the huddle around the prince, drew back a little – but his eyes were fixed firmly on Bruce. The King, about to storm the man into the rushes and out of the castle for his impudence, paused.

He had heard rumours about the lord of Annandale, of course, but whispered by Bruce's enemies . . . still, it might pay to let this hound run a little. Besides, his wayward son and that bastard of a serpent, Gaveston, were watching, so a lesson in kingship might be timely.

'You have something to say, sirra?' he rasped and Bruce saw Malenfaunt quail a little, lick his lips and flick one snake-tongue glance sideways. Bruce followed the glance and came into the sardonic face of John the Red Comyn.

'I merely insist, Your Grace, that all Scotch are thieves,' Malenfaunt said, almost desperately. He was not so sure as he had been concerning this. Bruce, he had been told, was no true knight, preferring the German Method of fighting, and his reputation as the second best knight in Christendom was badly earned. Malenfaunt had seen for himself the tactics used and paid for them. Or Badenoch had, since the ransom Bruce had demanded was beyond the means of any Malenfaunt.

'All Scots, my lord?' Bruce answered softly, with a wry smile and Malenfaunt felt the surge of anger in him, the flaring rage against the man who had cozened him out of the Countess of Buchan years before, who had laid him in the mud yesterday with a foul trick. It was the sneering smile on Bruce that angered Malenfaunt and anger was as good as courage for what he had been set to do.

'Some more than others,' he replied. 'Thieves of honour especially, who swear one thing and do another at the expense of their better's mercy.'

That was clear enough and even Wishart's warning hand on his arm did no good. Bruce shook it off and any sense with it.

'You will defend that, of course, before God,' he replied and Malenfaunt felt the cold, sick slide of fear in his belly. Bruce did not seem afraid at all, for a man who could not fight like a true knight . . .

'In your beard,' he spat back. 'God defend the right.'

'Swef, swef,' Wishart demanded, attempting to patch the tearing hole of this. 'The King forbids such combats *à l'outrance . . .*'

'Usually,' the King replied and staved in the hull of Wishart's hopes. Usually. The King had not meant matters to go this far, yet he had recently removed Bruce from the sheriffdoms of Ayr and Lanark because of the whispers, seeing the dangers in handing too much power to the man.

He felt a sharp pang of annoyance and sadness; he did not want to lose Bruce to his own foolish ambition, so perhaps a humbling would be good for him. It was clear this Malenfaunt creature had been set to the task by Bruce's enemies, but he could be leashed by a king. He would have a word with both men, make it clear that, despite the use of edged weapons, death was not the finale here – though defeat in the sight of God would be humbling enough for either of them.

Afterwards, reeling with the surprise of it, Bruce was still wondering how he had landed in such a mire. Wishart was sure of how – and why.

'You lost yer head, my lord,' he declared bitterly and Bruce had to admit that was true enough, cursing himself for it.

'A family trait,' he managed lightly. 'I thought my brother

Edward had stolen most of it for himself, mark you.'

'No laughing matter,' Wishart spat back. 'It is clear who has put this Malenfaunt up to it – Badenoch and Buchan both gave him the siller that ransomed him from his tourney loss. Now he is in debt to that pair and flung in like a dog in a pitfight.'

'They must rate him highly, then,' Bruce replied sourly, 'if they think to humble me using such poor fare.'

Wishart waved an impatient hand and broke fluidly into French without missing a heartbeat.

'They win, no matter the outcome. If you beat Malenfaunt, then Buchan and Badenoch have revenge on the man who captured the Countess of Buchan and held her to ransom. If you are defeated, they have humbled you. Better still for Badenoch if you were killed in such a combat – and those will be Malenfaunt's instructions, mark me.'

He broke off and shook his head sorrowfully.

'And The Plantagenet, of course, permits it in the hope of bringing you tumbling, my lord earl,' he added. 'Mark me, the King will send word soon that you are not to kill. He will send the same to Malenfaunt – though that one may ignore it. But a defeat over such a matter will ruin your honour, leave you ostracized at court, denied the peace of God and so left at the mercy of the royal favour.'

'If he defeats me,' Bruce declared, then frowned and shook his head. 'Malenfaunt is a brave man, for all that, to put himself, with no great reputation as a knight, against me.'

Wishart snorted. In times of stress, Bruce noted wryly, he reverts to his roots and the lisping French was banished like mist.

'Think yersel' all silk and siller? Aye, mayhap – second-best knight in Christendom after the German emperor? When was the last time ye jousted *à l'outrance*, my lord earl? Using the French Method and bound to it?'

Bruce thought and the sudden, thin sliver of fear speared him. A long time, he had to admit. The French Method –

charging home on a warhorse trained to bowl a man over – was one he had used as a youth on the tourney circuit.

Then he had learned the German Method – riding a lighter horse, avoiding the mad rushes of French Method knights and attacking from behind or the side in the *mêlée*. It was called 'German' as a sneer by the French, for everyone knew it was a Saracen trick learned by crusading German knights of the Empire and brought back by them. Better for prizes and sensible in war, it was not considered honourable for the *nobiles* of the civilized world to the west. Worse even than that, it was not French.

Acceptable – barely – in the whirl of the *mêlée*, it was not permitted in that perfect contest of skill and bravery, the joust, which was the epitome of the French Method, preferred by the young and daring.

This joust was *à l'outrance* and there was no German Method permitted at the edge of extremity.

For God was watching.

Lincoln
The day after – The Feast of St John the Evangelist,
December, 1304

It was cold, so that the King was ushered to a seat with heated cushions and swathed in warm furs alongside his wife. In the striped pavilion, with the horse gently steaming and two coal braziers smouldering, Bruce saw the leprous sheen on his maille as the trembling squire helped him into the jupon emblazoned with his arms.

The horse shifted, clattered bit metal and champed froth. Bruce eyed the beast, which had been given to him by his brother since he had no decent warhorse for a joust like this. Castillians his were, fine, fast and strong but no match in a stand-up fight with something like this terror, all muscle and vein like an erect prick, with heavy legs and hindquarters. A Lombard, crossed with Germans, his brother had told him – black as the De'il's face and called, with bitter irony, Phoebus.

Somewhere outside, Malenfaunt stood with his own horse in a similar pavilion; custom decreed that neither should see each other once the processions and oaths and mummery of it all had been concluded, save at the very moment of combat. The mummery, Bruce thought to himself wryly, had possibly been the worst part of the affair.

The King had processed, the witnesses and bishops and officials of the tourney had processed, the ladies of the court had processed – including the stiff, disapproving Elizabeth. When presented with the news of the affair from her husband, she had raised one scornful eyebrow, and had spoken not one word to him in all the hours since. He could scarcely blame her – her honour was braided with his own and if he fell from grace, so did she.

Speeches had been exchanged, blessings given, oaths made regarding the anathema of using weapons forged by spells, or with spells placed on them. Lances had been measured, so that neither had an advantage and, for the same reason, agreement had been reached over the number and type of weapons carried – it was, as always, three lances, the same axe each, their own sword and a dagger or estoc of their choice.

After those had been exhausted or broken, it would be fists and teeth, Bruce thought grimly.

The rules regarding the conduct of squires and the hundreds who thronged to watch had been read out – no-one horsed on pain of death, no-one else armed on pain of death or loss of property – for this was no raucous entertainment, but a solemnity of chivalry to decide which knight was favoured by Heaven. It was decreed by custom and Law and, therefore, by God.

Bruce, moving stiffly and talking in single words, was aware that all the procession and pomp and conspicuous legality was because, when all else was done, there were no rules at all in that rectangle of tilt field.

Outside his tented pavilion was a low hum like a disturbed byke; they were removing the altar, crucifix and prayer book on which each man had sworn to defend the right of his honour before God. Bruce nodded for the squire to leg him up on to Phoebus and the horse, knowing what was expected of him, trembled a little, baiting on the spot so that the splendid drape of his covering flapped. Bruce settled himself with a creaking of new leather.

'*Faites vos devoirs*,' a voice called and the squire handed Bruce up his helmet.

'*Faites vos devoirs*.'

The squires dragged back and fastened the flaps of the pavilion and the crowd spotted him, swelling up to a roar of approval, drowning the final ritual call for both men to 'do their duty'.

The two caparisoned beasts moved out, led and flanked by squires, on to a tiltyard cleared of snow and laboriously sanded. The Tourney Marshal waited with one white glove in his raised hand. He paused; the crowd fell silent.

At least this is the last act of ribaldry, Bruce thought, and glanced at Malenfaunt, seeing how pale he was and how his face, framed in maille coif, seemed clenched like a fist. He wondered if his own was as stiff and tight and if the reason for appearing unhelmed was less to do with making sure the combatants were who they were supposed to be than for each of them to savour the fear of the other.

'*Laissez-les aller*,' the Marshal said, dropping the glove. Let them go. The squires bustled, handing up shield and lance; the first was slid through two straps on the left arm, the latter rammed firmly into the fewter attached to the stirrup.

Bruce half-turned to where Elizabeth sat, raised the lance in salute, seeing his squires scatter from him. The handing of the lance was the last allowable contact from human hands that either would receive until matters were over.

He took his helm from his saddle bow and slid it over his head, plunging himself into the dark cave of it, split only by the framed rectangle of view from the slit. His breath, magnified, wheezed in and out and he tried to slow it, feeling the end of his nose rasp against the metal. Opposite, the inhuman steel face of Malenfaunt stared blankly back at him.

From now on, Bruce thought, we are alone in this. Save for God.

Woods at Pittenweem
The Feast of St John the Evangelist, December, 1304

If it was not for the bad luck, Bangtail thought to himself, I would have no luck at all. It was bad enough having lost the cast of a dice to the Dog Boy without having the sour memory of losing the last of his dignity to the chiel as well.

Now Dog Boy was riding back to the comfort of Edinburgh and on to Sim at Herdmanston while Bangtail Hob, once the Dog Boy's better in every way, followed the guide up a muddy trail in the freezing cold.

Once, but no longer. The memory of it burned him with shame and loss. He had woken, warm and languorous in the tangled bed under the eaves of Mariotta's Howf in Kinghorn only this morning. A glorious, roaring night it had been, him and the Dog Boy both; Mariotta's was a favourite of Bangtail's and had been for years after Mariotta herself had gone to the worms.

He had woken in time to hear the rhythmic beat and grunt and squeal, in time to see the quine from last night sit up and stretch and yawn, her body white and marked here and there with ingrained dirt and the bruising of too-rough hands, but lithe still. She turned, smiling with a deal of teeth left, as he grunted upright and rubbed his eyes. The bed shook.

'Sorry to have been sae much trouble,' Bangtail growled,

nodding at her bruises. The bed rattled and the squeals grew louder but Bangtail could not see behind the quine.

'Och,' she said gently, patting him like a dog, 'ye were no bother, Bangtail – ye nivver are. It is the youngster ye brought that is loosening all our teeth.'

And there it was, laid out like bad road for Bangtail to glower on. Dog Boy, still ploughing exultantly and Bangtail who was 'nivver any trouble'. His years whirled up like leaves and crashed on him like anvils; he had aches and the thinning hair on him was less straw and more silvered. He had to roll out of his bed most nights to piss.

He was old.

So it came as no surprise when the throw of dice – to see who would go with the Wallace guide, for only one was permitted – went against him. Grinning, Dog Boy saddled the garron and rode off back to Herdmanston, leaving Bangtail sour and scowling into his ale.

An hour later the Wallace guide had arrived, sleekit and slinking – as well ye might, Bangtail thought, wi' half the country huntin' ye like a staig. He went out, saddled the garron and rode to where the guide had hissed to meet him, then watched the man wraithing from cover, twitched as a coney in the open.

The man had no horse and started to run ahead, a long, loping wolf-run born of long use – and that was the measure of how far Wallace's band had sunk. Without horses, they could no longer strike hard and fast and vanish. Without horses they were mere outlaws, locked to a place and easy to track.

The running man, in hodden wool with more stain than colour, said little, which suited Bangtail, brooding on his lot and the new reality of his life. Deliver the message from the Bruce, he said to himself, then get back to Herdmanston and begin huntin' a new life, that included his own ingle-nook and a good wummin. The thought of dying, alone and cold and old, made him shiver. The thought of a wife made him shiver, too and he did not know which one was worse.

The guide vanished. Bangtail stopped the garron and sat it for a moment, staring at the hole where he had been and then, in the trees to his left, the shadows merged, edged themselves, took shape and stepped from the gloom; Bangtail's mouth went dry.

Dark with the long grime of old dirt, wearing worn cloth, odd tanned hides, strips of fur, raggles of rusted maille and metal, they had skin the colour of old bog water, where you could see it through the tangle of hair and beard. They had spears and axes and round shields – one or two carried the shields of knights and Bangtail knew where they had come from. Some of them were women, he saw suddenly and swallowed hard at their eyes.

'Christ be praised,' Bangtail whispered.

'For ever and ever,' answered a cheerful voice and one man stepped from the others. His nose was broken and he was taller than the others, but he was not Wallace.

'Noo ye ken we are not bogles,' this one said in a broad growl of Braid and the others laughed, a sound like whetting steel with no mirth in it at all. Then Broken Nose gave a signal and Bangtail obeyed it, climbing off the garron, seeing the others close in on it with feverish eyes. He did not think he would get it back, nor the pack with his spare clothes, nor the weapons they took from him and the thought made him uneasy.

Wallace was easy enough to recognize when Bangtail arrived in his presence – head and shoulders taller than the others, dressed no differently save for the hand-and-a-half slung carelessly from one shoulder. Yet he was etched like a blade, elbows and knees knobbed on too-thin flesh, the muscle on him corded.

'Ye are Bangtail Hob,' Wallace said and had a nod in reply.

'Ye are seekin' me, it seems. Whit why – to join us?'

'God, naw.'

The cry was out before Bangtail could smother it and he

heard the growl from them, saw the cold-eyed, curled-lip gleam and started to back out of the hole he had walked himself into.

'I have done my fighting with ye,' he answered, trying to make amends and having to drown the spear in his throat with swallowed spit. 'At Cambuskenneth and again in the trees at Callendar.'

'Ye were there?' Wallace remarked and Bangtail bridled at the mild sneer in it.

'With lord Henry o' Herdmanston. We saved yer skin yon day,' he answered harshly.

Now Wallace remembered and the cold stone of what had to be done sat in his belly even deeper. He remembered the day and how the brace of Templar knights had almost ridden him down save for the skill and courage of Hal of Herdmanston and another – Sim Craw, that was it. Sim and his big latchbow. And this one, or so he claimed. Wallace tried to see this Bangtail's face on a man that day but could not make it work.

'So – ye do not wish to stand with us, wee man,' he said lightly. 'Why, then, are ye here?'

Bangtail breathed in.

'The Earl of Carrick bids ye friendship and his regard and offers what help ye might need to quit the realm for your own safety for there are those who would do you harm and give you in to the English.'

It was delivered all of a piece and Bangtail could not get the words out of his mouth fast enough. There were growls and it was not Bangtail's feverish imagination that heard dissent. Wallace was silent for a time, then shifted.

'Well, ye have delivered Bruce's message. He has gave me it afore, but refuses to listen to any of my answers. Mayhap he will listen to this one.'

Bangtail's skin crawled when Wallace said no more and the man with the broken nose grinned, wolf sharp and evil.

'I came here thinkin' this to be a perjink well-conducted meet,' he hoarsed out. 'Held by an honourable chiel.'

Wallace nodded, almost sadly. Men grabbed Bangtail's arms and he struggled briefly, his heart pounding. He could not believe this was happening.

'Ye thought wrang-wisely,' Wallace said, gentle, bitter and sad, a note that chilled Bangtail to his belly. 'We are trailbaston. Outlaws. You see how it is – we need time here an' if I let ye loose, we will have to be on the move. Besides – yer master needs my answer.'

'I will say not one thing about your presence here,' Bangtail protested and was appalled at the whine that had appeared in his voice.

'So you say,' Wallace replied flatly, 'but there was a man with ye and there may be more. I have others to think on besides my own self.'

'I fought for you!' Bangtail howled, seeing it now and struggling, far too late. Broken-Nose, grinning, started to unsheath a dagger and Wallace laid a hand on his wrist. For a moment, hope leaped like a salmon in Bangtail.

'No,' Wallace said firmly, then drew his own. 'He deserves this at least.'

The blow drove the air from Bangtail and he sat, released from the arms, trying to suck in a breath and leaking snot and tears. Then the burn of it hit him. Then the pain. He found himself on his back, staring through the latticed trees, feeling a wry laugh bubble in him at the thought of how this had come about. Two threes instead of two fives and here he was in his worst nightmare – dying alone, cold and old . . .

'Hang him from yon tree near Mariotta's place,' Wallace ordered Long Jack, feeling as if he had been slimed with someone's sick.

'You were not always as hard,' said Jinnet's Jean, starting to strip Bangtail of his welcome clothes and boots. Wallace said nothing, though he wanted to snarl that he did it for them, though it choked him.

Freedom, he thought. This is what it feels like.

CHAPTER FIVE

Lincoln
The Feast of St John the Evangelist, December, 1304

It was all familiar, but tainted with the rust of long neglect and Bruce was alarmed by how fumbling he felt. He saw the distant shape of Malenfaunt on a powerful, arch-necked beast – not his own, for certes; Bruce wondered if it was one of Buchan's, or even one of the King's.

He saw the sudden clench and curl of it, knew that Malenfaunt was spurring the beast and, with a sick lurch, dug his heels in to Phoebus, feeling the huge muscled rump gather and spring, almost rocking him backwards so that the lance wavered wildly.

Seventy ells separated them and they were at lance-length in the time it took to say '*Sire Pere, qui es es ceaus*'. Bruce saw his lance slide over the top of Malenfaunt's shield and miss his helmet by the length of a horse whisker – then the clatter of lance on his own shield slammed him sideways, reeling him in the saddle. Phoebus faltered, lost rhythm and rocked Bruce back upright before cantering on.

Stunned, shocked, Bruce fought the horse round. Christ's Bones, he shrieked to himself, his breathing a thunderous roar inside the helm, what madness drove me to this? Possession by some imp of Satan?

The Curse of Malachy, a voice nagged at the back of his mind.

Then Phoebus was round and he was thundering back down the tiltyard, trying to keep the long ash shaft's bouncing point somewhere in the region of Malenfaunt's unscarred shield.

Malenfaunt, snatching up his second lance from the rack, was blazed with a relief bordering on the exultant – Bruce was inept. He could not fight like this, as Buchan had said and that lance stroke was one a still-wet squire would have scorned.

He wrenched the head of the beast round, feeling it fight back against the cruel barb of the bit and cursing it until he deafened himself in the helmet. Then he levelled his lance and rowelled the animal into a great, leaping canter, hearing his own voice howling.

Bruce saw the mad plunge of it and felt, as well as the fear, an anger that burned it away like morning mist. He was an earl, one of the recognized best knights of Christendom and would not be made afraid by anyone. He sat deeper in the cantled saddle, straightened his legs out in the stirrups, urged Phoebus with his weight alone and sprang forward.

They clashed and the crowd roared at the perfection of the strokes, two lances burying their leafed points in each shield and shattering with a simultaneous crack that shivered splinters higher in the air than anyone could have thrown.

Bruce rocked with the blow and Phoebus staggered sideways, crossing feet over each other, at first delicate as a cat and then stumbling like a drunk. Malenfaunt felt his head snap and his teeth cracked wickedly on his tongue; the horse was flung from a canter to a dead stop and sank back on its powerful haunches, skidding furrows along the sand.

Bruce reached the far end, reined round, sobbing for breath. He threw down the splintered lance butt, worried the shattered point out of his shield and flung it away, more to give him and horse breathing space than anything. At the far end, he saw Malenfaunt drop his own shattered lance and seem to sit there while the horse snorted and shifted beneath him.

Had he given in? Too injured to continue? In his heart, Bruce knew the lie of it; this was *à l'outrance* and there was no giving in at the edge of extremity, until one or the other was forced to it, for a loss here stripped you of honour and dignity. Under the rules, it stripped you of life, too, since your opponent had the right – the duty – to kill you and the very least that could be expected was that the tongue with which you swore your falsehood to God would be removed.

For God was watching.

So also was the King and he had sent a stern-eyed squire to inform Bruce that there was to be no death in this and that his opponent had agreed to the same. Mistakes can be made, Bruce thought grimly to himself, at the edge of extremity.

Malenfaunt was now realizing how great a mistake had been made and that Bruce had all the skills others claimed for him – he had just been faltering until they came to him. From now, Malenfaunt thought with a sick sensation that threatened to loose his bowels, Bruce would be deadly with the lance – so best not to give him the advantage.

Bruce saw the flick of wrist that brought up the wicked axe from the saddle-bow. There were three lances permitted and he had two still in the rack. There was no rule that said he had to give up the advantage – but God was watching. More importantly, all the other knights were watching.

Bruce unsnagged his own axe and the two great warhorses came forward again, slower this time.

They circled, hacking at each other, slicing splinters and chips from shields in a chivalric *estampie*. The axes locked heads now and then, a furious tugging, silent save for the grunts that could be heard even over the crowd.

The axe was a wicked affair, three feet of wooden shaft with a sharp curve of blade on one side and a wicked pick-spike on the other. Another foot beyond the top was encased in a leaf-shaped spearpoint and the butt had a six-inch spike. It was designed to cleave helmets, spear through maille links, slip a point under the joints of fancy new plate vambrace and pauldron and open it like shelling crab – and Bruce loved it.

Malenfaunt realized this after the first few cuts and, by the end of the first two harsh minutes he was sobbing for breath and in fear, his flesh ruching up under all the metal in terror at what that skilfully wielded weapon would certainly do, sooner rather than later.

In desperation he cut down on the head of Bruce's horse and shattered it to blood and brains. Phoebus barely made more than a high-pitched grunt before all four feet went out from under him and he fell like a dropped stone.

The crowd roared anger at such a foul, unchivalric stroke – but there were no rules in that sand-scattered arena and Bruce, kicking free of the stirrups and rolling with *mêlée*-practised ease, knew it.

He knew, too, as his unlaced helm flew off and rolled away, exposing his red, sweated face, that he was in trouble.

The moors south of Yorkshire
The Feast of St John the Evangelist, December, 1304

The moors here in England were no different from back home, Malise thought bitterly. A tapestry in mottled black and white, patched here and there with the last faded russet of old bracken, studded with stones dark as iron. Neither should be travelled in this season.

He glanced at the pewter sky, pregnant with snow and worried that it would fall on him like a shroud before he reached the safety of the Priory of Lund, yet one more knot in the long rope that Lamprecht trailed behind him.

Find him, Buchan had ordered on the day he arrived to cart

his wife off to a nunnery in Perth – at last, Malise thought viciously. Not before time, too, though the freedom he had envisaged on that day had been twisted by the loss of her. It was a witch thing she did to him, he had decided, a cauldron-brewed spell that made him think only of her until his groin ached and he had to take it out on some dirt-patched whore.

Precious few of those in this plod through the winter north after the pardoner, he thought, and the Christ's Mass gift of horse and silver from a strangely desperate Buchan had only gone a little way to balming the pain of journeying at this time of year.

Find him, Buchan had ordered, for it was plain Bruce was now involved in the deadly game. Find the pardoner, and find out what he was doing with Bruce and why the relic of the Black Rood was involved in it. Discover why Bruce was involved in it. Find the proof.

Malise mourned it all bitterly. Lamprecht, the wee dung beetle. The last time we met he made my life a misery and now here he is bringing bad cess to it once again. I will put him to the Question, right enough, he thought.

First, hunt down the pardoner – not that it was hard to follow his trail. An ugly wee man with the conch of Compostella in a broad-brimmed hat, a strange way of speaking and a scrip full of wondrous relics could not hide in the places he preferred to haunt.

Malise had already discovered simple priory priests in possession of lead amulets stamped with Caspar, Melchior or Balthazar and guaranteed proof against plague and ague, not to mention an abbot convinced he had a feather from the very wing of a seraphim. All sold by Lamprecht and proudly shown to Malise, who had also learned of two other men asking about the pardoner; he was sure one of them was Kirkpatrick.

Malise had come across the bridge at York, along the Micklegate to the Bar with its empty-eyed corpse-heads – rebel Scots, Malise knew. Malise kept his lips clenched and his accent hidden until he had passed through and on to the Tadcaster road.

At St Mary's in Tadcaster, Malise had learned that Lamprecht had sold the toebone of Moses, attested by a Templar-sealed parchment, and was moving on south. Malise had lost a day going in the wrong direction before he realized that the little coo's hole of a pardoner was headed for London, slipping from abbey to priory and moving swiftly for a man on foot and with no fear of the weather.

Doubling back through Tadcaster, Malise was sullen at the pardoner's lack of regard for what a north winter might do; ignorance is bliss, he thought and Lamprecht would pay for it when the north stormed out snow and froze his black heart.

Yet he knew the De'il looked after his own and the little pardoner would not suffer. Piously – fervently, as the first flake wafted on to the back of his gloved hand – he hoped God was also watching. He needed God's help, for sure, since he had found out one more valuable item in doubling back.

There was someone else on the trail of the pardoner, ahead of Malise now, someone well mounted on a black horse and with a sword of particular type, incised with a cross on the wheel pommel.

A Templar sword.

Lincoln
The Feast of St John the Evangelist, December, 1304

He was on the wrong side of his dead horse, for the axe lay on the other and all Bruce now had was a forearm's length of thin *estoc*, an edgeless weapon too long to be a dagger and too short to be a sword, but perfect for sliding in a visor slit, or punching through maille. Against an axe-armed man on a horse it might just as well have been a reed.

Malenfaunt was in a fever of triumph, tearing at the horse's mouth to get it round, raking it cruelly to repeat the process, charge down his victim. Bruce was down, weaponless, unhelmed and helpless – he had won . . .

Bruce saw it in Malenfaunt's frantic movement. Nothing left but the German Method, he thought grimly and positioned himself, feeling the desert of his mouth and the wrench in his guts.

The crowd was a bellowing beast as Malenfaunt came at him, all hooves and wicked axe, reversed so that the pick, brought hard down by a man raised up in his stirrups for the leverage, would spear through metal *cervellier* skull cap, the maille coif beneath it, the padded arming cap under that and, finally, the skull of his victim. Like a lance through a bladder, Malenfaunt exulted . . .

At the last, Bruce sprang to one side – to his right, away from the axe. He heard a metalled scream of frustration from under Malenfaunt's helm – then watched as the horse ploughed on, into the dead Phoebus.

Malenfaunt was horrified as he felt his mount balk, stumble and then seem to sink, trying to thrash and heave back upright from its knees, while Malenfaunt perched in the saddle like an egg on a stick. In his panic he did not wait to find out if his mount fought free from the tangle of dead horse and drapery – he kicked out of the stirrups and stumbled to the ground.

The crowd roared their approval and both men closed with one another, Bruce shieldless and with his long, thin *estoc*, Malenfaunt with axe and shield. They moved cautiously on the kicked up sand.

They circled, Malenfaunt swinging in vicious swipes, Bruce crabbing away, looking for an opening. Malenfaunt heard his own breath rack and sob, deafening under the helmet, where the heat was smothering him and the sweat starting to run in his eyes. He realized, sickeningly, that he could not keep the axe in motion for much longer, that he would have to stop, to rest . . .

Bruce struck when he saw the weary arm sink, an adder's tongue flick of metal that speared through the maille of Malenfaunt's forearm, grating on the bone. He heard the man's muffled howl, the arm was whipped away and the axe sailed from nerveless, gauntleted fingers. Bruce closed in as Malenfaunt stumbled away, lashing with his shield, batting the striking point away from him while he fumbled.

He came up with a dagger, just as Bruce took a shield swipe on his own arm. The blow numbed it and he cursed, fell back, the *estoc* tumbling from his hand. Gasping for breath, both men seemed to pause – then Malenfaunt, seeing Bruce unarmed, gave a high shriek and lunged forward, smashing with his shield at the same time as he cut back with the dagger.

Bruce, in pain and off balance, saw the wink of it too late. It came at his shoulder, glanced off an aillette and went through the hood of the maille coif into his right cheek. He felt the tug of it, felt – shockingly – the cruel length of it like a bit in his mouth, felt it pink a tooth. The edge slashed his tongue and his mouth was full of blood.

The crowd howled – the King sprang to his feet and Badenoch lurched forward, bellowing at Malenfaunt to kill him. Malenfaunt roared exultantly and stepped back, leaving the weapon in the wound, throwing up both hands as if to announce that he had won. He paused, a little dazed it seemed, by this turn of events, then half-turned as if to go for his axe.

The shock of seeing Bruce reach up and remove the dagger unmanned him. The man should have been on his knees from the agony of it – Christ's Bones, the blood was pouring down his face, streaking the chevronned jupon . . . Malenfaunt staggered back, caught his spurs and fell.

There was a moment when the pewter sky, patched with iron clouds, swung wildly and Malenfaunt lay, trying to believe what he had seen. Magic. Had to be – the Devil looks after his own. Then the sky was blotted and he felt a shape settle on him, driving the air from his lungs and pinning him.

Bruce straddled Malenfaunt, his knees crushing Malenfaunt's arms into the muddied sand, and he heard desperate, babbled words come from under the helm. Comyn, he heard. Lord of Badenoch, he heard. His idea – he knows of your bid to be king of the Scotch. The King said not to kill you, he heard. To spare you. He told you the same, I know. Spare me . . .

Bruce let the words wash him, grim and uncaring as rock. I yield, he heard. He should heed that one. God was watching, after all.

More to the point, Badenoch and the rest of the Comyn were watching, so he lay closer, his head on Malenfaunt's shoulder like an embracing friend, took Malenfaunt's leaf-shaped dagger, bright with his own blood and shoved it up under the bucket helm to where it grated on the coiffed chin. He felt the man buck and start to shake his head from side to side, his metallic pig squeals increasing, his babbled desperation wilder still.

Then he put the heel of his hand on the hilt of the weapon and slammed hammer-blows until he felt it pop through the links, the flesh of the chin, then the tongue and the roof of Malenfaunt's mouth. He knew that because the blood spurted and the babbling was so high only dogs could hear it. Then there was only a sickening 'thu . . . thu . . . thu' from a man whose desperate speeches were now all pinned.

The crowd was a great roaring beast, feeding on the pain and the blood.

One more blow would drive it up into the stem of the man – Bruce stopped then, for it was a message he was sending, not death.

He wobbled upright feeling the world whirl. The blood drooled from his mouth as he turned, half-blind like a blinkered horse; the crowd fell silent at the sight of him, at the twitching, moaning ruin that was Malenfaunt and into it, as loudly as he could muster, Bruce completed the bloody mummery of the day, spouting gore from his cheek with every word.

'*Ai-je fait mon devoir?*'

The Marshal nodded but it was the throated roar of the crowd that revealed that Bruce had done his duty. Released like arrows, the squires and his brothers raced for him, even as his legs finally gave way.

Nunnery of the Blessed Saint Augustine, Elcho, Perth
Feast of the Blessed St Fillan, January, 1305

They had arrived in daylight when it should, to suit the mood and the deed, have been darkest night, she thought. A rare day as well, silvered with a weak coin of a sun fighting through the iron sky to shine on the enchantment of Elcho.

She and the escort of her husband's grim dog-soldiers, all swagger and lust, came to it past herb banks and trellised rose bushes, black and clawed now but, she knew, a riot of beauty in the spring and summer. There was a carp pond, half-frozen and, beyond that, a cobbled path they had to walk to reach the nunnery, a series of stone buildings, some of the stones yellow, others rich pink, like jewels in the black-brown of it.

Arrow-slit windows and a stout door told much of how it had survived and the woman who came to the gate revealed more without saying a word. She was dressed in plain grey homespun, but wore a small gold cross on a chain about her neck. As tall as me, Isabel thought, and pale-haired under the headcover if her brows were anything to go by. Not white, though – in the plain, shapeless clothes and veil it was hard to guess her age, but Isabel thought her not greatly older than herself. She moved with dignity and bowed to Isabel.

'The lord of Buchan craves shelter, lady, for his countess and protection from the world. He begs you instruct her in the ways of God.'

The *serjeant* said it by rote, having memorized it in mutters all the way here. The woman did not even look at him, but at Isabel.

'I am the Prioress Bridget,' she said simply and held out both hands. 'Welcome. Are you with child?'

Isabel, taken aback, almost shook her head, then recovered herself.

'If I was,' she answered with bitter haughtiness, 'I would not be here. And I am the Countess of Buchan.'

The prioress did not blench, merely nodded a receipt to this reminder of their station, but remained still as an icon, arms folded in her sleeves.

'If you were,' she answered blandly, 'and are sent here, then it would not have been the Earl's child.'

'Countess,' she added, with a slight, wintery smile, then looked at the scowling, shift-footed thugs.

'Your task is done. You may leave the lady's baggage – Elcho is no place for men.'

The *serjeants* went, dismissed like the dogs they were; Isabel smiled, liking this prioress, yet recalling the other time she spent in a nunnery in Berwick as a prisoner of Malenfaunt.

She turned, to take a last scornful look at the retreating backs of her husband's thugs and saw another grey woman shut and bar the heavy door; she knew then that this was no different than the last time – save that the nuns here were truer Brides of Christ.

The prioress smiled softly, gentle as falling snow and just as cold.

'Your husband sent word of your coming,' she said. 'Now we have established that an unwanted child is not the reason for your arrival, we may thank God for His guiding you here. We are to care for you and instruct you in the ways of God's love. *Victoria veritatis est caritas* – the victory of truth is love.'

Isabel followed her meekly, past where women, unveiled, shaved heads revealed, wore stained sacking overserks and worked with lime water and sinopia at marking out a fresh plastered wall for painting; the blood-red sinopia ran in sinister

106

runnels, swiftly halted by squirrel-hair brushes before they could besmirch the glory of the Raising of Jairus' Daughter.

Red lead and cups of gold dust for the halos lay nearby, showing the wealth of Elcho, and Isabel wondered at what Buchan had paid for this, her final instruction.

Her quarters were simple, but comfortable. The prioress pointed out where the wash place was, and the latrines, showed where meals would be served, and told Isabel how she would be called by the ringing of the bell.

There was no need to show where the chapel was, for the sound of chanting revealed it; the prioress offered another thin smile.

'*Qui cantat, bis ora,*' she said – who sings once, prays twice.

Alone, Isabel sank on the bedplace, feeling good springy heather and thick warm wool plaids. There was wood stacked beside the fireplace, but it was unlit and her breath smoked; a pair of panting nuns sweated in with her meagre baggage, all that had been garnered in the brief moments between her husband's brusque instruction and her own departure from Balmullo.

There had been little time to do anything, but she had used it as wisely as she could. A quick press of coin and token into the hand of Ada, a whispered, urgent message and the swift secreting of a bundle in the depths of her cosmetics.

She hoped it would be enough, the first to bring rescue, the second to bring some succour and, after a moment, she hunted out the bundle, unwrapping it to reveal the contents, the remaining five bright berries of blood on the snowy linen.

Wallace had shoved them at her in the cold half-light of the hall on the morning he had limped away from Balmullo.

'For yer love and care, ye mun have need o' this, lady,' he had said, 'though sell them abroad and tell only those ye trust that ye have them. They are no use where I am bound, since no-one has the coin or the will to buy them in this country.'

The sixth ruby Apostle she had sent with Ada glowed

brightly in her mind and she wondered who was there, clasped in the warmth of her tirewoman's considerable cleavage. James the Greater? Matthew? Peter?

'May the saints bless your sleep,' the prioress had said portentously on taking her leave and had been puzzled at Isabel's sharp reply.

'I have no need of them – I have Apostles to bless me.'

The ruby nestled in the warm down of Ada's bosom like a blood egg, shining with soft hope as she hurried through the night.

CHAPTER SIX

Holebourn Bridge, London
The Invention of John the Baptist's Head, February, 1305

The rain came across the Fleet like a curtain, a thin, stinking mist of tar, salt, pickle and fish. It collided with the rich odour of meat and dung, pie shop and bakery, hissing on the smithy fire, rattling the flapping canopies of the stalls along the river.

Folk fled it, grey shapes scampering, looming out of it with faces soft as clay, baggy-cheeked and scowling, the women barrel-bottomed and harsh-voiced. Hal didn't understand them, didn't like the place, not even the comfort of the Earl of Lincoln's Inn which they had just left, and thought the best of London lay back with the unseen St Andrew's church where they had paused for word of Lamprecht.

Kirkpatrick, squinting from under a loop of cloak, grinned at Hal's expression; the wee lord had never been in London before – Christ's Blood, he had never been south of York – and the sights and sounds and stink of it were as stunning to his sense as a forge hammer on the temple.

Even to Kirkpatrick, who had been here twice before, it was hard to take. Tinkers, furriers, goldsmiths, hemp-sellers, all with the crudely-daubed bar over their stall to show what they were, bellowed against the calls of butcher and, above all, the horse copers, for this was the southern edge of Smoothfield, main market for livestock and the sale of prime horseflesh.

The frenetic throng was thinning as folk huddled in shelters from the rain, leaving the muddy, shit-clogged roadway to carts, barrows, litters. And the doggedly foolish like us, Hal thought bitterly as the rain wormed down his back.

'Sty Lane,' Kirkpatrick declared, pointing the fetid entrance to an alleyway. Hal wanted to know how he knew that, but did not bother to ask; Kirkpatrick's skill at finding places and people had long since earned respect from Hal. Still, he did not like the look of the place, where the houses leaned in and blocked the sky, making it a dark and dangerous cave.

Two men came out of it, carrying the split carcass of a large pig, leaking rain-watered blood on to the sacking of their shoulders – which at least proves Kirkpatrick is right, Hal thought. Right, too, about Lamprecht making for here like a dog back to its own sick, though that had made no sense at first, even as they trailed him down to St Andrew's and then the Purpure Lyon.

'The little by-blow will offer this Mabs back the half-cross he has,' Kirkpatrick had growled in answer. 'In return, he will want passage to France, or Flanders or even Leon if he dares the crossing.'

'Because that's what you would do?' Hal had queried, speaking in a soft hiss so as not to be heard by the muttering growlers and drinkers in the inn. They spoke French for the same reason and Kirkpatrick had laughed.

'Because it is what I would not do. But I am clever and Lamprecht is not only afraid, he is as idiot as a moonstruck calf.'

'He may have gone to Dover,' Hal pointed out, not so convinced of Lamprecht's stupidity. Kirkpatrick shrugged.

'Without coin he can squat on the shingle and try to wish up a ship until we come on him, then.'

110

The more Hal looked at the rain-misted cleft of Sty Lane, the more the Lyon's now-distant fug-warmth called to him. The Earl of Lincoln's Inn had been the last haven for Lamprecht, two nights before; no-one called it anything other than the Purpure Lyon thanks to the sign, the arms of the Earl of Lincoln, nailed over the door. Lincoln owned it as he owned a deal of the land round it, but Hal doubted if the Earl had ever been in it. Which was a pity for him, since the roast goose had been a joy, with raisins, figs and pears in it. A barnacle goose, for it had been a fish day and that was aquatic, as any priest would tell you . . .

Kirkpatrick was on the move and Hal, flustered, shredded his dreams of food and followed on, hoping the rest of the plans made in the Lyon moved as smoothly.

The rain was flushing filth out of Sty Lane like a privy hole drain; Hal's boots sloshed through a gurgling brown mess and the place stank, so that pushing into it made him open his mouth so as not to have to breathe through his nose.

Kirkpatrick stopped and Hal almost walked up his heels. There was silence save for the hiss and gurgle of rain and the squeal and honk of unseen pigs; sweat started to soak Hal from the inside at the sight of the grey shapes looming up in front of them.

Six he counted, their faces blurred by rain and beards and grease. Three wore broad-brimmed hats, turned up at the front and pinned so that the soaked droop of them would not blind them. Two wore coif hoods of rough wool, one a hat trimmed with ratty fur, all had the sacking tunics of slaughtermen, dark with old blood. Every one had a naked, long, knife.

'Oo are ye and what d'yer wish in Sty Lane?'

Hal struggled with the thick accent, knowing it was English but unable to make it out without squinting. Kirkpatrick, seemingly easy, offered a smile and a spread of empty hands.

'Looking fer Mabs,' he declared. 'Heard there was work for lads as was not afraid o' blood.'

Which could mean much or little to slaughtermen, Hal

111

thought, half crouched and silent in his role in the mummery. The rat-furred hat swivelled to take them both in, while the others circled in a ring; used to herding pigs, Hal thought wildly, his mouth dry, his heart thundering in his throat.

'Sojers,' Rat-Fur declared and then spat sideways. Kirkpatrick shrugged.

'Have been, will be again if the shine is right. We knows the way of it, certes.'

Warned, Rat-Fur held his distance while the rain plinked and splashed. Then he nodded at Hal.

'Tongueless, is he?'

'From the Italies,' Kirkpatrick countered smoothly. 'Knows little of a decent way of speaking.'

Which hid Hal's Scots accent.

'Where did you hear about Mabs?'

The question came sudden as a hip-throw, but Kirkpatrick was balanced for it.

'Old friend,' he replied and winked. 'Lamprecht. Ugly bastard of a pardoner. Said there was work in Sty Lane, with Mabs. Izzat yourself?'

Rat-Fur chuckled, glanced swiftly to his left. Oho, Hal thought, there is someone unseen jerking this one's strings.

'Not me,' Rat-Fur said, while the others laughed, though there was little mirth in it. 'Come and meet the bold Mabs, then.'

Cautious, sweating, Hal followed Kirkpatrick, who followed Rat-Fur, with the others closing in so that the flesh from the nape of Hal's neck to his heels crawled with the unseen presence of them at his back. They went sideways, into a place of unbelievable stink and squeals from pigs jostling each other, as if they sensed that these men were slaughterers. That or the smell of old porker blood from them, Hal thought . . .

They halted. Rat-Fur leaned on the enclosure fence, where slurry slopped under a fury of trotters, then turned and grinned his last few ambered teeth at Kirkpatrick.

112

'Mabs,' he said. For a moment Kirkpatrick was confused – then a huge hump of the stinking slurry moved and the biggest sow he had ever seen lumbered forward, making him recoil; the slaughtermen laughed.

'Mabs,' said a new voice, 'smells new blood and wonders if it is tasty.'

Hal and Kirkpatrick whirled and saw a lump of a woman with the biggest set of paps either of them had seen – bigger even, Hal thought, than Alehouse Maggie's. She had a face like unbaked bread, grey and doughy and shapeless, though the cheeks were red with windchafe and drink. Her eyes were buried raisins.

'Mabs,' she repeated, looking fondly at the huge sow, which had now rolled over and was luxuriating in slurry, her line of fat, dangling teats dripping.

'Queen of the Faerie,' the woman went on wistfully. 'Her name and mine.'

'Ah,' said Kirkpatrick, struggling. 'Indeed.'

'Mistress Maeve,' Hal interrupted smoothly, giving the woman her full queen's name and forgetting himself entirely. 'We come seeking one Lamprecht, whom you ken. D'ye have word for us on his whereaboots?'

Kirkpatrick closed his eyes with the horror of it. The woman's currants turned from the pig to Hal.

'Now that is the strangest Italies I have heard spoke,' she declared. 'Much similar to Scotch, if me ears are working.'

Her men growled and seemed to loom closer. Kirkpatrick put a hand on the hilt of his dagger.

'Stand back,' he warned. 'My friend has the right of it – we seek only Lamprecht, nothing more.'

'And the Rood,' Hal added, so that Kirkpatrick cursed him to silence.

'Wood?' queried Mabs.

'Rood,' repeated Hal before Kirkpatrick could stop him. 'That what was in the reliquary ye split between Jop and Lamprecht.'

113

Christ's Bones, Kirkpatrick thought, feeling his palm slick on the knife, he has doomed us all.

'Lamb Prick,' Mabs said slowly, rolling the name like a gob of greasy spit round her mouth, 'is not welcome here. Nor that big whoreson dolt Jop, Gog's malison on him – though I am told he is dead.'

She spat and looked slyly at the pair of them.

'King's men took him, or so I was told. Put him to the rack and the iron, or me name is not Queen Maeve. An' 'ere yer are,' she added, gentle as a poisoned kiss, 'come lookin' fer me.'

She thinks Jop spilled his all and that we are King's men, Hal realized and started to deny it. Kirkpatrick, seeing his mouth open and fearing the worst, leaped into the breach of it.

'Well,' he managed through clenched teeth. 'An error. No harm done . . .'

'No?'

Kirkpatrick knew, with sick certainty, that there had been a great error and he was the one who had made it. Lamprecht was nowhere near here and Mabs would not want folk walking out of Sty Lane who could chain Jop and Lamprecht, Mabs and Sty Lane and robbery of the King's Treasury in one shackle.

She leaned against the fetid timbers of the sty and gazed fondly at the giant sow.

'Yes, yes,' she crooned. 'You are a greedy girl . . .'

Her giggle, strangely young and girlish, was chopped short by a thin, high whistle from Kirkpatrick as he sprang forward and Mabs reeled back. Rat-Fur slithered to put her behind him – but Kirkpatrick's blow was no slaughterman's cut, it was the flick of a killer.

Rat-Fur staggered away, choking and holding his throat, a thin jetting of blood forcing itself between the clench of both his hands. Both Mabs were squealing as loudly as each other and men were shouting – one of the big-hatted ones ran at Hal and he slashed the air, forcing the man to a skidding halt. For a few steps Hal danced awkwardly with him, slithering in the clotted mud, then the man bored in, a great slack, foolish grin splitting the tangled hair of his face.

Hal was no knife fighter, but he knew a few tricks. He raised his arm as if to strike, then lashed out with his foot, feeling it collide high up on the man's thigh. It missed his cods, but the pain jolted him, deadened the leg so that he fell and then lay, one hand raised like a knight demanding ransom for yielding.

'Please,' he said. 'I have daughters . . .'

Hal stopped, the dagger poised. The man got on one knee, then lashed with his free hand, a sharp knuckle that slammed into Hal's already damaged ribs. The pain whirled through him like fire, a blinding shriek that took him to his knees in the shite; he heard the man snarl, saw the long butcher knife winking.

Stupid, he thought. Should have just killed him.

Then there was a sudden spill of bodies, men with the lower part of their faces covered, wielding long swords and the wrists that knew how to use them. The man facing Hal half-turned, gave a short scream and tried to run; the better portion of a good blade flashed into his ribs, spraying gore as it came. As he fell away, the man holding the blade let it slide out with a soft suck and grinned with his eyes – even without the mask, Hal knew Edward Bruce.

The men brought by Kirkpatrick's whistle came up fast and hard, muffled as much against the stink as recognition. There was a flurry of cuts and screaming, then Hal turned to see that Mabs, trembling and on her knees, was the only one left; only she and the pigs squealed in terror now.

'God disposes,' Kirkpatrick said to Mabs. 'How fast the world turns, eh Mabs – one minute you are planning the diet of your pet. The next, you ARE the diet of your pet.'

'Wait,' said Mabs, looking from Kirkpatrick to Hal and then at the rest of the grim, masked men who had appeared. Armed like King's men, she thought, but hidden against recognition, so not them. If not Longshanks, then there was a chance to deal . . .

'Wait? For what? Friendship? Something deeper?'

'Enough,' growled the muffled voice of Edward. 'This is no place to be toyin' with your food, man. Eat the porker, or leave her on yer plate.'

Men laughed as Mabs whimpered and appealed to the one man who seemed detached and unconcerned.

'The Rood. The Rood, lord,' she said. Hal, nursing his ribs, was taken by surprise; he had been watching the giant sow, seeing her unconcerned and luxuriating. *Sae cantie as a sou in glaur* – happy as a pig in muck. It had been a phrase he thought he had understood until now, when he had seen a sow of this size luxuriating in her filth.

Mabs' desperation jerked him from the reverie, stunned him with a shock like cold water as to how he had been standing in the midst of all this, daydreaming.

'The Rood,' he repeated and Mabs leaped on it, worried it with feverish hope.

'Jop and Lamb Prick had it, sir,' Mabs wheezed, nodding furiously in agreement with her own words. 'I gave Lamb Prick the little bitty wood in the thing, sir, of being more account to him than me. Jop wanted more and persuaded Lamb Prick to steal the cross with the stones. A murrain on them both.'

Hal blinked as the words sank in like rain on a desert. He tried to straighten, felt something tear and gasped, so that Kirkpatrick turned to him, frowning.

'Is that all of it?' Hal managed.

Her head threatened to nod itself from her shoulders, her huge breasts shook.

'Round his neck on a string. It is no more than finger-length, lord.'

Kirkpatrick and Hal exchanged glances. It was good to have matters confirmed, but no joy to be reminded that it had been under their noses at the start . . .

116

'Faugh,' said Edward Bruce. 'This place stinks and is dangerous – time we were away.'

Mabs saw the look in Kirkpatrick's eye.

'Wait,' she said. 'Wai –uurgh.'

It was done before anyone could blink – a short thrust and a heave, enough to knock her off-balance. She rolled like a boulder through the flimsy sty fence right to the trotters of her surprised namesake, still squealing.

The fresh blood hit the sow's nostrils, and all the others raised their snouts, while Mabs struggled with the mud, floundering on all fours like a new and even bigger sow.

They left, Hal trying to blot his ears to the sound of the pleading shrieks, then the grunts; he could not tell whether they came from an agonized Mabs or from the enthusiasm of chewing pigs.

Cantie as a sou in glaur, he thought, then shivered, glad of the rain sluicing on him like cleansing balm and outside air to breathe.

Nunnery of the Blessed Saint Augustine, Elcho, Perth
Feast of Saint Mauritius, the martyred Knight, February, 1305

God turned his hand over and changed the weather. When Sister Mary Margaret woke beside Bets the milcher, she heard the pea-rattle of the rain and did not want to leave the warm snuggle of her charge, the cow. But it was the water in her bladder that had roused her, so that she cursed, then rose up, shivering and offering apologies to God for the blasphemy.

Bets stirred and Sister Mary Margaret, hunched and stiff, rubbed the curled nap between the horns; she much preferred sleeping here in the byre than her cell and, though the others carped about her appearance and her smell, she did not care.

Did she moan about the stink of paints and the smears on their habits? She did not. Her skill lay with beasts and not pictures on walls and she offered it up to the glory of God daily.

The wind and hissing rain smacked her as she opened the byre door and there was a moment when she blenched, considered hiking her clothes up and doing it there in the warm straw – after all, the cow did. Who would know that she had not scampered all the way to the privy?

God would know. She took a deep breath as if to dive into a pool – I have not done that since I was a wee girlie, she thought incongruously, just as she ran into a door.

Stunned, she recoiled, bewildered, for there was no door where she moved – she knew her way round Elcho blindfold. The door moved and she caught her breath at the great wet bulk of shield that towered over her. The owner flicked his massive mailled shoulders and slithered the shield on to his back with a hiss that drowned the rain, then he stuck one huge, armoured hand down to her.

'Ye are all wet, sitting in the rain, Sister. Rise up.'

Sister Mary Margaret was hauled upright; she was aware of being wet and that some of it was warm, so she had pished herself after all.

'My name is Sir William Wallace,' the man said, smiling like a wolf. 'I seek a wummin and a particular yin among so many. A countess no less. Can you assist me, in the loving name of Christ?'

Sister Mary Margaret had no words. Behind the giant, she saw other men and, in the midst of them, a slight dripping figure, flinging an axe blade stare at her. A woman, come with armed men – the prioress will needs be informed, she thought . . .

'I am sure you can assist me, Sister,' the giant said, cutting through the mad whirl of her thoughts and Sister Mary Margaret realized, suddenly, that the days of the prioress were probably over.

Her hand flew to her mouth and smothered the sudden,

118

savage scream – but she managed to point to where the Countess had been quartered. The giant grinned.

'*Pax vobiscum*, Sister,' he said and left so suddenly that Sister Mary Margaret sat down with a squelch. Relief washed her like the rain.

In the cloistered heart of Elcho, the sisters were running and shrieking as men spilled in, reeking of sweat and old blood, woodsmoke and feral lust. The prioress stood, her heart thundering like a mad bird, and stretched out her arms protectively, just as the Countess of Buchan came up behind her.

'Stay behind me, Countess,' she declared, throwing out her chest as a giant stepped forward, huge sword in one grimed fist and a twisted grin on his face. 'God will save us.'

'You have been called many things, Will Wallace, but never God Himself before,' the Countess declared and pushed past the astounded prioress, who was shocked to see the great ogre with the sword take the Countess' hand, delicate as any courtier and raise it to the mad tangle of beard.

A small figure emerged from behind the giant Wallace and the smiling Countess recognized her tirewoman Ada beneath the sodden hood of the cloak, embracing her.

Isabel turned to the pale, open-mouthed prioress and felt a wash of sympathy for what she had brought down on them. She quelled the feeling, ruthless as those who hunted nuns and food and drink through the sacred shadows of Elcho. Here was a wee wummin who had taken money from her husband to hold her as prisoner in the name of God.

'Brace yourself,' she said viciously to the prioress. '*Victoria veritatis est caritas* – the victory of truth is love.'

Outside, Sister Mary Margaret found a hand taloned on her shoulder and lifting her from the soaked ground. An eldritch face, scarred and gleaming wet, thrust itself at her, grinning, the broken nose dripping.

'You will catch a chill, quine,' Lang Jack declared and

glanced at the open door of the byre. 'We mun get you in the dry and oot of those wet clothes.'

Now Sister Mary Margaret screamed.

The Bruce House, London
The same night

The waxed paper windows turned the room to amber twilight even at midday and let in both the cold and the clamour from the Grass and Stocks markets; Hal could even hear the whine of the beggars on the steps of St Edmund's Garcherche opposite and, naked to the waist, wished he could move closer to the brazier, a glowing comfort perched on a slate slab on the wooden floor.

The physician finished bandaging Hal's ribs, dipping his fingers in a basin and drying them fastidiously on a clean linen square as he turned to Bruce.

'Your man,' he said, haughty and dismissive, 'has re-opened an old wound. I have fastened it and will give him a salve and two mole's feet, for protection against infection in the bone.'

He paused, then looked steadily at the Earl, ignoring Hal's sullen scowl at the term 'your man'.

'In your own case, the tooth is healing nicely and your tongue is undamaged,' he said. What was unsaid crouched between them like a rat on a corpse. Edward Bruce, oblivious to the exchange, laughed nastily and clapped his brother hard on the shoulder.

'More than can be declared for your opponent,' he growled. 'I am told he gabbles like a bairn.'

The physician turned fish eyes on him. He was called James and came, he claimed, from Montaillou, which most thought simply a village in France. Those who knew, all the same, could tell you that Montaillou lay smack in the middle of that Langue D'Oc stronghold of the Cathar heresy which the Pope was scouring from the world.

120

James of Montaillou, Bruce mused to himself, was mostly a lie. He claimed to be a physician but had attended no university and was, at best, an inferior breed of skilled barber-surgeon. He claimed to be a Christian, but should, in truth, be wearing the compulsory yellow cross of a heretic Cathar.

'I have it that Sir Robert Malenfaunt may never speak properly again,' James commented, with more than a sting of mild rebuke in it. 'His palate is pierced and his tongue slit longways into two halves.'

His audience winced. Bruce managed a wan smile, the square of linen held to his cheek in what was becoming an ingrained habit; the gleet from the purpling-red half healed cicatrice was clear, yet stained the square a foul yellow, tinged faintly with pink.

'God preserve him,' he said thickly, though there were few present who thought God had much to do with Sir Robert Malenfaunt, who had so clearly been abandoned by Him on that tourney day.

'Deserves that at least,' Edward Bruce growled, 'and a mark of God's Hand that he suffered it as a result of the battle and not afterwards, for losing in the sight of the Lord.'

But the worst injury done to him then is the one I fear myself, Bruce thought – the shunning by your peers.

James of Montaillou left and, after a blink or two of silent messaging to Edward, the rest of the *mesnie* clacked across the boards, leaving Bruce alone with Hal, Kirkpatrick and his brothers Edward and young Alexander.

'So this Lamprecht is lost to us,' Bruce declared bitterly. 'And the Rood with him.'

'We'll spier this wee pardoner out,' answered Edward determinedly, only to have his elder brother savage him with a glance like a lance-thrust.

'You should not have been there yester,' he declared, the words mushed by anger and pain. 'Scampering around in pig shite like some callow boy.'

121

Edward's smile was wide, but razor thin.

'I thought to mak' siccar it was done right,' he declared and Kirkpatrick, hearing the phrase, spun round, glaring at him.

'What mean you by that?' he spat back, heedless of the protocols of rank. 'D'you imply that it would not have been well done without ye?'

'You needed our swords, certes, from what I saw,' Edward snarled back, equally disregarding the differences in their station.

'Who was it planned for such and summoned you?'

'First time the dog has ever whistled up the master . . .'

'Enough.'

Bruce's voice was harshened by pain and a slap across both their faces, so that they subsided, glowering.

'With or without you, brother,' Bruce went on sternly, 'the matter was not well done. And if you had been caught in it, all of us were ruined. Christ's Bones – here you are arguing with a lesser rank like some drunken cottar and showing exactly the same disregard for station and dignity as you did in Sty Lane. It is not just yourself you risk nowadays, Edward – it is the Bruce name. My name and rank more than yours.'

Hal, fastening his belt back round his tunic, saw Kirkpatrick's sullen scowl at being no better than 'lesser rank'. He also saw Edward chew his bottom lip to keep silent; he knew why, too – the rumours of it were whispers within the *mesnie* that here was a man who wanted at least one of the titles his elder brother held and was not going to get it until that brother had the compensation of a crown. Only ambition outstripped Edward Bruce's recklessness.

'We must find and deal with Lamprecht,' Bruce went on; Edward, still blunt as a hammer-blow, voiced what that really meant.

'We have to kill him,' he growled, 'before he can tell others what he knows.'

'He can tell no-one, my lords' Hal replied carefully, 'without

122

giving away his own part in such affairs. Better to let him crawl away to a hole across the sea.'

'He will tell all he knows if put to the Question,' Bruce pointed out, patiently because he valued the Herdmanston lord and did not want to slap him down, as Edward was about to do until a look from his brother clapped his lips shut.

'The pardoner is clever,' Bruce went on, 'but greedy. He will try and sell that reliquary treasure, or parts of it. Even the sight of one of those Christ-Blood rubies will trap him. Besides – there is the matter of the Rood itself. He has it. I want it.'

He looked from one to the other of them like a stern father.

'Aye, weel, Your Grace,' Hal said sourly. 'Whatever his business wi' us, it is concluded and it is my opinion that Lamprecht will consider himself safer abroad now he has failed to discomfort myself and Kirkpatrick – and Your Grace's honour. I dinna think his revenge runs so deep as will have him try again. I understand he was birthed in Cologne – mayhap he will return there wi' his prize.'

'Comyn will not let him,' Bruce replied and the cutting blade of that was too sharp to answer. Bruce let the silence slide for a moment, the thoughts piling up behind his eyes as he removed, studied, then replaced the cheek pad.

'Buchan has sent his animal Malise after Lamprecht, and Red John Comyn works hand in glove with his Comyn cousin, the Earl,' he said eventually. 'If all they suspect is that the pardoner has information contrary to my comfort, it will be enough to keep them searching. If Red John suspects the presence of the Rood, he will want it for himself and his own plans for the throne of Scotland. He will not rest until he unearths it.'

Bruce removed the pad from his cheek, inspected it and put it back, his eyes bleak as a winter sea. For a moment, Hal saw the ugly wound and blanched at it, then the trailing *conroi* of his thoughts took him to Malenfaunt and the duel, incited by Buchan and Comyn.

For Buchan it had probably been in response to the business

of Isabel, whom Bruce had ransomed from Malenfaunt while pretending to be Isabel's husband and using that man's own money. But Buchan had not had his countess back – Hal had got her, however briefly.

In turn, he thought bitterly, that act, for Bruce at least, was revenge for the time when Red Comyn had taken Bruce by the throat in public and threatened to knife him. Now it came to Hal, sudden as sin and just as thrillingly blasphemous, that perhaps English Edward was the best strong hand the unruly kingdom of Scots needed for, without it, the realm was already in a war with itself, played out in a mating-snake writhe of plot and counterplot, dark knifings and treachery.

'Matters are not lost,' Kirkpatrick said into Hal's thoughts. 'I can find Lamprecht – but not with Sir Hal in tow.'

He looked into Hal's outrage and shrugged.

'Your idea of stealth and cunning in these matters is limited to not shouting who you are at the top of your voice,' he said, half apologetically and in French, which softened the bile of it. 'Besides – you are hurt.'

Bruce looked from one to the other, removed the linen square and studied the stains, then replaced it.

'Kirkpatrick,' he said, 'shall stay in London and seek out this Lamprecht. Hal – go back north. The men you sent must have found some trace of Wallace by now. Find Wallace, and take care of your wound, for I have need of you yet.'

Hal nodded; he had had enough of London's stew of streets and alleys, while his ribs ached and burned in equal measure, so he leaped on Bruce's suggestion like a fox into a coop. He and Kirkpatrick headed for the door, pausing to offer passage to one another with exaggerated courtesy.

Bruce watched them go, shoulder to shoulder like two padding hounds who snarled and growled at each other, yet seemed capable of springing to each other's defence in an eyeblink.

He sent Edward off with some soothing words about his

prowess and sighed when the door closed on his back, leaving him with Alexander. The youngest and yet the one he trusted most.

The Curse of Malachy, he thought bitterly, is to have all the attributes of greatness handed to you by God and have to accept recklessness with it. Thank Christ and all His angels that he was not as reckless as brother Edward, who had been slathered with most of that - but the sudden stab of pain from his missing tooth was a reminder of his own rash fight with Malenfaunt.

'Does it hurt?' Alexander asked and Bruce felt a wash of panic and revulsion at the reality of the stained linen square and his cheek.

'My tongue burns like the very De'il,' Bruce replied laconically. 'At least the rough edge of that tooth is no longer a nag on it.'

The careful answer masked the truth. Alexander nodded, then flicked his fingers in an impatient gesture for his brother to remove the pad. He bent, inspected, then straightened with a sombre nod and face so at odds with his youth that Bruce almost grinned. Almost. A smile stretched the cicatrice into a gape; in all the weeks since the tourney, it had barely managed to close on itself and Bruce knew that Alexander and his physician feared infection.

'The Curse of Malachy,' Bruce said suddenly, though he contrived to make it light and laughable. Alexander did not laugh and finally voiced the truth of matters.

'The cheek does not hurt at all?'

Bruce shook his head, swallowed the rising panic. No pain when the knife had gone in. No pain when he had plucked it out. None at all when James of Montaillou had apologetically pulled his mouth aside to file down the pinked tooth, though the pain of that was a screamingly agonizing memory. Folk had marvelled at the stoic bravery of the Bruce, who felt no pain.

No pain in a cheek deadened. The irony, of course, was that it had saved his life, for Malenfaunt's blow should have reduced him to a blinding agony of tears and snot, leaving him at the mercy of a killing stroke.

'Lepry,' Alexander said, a slapped blade on the table of Bruce's wild thoughts. Bruce said nothing, but the bleak truth of it was part of the Curse of Malachy.

'Only you and I and James of Montaillou are party to that suspicion,' he answered at length. Alexander, the scholar, had worked it out almost as swiftly as Bruce and the physician; he nodded, his eyes welling with a sympathy Bruce did not care to see. Too much like the look you give a dog you have to put down, he thought.

'No-one else must know,' he managed to rasp out and saw Alexander's eyebrow raise.

'Not your wife, brother?'

Not her, with her coterie of tirewomen spying for her, and her wee personal priest sending back the doings of the Bruces to the Earl of Ulster. From there, Bruce was sure, it arrived in the hands of Edward Plantagenet in short enough order.

He felt a crushing sadness at the mire she and he were in, how their life had become polite in public and distant now in private; the excuse of his wounds kept them in separate bedchambers as much as Bruce's fear of the sickness he might have – a leper's very breath was poison.

Alexander knew all this and required only a sour glance from his brother.

'Not Edward?' he persisted and now the glance was alarmed.

'Especially not brother Edward.'

Especially him, the rash hothead who would ride through the fires of Hell to fetch Holy Water to heal his big brother – and turn every head to watch the glory of it as he did so.

Leprosy. Bruce pressed the linen to his cheek and stared blindly at the yellowed window, as if he could see through it to the street of the Grass and Stocks markets, the new, still-

126

scaffolded houses of the Lombard goldsmiths and on up to Poultrey.

Where Buchan had his own house, lair of all Comyn activity in London; they would pay any amount, dare any dishonour, to discover that their arch-rival had even the suspicion of such an affliction.

Moffat, Annandale
Feast of Saint Kessog, March, 1305

Wallace was woken by the cow struggling to her feet. By the gleam of daylight smearing through the smoke-hole he saw Patie's woman kneel by the firepit to blow life back into the banked peat smoulder.

One of the brood of bairns wailed as he shrugged out of the door into a muggy morning where colour slid back to the land. For a moment he stood, listening, turning his head this way and that, but only the chooks moved, murmuring in their soft way.

Eventually, he unlaced his braies with one hand and, grunting with the pleasure of it, pissed on the dungheap; it was the first time this year, he noticed, that it did not steam.

The sound shut off his stream like a closing door and he half-turned, but it was Patie, coming up to join him and, for a moment of still peace, they both wet the dungheap.

'Fine day comin',' Wallace growled and Patie nodded.

'A seven-day o' this,' he answered thoughtfully, 'an' I will sow peas in my own strip. Mayhap even oats. Pray to Goad there is no blight.'

Then he turned his big heavy face into the crag of Wallace's own.

'There is gruel to break yer fast.'

Wallace nodded, then rubbed the greasy tangle of his chin ruefully.

'I have no siller left to offer ye,' he said and Patie nodded sorrowfully, as if he had expected the news.

'An' ye a dubbed knight, no less,' he answered, shaking his mournful head on the inequity of it. 'Whit happened to yer siller, then? Wager or drink?'

Wallace laughed, remembering.

'The most o' it went on a wummin,' he said and Patie sniffed. Hawked and spat.

'Worth it, was she?'

'She was,' Wallace agreed, the image of her sharp and blade-bright in his mind when he had come to the priory weeks before with his handful of scarred, filthy army.

'A coontess, no less.'

It was the last shine of glory and tarnished even then and he had known it was all over even as he stood, hip-shot, while the nuns of Elcho squealed and ran. He had tossed the red robin's-egg ruby carelessly back to Isabel as she clasped her exhausted, trembling tirewoman, Ada, with her free hand.

'I will take ye to Roslin,' he had told her. 'Ye will have to make yer own way to Herdmanston – I am no' welcome there in these days.'

She had nodded, not knowing the why of it and too relieved to be free to do any asking. Wallace did not offer an explanation.

Patie's final grunt shook him back to the moment and the dungheap; he saw the man was looking at the scarred pewter sky with a calculated, expert squint.

'A good crop, if there is little rain and less war.'

'No war, Patie,' he answered and could hear the sorrowed loss of it in his voice, so that he was almost ashamed. No war, for his men were scattered and gone after taking Isabel, Countess of Buchan, to Roslin – Long Jack Short, Ralf Rae and the worst of them were briganding out of that old stronghold of outlaws, the Selkirk forests. Jinnet's Jean and others were probably hooring with the English in Carlisle and robbing them blind when they could.

And he was here. Once he had ruled the Kingdom as sole Guardian, now he sheltered in the mean holding of a sokeman of his sister's man, Tham Halliday, Laird of Corehead, because the castle itself was under watch. Soon, he knew, he would move to a house in Moffat, or another near Glasgow, those hiding him risking the penalty of harbouring, lying low until . . .

What? The thought racked him, as it had done from the moment he had woken to find most of the remaining men gone. Those left, he had realized, were starving and wasted, so he had given them what coin he had and watched the last of them melt away.

France, perhaps. The Red Rover, de Longueville, would get him away as he had done in the past and he and that old pirate had fought there before – but the French had given up as well and now no-one opposed the English; the idea of that burned him, but the old fire of it had little left of the great body to feed on save heart.

There was nothing in France for him – other than the relief of the Bruce; he almost managed a smile at that, but could not quite manage it, or the spit that went with it.

'No war, Patie,' he repeated.

Patie fumbled himself shut, wiped his fingers on his tunic and nodded meaningfully.

'I would lay that aside, then, while ye break yer fast,' he grunted. 'Ye are scarin' the bairns.'

Wallace looked down, was almost astonished to see the hand-and-half sword clasped in his right fist, so much part of him for so long that he no longer recognized it as a presence. He had woken with it clenched there, walked out of the mean hut with it and stood pissing with it. He had learned to do so many things left-handed, because the right was always occupied by that weapon. Naked, notched and spotted with rust, it was as done up as he was himself – yet sharp and ready.

He remembered cutting men down at Scone with it, carving

129

bloody skeins off the fine English knights at Stirling's bridge, slicing through the jawbone of the Templar Master, Brian de Jay, in the forest of Callendar.

His sword, so much part of him for so long, quenched in blood and wickedness, he thought. Now it was no more than a monstrous frightener of bairns.

Like myself.

Church of St Thomas of Acon, London
Thursday of Mysteries, April, 1305

He had risked it and was sure the dice had gone against him. When Lamprecht reached the herber's stall he looked round and was sure the cloaked man was the same one he had seen. He was sure, also, that it was Kirkpatrick; there was something sickly familiar in the oiled way the man moved, turning sideways, stepping careful as a fox and never bumping or being jostled.

Money, thought Lamprecht bitterly. Always the driven curse of a poor man, it had lured him to the Church of St Thomas of Acon on the day he knew alms were liberally handed out for the celebration of Christ's Last Supper on Earth. And here is me, he thought, with a ransom of rubies and so unable to make use of it that I am worth less than a beggar's cloak.

Even as he waited for the chimes to open the City's posterns, he had known that it was a bad idea, that he should have stayed in St Olave's and waited for a suitable ship to take him away from these shores.

Yet the pretence of being a lowly painter was a strain, while the skin-crawling horror of knowing that a Scotchman was on his trail like a relentless gazehound was more than his nerves could stand; he should never have revealed himself to Kirkpatrick and Bruce and that Herdmanston lord at all, he knew now – but the chance of revenge had been too sweet a taste to resist.

The bell rang an hour before sunrise and the City's wicket gates opened to the basket-carrying hucksters, the labourers, the journeymen, the beggars – Lamprecht hidden among them – and all the rest who lived in the stinking shadows of the City. And the shadow in the shadows, who trailed him, a presence like the crawl of cold sweat down Lamprecht's spine, which sent his neck straining side to side in a desperate attempt to pick him out of the crowd.

El malvogio, ki se voet te tout, a nou se voet – the evil one, who is seen by all and is not seen.

At which point, he was seen having seen. Suddenly, across the chafering throng of Ironmonger Lane there was only himself and the dark hole in the raised hood where he knew the eyes were; he fancied he could see through the cloak to the shining bar of steel hidden beneath.

So he ran.

Slow-worm blind at first, skidding through the muddied slime and the throngs until, like a dash of cold water, he caught the shocked, suspicious faces and brought himself to a halt; a running man in a crowded street was a thief or worse.

The lane was a maze that led to the sudden, broadening rush of the Cheap, already thick with stalls and people. He forced himself to walk, hurried but not fast and tried not to look constantly over his shoulder.

There were two of them now, he was sure. He stopped at a cheese stall, peering through the great wheels; yes, two of them. Perhaps more . . . in his mind, every man suddenly became a sinister hunter.

'Is there a lover's face in that?'

The voice, rasping sarcasm, cut into his panic and, strangely, quelled it; the cheesemonger glared at Lamprecht.

'You will wear a hole in that fine cheese with such staring – do you buy, or just look?'

Lamprecht offered a wan smile and moved away, half-fell over a large dog and was forced to jump it, colliding with something

131

huge and soft, which staggered a little then cursed him. He looked up into the baleful glare of a fishwife, scales glinting on her folded forearms and a wicked gutting knife in one fist.

'*Perdonar*,' he said, with an apologetic smile, but it was the foreign tongue that deepened the suspicious frown – and gave Lamprecht his idea.

'*El malvogio. Lo baraterro. Se per li capelli prendoto come ti voler conciare.*'

Rosia Denyz was a pillar of Cheap, a hard-mouthed matron who had dealt with every attempt to rob, coerce and cozen her for twenty years, so that few now treated her with anything but respect. She did not understand foreign tongues, but she knew curses when she heard them. When the ugly little man grabbed up one of her own fish and struck her in the face with it, she was so astonished that he had gained ten yards before she found her voice.

'Thief,' she bellowed, even though the fish was at her feet, giving the lie to it.

Across the other side of the market, Kirkpatrick saw the crowd boil like a feeding frenzy of shark, cursed the daring cunning of the little pardoner and headed after him.

Briefly he was balked by a string of horses coming from Smoothfield and beginning to get skittish at the crowd baying after an unseen thief – then he caught sight of Lamprecht, sprinting back up Ironmonger Lane.

He made a move past the flicking tail and shifting hindquarters of the last horse and slammed into a figure, the pair of them reeling back. Cursing, Kirkpatrick made to go round him, then drew up short, staring into the equally astounded face of Malise Bellejambe.

It took Malise a droop-mouthed moment to recognize Kirkpatrick through the grime and the dirt, the tunic that was more stain than cloth and a hooded cloak that was more sack than wool. When he did, he squealed, only later feeling a wash of shame for it, and ducked behind the man at his elbow.

Kirkpatrick saw this one, bemused, half turn to see Malise scuttling away in pursuit of Lamprecht, then turned back into the half-crouched figure of Kirkpatrick, who now realized that the man was with Malise. No henchman thug, he thought, a *serjeant* no less, wealthy enough to own a decent set of clothes – and a sword, which he hauled out just as the crowd jostled up, the cry of 'thief, thief' thundering joyously out.

The sight of the sword balked them, spilled them round the man who held it like a stream round a rock. People yelled at him to watch what he did with that blade – then the shriekers at the back, unable to see anyone who looked like their prey, spotted the wink of a drawn blade and decided that this was enough to mark their man.

The *serjeant*, surrounded, slashed wildly and sealed his fate with the first spill of blood; the baying mob, ignoring the flailing sticks of the bailiffs and the wild hornblowing of red-faced beadles, seemed to surge on him like a tide.

Kirkpatrick slid away, moving fast but not running; ahead he could see the bobbing head of Malise. Keep him in sight, Kirkpatrick muttered to himself, a litany that kept the curses damped; he had not spent all this time living like a beggar to lose Lamprecht now. Keep Malise in sight and, let him lead on like an unleashed rache.

Malise felt Kirkpatrick at his back like the heat of an unseen flame, but did not dare turn to look for fear of losing sight of the fleeing Lamprecht, beetling along the Lane. He slammed into a Crutched Friar, stammered apology and had back a less than holy spit of viper venom – when he turned back, Lamprecht was gone.

Lamprecht, sweating and gibbering to himself like a madman, knew only that he was pursued by everyone and that, if he started to sprint like a frantic hare he was a dead man. He fought the urge, sidled round a stall laden with red slabs of meat, collared with succulent yellow fat and only briefly flicked his eyes to them where before he would have stood and drooled.

He should have left London ages since, but was, in a bitter irony that did not escape him, the richest pauper in the country, his bag full of unsellable bounty and his purse full of nothing but wind. He had to get away.

Now he was pursued – he half-turned at a stall full of cabbage and celery and saw Malise, knew the man at once and was transfixed by fear. Him too? Christ's Wounds – the Comyn had determined to hunt him out as well . . .

Lamprecht found himself staring at the shambles, realized he was at the place where offal was sold and the stalls were rich and ripe and dripping with heart and tripe, sweetbreads and kidney, pale white, blue-veined collops in strings and folds. Flies hummed like the murmur of chanting priests and the entrail piles on the stalls slithered over each other like glistening, mating snakes.

When Kirkpatrick came up on the place a moment later Lamprecht was huddled in the lee of an oxcart, mere feet away. If Kirkpatrick turned, he could not fail to see him . . .

Kirkpatrick felt it more than he saw it, a chill on the side of his neck and he whirled in time to see Malise launch at him, all snarl and feral scything with a blade that seemed to whine through the air, so that Kirkpatrick had all he could do to avoid it.

'Ye hoor's slip,' Malise bellowed. Seeing Kirkpatrick hauling out his own blade, those nearest shied away, shouting, and a butcher called out to his companions that there was trouble.

'Ye bloody-handed, cat-wittit crawdoun . . .'

It was a roaring invective to put fire in his belly; Kirkpatrick knew it as the sparks flew from their clashed knives and they circled in a slow-stepping half-crouched dance.

'Here, here,' said one of the fleshers indignantly and made the foolish move of stepping forward with one hand out to separate the combatants – then he reeled back, shrieking and holding his hand, the blood welling up where Malise had cut him.

'Murder, murder . . .'

The cry went up just as the ones of 'thief' were fading into the distance and it was enough to fan the old embers into fresh flames; the baying horde surged out of Cheap, a wave that tossed aside a ragged, bloodied corpse that had once been a *serjeant* and left the gasping, weary, flustered beadles and bailiffs in its wake, washed up like flotsam.

Lamprecht could not believe his fortune when Malise attacked Kirkpatrick and kept those black eyes from him. He slithered right under the oxcart, jammed his fingers up between the boards and lifted his feet up in an awkward, splay-kneed stance, on to the axle. In a second they were moving and he almost laughed aloud at his cleverness, for he had realized in an instant that the oxcart owner would want beast and vehicle well clear of damage from a riot and men fighting with naked blades.

The cart lurched away from the shouting butchers and their shrieking customers, away along the lane, swaying and ponderous but fast enough for Lamprecht, who clung on underneath, like a barnacle to a hull.

He did not see the crush which spilled over a butcher's stall, the flood of contents like a glistening shoal of fresh-caught eels. He did not see Kirkpatrick, leaping back from another wild Malise swing, collide with someone's back, slip on the coiled guts and offal and disappear into the mass of it. He did not see Malise flung away from Kirkpatrick, losing his knife but slithering out of the fray and up an alley.

The oxcart driver wanted to see it; Lamprecht felt the cart stop, heard the man climb laboriously up into it, swing over and drop – then the world exploded in howling pain as the driver's thick-soled wood and leather clogs ground Lamprecht's plank-clutching fingers to pulp.

He shrieked, which made the driver move to the side to find the screamer beneath him, allowing Lamprecht to tear his fingers free and fall to the cobbles. He scrambled out, whimpering and stumbled away, ignoring the shouts of the driver, nursing his broken fingers and blinded by pain – by sheer animal instinct he headed for the one refuge he had known for some time now.

Malise, wiping his mouth and aware that he was covered in blood and guts and shit, sidled out of the alley and along the fringes of the howling maelstrom that was now Ironmonger Lane; somewhere in there, he thought to himself with a grim, hot glow of malevolent satisfaction, was Kirkpatrick – another second and I would have had him, liver and lights.

Reminded of his lost dagger, he instinctively looked down and round for it – then caught sight of a familiar figure.

Lamprecht, hands tucked under each armpit. Headed for Old Jewry, Malise thought. The little shit, putting him to all this trouble.

Kirkpatrick was still on Lamprecht's trail. He had not drowned in the writhing, sodden spill of animal entrails, but fought out from it with his dagger still in his fist, surfacing like a breaching whale into the rat-eyed stare of a thief stuffing offal in his jerkin before darting off.

Kirkpatrick hid the dagger, skated his way across the slip-sliding cobbles between the struggling, bellowing fighters. He ducked a swung fist, half-skidded on the slimed cobbles past a shrieking harridan and was out of the struggle, moving swiftly along the side of buildings, then up an alley in the wake of the hurrying Malise. Old Jewry, he thought. They are headed for Old Jewry.

Old Jewry was a sinister place, abandoned a decade before when Longshanks had expelled the Hebrews from England, immediately plundered and now left to the rats and the rain and the wind. Houses, boarded up when their owners fled, had been ripped open like treasure kists, though they found precious little of worth left from a people too used to fleeing in a hurry with all that was worth taking.

A few folk had moved in, the desperate poor who preferred to shiver from fear of what heathen devilry still lurked in the shells of Jew houses than from the cold and wet of no shelter at all.

At the end closest to the lane, where the houses huddled round St Olave's like children round a mother's skirts, a few Lombard goldsmiths had moved in. They were the unlucky spill of Longshanks' generous invite, who came too late to reap the benefits of the fine houses along the Street of Lombards and were now trying to raise the status of Old Jewry by donating generously to St Olave's.

The old church had been there forever, Kirkpatrick knew, a refuge for Norwegians who came to the City – he knew this because the Bruce's relations used it. He frowned, for the tall ragstoned edifice was where Malise was headed, sure as a night ship to a beacon.

Old Jewry in daylight was bad enough, Kirkpatrick thought as he crabbed up the overgrown street, with the gaping doorways leering at him and the half-splintered window shutters seeming to glare balefully, like injured eyes. At night, it would be a place of horrors, real and imagined, and he was glad to reach the sanctuary of St Olave's, sliding through the open doorway into the dim and cool illusion of safety, all balm to his sweating fear.

Voices. He paused, feeling the sweat slide down his back, but he forced himself to speak when he saw the owners of the voices – a priest in black habit and scapular, tall, gaunt and angular, arguing with a white-haired, red-faced man in paint-stained tunic and hose which an apron, as riotously daubed as Joseph's Coat, had failed to protect.

'Ho,' Kirkpatrick hoarsed out and both men whirled, startled.

'Is this some alehouse?' The red-faced man thundered, staring accusingly at Kirkpatrick, 'where folk can rush in and out as they please?'

137

'There is a riot in Ironmonger Lane,' the priest said gently, adding woefully, 'again.'

'Have folk come in here?' Kirkpatrick demanded in a rasp even he did not like. 'A scuttling little man followed by another, black and spider-like?'

The priest looked him over and Kirkpatrick felt a spasm of irritation at how he must look; it had been bad enough when he was disguised as a beggar, in sackcloth hood and torn old clothes which stank of the cabbage smell you get from marinading in your own farts. Now he was slathered with fluids and watery blood and grease, so he realized he was unlikely to get reasonable treatment – the red-faced man confirmed it.

'Who the Devil are you, sirra?' he demanded truculently, but the priest held up one placating hand for he had heard the voice, at odds with a beggar's look. No whine or deference in it – on the contrary, it had the tone and timbre of command so the priest stepped carefully.

'Ekarius came in. Another followed him, asking after him as you have done.'

'Who is Ekarius?' demanded Kirkpatrick and the red-faced man elbowed the priest aside.

'My assistant – and who are you?'

'Assistant what?' answered Kirkpatrick and the red-faced man went purple, drew some of the fat from his belly to his chest and puffed up like a pigeon.

'I am William of Thanet, Master artist,' he bellowed. 'I will not ask again . . .'

'Neither will I.'

Kirkpatrick showed him the dagger; even at six feet of distance it pricked a hole in the man's pompous bluster and he sagged and sputtered. The priest made the sign of the cross and said: 'Christ be praised.'

'For ever and ever,' Kirkpatrick answered, then jerked the dagger meaningfully.

'Ekarius mixes paints for Master William,' the priest answered quickly and the dumbed William nodded furious agreement.

'Little man, speaks strangely, says he is a pilgrim from the Holy Land?'

'As to that last, my son, I could not say,' the priest declared and William of Thanet found his voice.

'From Cologne,' he spluttered. 'He has seen the church of St Maria Lyskirchen, as have I – he can recall some of the frescoes and is helping me recreate them here . . .'

He waved and Kirkpatrick saw, for the first time, the great, intricate webbing of scaffold clawing up two of the walls, half masking Christ in His Glory and The Last Supper. Cologne – well, that fitted at least – Ekarius was almost certainly Lamprecht.

'Can he paint?' Kirkpatrick asked, bemused and William of Thanet exploded.

'Christ in Heaven, no – he simply recalls figures and positions I have forgotten. I let him limewash, mind you. When he is not darting around . . .'

'Where is he now?'

Both men pointed upwards.

'He has made a nest up there,' snorted William. 'Like a squirrel.'

Kirkpatrick looked up, then back at the men.

'It would be best,' he said, 'if you went about your business elsewhere for the moment.'

'It would be best,' the priest answered firmly, 'if you were to hand me that dagger and kneel in prayer.'

William of Thanet knew that was not about to happen and dragged the priest away. At a safe distance they would run and fetch a bailiff – if they could find one in all the ructions and if they could find one willing to enter Old Jewry even in daylight.

Kirkpatrick found the way to the net of lashed poles, a

series of slatted wooden rungs with ropes hung on either side as handholds; when he looked up, the edifice towered above him, the height of a good castle wall and, to his left, another scaffolding dappled the half-finished Annunciation with light. He bounced a little, testing the first rung and swallowed a dry spear in his throat as the entire cat's cradle of wood swayed alarmingly.

Sixty feet above Malise felt it just as he closed in on the whimpering Lamprecht, who was huddled in the darkest corner among pots of limewash and long brushes; the stink of paint and flax seed oil caught his throat and stung his eyes so that his frayed nerves sprang to a temper he had to fight to control.

'Lamprecht, you stinking little goniel erse o' a hoor slip . . .'

Lamprecht heard the voice and found some rat courage.

'*Non aver di te paura, malvoglio. Tocomo – er tutto lo mondo fendoto . . .*'

Malise cursed; he had no idea what Lamprecht was saying, but he heard the shrill, desperate threat in the voice and swallowed his ire until it all but choked him.

'Lamprecht,' he said soothingly in French, which he knew the little rat understood. 'Listen to me – I am here to help you . . .'

'You come to kill. Everyone she wishes to kill Lamprecht. *Fater unser, thu in himilom bist . . .* '

Malise heard the whine of him, heard also the descent into muttered German. Then he felt the sway of the platform and knew at once what had caused it.

'Oaf,' he hissed. 'Unhalesome capernicous gowk . . .'

He caught himself again, forced French between the grind of his teeth.

'Who is my master, imbecile? The Comyn Earl of Buchan, kin to the Comyn Lord of Badenoch and both of them seeking only to reward you for what you know. Why in the name of God and all His angels would I wish you harm? I wish only to keep you safe from the imps of Satan that the Earl of Carrick has set on your trail.'

Lamprecht, despite the screaming agony of his fingers and his crawling fear knew Malise almost certainly lied, so he shrank away and babbled; the platform swayed again and Malise was suddenly there, close enough to touch, his face lopsided with rage.

'There,' Malise declared, throwing one dramatic arm back the way he had come, 'is the man who wants you dead. Tell me what you know . . .'

'*Hilfe* . . . save me first,' Lamprecht whimpered, seeing a bargain to be made, even now.

Kirkpatrick was trembling and slick-wet when he finally hauled himself over the lip of the platform. Christ in His Heaven, he thought, whom I will surely meet two steps from here, I am so high.

He started to tremble his way to his feet, marvelling at how anyone could climb that spider's web of wood every day . . . not for all the siller in the world, he thought, starting to pick a way over the coiled rope and paint-slathered pots.

Then the world hit him and he reeled, caught desperately with one hand and felt cloth, felt it tear, then fell, rolled and slid over the platform edge – and stopped, hanging by the snag of his sackcloth cloak. Something black fell past him with a shrill cry.

Malise thought he had succeeded when he rammed into Kirkpatrick, catching him unawares and driving him to the edge of the platform – then, just as the man teetered on the brink, Malise felt the clawing hand grab his sleeve, tugging him off balance and they staggered until it tore. Malise, feet tangled in a coiled rope, felt himself falling, flailed wildly at the air – then clattered to the plank walkway and rolled over the edge like a stone.

There was a sickening, bowel-opening moment of plunge, when the dim flagstones of the floor screamed towards him –

141

then the rope-loop cinched tight round the ankle of his shoe and, the other end fastened to the winch for raising heavy loads, he swung like the pendulum of a bell, clear across the space of the nave where the white, open-mouthed blobs of the priest and the Master limner sped below him like strange birds.

He hit the other scaffolding with a sickening crash that drove sense and the air from him, swung back, spinning while the lashed wood creaked, cracked and finally collapsed in a rolling thunder of noise and dust clouds. On the way back again, his shoe slipped off releasing the loop and he fell the last little way like a bag of rags, rolling heavily to the feet of the astounded priest.

Above, Kirkpatrick heard his cloak start to rip, flailed in a panic to get a handhold and heard it tear even more, so that he dropped a foot. One hand reached up and grasped a pole, just as the cloak tore in two; he hung, feeling the savage pain of his own weight tearing his arm from the socket. He looked up at the sound of a step, saw Lamprecht leaning over, brown with wide grin.

'*El malvoglio*,' Lamprecht said and wished he had a knife – wished he had unbroken fingers to be able to hold it. That gave him an idea and his grin grew wet and red; he raised his foot to bring it crushingly down on Kirkpatrick's fingers.

Kirkpatrick braced, knew he would never resist the pain of it, that he was about to take a long, hard fall into Hell itself . . . looked up into the leering face for one final curse on the ugly little shit . . .

The face changed in an instant, to one of absolute bemusement, staring down at the length of bloody steel which had just sprung out of his belly. It disappeared with a sucking sound that seemed to cut some hidden string inside Lamprecht and the little pardoner slumped sideways, mewling.

Kirkpatrick, blinded by sweat and pain, saw a black-gloved hand grasp his wrist, then a tremendous strength hauled him up and on to the platform, where his legs refused to carry him; he sat, shaking, looking at the twitching remains of Lamprecht.

The man who had killed him was all brown and black, wiping the length of sword clean on Lamprecht's tunic, so that Kirkpatrick saw the pommel of it, the Templar cross clear. The man's black spade beard split in a grin as he tore free what was around the dying pardoner's throat, already slick with his own bloody vomit.

'Rossal de Bissot,' he announced in French, then jerked his head back the way he had come. 'You should have realized how a fat painter would get to his workplace and saved yourself a climb. Now we must hurry and use the same counterweight lift – this place is carnage, no?'

CHAPTER SEVEN

Herdmanston Tower, Lothian
Six days to Midsummer Eve, June, 1305

Hal and the Dog Boy came up on Herdmanston under a low sky like a bruise, the weather hot and heavy and the garrons moving as if underwater. Thunder growled behind the hills.

Hal came, pale as milk from the fever which had forced him off the road from York to Whitby and into the care of the Augustinians at Kirkham. It was there that the questing Dog Boy found him and brought the news of how Wallace had red-murdered Bangtail Hob.

Now the pair of them rode down into the huddle of buildings clustered round Herdmanston, where children left off making a fat straw man for the midsummer bonfire to run up and gawp. I am a stranger, Hal realized, looking at a fat-legged toddler with a finger stuck up one nostril. There are bairns here too young to have ever laid eyes on me in the flesh.

Herdmanston bustled, all the same, was scattered with sawdust fine as querned flour and smelled of new wood and pitch; men waved to the lord of Herdmanston from the roof where they were making the trapdoor watertight.

Some matters were the same; Alehouse Maggie, all bosom

144

and folded arms, gave him a wide grin and then swaddled him as if he was a bairn and not her fealtied lord; men in sweat-darkened serks jeered and chaffered, as much glad for the excuse to stop work as the sight of the bold knight of Herdmanston gasping for breath and demanding Maggie leave off and watch his ribs, which were tender yet.

Sim Craw arrived, his iron-grey curls and beard frosted with wood shavings, his own grin wide and his wrist-grip iron hard; Hal, for the first time in a long run of days, felt a glow of peace descend on him.

Yet not all was the same. Bet The Bread was gone, taken by the bloody flux – now her daughter, as willow-wand slim as Bet had probably been in her own youth, bobbed nervously at Hal, announced herself as 'Bet's Meggy' and went away beaming and strutting when she was confirmed as Herdmanston's cook and baker, the place her mother had once occupied.

'There are some other matters,' Sim said, when they were in the cool of the big hall and left alone with bread, cheese and leather mugs. 'Yon Malenfaunt has had to end his legalling ower his writ, for one.'

Hal nodded; it had hardly been a surprise. Longshanks had confiscated Herdmanston years before from the rebel Hal and handed its care to Malenfaunt, though the ownership was a parchment gift only. Malenfaunt, in all the years since, had never been capable of claiming it – but, since peace had broken out he had agitated through wee canting lawyers for the exercise of his rights.

It had been a nagging stone in Herdmanston's shoe – but defeat at the hands of Bruce had stripped Malenfaunt of honour, dignity and support and now he had quit the case. At least some good came of that ill-fated joust, Hal thought, remembering the sickening sight of Bruce's cheek.

'Earl Patrick has refused the use of his mill – happily, Sir Henry is letting us mill at Roslin,' Sim went on, spraying bread as he spoke.

145

Hal was not surprised at Patrick of Dunbar's decision – the Herdmanston Sientclers were supposedly fealtied to Patrick, Earl of March, but had defied the determinedly English-supporting lord at every turn. The Earl had had to grit his teeth and welcome Hal back at every turn, too, as part of the peace terms with Longshanks, so any petty slight he could visit was grist to his mill, as Sim declared, proud of his cleverness.

'Dog Boy needs confirming as a cottar,' Sim continued when Hal seemed not to have recognized his word skill, 'now that ye have manumitted him from bondage. He would not ken ploughshare from auld heuch, so I have kept him working with the dugs for money payment – Sir Henry sent a brace o' braw wee deerhound pups which have grown leggy since an' Dog Boy loves yon animals.'

Hal, feeling at ease from pain and care, sitting in his own rebuilt hall, could only smile at it all, the comforting balm of the familiar, of Herdmanston at work and far removed from the maelstrom it stood in – yet the next words drove the old chill back in him.

'Kirkpatrick came,' Sim said, frowning over his mug. 'There was a stushie in Lunnon, it appears, where yon wee pardoner was killed dead an' that hallirakus likkie-spinnie Bellejambe seems as good as. I would surmise so, since Kirkpatrick looked like a week-auld corpse himself and he the victor of the tourney atween them.'

So the pardoner was dead. Hal felt relief that it had happened, more that it had not been him who'd had to do the deed – and guilt at feeling both.

'Christ be praised,' he said.

'For ever and ever,' Sim replied, then cleared his throat.

'Kirkpatrick is now away to Sir Henry at Roslin,' he went on, 'charged with pursuing "the other matter" – I jalouse this is the same matter Bangtail died for.'

Hal met his eye with one of his own, as hard as glass so that Sim's eyebrows seemed suddenly to shoot up to avoid colliding into a frown. Curved as Saracen scimitars they stayed that way for a long moment, then he nodded.

'Aye, weel,' he growled. 'I have had men out, making discreets and riskin' nothing. Every spoor says that Wallace has gone to ground and his men scattered. He has not been seen since he arrived at Roslin a while back. Mayhap this is the end of him.'

'Wallace is never ended,' Hal replied tersely, then forced a smile.

'Wallace came to Roslin?' he asked and shook his head. 'So even Sir Henry keeps secrets from me – is there any good news in this dish of grue?'

He paused apologetically, then waved a hand which encompassed Herdmanston and everything done to it.

'Apart from all this, which is sweetening indeed – more power to you for it, Sim Craw.'

Sim, muttering pleased, waved a dismissive hand, then laid his leather mug down, slow and careful, a gesture Hal did not miss.

'There is a last matter,' Sim said, 'but I leave it to yourself as to the good or bad news in it.'

Hal paused, then forced a smile.

'Weel, I am sittin', so the shock will no' throw me on my back. Speak on.'

'Sir Henry kept the news of it until now, when he thought you better suited to the receipt of it. Wallace brought the Coontess to Roslin and, if ye send word, she is almost certes headed here.'

Herdmanston Tower, Lothian
Midsummer Eve, June, 1305

He sent word, would have dragged Hermes from Olympus to deliver it faster if he could. Then he waited, limping up and down and fretting, leashed only by the certainty that, if he stormed over to Roslin, he would shatter something delicate as a glass web.

The days slid away, thunder-brassy and hot and still she did not come. Tansy's Dan and Mouse lugged four of Herdmanston's fat porkers to the barmkin green and cut their throats.

Then they, Ill-Made Jock, Dirleton Will, Sore Davey and others skinned and jointed them, cramming them into cauldrons for boiling while the grass grew greasy and red; Dog Boy whipped up a pig's head and danced with it, rushing at the young bairns and roaring while they ran away with squeals of delight.

Tansy's Dan strung entrails round him like ribbons and joined in, dancing barefoot with the Dog Boy on the blood-soaked grass, the pair of them shrieking with laughter, gore splashing them to the knees. For a time, the lust of it leaped from head to head like unseen lightning so that the knowledge of the feast to come and the peace to enjoy it and the dizzying freedom from work sent everyone giggling mad; they grabbed pig heads from one another, pretended to be charging boars, swung them by the ears and sprayed crimson everywhere.

Toddlers, sliding and slipping on unsteady legs, were blood-drenched head to toe. Young babes sucked on kidneys, their mums red-lipped as *baobhan sith* from eating liver.

And still she did not come.

Donachie, the Earl Patrick's man, rode over with a black-eyebrowed scowl and a demand for owed tolts and scutage, but that was simply the Earl's latest stirring of the byke he saw in Herdmanston; Hal sent him off home empty-handed and reminded him of the legality of matters.

The children promptly added scowling black eyebrows to their straw effigy and Father Thomas, though no Herdmanston man born and bred, preached a sermon in his rough-walled church about how Adam and Eve did not have to plough, sow

148

or weed for any lord, then had to add enough embellishment to show how Sir Hal of Herdmanston was practically kin to Jesus and should be so served.

And still she did not come.

Then, in the dark of Midsummer Eve, the fire was lit, the straw man burned, the boiled and roasted pigs eaten and the ale drunk. Bet's Meggy, in a green dress festooned with madder ribbons, pranced barefoot with the straw stallion mummer head in the Horse Dance, elegant and feral.

She led the procession of flaming brands into the fields, Father Thomas stumping determinedly after with his fiery crucifix, so that God was not forgotten in it; everyone was festooned with garlands of mugwort, vervain and yarrow, cheering and reeling and beaming, greasy-cheeked and red-faced.

Later still folk leaped the bonfire flames, or daringly rubbed fern seed on their eyelids in the hope of seeing the *sidhean* on this night when the veils between worlds were thinnest – with rue clenched in their fists to prevent them being pixie-led and never seen again.

And, finally, she came.

Slowly, up the steps from the hall, where a visiting Kirkpatrick greeted Sim Craw and others with a twisted smile and accepted strong drink, she climbed to the folly of the topmost room in the tower, her feet leaden and her heart fluttering like a trapped bird. She felt breathless and had to stop once for fear of fainting and wished she could loosen the barbette and goffered fillet on her head.

It was dim. There was a crusie flickering, but the light in the room was mainly the full, bright moon and the flare of the bonfire through the tall unshuttered folly of window, so that he was a stark shadow there and no more. She stopped then, one hand to her throat.

He saw her head come above the floor level, caught the flame glint in the russet of it so that his breathing stopped entirely for a moment and his heart, which had been thundering so loudly he was sure they could hear it outside, seemed to catch and cease.

'Isabel,' he said, his voice a rasp.

She backed away, not ready for this, not ready for any of it. Five years since she had been here . . . five years since she had even set eyes on him at all, or he on her; she smoothed her dress, touched her hair with an unconscious gesture.

She heard him move, then the crusie flared more brilliantly and he set it down on top of the kist at the end of the great canopied bed; new, she thought wildly. Not the one she remembered, though she remembered the nights in it. Could not move any further than the first step into the room.

He was thin, the fine perse tunic loose on him. His hair had more grey in it than she remembered and she touched her own again, as if to feel that the artifice that held it to its old colour still worked. His eyes, though, were the same grey-blue, but it seemed as if more ice had crept into them than before and they were fixed on her with an intensity that made her reach one hand to her throat.

He said nothing and they stood there, while the midsummer shrieks and laughter echoed faintly and the amber shadows danced.

'Am I so changed?' she managed at last and was irritated by the tremble in her voice, like some maid clutching St John's Wort for the promise of a future lover.

There was silence, so long she felt the crush of it.

'Lamb,' he said eventually, soft as a lisp. 'My wee lamb.'

It broke her, closed her throat, sprang tears. She did not know who moved, but she felt the strength of him, the wrap of his arms, the smell of sweat and wool, woodsmoke, vervain, leather and horse.

Then they were half-weeping, half-laughing, telling each other what they had missed, how they still loved, babbling into one another's speech so that, in the end, the words themselves did not matter, but simply trilled like a stream of balm.

150

Like music, he thought, drenched and drowning. Like music.

They talked and loved, laughing because the long, full gown had sleeves she had been sewn into and he had to cut them free, while the elaborate fillet which had taken so painstakingly long to arrange in her hair, was sloughed away like the years between them.

Later, she learned of Lamprecht and Bruce; he learned of her put-aside by Buchan. They swore never to be parted, even if the world went up in flames.

She found out his doings with Kirkpatrick, who had brought her here. He found out about her rescue from Elcho by Wallace; she saw the grim set of those iced eyes at the mention of his name and knew why.

'Bangtail,' she said and heard him grunt in the dark. Then she sparked life into a tallow and, by the guttering yellow of it, showed him the Apostles, six baleful red eyes staring back at them as they both huddled, half-naked and half-afraid in the flickering dim.

'A generous gift,' he admitted grudgingly, stirring the blood-drop rubies, 'but against the life o' Bangtail Hob, it weighs less than a cock feather in the pan.'

'It was a hard thing for the Wallace to have done,' she admitted, shivering in the fresh breeze that swept suddenly through the tall unshuttered windows, a relief from the leprous heat that, just as quickly, puckered skin to gooseflesh. 'Yet there is good and honour in the man, as you know.'

He drew a bedspread tenderly round her shoulders.

'Aye, lass, I ken it – God forbid I have ever to face Wallace in person, though it is what we are charged with, Kirkpatrick and I. Better us than men from English Edward.'

There was a long silence, broken only by the slough of wind and the sudden rattle of rain, bringing distant shrieks from those still hooching and wheeching round the dying midsummer bonfire.

Then she stirred, as if gentled to life by the wind itself.

151

'I know where Wallace is,' she said, almost sadly.
The thunder slammed a seal on her betrayal.

St Bartholomew's Priory, Smoothfield, London
Feast of the Visitation, July, 1305

Red John Comyn stood hip-shot beside the elaborate tomb to Rahere, first Prior of St Bartholomew's, tapping one high-heeled, booted foot impatiently. Around him were shadowed figures, far enough away not to overhear if voices were kept low, close enough to intervene if it became necessary.

It could easily become necessary. Ostensibly buying prime horseflesh at Smoothfield, one of the premier markets of Europe, Red John was here to meet Bruce – at his request. An elaborate ritual dance of exchanged messages, barely disguised hostages and the agreement of neutral ground had brought Red John here, beside the black-robed recumbent figure of Rahere, stone hands piously clasped.

There were no other folk here, kept away even during such an important feast day in one of the popular priories of London, which showed the power of the Comyn and Bruces. Plantagenet will hear of it, all the same, Red John thought, which is a risk worth taking to find out what happened.

Above all he wanted to know what had happened – Bellejambe had arrived back, staggering and broken, having dragged himself away from St Olave's before the King's men came down on it and found outraged priests and the dead body of a pardoner. Bellejambe did not know how the pardoner had died – or how Bruce's man had survived – but what information Lamprecht had was now lost to them.

Which was an annoyance Red John thought with a sharp pang of bitterness. But at least droop-eyed Edward Longshanks knows nothing of any Comyn involvement in the matter – else I would not be here, he thought. There was annoyance, too, at how he had been left to pick up the pieces while the Earl of Buchan, ostensibly seeking out his wayward countess yet again, had used the lie of it to flee to his own lands, just in case.

There was a flurry, a clack of leather on smoothed flagstones; Red John's men, bland in plain clothing, stiffened like scenting hounds.

Bruce had arrived.

He came up swiftly, with the air of a man with better things to be doing, but that was mummery – Bruce was swift because he wanted this dangerous liaison over with, for a whole ragman roll of reasons.

Yet there was savour in the moment, handed to him from the wreck of a bad day which had brought Kirkpatrick hirpling home with tales of riot and chase, brawl and murder – and a Templar, who had arrived in time to kill Lamprecht and save Kirkpatrick.

'The Templar knight has the Rood and the contents of the pardoner's scrip, gilt reliquary, Apostle jewels and all,' Kirkpatrick had said, once James of Montaillou had finished tutting and treating and left them alone.

'He tells me his name, which is Rossal de Bissot, and that he will bring the Rood when the time is right.'

He paused and eased himself gingerly in the chair; the sweat popped out on his forehead, fat drops that he dashed away with an irritated hand.

'It seems the Templars are up to their neck in this.'

A neck on the block, beset by rumours of papal displeasure and French spies actively seeking proof of heresy, as Bruce pointed out. Which was no soothe to Kirkpatrick's bruised pride and cracked ribs, Bruce saw. The taste of failure was bitter in the man's voice; Bruce heard and it was best that he knew all was not lost – just the opposite, in fact.

'Rossal de Bissot is clearly working for the safety of his Order,' he informed the whey-faced Kirkpatrick. 'Bissot is a much-revered name within the Poor Knights.'

'Aye, weel – revered or not, he will not be backwards in coming forwards,' Kirkpatrick answered sourly. 'He will want advantage from handing you what you seek, my lord – it is not wise to mire yourself in the doings of the Poor Order.'

Bruce said nothing, merely stroked his injured cheek, perpetually hidden now under a plain hood. It was clear that this Rossal was holding Lamprecht's loot; the Apostles were gone – save the one the pardoner had handed over in a loaf – and, worse still, the Rood was gone and it was little comfort that it lay in the hands of the Templars. Still, the Bruce involvement in all of it was safely locked up behind the kist of Lamprecht's dead mouth.

Best of all, the Comyn had been left floundering and, shortly after speaking with Kirkpatrick, Bruce had sent out word for a meeting with that family – and then dispatched his brothers and Kirkpatrick back to Scotland.

He had also sent off Elizabeth and her women, which had been a more disagreeable task altogether; he had not even seen his wife, only Lady Bridget her tirewoman, who had informed him that her mistress was not inclined to leave the comfort of London for the cold north.

He had bitten down on his angry tongue, though enough anger spilled into his eyes to set the tirewoman back a step and pale her cheek. His quietly delivered ultimatum had been taken to his wife, and very soon he could hear the flurry of them packing – but the victory in it was a sour taste.

Now he clacked across the floor to Red John, leaving a suitable hem of his own *mesnie* at the fringes of Rahere's tomb. He studied the frowning wee man with his red-gold curve of beard quivering as if he barely held some unseen force in check. He looked like a man in the wrong clothing, from the foppish hat on his close-cropped head down the silk and fine wool to his vainly-heeled boots – Bruce was wary; this was the man who had sprang at his throat before and the memory of it burned shame in him still.

'Was he one of yours, the man killed in the riot in the Cheap?' he asked and Red John curled his lip in something which might have been sneer or smile.

'He was not. That was one of Buchan's own, a fine man from Rattray who will be much mourned – how is your own man? I hear he was much battered about.'

'He is in good health. More so, I understand, than your Bellejambe.'

Red John smiled, warmly this time.

'Again, Buchan's man – and he is sore hurt, but will survive with Heaven's help and good broth.'

'Christ be praised,' Bruce replied laconically.

'For ever and ever.'

'I suspect God's Hand will be withdrawn from him, all the same,' Bruce went on, flat and vicious. 'Failure is a poor option in Buchan lands.'

'*Go dtachta an diabhal thú,*' Comyn hissed, looking right and left.

'If the Devil does choke me,' Bruce answered, also in Gaelic, 'it will be a Comyn hand he uses.'

Which was enough of a reminder of Red John's previous throttling anger to bring the fiery lord of Badenoch to the balls of his feet; he sucked in a deep breath.

'What do you wish in this matter?' he demanded, still bristling like a ginger boar. 'Why for did you call this meeting?'

They sibilated in Gaelic now, the better to confuse any passing monk who, consciously or accidentally, breached the glowering ring of faces and came close enough to hear; there was chanting somewhere, for the celebration of the Visitation, and monks scurried to and fro with little flaps of sound.

Bruce waved one hand and, despite himself, Red John followed it with his eyes until he saw it was empty of blade.

'Longshanks is no fool and will have learned of what happened. It is enough for him to leave off wondering and descend on vigorous seeking of answers,' Bruce replied

155

viciously. 'He will see where your thoughts run, my lord. The Comyn looking to foil the Bruce? He may not consider this another tourney in our personal quarrels – he may think one or either of us plot against him, which has ever been his way. I am loyalty writ large and gilded, my lord – but yourself and Buchan have been a single thorn to him not long since and he will consider you are about to fight him again.'

'We were fighting for Scotland before you and will after you,' Red John replied savagely, then slapped his silk-quilted chest. 'Comyn and Balliol, my lord Carrick, holding true while you waver and turn whenever it suits you. *Titim gan éirí ort.*'

May you fall without rising – a good old Gaelic curse that Bruce recalled his mother uttering, so that the memory of it made him smile a little; the sight threw Red John off his course.

'Aye, you have resisted Longshanks fiercely,' Bruce agreed, 'so that your wife will be no guard against his belief that you will do so again.'

Red John's eyes flickered at that; his wife was Joan de Valence, sister to Aymer and daughter of the King's own uncle. Red John Comyn must be a fretting annoyance to the de Valence family, Bruce thought – almost as much as he is to me.

'This must end,' he said flatly. 'Enough is enough – our feud is ruining the Kingdom, which needs a strong hand. It needs a king, my lord.'

'It has a king,' muttered Red John. 'A Balliol, not a Bruce.'

'Unmade by the same hand that raised him up,' Bruce answered and saw the bristling over this old argument; he waved it away with a dismissive gesture.

'We may debate it until Judgement Day,' he growled, 'but the Gordian Knot of it can be cut simply enough.'

They stared at each other and Red John grew still and quiet, leaning back slightly to look at Bruce – pale for such a dark man, Red John saw, with the tight dark green hood framing his face tightly, the spill of it like moss dagged on his shoulders.

To hide the scar on his cheek, he thought, from Malenfaunt's blow – *marbhaisg ort*, a death shroud on you, Malenfaunt, he thought. If you had done your work as you were paid to this man would not be such a stone in my shoe.

'You have such a sharp edge, then? One to cut away a king?'

The question made Bruce's eyes glitter and Red John caught his breath. God's Bones, he has, right enough, he thought. This Bruce is planning to usurp a kingdom.

'There is support for it,' Bruce replied guardedly, seeing the astonished curve of Red John's eyebrows. 'More than you perhaps realize. Together we will be a stronger flame than apart – but even without that, it would be better, at least, if our fire was not being thrust in one another's face.'

'Are you saying you will stop plotting against us? That there will be peace – or a truce at least – between our families?'

'I am.'

'So that you can make yourself king of Scots and usurp my kin?'

Bruce hesitated.

'So that a king might be found who is better fitted to the task than John Balliol,' he replied carefully.

'What do the Comyn and Balliol get from this?' Red John asked with a sneer. 'Apart from a royally angered kinsman and a dangerously powerful Bruce.'

'No mention of your plotting beyond these walls,' Bruce declared, waving the document. 'A free hand with your own lands and rewards from a grateful sovereign.'

'Do I seem afeared to you?' Red John sneered, waving one wild arm. 'Tell your tales to Longshanks and see if he has the belly for another fight in Scotland, which is what it will cause. See then how your careful wooing of the gullible will stand when it is known that you have plunged them back into war and, yet again, waver on where to stand. And we have a free hand in our own lands already, as well as a grateful sovereign in John Balliol.'

'It is not Longshanks you should fear,' Bruce answered, his cold eyes on Red John's hot face, so that the air between them seemed to sizzle. 'It is the Community of the Realm.'

That made Red John blanch a little and Bruce saw it with a savage leap of pleasure that he had trouble disguising. Red John was silent for a long time, staring at the effigy and its elaborate tomb, the armorials all faded beneath the flaking wood of the ogee arches.

'Did you know Rahere was a wee clerk in the service of auld King Henry?' he asked suddenly, breaking from Gaelic to braid Scots. 'Steeped in venery, it is said, but he proved useful to the sovereign and so was raised up.'

He turned to the tomb, one encompassing arm taking in the kneeling canons, reading their stone Bible at the feet of the recumbent figure.

'Proof positive that any chiel of poor account can rise to the greatest if he is willing to any sin.'

Bruce clenched his teeth on his anger, the sickening tug of the cicatrice like a dash of iced water down his veins. He waited.

'I will consult with the Earl of Buchan on the matter,' Red John declared eventually in French.

'You are the Comyn who matters,' Bruce answered and Red John nodded, almost absently, then offered a terse, thin smile.

'You will hear from us, never fear.'

Bruce watched him walk away on his vain boots, to be folded into his cloak of hard-faced men. Incense wafted in the air and the chanting grew louder as Bruce's men waited, tense.

He had not been a clerk, Bruce knew. Prior Rahere, founder of St Bartholomew's, had been a jester and laughter had raised him up. That and the advice of a wise fool.

Bruce peered at the words on the stone Bible - Isaiah, Chapter 51, 'The Lord shall comfort Zion . . .' - wondering if he had been wise or a fool to reveal so much to the Lord of Badenoch. He wondered if the Lord of Badenoch had been moved from his position any. Or if he dared move himself, in pursuit of kingship and despite the Comyn.

'You will have to move soon, lord of Annandale,' said a voice and Bruce whirled to find the sub-prior close by, arms folded into his robes and seemingly blissfully unaware of the wolves hovering at his back.

'God wills it,' the sub-prior said piously.

As Bruce continued to stare, blinking in wonder at this strange prophet, he added apologetically, 'You are blocking the processional, my son.'

St Mary's Loch, near Moffat, Scottish Border
Vigil of St Palladius, July, 1305

They came along the shore of the loch, with the bare hump of Watch Law on their right and the darkly wooded Wiss across the mirror mere, reflected dizzyingly so that the world seemed upside down.

It was a long cavalcade which made those who encountered it leap to their feet, thinking that so many riders could only herald the return of red war to their little part of the world. The half-dozen of the English garrison at Traquair had run off at the sound, only returning, half-ashamed and not speaking of it at all, when they found that the mounted horde of Wallace consisted of five men, a woman and a herd of some fifty horses, sound and stolid stots and affers being driven to the market at Carlisle.

'Every venture I take with you,' Kirkpatrick muttered to Sim Craw, not for the first time, 'seems to consist of starin' at the spavined arse of livestock that God has forsook. Nags or kine with shitey hurdies.'

'Ca' canny,' protested Stirk Davey. 'There is some prime horseflesh here – Fauberti will wet himself at the sight, like a wee ravin' dug.'

Stirk was as rangy and lean as a stag on the rut, all nervous energy and concern for his charges, one of which was the prime horseflesh he spoke of. This was a fine, cold-bred *destrier* called Rammasche, which was the name you gave to a wild hawk. An entire – a stallion – he was not exactly destined for the fine hands of top dealer Fauberti in London, but would still fetch good money in Carlisle.

The rest – palfreys, rounceys, everyday stots and carter's affers – were a good cover for a group trying to creep into Moffat to find out if the Countess was right and Wallace was secreted at Corehead Tower – the horse droving road to Carlisle and the south led straight past the place.

Being here nagged Kirkpatrick, because it was a lick and spit away from Closeburn, seat of the Kirkpatricks and held by his namesake, who had no love for the rebel Wallace and would as soon hang them both side by side.

Isabel, however, merely smiled at his fears, though she was the other rub on the fluffed fur of Kirkpatrick's nerves – the Countess of Buchan, striding along in ungainly leather riding boots and a plain dress, which she tucked up to ride astraddle when the fancy took her.

Wearing a threadbare hooded cloak, red-eyed from woodsmoke, having cooked for all of them over an open fire, like any auld beldame wife of a horsecorser.

It was a perfect disguise, admittedly – Buchan would not be looking for his wife here – but not only was it simply delaying the inevitable, it was not right that a noblewoman of the realm should be chaffering and handing out bowls to the likes of Dog Boy and Stirk and himself.

Hal, of course, didn't mind – it had been his idea – and Kirkpatrick, not for the first time, shook his head over how the lord of Herdmanston was mainly for sense, save over this woman.

Still, he thought, she has at least one good use in her for me and he had put it to her one night when she was alone at the smoking fire where she was cleaning bowls and horn spoons. Squatting companionably beside her, at length he said, slow and careful as a man walking on eggs, 'It would be better, do ye ken, if I saw to the Wallace alone.'

She wiped the last bowl clean, tucked a stray tendril of hair back under her hood and looked at him for the first time, waving away insects drunk on woodsmoke.

'Hal did not come all this way to stand by while you speak,' she said.

'Why did he come?' demanded Kirkpatrick, low and urgent. 'That is the question begging here.'

'No harm will come to Wallace,' she answered firmly – more firmly than she was actually sure of, if the truth was known. But it was known only to her and to Hal and Kirkpatrick simply had to take the face of it – which he did, scowling.

'I will hold you to it, mistress,' he said. 'I do not want any brawl between Hal and the Wallace over Bangtail Hob, for there is no telling which of them will come out the other side of it alive and no matter which it is, all will be in ruin.'

'I wish this was for the concern of the lord of Herdmanston,' she answered sharply, 'but I know it is because of Bruce's plans, whatever they are. You forget how well I know him.'

'I do not forget how well you know him,' Kirkpatrick answered. Others were moving towards the fire.

'I pray the blessin' o' heaven on ye, lady, that the lord o' Herdmanston has forgot that fact entire,' he added viciously as he wraithed away.

They had not spoken since, in all the long days down through Peebles and Traquair, into the forest vastness that had been the Wallace stronghold and was now no more than a lair for the ragged remnants, gone back to brigandage.

By the time they circled the animals near St Cuthbert's Chapel, while Stirk Davey was haggling grazing payment with the monks, it was clear that word of them had gone out; among the Moffat gawpers were two or three riders, who came no closer than long bowshot, looked and left.

Patient as a stone in a river, Kirkpatrick moved among the chiels and monks, chaffering and exchanging news, dropping the name Wallace in now and then to see whose eyes narrowed or widened.

As dusk crept in, he came to the fire as they gathered for thick soup and oat bread. Red-dyed by the embers he spoke without looking at any of them, as if he muttered into his bowl.

'We will be visited tonight and they will come armed, though they will do us no harm unless we leap up and threaten them. Hal and I will go with them and if we are not returned within two hours, you must talk among yourselves as to what is best.'

Then he looked up into the great broad grin of the Dog Boy and managed one in reply.

'Get quickly to the meat of it, where you come looking to lift us safely out of their *donjean*,' he added and had back a low laugh or two for his pains.

The visitors came later than Kirkpatrick had expected, shadows against the black, a faceless voice thick with suspicion and menace.

'Bide doucelike. If as much as the hair on the quim o' yer wummin twitches, ye will rue it.'

For a moment, all was still, frozen – then the slim rill of a woman's voice sluiced away the terror.

'Lang Jack Short,' Isabel said, firm and fierce. 'At our last meeting, ye would no more have discussed my nethers than you would have refused the meat and ale of my hospitality at Balmullo the night we fixed Will Wallace's leg.'

Hal almost cried out with the delight of it; if he was not already in thrall to her, he would have loved her for this moment alone; there was a pause, then a face, broken-nosed ugly, shoved itself into the embered glow of the fire,

'Coontess?'

'The same,' she answered tartly. 'Here to see Sir William. So less of your sauce, Lang Jack and do what you have been bid.'

'Bigod,' Sim Craw admired, 'it never fails to maze me how such a well-bred wummin kens every low-born chiel from here to beyond The Mounth.'

It was a slash through Long Jack's spluttering and Hal broke in before it boiled up to something ugly.

'Take us to Wallace,' he said. 'Myself, the Countess and Kirkpatrick.'

'A Bruce man?' Long Jack spat back, leaping on this fact to save his face. 'I am as likely to shove my dirk in the Wallace hert.'

'Ye are skilled at that,' Hal replied, losing his own temper. 'Bangtail Hob will testify to it afore God.'

'Swef, swef.'

The new voice rolled over the tension like a flattening boulder and the figure who stepped out of the dark was as large, a barrel-shaped man whose hair furzed out from under a confection of hat. He had a face dominated by a fat nose that drooped like a pachyderm's over a sprawl of moustache, shrewd, heavy-lidded eyes and a way of swinging his head like a blind, hooded hawk when he turned. Hal knew him at once.

'Sir Tham Halliday,' he said and had back a nod before the head swung back, the gaze almost as heavy as the hand he laid on Long Jack's shoulder.

'Bring them, as Will bidded.'

Scowling, Long Jack turned and led the way, while Sim, Stirk Davey and the Dog Boy looked at each other and then into the dark, which hid a multitude of sins clenched in a horde of unseen hands.

The meeting, when it finally came, was a strange affair and Isabel noted it mainly because of the shock at the sight of Wallace and for the reversal of characters between Kirkpatrick and Hal.

Wallace was slumped in a curule chair, a pose that Hal

remembered well enough for it to pain him; the hand-and-a-half, he noted, was hung, scabbarded, on a wall and that was a difference from before, for Wallace would once never have allowed the hilt of that weapon more than a fingertip from him. Hal wondered if the belt that it hung from was really made from the flayed skin of Cressingham, the English Treasurer of Scotland who had died at Stirling Brig.

Wallace was gaunt, wasted, galled with too much bone at knee, elbow and cheeks. His eyes were the worst part of him and everyone saw it. They were the washed-out eyes of a netted fish in opaque waters, slightly bewildered and infinitely weary. They brightened at the sight of Isabel and a smile split the close-cropped beard; his hair, too, was all but shaved and he saw the shock this gave the Countess.

'Shorn,' he said ruefully, 'like an old wether. Nits and lice – it is good to see you, Countess. I see you have leaped the dyke.'

She could not reply for the sight of him and Hal stepped into the silence.

'You have my thanks for the rescue of her,' he said in the French Wallace had offered up. The poor coin of his voice rang hollow even to his own ears.

'Aye, well,' Wallace replied laconically. 'I think that comes true from the Countess and only from politeness out of yourself.'

'Bangtail Hob,' Hal said and Kirkpatrick sighed, started forward with his mouth opening to block the breach of the conversation. Wallace spoke over him, silencing him before a word got out.

'Aye, Bangtail was a sadness,' Wallace admitted. 'Necessary, all the same, else he would have told where we were. I had tired and sick folk who couldn't spend another night in the cold and wet.'

'He fought for you once,' Hal reminded him savagely. 'He would have said nothing.'

'He would have told the next hoor he lay wi',' Wallace

164

replied wearily, breaking into Scots. 'And if ye were no' blind with grief ye would ken this.'

'Ye might have held him for a day or two,' Hal insisted hotly. 'He helped save yer life, in the name of Christ.'

The eyes flashed, the old fire escaping from under hooded lids, but diffused like pump water from a spout blocked by a finger.

'Long hundreds have done so. Thousands. The dead pile up round me like leaves in November.'

He leaned forward a little, tense as a hound on a leash.

'Freedom,' he said hoarsely, 'is never got for free. It is paid for in suffering, more by some than others. Yet *"dico tibi verum, libertas optimum rerum"* – which is, afore ye say it yerself, everything I ever learned training as a priest. And these words ye ken already, Hal of Herdmanston.'

I tell you the truth, the best of all things is freedom. Hal had no answer to it.

'Fine words,' interrupted Kirkpatrick, the Latin lost on him, dropping the bag into the silence with a heavy, solid shink. Wallace turned the weary gaze on him.

'The Earl of Annandale and Carrick,' Kirkpatrick said softly in French, 'sends this for your regard. Enough coin to pay for passage to France.'

'Why would the Bruce think I need his coin?'

Kirkpatrick smiled thinly.

'To add to the safe conduct letter the Comyn extracted from the Pope, in the name of King John Balliol,' he replied. 'Now you can flash the Bruce coin back at them and avoid being shackled by obligements to either one.'

'Or end up manacled to all of ye, in the mire of yer damned feud,' Wallace countered.

Kirkpatrick shrugged.

'Bruce has made his peace with the Lord of Badenoch. There is no feud.'

That was news to everyone, including Wallace, who sat and

scratched the remains of his beard, so clearly wanting one long enough to stroke that Isabel almost laughed.

'There is, it seems,' he said, the aloes of it so thick that every mouth could taste the bitterness, 'no good reason for my remaining in the Kingdom. Everyone wishes me quit of it.'

He offered a twisted smile.

'One day you may find as I do, *gentilhommes*, that it is not so easy to be quit of this kingdom. Only in death.'

Kirkpatrick took in a deep breath. Wallace would do it; he would go. In all probability he would go to France and use the same method he had used before, tried and true; for a moment, he felt the sharp, sick pang of what he was doing – then shoved it ruthlessly to one side and pushed the heavy bag forward.

'My task is done,' he declared and Wallace laughed, though it was cold.

'I would thank you for it,' he replied lightly, 'but here I am, thinking you had a sharper argument if I had refused.'

Kirkpatrick did not even blink, merely held out his arms, hands dangling loose at the wrist, in an invitation to be searched. Isabel knew there was no hidden steel on him and, with a leap of fear, realized she could not be so sure of Hal, even though everyone had already been examined, save her.

Wallace caught her eye as he turned his head. There was a pause, then he focused on Hal.

'And you, lord of Herdmanston,' he said heavily. 'Is your task done?'

Hal felt the moment, the iron rods of Bangtail and Falkirk's wood and Stirling's brig all twisting and forging to a point, sharp as the weapon hanging on the wall. He felt the hilt of it in his hand already, burning his swordfist as if suddenly fired red hot by the rage in him. He wondered if he could get to Wallace's own sword in time, before the battle-honed Wallace reacted. He was weakened and weary, but he was still Wallace, a giant with fast hands and strong wrists; Hal remembered him at Scone, whirling the hand-and-a-half in one fist.

The moment passed; the tension deflated and Kirkpatrick found he needed to breathe.

'In the name of Bangtail Hob, my task is not done and I will needs live with that,' Hal hoarsed out, meeting Wallace's gaze. 'But yours is. Get ye gone, Sir Will. Your price for freedom has cost too many good folk their lives and the promise you made for it stays unfulfilled.'

He turned and left like a cold wind. Isabel saw that the slash of those words had wounded Wallace deeper than any dagger could, saw the stagger in the man, like a ship caught sideways in a gale. Then he recovered and drew up a little in his seat, managed a shaky smile.

'Ye'll need a strong hand with yon yin,' he said to Isabel and she nodded, his face blurring through the springing tears, so that she turned away.

Kirkpatrick was left alone with him and the thought was bitter irony. Once this would have been an opportunity needing only a moment and a blade . . .

Instead, he nodded to the fallen giant and left. The true weapon was snugged up under the real coin in the bag, as vicious as any knife, a winking red eye of betrayal. Wallace would nurse his pride against need and would never consult the innards of that bag until forced to it. In truth, Kirkpatrick thought, he would not consult it at all; the men who would come in the night, sooner rather than later, would do that.

Outside in the drenched night, Kirkpatrick sucked in a breath and twisted a small, half-ashamed smile on his face. He now knew the true name of at least one of those jewelled Apostles – a ruby called Judas.

CHAPTER EIGHT

Herdmanston Tower
Invention of St Stephen, August, 1305

Lammas came and went, with trestles on the green groaning with meat, bread and cheese. The harvest had involved everyone, lines of men with scythes, gaggles of women and bairns gathering and tying and stooking.

Hal, stripped to the waist, joined in and, for some hours, reduced his world and the problems in it to a green wall and an avenue of amber stubble. Sim Craw on his right, Ill-Made on his left. Blisters swelled and broke on his hands, life became pain, in the back, across the shoulders.

At the end of it, Hal was sorry to have to leave, drenching himself with water from a bucket handed by a giggling Bet's Meg, while the men competed for the kirn, the last cut of corn, and drank deep of Maggie's new brew, frothed and thick as soup.

Increasingly mazed, they threw their scythes at the last stand until Dog Boy cut it through; grinning, he presented the sheaf to Bet's Meg, who would make it into the kirn-baby, a sure sign that she was next for wedding.

Next for bairning, Hal thought, for sure – Dog Boy was

ploughing that willing furrow already, he was sure, just as Sim Craw and Alehouse Maggie could be heard all over the tower.

The whole world was rutting, he thought, including himself. He lay with her russet spill of hair across his chest, aching and exhausted in the best way, from work and love. The wool was good, the harvest was good, the only deaths were those expected and the rents for Roslin ready for the start of next year, in March.

Yet the nag was there, of when the blow would fall and how hard and who Buchan would get to do it. There was no question of the Earl openly demanding his wife back; she had been put aside in a nunnery, after all, like a discarded pair of shoes. Still, they were Comyn shoes and stepping into them gained parts of Fife, so they would not be left in a corner of a tower in Lothian for long.

A hoolet screeched, threading the night with terror. A wind blew, cool and holding the promise of rain, rattling the shutters of that folly of a window, built by his father for his mother and a breach in the defence of a tower. Hal thanked his da for it, all the same, as his mother had when she sat in the nook of it, sewing and looking out. Now Isabel did the same.

If there was no war, he thought, sliding towards sleep, I would not worry so much about that silly window. But Bruce is moving and war is on the wind . . .

He wondered, sinking into the sweet softness of sleep, where Kirkpatrick was.

Next day, he tried to slough off the unease with a deer hunt, though the chances of success were slight and the manner of it was not to his liking – a 'bow and stable', which was usually the province of the old and infirm. I am both, he had to admit to Sim Craw, who merely grunted as he climbed aboard his garron and heaved up his monster crossbow across one shoulder. Only Dog Boy, young and fit, revelled in the moment of it, in sole charge of the deerhounds he had been training.

They rode out to Roslin's deer park through a glory of

stubbled gold where rooks and crows rose up, protesting loudly. They nodded to wardens and shepherds while clouds swelled over the land from the Firth.

'Weather is comin',' Sim noted, when they were in the deer park's coppiced edges, negotiating the formidable earth barriers and leaps that allowed the roe and hart in but not out.

'Is it now?' Hal noted mildly and with some humour, for Sim Craw fancied himself a foreteller of rain and storm though the truth was he would know it poured at the same time as everyone else.

They paused at the entrance to a long, coppiced stretch, while the two deerhounds panted with lolling tongues, tasting the stink of the wolf head nailed high on an oak. It was a warning to poachers on two or four legs, Hal knew and would have paid it no regard – save that the sight reminded him of Wallace.

'It is how every wolf's head ends up,' Sim declared when Hal spoke his thoughts. 'Unless it is wise enow to run out o' the country entire.'

It was then that the roe leaped from one side of the wood, paused to stare at them, no more than a lance-length away, so that Hal swore he saw himself reflected in the beautiful deep pool of perfectly-fringed glaucous eye.

Then, with a powerful heave, it leaped up into the far side of trees. After the first stunned moment – the dogs shot forward, baying exultantly, ripping their leashes from Dog Boy's hands.

'Ah, ye hoor slips . . .'

Dog Boy danced with the pain of the weals on his palms, cursing his charges who disappeared into the trees, trailing leashes and howls. Sim Craw, reeling with laughter, almost fell from the garron, which set Hal laughing and even the Dog Boy joined in, alternately blowing on his palms and on the hunting horn, the sound he had been training the dogs to return to.

What had sent the deer out into the path? The question was rolling like spit on Hal's tongue when he felt the garron judder as if kicked, felt it rise up under him with a shriek – then there was only a birling of sky and trees and a great blast of pain as he landed, driving the breath from him and the pain of his half-healed ribs through him like a lance.

Sim Craw knew in an eyeblink what had happened, so that the two men who spilled from the trees, one casting aside the crossbow and dragging out a long knife, came as no surprise to him.

He kicked his own horse hard, feeling its shock and the surge of it, then rode at the men. They balked; one had a spear and waved it, but Sim Craw hurled the heavy, unloaded crossbow at him, spilling him backwards even as Sim launched himself from his horse at the second man, dragging out his own long knife and roaring like a mad bull.

Hal, struggling and wheezing upright, slapped a dazed Dog Boy hard on the shoulder as two more men closed in, all wild hair and red mouths and frantic, desperate eyes and sharp steel in their hands

The one who came at Dog Boy thought he had rolled winning dice, for he saw a strapping youth, but one with no weapon on him; his snarl was a feral grin, which he lost when Dog Boy rammed his hunting horn in it.

Yelping, the man went over on his arse; Dog Boy stepped forward, booted the man perfectly in the cods, then sprang on him to tear the long knife free. They rolled in a maelstrom of wet leaves and mulch.

The man who came for Hal was the biggest bastard of them all, and armed with a spear. He knows how to use it, Hal thought to himself, seeing the hold the man had on it; Hal struggled to get back the breath driven out of him, but the man bored in, flicking the spear like a snake's tongue, using the slicing edge of the head as much as the point.

Something slammed Hal sideways; the rump of his own plunging garron, mad with fear and pain; there's traitorous for you, Hal thought and watched the butt end of the reversed spear come at him, clipping his thigh and throwing him the other way.

Babbling and dribbling, face twisted from the pain, Hal reeled away, fumbled his sword out at long last and had it clear of the sheath in time to fall over backwards like a great felled tree. The big spearman gave a howl of triumph, spun the spear back to the blade end with a masterly flick of the wrist, then took it in two hands and raised it high for the killing stroke.

Stupid, Hal thought with that part of his mind not shrieking with the exultant realization of the man's mistake. He drove the sword into the man's keg belly, rammed it hard, for the point was a little blunt, rammed it hard until he felt the jar of it hit backbone.

The big man's howl turned to a querulous whimper, he dropped the spear and went into a panicked jerking, as if getting rid of the bar of iron driven into him would put things back the way they were.

His writhing tore the sword from Hal's grasp and he could only lie there and watch as the man realized nothing was going to be put back and that the sword wasn't coming out. The sheer unfairness of it all roared enough anger into him to keep him stumbling forward, even as his legs were failing. Hal felt himself plucked up in an iron grip, a fist hauling him up into the dying rage of the man's bearded face, a second raising up like a forge hammer to come down on Hal's face.

The little knife went in the man's ear. In and out, faster than an adder's lick and Hal was suddenly drowning, flooded with blood and the man's own last flecked froth, so that he panicked and thrashed against the falling weight until, mercifully, it was gone and he rolled over, retching.

'Aye til the fore,' said a voice and Hal cleaned enough of his eyes to see, red-misted, the grin of Dog Boy, bloody dagger in one hand. He is getting awfy handy at stickin' folk in the lug, Hal thought and flopped back on the grass until Sim Craw loomed over him, dangling two bags.

At first Hal thought wildly that Sim had cut the bollocks from his victims, then realized that the bags were purses.

'Taken from each of they moudiewarts,' Sim growled, shaking the sweat runs from his face. 'The same amount of coin in either, give or take a farthing.'

'Aye,' Dog Boy echoed, almost cheerfully, looking up from searching the others, 'it is the same here.'

Hal and Sim looked at each other, then Hal took the proffered arm and was hauled back to his feet.

'Buchan,' said Sim and Hal nodded, wiping the streaks of the big man's blood from his face. Sent by Buchan, for sure, even if they were fealtied to Earl Patrick of Dunbar, or Badenoch, or some other lord who owed the Comyn favours. Of course, none of the four dead men were identifiable and none were simple brigands – with so much coin a brigand would be drinking and hooring, not taking on three armed men in a wet wood.

The deerhounds came loping back, slinking ashamedly under Dog Boy's gaze.

'Well ye might,' Dog Boy admonished, while the hounds sank to their bellies and crawled to him. 'Where were ye when ye were needed? Ye didna even get the stag.'

Sim, chuckling and tucking away purses and anything else of value from the dead, could not be persuaded that it had not been a good day, even if the string of his hurled latchbow was half-severed and so wholly ruined.

Hal helped drag the bodies off the path and into the trees, for they would not be reported save to Bruce and their vanishing would keep others from the same hunt for a while – why pay more men when you have four already on the spoor?

He will come at you sideways, like a cock on a dungheap. Hal heard the warning words of his father about Buchan, trailing down the long years like chill from an open grave.

The fortress at Kirkintilloch
The same evening, 1305

The hand was grimy even in the dark, the face half-shadowed, half-gore in the sconce light, so that the twist of nobbed nose gave Lang Jack the look of a weathered gargle, spewing high under the eaves of some church.

It was an apt look for him, who had vomited all the venomous bile he had stored up about Wallace and his failures and perceived betrayal - bokked it up for a purse of gold until all he had left to spit out was a time and a place. Kirkpatrick dropped the purse in the hand, which closed like a trap, weighed it, then made it vanish. Lang Jack nodded and wraithed into the dark, while the rain gurgled through the gutters and merlons of the fortalice, turning the old wood black.

Kirkpatrick turned his face briefly to the lisping cool lick of the rain, then shook himself like a dog and walked back under the gateway and into the maw of the place.

In a room smoky and sick with tallow light, he came on Sir John Menteith slopping wine into a pewter mug.

'I wish ye had not brought this to me,' the knight declared and Kirkpatrick sighed, since it was not the first time Sir John had said it. That had been when Kirkpatrick had brought the where and when and how of it all, laying it in front of the man appointed Governor of Dumbarton Castle by Longshanks and so responsible for the area. Responsible for the arrest of a betrayed Wallace, lying in a house not more than a handful of miles away.

Four hours later, the soldiers – all English of the garrison, for Menteith could not trust the Scots in it to carry it out – bundled a giant in chains back through the door, with only minor bruises and one slashed arm to show for it.

'You are the man of the hour and place,' Kirkpatrick said to him – again.

'They will revile me for it,' Menteith answered bitterly and Kirkpatrick frowned. Sir John Menteith – and his brother, Alexander – were already reviled, for throwing off the Stewart name and adopting that of Menteith. False Menteith was the least of the epithets hissed at the back of Sir John and the arrest of Sir William Wallace was neither here nor there in it.

'You will be raised by it,' he replied. 'King Edward will see to that, advised by his good men in the Kingdom – the Earl of Annandale being one of the more powerful.'

Menteith had long since worked out that, no matter who ruled in Scotland, his rise was assured, because of a handful of soldiers and a secret night descent on a lonely house.

Yet Kirkpatrick sensed the wavering in Menteith, saw him swill the wine as if something foul would not be washed away from his mouth. The knight did not care for it – but Kirkpatrick had planned for this, too, so that the news of the betraying Apostle, the Pope's letter, the bag of coin – though not where it had come from – was already known to Longshanks.

Wallace, snatched timely from an escape, to be paid for by the proceeds of robbery from the King's Treasury? With a safe conduct from the Pope so vague it could easily be ignored? It was a tale that could not fail – all Menteith had to do was deliver the man safely to those who would take him south to London and he could not avoid doing that without ending in irons himself.

Menteith knew it, too, for all his desperate wine-swilling.

'Will you see him?' he demanded and Kirkpatrick tried not to react violently at the suggestion.

'Best he does not know of my part in it,' he said, as if the entire affair did not hang on Wallace knowing nothing of Kirkpatrick's involvement, which would lead him to the Bruce part in it.

'Best to let him believe Lang Jack did him in. That way, word will get out to those Wallace men left and there will be further division among them – and no further rebellion in this part of the realm.'

Menteith nodded sullenly and Kirkpatrick eased a little. If Wallace discovered that Kirkpatrick had betrayed him nothing would convince him that Bruce had not ordered it and there was no telling what secrets he might spill.

This way, the Wallace was sent off, growling and tight-lipped, for a date with the executioner, while Lang Jack would last as long as it took for Kirkpatrick to track him to a dark alley, reeling drunk with his new riches. No-one would mourn the traitor who had led Wallace to the English, or help find the vengeful killer.

And Bruce had his road to the throne unblocked.

A big risk, of course – but Bruce had sat, quiet and still when Kirkpatrick had voiced this, the pair of them alone.

'He will not betray anyone he believes holds the freedom of the Kingdom in regard,' he had replied and so clearly, breathtakingly, considered that to be himself that Kirkpatrick had no answer to it. He had left Bruce kneeling, head bowed in prayer, or penitence, for what he was about to do.

Or mayhap he tries to appease the Curse of Malachy, Kirkpatrick thought to himself with a bitter twist of humour, for forcing him to weigh his soul with so great a sin. I doubt he will, but it would be good of him to offer a prayer for the sins he has heaped on my soul.

He stepped out into the rainwashed night, wanting to put distance between himself and the shackled giant he could feel through the stones of the keep.

Yet, all the long, wet night's ride away from the place, he felt the heat of Wallace's unseen, accusing stare through the dark of his prison and felt something he had not felt for a long time, something calloused over long since and now split open, raw and red.

Shame.

*   *   *

He stared at the stones as if he could dig through them with only his gaze, as if his eyes could search out those left and shame them into rescue.

In the dark, he knew most of them were dead. Those who had stuck by him, that is – the others would deny him faster than Saint Peter did Christ. He crossed himself for the blasphemy, but could not stop the wry thought creeping in, that even God had forsaken Will Wallace faster than he did Christ on the Cross.

Who else had forsaken him? He thought of them then, the faces coming at him like dead leaves whirling in a wind. Fergus the Beetle, arguably the most loyal of all, had died of the coughing sickness last winter, slick with sweat and pain and fear and still able to call Wallace 'the best chiel he had ever walked with'.

There had been others there to meet Fergus when he slipped into God's Grace, good men – aye, and women as well – who had followed him for the belief in it. They had fought and laughed, taken hunger and plenty in equal measure and had found the understandings that come with a life so close together, so shared in the one desire – a good king in a realm that was their own.

Gone. All gone, snuffed like a guttering candle and the best part of him with it. He looked at his hand, grimed and shackled; once it had slashed Hell into his enemies, had pressed an arrogance of seal into letters on behalf of the Kingdom. Now it was fastened to the wall of the cell they called Lickstone, because the only way of quenching your thirst was to suck the damp from the run-off near the lintel.

He knelt in the darkness, shivering and silent and wondered who had betrayed him. Lang Jack Short, of course – but he would have been put to it, by appeals to vengeance as much as a fat purse. Should not have broken his neb before, Wallace thought. Even if the wee moudiewart bastard had deserved it, carping on and on about what should be done and what should not, as if he had been leader . . .

Leader of nothing now. Left to pay the price for it – his fist closed, as if on the hilt of the sword he no longer had. Everything worked for, gone like smoke.

Like dreams.

Who had betrayed him? A woman, possibly, though he could not recall any he had treated particularly badly – nor any he had loved particularly well.

Menteith, mayhap. No, he was only the luckless chiel who had to carry it out and was clearly unhappy at it. He had come to Wallace not long after he had been huckled into the cell, loaded with enough chains to stagger a pachyderm. Poor Sir John, Wallace had thought at the time, seeing the man standing with his mourn of a face and his feet shuffling in the filthy straw, trying to summon up the words to say how sorry he was.

'When you decide that peace is best at any price,' Wallace had told him, 'the price you pay is in chains.'

'It is you in chains,' Sir John had spat back, unable to contain his pride, even now.

'Here,' Wallace had replied, shaking his shackled wrists, not yet fastened to the wall.

'No' here or here,' he added, touching his heart and his head.

Clever Will, who could not button his arrogant lip. Menteith had flushed to the brim of his fading hairline and ordered 'the prisoner' fastened to the wall.

Not Menteith, then. Buchan or Badenoch, playing some cat's cradle game of their own in which they saw Will Wallace's end as some new beginning for the Comyn.

But if it was new beginnings we are speaking of, he thought to himself, then Bruce is at the heart of it. He heard himself say it, clear as running water, when they had crossed swords at Haprew.

178

If I remain, you cannot get started.

In the end, it did not matter which black heart had done it, for he knew that his time was done and that all he had fought and bled for – aye, and all the bodies he had stepped over, on both sides, to achieve what he did – was come to nothing.

Freedom was as far from the Kingdom as it now was from himself and he knelt in the sodden dark and felt the black years of it leak from him in a series of hacking sobs, a brief collapse into pity for poor Will Wallace, abandoned and alone and facing sure death.

Just as quickly, he reeled back from it. A last few sobs, a snort of snot into the back of his throat and he hoiked out his fear and loss in a disdainful spit. That life was gone and what was broken could not be mended. All he could do now was die well, so as to leave some flame for others to follow.

He knew they would – and if they had to do it over his body, then it was no more than he had done over others. It does not matter if I fall as long as someone else picks up my sword and keeps fighting.

He climbed unsteadily to his feet, though there was no-one to see. Better to die standing than live on your knees.

London
The Vigil of St Bartholomew, August, 1305

The great pillared aisles sweated with those craning to see, genuinely curious even if many had only come because the King wished it. They watched him, sitting in state, in ermine and gold circlet, one hand stroking his curled silver beard, the drooping eye like a sly, winsome invite to the giant who stood alone and overloaded with chains on the top step of Westminster.

The great and the good, crusted with finery and stiff in their curule chairs, stared back at Wallace with fish eyes while le

Blound, Mayor of London, cleared his throat and read the indictment, uncurling the considerable roll of it as he did so.

'. . . trial at Westminster before Johannes de Segrave, P. Maluree, R. de Sandwich, Johannes de Bakewell, and Jean le Blound, Mayor of the Royal City of London, on the vigil of St Bartholomew, in the thirty-third year of the reign of King Edward, son of Henry . . .'

Bruce watched Segrave, who had brought Wallace to London in an overloading of chains and would take away the pieces of him afterwards – and be handed a purse of silver for his expenses.

Bruce wondered if there were thirty pieces in it, which would be in keeping with the mummery of the affair – he looked at the figure on the steps, sagging with exhaustion, dripping with shackles and crowned with a wreath. Oak, to signify that he was king of brigands and had dared try and usurp the rule of Scotland from King Edward.

A poor decision, he thought to himself. Edward has made a mistake and one which will rebound on me, too, for that oak wreath gave Will the air of Christ himself, bound and scourged and crowned with thorns – and this day might be dedicated to St Bartholomew, but it was also the Feast of St Longinus, the defiant soldier who had thrust a spear into Christ's side for mercy and was later martyred as a Christian.

A Christ-like Wallace did not bode well and Bruce, even as he marvelled at the strength still left in Will, frowned at the thought of him as a martyr in the name of King John Balliol.

Treason, murder, robbery, incendiarism, the felonious slaying of William de Heselrig, Sheriff of Lanark . . . the long litany of it rolled on, interrupted only once, when Will raised the bruise of his face.

'Treason?' he thundered back, taking everyone by surprise with the power in his voice. 'I never swore to you, Longshanks. John Balliol is my king. Treason there never was.'

Mayhap – the wee legals could argue the finer points of it

until Judgement Day. Yet there is enough, Bruce thought, in all the rest.

'. . . and after this, joining to himself as great a number of armed men as he could, he attacked the houses, towns and castles of that land, and caused his writs to run through the whole of Scotland as if they were the edicts of the overlord of that land . . . and he invaded the Kingdom of England and especially the counties of Northumberland, Cumberland, and Westmorland, and all whom he found there loyal to the King of England he feloniously slew in different ways . . . and he spared no-one who spoke the English tongue, but slew all in ways too terrible to be imagined, old and young, brides and widows, babes and their mothers . . .'

Edward, brooding as a raven waiting for a sheep to die, listened to the meticulous detail of it all, thinking only of the one felony which remained unmentioned and never would be, though the single eye of that ruby Apostle glinted balefully in front of the King every day.

By God's Holy Arse, this Wallace had contrived to reach out from the north and rob him in his own treasury – the sly, ingenuous term 'brought unease to the King' was a shouted laugh of understatement.

Wallace said nothing more in answer to any of the charges, which brought a deal of cold satisfaction to Edward. Did he think a legal wriggling off the hook of treason would save him?

Bruce sat and looked at the stone face of Wallace, his thought racing like wild horses. He once vowed to march on London, Bruce recalled, so this was a sour jest by God on the man – the best view of Edward's capital, elevated above all of London, was hanging where the crows circle the gate spikes.

'So resolved that the above-mentioned William Wallace should be dragged from the Palace of Westminster to the Tower of London and from the Tower of London and thus through the middle of the city to the Elms at Smoothfield

181

and as a punishment for the robberies, murders, and felonies which he has committed should there be hung and afterwards decollated. And because he had been outlawed and had not been afterwards restored to the King's peace he should be beheaded. And afterwards as a punishment for the great wickedness which he had practised towards God and His holy church by burning churches, vessels and reliquaries, his heart, liver, lungs, and all internal organs should be thrown into the fire and burned . . .'

Segrave read the verdict loudly, smugly, revelling in his moment in the light, with his king approving at his back and his son, Stephen, admiring on one side. Bruce, even though he had been expecting such a verdict, winced at little, so that Monthermer glanced sideways, feeling the jerk.

'Harsh,' he murmured, 'but fair enough. This should set the seal on matters. There will be no rebellion in the north again and that land might raise some sensible chief to advise the governor, Sir John de Brittany. Good – now that this Passion Play is ended, we can go and find some wine.'

Bruce offered the man a smile. He liked Monthermer – counted him a friend – but he was Edward's man, which tie limited how far Bruce's friendship went.

'I will join you presently,' he said, received a shrug and a stare in response as he went out in the throng, nodding here and there, acknowledging a bow, feeling his hooded face numbed in a fixed smile.

He thought to go alone, just another hooded figure in a crowd following the sorry mess that was Wallace dragged on an oxhide by four horses all the way to Smoothfield, through the gawpers who had gathered to jeer and those who just wanted to get out of the path of it, not realizing who was dying in Cow Lane.

Even those ones fell in with the mob, for Wallace was now a grim-faced freak that they wanted to hear scream, would applaud like an audience at a performance of mummers. It was the last look Wallace would get of his fellow man, a thousand black-rotted mouths spitting and jeering, shrieking at the hangman to get to the next act, the handful of privates held high and dripping.

Bruce, elbowed sideways and jostled, scowled at the man next to him and the man disappeared, replaced by Kirkpatrick.

'Ye are at risk in all this,' he said and Bruce, his thoughts fevered, realized he was easy prey for a secret blade in the crowd. He did not care, felt that it did not matter much and his head echoed with Wallace's words at Happrew, delivered with the lopsided cynical grin, as if he had known all along how matters would turn out.

If I remain, you cannot get started.

Kirkpatrick saw it in Bruce's eyes as the executioners began their work on their victim, turning God's brilliant creation into offal, unwrapping the secret, the mystery whose viewing changed everyone who saw it, the cloak of skin drawn back to let the light walk where it had no right to step.

Wallace threshed and kicked and gurgled on the gallows. Not quite dead when they cut him down, he was not dead enough when the executioners, expert surgeons in their way, sliced his cock and balls off, holding the bloody mass up for the gawpers to shout at in triumph.

He was certainly not dead when they opened his belly and drew out his tripes and, with horrific marvel, they heard him protest only once, when the assistants drew back his arms so that the ribcage was raised enough for the executioner to reach in through the gaping belly wound and up to grasp the heart.

'Ye are gripping my arms too hurtful,' he said and neither Kirkpatrick nor Bruce could speak for the choke of listening to a man complaining of his elbows as another's hand clawed at his still beating core.

Bruce did not know why he was there. He had had half an idea to catch the last look of Wallace, to stare the man in the face at least, to share the final pain. Now he did not want to be seen by him while they gralloched him like a stag and the blood grew sticky and deep enough to suck the shoes off one of the executioners.

His mind, flashing like a kingfisher wing in sunlight, spun him back years, to a night by a campfire with the men from Herdmanston, one of whom – a ragged wee lad, no more – had questioned him about the vows of knighthood.

He recalled it vaguely, for he had been drunk – but he remembered the bitter bile of realizing how many of those vows he had broken even then, even as he listed them solemnly, dropping them like water on to the upturned petal of a dirt-grained face that thirsted for something finer.

Dog Boy, he recalled suddenly. The lad had been called Dog Boy. Didn't even own a real name, yet had made me feel less than he.

He felt the same way now and, in the end, stumbled away, the thick metal stink and the flies in his mouth, so that he spat and had to stop himself from gagging. Then, eventually, he straightened, looked ahead and walked away from the baying and the blood, only half aware of Kirkpatrick at his back.

Who would know Hector, he litanied to himself all the way back to safety, if Troy had been happy?

CHAPTER NINE

Winchester Castle
Feast of St James the Almsgiver, January, 1306

Feeding the Hungry. Clothing the Naked. Burying the Dead. The bright hangings wafting gently in the thin breeze of the cathedral glowed with a piety that could not balm the anger of the droop-lidded king of England.

'Is he likely to say more?' Edward demanded and Monthermer looked apologetic.

'He has been put to the Question at length,' he answered carefully, 'but all we know is that he is called Guillaume of Shaws and was a notary in the service of Bishop Wishart. If he had not gotten himself stinking drunk in Berwick and babbled, we would not even know that much, your Excellent Grace.'

'A notary,' Edward muttered, sitting in the wool-swathed chair of Lancelot, both hands flat on the table. Somewhere, drifting on the iced wind, the slow, rolling chant of the monks celebrating the feast day clashed with the clamouring masses begging for the alms that had brought them in ragged flocks.

Edward wished they would shut up, but did not voice it aloud; he was already aware that his reputation for magnanimity, piety and regal magnificence had been badly

185

damaged by Wallace. He had been matched up against a rebel outlaw from the wild land of Scotland and ended up looking mean and petty; the thought burned him, an ember irritation in his bowels which even the thought of this great Round Table he'd had made could not balm.

A splendid thing, the table. For a tourney in celebration of Arthur and the Grail, though Edward could not remember when that had been. When he had been enthused for tourneys and the ideals of Arthur, he supposed, which had all dissipated after Eleanor died.

'With respect, father, surely all we know is that this man spoke rebellion in his cups. Why is he considered as more?'

Edward looked at his son, taking in the violet silk of him. Before this one, he thought. I had this table made before he was born, when I was young and strong and the best knight in Christendom, when I thought of all the powerful sons I would make to glorify the Kingdom I would create here.

Now there is this one, the only one God saw fit to leave standing, so no doubt He has a plan for him. I cannot see it, he added to himself and sighed, taking on the wearisome burden of educating the boy in the staringly obvious.

'A notary of Wishart? Young, well-educated with a neat, perjink beard, a knowledge of letters and Latin and with ambitions thwarted and a deal of resentment. He did not growl rebellion, he babbled of plots, involving folk of high degree.'

His voice, rising as he spoke, was finally brought under control, but with difficulty, so that his son took a step back, then recovered himself.

'Gaveston says . . .'

'Gaveston says, Gaveston says.'

It had been a mistake and the younger Edward knew it as the spittle flew from his father's lips.

'Gaveston can kiss my arse,' Edward thundered. 'As I hear he has been doing to your own.'

'The prince,' Monthermer interjected smoothly, 'simply

means, I am sure, that we have no firm proof that this man plots anything other than vague vengeance against Bishop Wishart, who dismissed him, it seems, for repeated drunkenness. The man actually laughed when he was accused of plotting with the Comyn against Your Grace.'

'Laughed?'

Monthermer inwardly winced; wrong revelation for the time, he thought and began feverishly to summon a way out of it.

'Laughed,' Edward repeated ominously. 'If you cannot even put a man to the Question but that he finds humour in it, it is hardly surprising we have no evidence. I suggest you wipe the smile from the man's face – take his damned notary beard with it if needs must.'

'He is dead,' Monthermer blurted out. 'Such was the questioning we put him to that he decided to stand before God rather than admit anything, my liege. We certainly have no firm evidence we can use as justification for dismissing the Earl of Carrick from Your Grace's pleasure.'

He allowed his voice to tail off, knowing the King would pounce on this, as a string dangled to a cat; Monthermer looked pointedly at the young prince, who nodded brief thanks and stepped away from the conversation.

'Bruce,' Edward said, staring at nothing. He liked the Earl of Carrick, but did not trust him in anything other than to oppose the Comyn.

'The Comyn,' he said aloud.

'Indeed, my liege,' Monthermer agreed. 'It seems uncommonly like it is that family who are still bent on causing trouble. But it is hard to tell – the Bruce and Comyn are at each other's throats.'

'They are all plotting,' Edward rasped. 'I can hear them, like mice in the rushes.'

Monthermer spread his hands and offered nothing better than an insincere blandness of smile.

187

Edward glanced up at the smooth, urbane Earl of Gloucester and did not trust him one whit more than any of the others, even those who professed unstinting loyalty. He trusted Monthermer at all because he held the title Earl of Gloucester only during the lifetime of his wife, Joan de Clare; it would revert to her son when she died and Monthermer's only hope of advancement then was for the King's benifice. Edward trusted in ambition and greed.

The Earl's advice was sound, all the same. Nevertheless, the thought of rebellion soured Edward; he was sixty-six years and eight months old, the oldest king England had ever had. His many territories were at peace, his authority was supreme and, for all his age, he was fit and healthy. God, he thought, has seen to it that I am preserved. For a higher purpose, surely.

The long-held urge for Crusade still fired his veins, held back by war and the rumour of war – by Christ's Wounds it would not erupt again like some festering ulcer and keep him from God's purpose.

He rose, stoop-shouldered and draped in a fur which failed to keep the cold from him, then scraped the heavy Lancelot chair back from the table. It came to him that the only time he had ever been warm in this place was when he and the Queen had almost died in the fire that ravaged it three – no, four – years since.

He'd pondered on it having been deliberately started, but eventually concluded that, like all plots, no-one would dare connive against his throne while he was alive. The idea sprang up like a soldier sown from Cadmus' dragon teeth.

'The mark of a man,' he declared suddenly, his smile fox-feral, 'is what he would do if he knew he could get away with it.'

'Indeed,' Monthermer answered, wary and none the wiser.

'I am due in Dumfries soon,' the King declared suddenly.

'A sheriff court,' Monthermer agreed. 'A mean affair, but a

statement of matters so that all the great and good Scots lords will attend, to prove their devotion to your liege.'

'And the not so good,' Caernarvon interjected, though he was ignored save for a warning glance from Monthermer.

'I will not attend,' Edward declared, drawing the fur round him. 'I feel a chill in my bones. I feel close to death's door, so that relics must be fetched for their efficacy and relief.'

Monthermer, puzzled, hovered uncertainly, then the light broke on him and he smiled admiringly.

'Indeed,' Edward declared like a lip-licking cat. 'Let us see what mice scurry out when they think this old puss is too done up to hunt them. Meanwhile – gather up every name this notary gave out. Put them all to the Question and see if they find laughter in it.'

Greyfriars Kirk, Dumfries
Feast of St Scholastica, February, 1306

His breath smoked, blue-grey in the frosted chill of the kirk and Dog Boy wondered why it was that holy places were never heated, as if it was a sin to be warm. In truth, Dog Boy was trying hard not to think of the wee Lincluden nun with the sweet smile and big eyes, the one who had giggled at him before being hurried off by an outraged matron with a face like a winter apple.

They should never have been at Lincluden at all, but Dumfries was stuffed to the rafters with the great and the good and all their entourage, so that the English justiciars had taken over the castle and the Vennel and the Comyn were in Sweetheart and Greyfriars, which belonged to them.

In truth, the Bruce had come with too many men – a hundred or so and few of them servitors, which was twice as many as anyone else – and so the Benedictine nuns of Lincluden, a mile up the Nith from the town, had had to scurry off and double

189

up in their cells, clucking protest and outrage as they were descended on.

In truth. Was there such a thing as truth left? Dog Boy doubted it, for all was mummery here; the retinues of the Comyn and Bruce, with their lesser and greater supporters, all walked round each other, stiff-legged and ruffed as hounds while smiling and calling out greetings through gritted teeth. They all openly snarled at the English, all the same.

And Hal, for all he stood wrapped in a warm cloak, hand on the hilt of a sword and guarding the back of the Bruce, had not wanted to be here at all. Dog Boy knew this because he had heard him say so, loudly and at length, when the rider had come to Herdmanston.

'I am his liege man, so he can summon me for service without thought. But each time I do this I put myself more at the mercy of the Earl in Dunbar.'

Dog Boy knew, vaguely, that Herdmanston belonged to Roslin first and the Earl Patrick second, but was not sure exactly how this worked. He knew, also, that Hal was talking to the Countess, because he always spoke clear English to her rather than Braid. Dog Boy also knew he should not be listening, but did so all the same, pretending to fuss with the deerhounds in case anyone happened by.

'Besides,' Hal went on, 'what of the other matter? Did he have a hand in Wallace?'

Isabel's voice was soothing and strong, laced with good sense and tinged with love – as good a balm as any Dog Boy had treated cracked paws with.

'If he did we will never know of it, so best not to dwell on that. Besides – we have our own guilt there.'

'I could refuse.'

Hal's voice was flat and cold as a blade in winter.

'He offers the usual pay,' he added, 'but we do not need it with what you brought. I could tell him to go to the De'il.'

'Best leave that hoarded up where we hid it,' she declared.

Her voice was soft, yet there was steel in it, like the fangs at the edge of a velvet maw, Dog Boy thought, afore it bites you. 'It is more dangerous in the light of day than in the dark and so cannot be of value in these times at least. Yet there is more to supporting Robert Bruce than siller, my Hal, and you know it. There is what happened in the deer park to set the seal on it, if even seal were needed.'

Hal had given in, of course and, when Dog Boy heard it, he turned his fondling of the hounds to a farewell. Next day, they had left Herdmanston – Hal, Dog Boy, Mouse, Ill-Made Jock and Sore Davey, leaving Sim Craw as reeve and having to ride off under the sour arch of his scowl at being left behind.

Now Hal stood watching the Bruce's back, feeling the cold seep up through the worn Greyfriars flagstones and wondering at the greeting he had had when he'd arrived, straggling into Lincluden under a pewter sky and a rain fine as spray.

'Stay close,' Bruce had said, the welted cicatrice on his cheek writhing like a lilac worm as he spoke. 'I will have need of good men I can trust here.'

The flickering rushlight did nothing for his face, nor that of Kirkpatrick at his back and the three of them sat in a sparse nun's cell like plotters.

Afterwards, Hal wondered how much had actually been plotted before he had arrived – or why he was needed in it. Once he might have gathered fifty good riders to him, hobilars all – but that was ten years gone and most were dead or too old and worn by war, while the young went with other commanders. Younger ones, Hal thought morosely, with more belly for the work of *herschip* raiding.

Belly, he realized, was what he lacked these days and nothing made it plainer to him than the day he rode a handful of men to Greyfriars, to find Bruce slithering himself into a maille shortcoat, hidden under the loose length of a brown wool *gardecorps*. The hood of it was drawn up and tightened under his chin to hide the cheek-scar from view; it wept still, that scar and Hal marvelled at how it never healed. Perhaps there had been poison on Malenfaunt's blade?

He dismissed that, remembering that Bruce had plucked the dagger from his cheek and rammed it under Malenfaunt's chin, into his mouth, pinning and slitting his tongue. Malenfaunt spoke in mumbles these days, Hal had heard, but had not suffered from any poison.

At the time, Bruce's hidden maille had seemed more than prudent, for this was an awkward meeting in a town dominated by Comyn and their supporters – the very kirk, Greyfriars, had been founded by Red Comyn's grandmother, the formidable matriarch Devorguilla, at the same time as she had laid the stones of an abbey so she could be kisted up alongside her husband. Sweetheart Abbey it had become as a result and a powerful icon of the Comyn.

Yet Bruce need not even have been here, sheriff's court or not, for Longshanks himself would not be attending – sick in a monastery, surrounded by the arm of St David, a portion of the chains of St Peter and a tooth said to be proof against the thunder and lightning of God's wrath.

'Mayhap he has over-exerted himself,' Kirkpatrick had said wryly when this news reached the Bruce cavalcade and those who knew that Longshanks' queen was pregnant again laughed.

Yet Bruce had sent riders off to request a meeting with the Lord of Badenoch not long after and no-one was the wiser over it – not least the Lord of Badenoch, standing there as straight and tall as he could make himself, arms behind his back to thrust out his chest and the red badge on it. *Gules, three garbs, or;* Hal smiled, as he always did when he recalled his father dinning the lessons of heraldry into a boy who only wanted away to the trout and calling fields.

Badenoch stood near the altar, watching the brown-clad Bruce cross the flagstones towards him. Like a monk's arsehole, he said to himself. Does he think dressing in a parody of piety would allay suspicion?

He was also aware of the men Bruce had brought into the church with him – three, as was permitted on either side, armed as befitted their rank, but unarmoured. Behind him, Red John had his uncle Robert, big and bluff with what appeared to be a squirrel settled in a dangled curve under his nose. Then there was Patrick Cheyne of Straloch, the best tourney fighter the Comyn had – and, for the provocation in it, the battered scowl that was Malise Bellejambe.

Red John had planned this last because he had expected Bruce to bring his shadow, Kirkpatrick – but his eyes narrowed when he saw Bruce's chosen men precede him into Greyfriars, stiff-legged as wary dogs. Seton was to be expected, a dark eagerness of a Lothian man married to Bruce's sister – but then came the Herdmanston lord, cuckolder of Buchan, which brought a surge of rage lancing through Red John. Followed by a youth of no account at all, one Red John knew to be no more than a kennel lad for Herdmanston and that was an additional slap of insult.

But his face was stone as Bruce came up, opening his arms wide to receive the kiss of peace.

Bruce saw the wee papingo that was the Lord of Badenoch, reaching on to the tippy-toes of his high-heeled, blood-red half boots to match Bruce's height for the purse-lipped lie of the cheek kiss, which only bussed air on both parts.

Red John wore a brimmed hat and a bag-sleeved wool cotte in dark green, with his badge on the heart side – the three gold wheatsheaves on red. Since the Buchan badge was blue, this red blazon gave the Badenoch Comyn lord his nickname.

'I understood we had a truce,' Bruce said when they had stepped back from one another and the launch into it took Red John by surprise, for he had been expecting more in the way of effusive pleasantries.

'Nothing was agreed,' he answered warily, then shrugged, 'but nothing has been done to you and yours.'

'Sir Henry of Herdmanston was set on by four men,' Bruce said, whacking the words out like blades whetting on stone. 'He was fortunate to escape with his life.'

Now he knew why the Herdmanston lord was here; Badenoch's eyebrows went up and he had half-turned towards Bellejambe before he could stop himself. Bruce realized that Red John had known nothing of the attack, which meant it had been arranged by Buchan on his own; the Lord of Badenoch would not like that, Bruce thought. He was the power in his family by virtue of his royal claims – but it must be hard to keep an earl leashed.

'Losing grip on your own hounds, Badenoch?'

Red John swallowed his temper and managed a shaking smile.

'Are the Comyn to be responsible for every brigand and trailbaston in the Kingdom?' he countered.

'No brigands these,' Bruce answered sharply, 'with the same amount of coin in each of their purses – payment for a deed. The price for them was high, mark you, since all are killed.'

'No doing of mine,' Badenoch replied, stung as much by the failure of the ill-planned event as by the event itself – and the fact that Buchan had embarrassed him with it. 'Besides – the Herdmanston lord has a private quarrel, as well you know.'

'Such quarrels risk much and gain little,' Bruce replied. 'A strong king in the realm would put an end to them, if he valued his crown.'

Red John sighed. Here was the meat of it, the same old litany.

'We have a king, my lord. He is called Edward. And if there is not him, then there is another, a Balliol one called King John, lest you had forgotten.'

Bruce leaned forward a little, his voice hoarse, his face, framed by the cowl of the hood, strained and seemingly anxious.

'The truth of that is clear,' he answered. 'King John is a

broken reed, unlikely ever to return to sit on a throne in this kingdom.'

Which was, Red John had to agree, a palpable truth but one to which he would never admit, least of all to a Bruce.

'The clergy of this kingdom require a king,' Bruce went on, galloping along on an argument which, Red John realized, he had long rehearsed. 'They demand one, for a kingdom with no king is not a kingdom at all – Longshanks has reduced Scotland to a land, my lord, subject to the laws of England and the bishops here will not have an English-appointed archbishop. They will not have a king interfering with the right of the Pope alone to sail in the Sees of this realm.'

'Sail in the Sees,' repeated Badenoch with a wry smile. 'Very good, my lord. Very good.'

'Not my own,' Bruce answered at once, which rocked Badenoch's boat once again; he was not enjoying the pitch of this conversation and fought to bring the helm of it back to a course he was more comfortable with.

'Bernard of Kilwinning,' Bruce went on, 'pronounced the words of that, together with the doctrine that a king of this realm has a contract with the community of it – and, if he does not fulfil it, the community is entitled to remove him.'

'I have heard all the wee priests of Kilwinning and Wishart and Lamberton cant this from every pulpit and market square they can reach,' Red John replied laconically. 'It makes little difference to the reality of matters.'

Now it was Bruce who was brought to a halt, blinking.

'The community are unlikely to choose a new king from any but a legitimate line,' Badenoch went on smoothly. 'Else any horsecoper or cottar – or a wee lord from Herdmanston – could put himself forward for it.'

He paused, looked at Bruce with a sly peep.

'Or Wallace,' he added poisonously.

'Agreed,' Bruce countered swiftly. 'You should know, my lord, that the clergy favour myself.'

Now there was a flat-out treason, breathtakingly brazen as a lolling whore, so that Red John had a moment, of which he was all too aware, of working his mouth like a fresh-caught fish.

'Wishart, Lamberton . . .' Bruce counted off the clergy of the realm on his gloved fingers, while Red John's mind raced. This had to have been agreed in a meeting. A plot, by God.

'So you see it clear, my lord of Badenoch. The tide flows in my favour. I realize that you have your own claims to this, but our feud with it defeats the purpose our bishops urge us to fulfil. That God urges us to fulfil. For the good of the realm, my lord, we must resolve this matter.'

Red John found his voice at last, though it was a twisted, ugly parody of it, hoarse with anger.

'You dare preach to me of the good of the realm,' he said, his voice so low and trembling that Bruce could barely hear it. 'You? You forget who it was who defended this kingdom, who put life and fortune at risk to fight. While you turned and twisted and bowed and scraped. What did we get from it, this honourable fight? Near ruin and imprisonment – I am only lately returned to freedom. Others are yet in peril, who would not bow the knee – Wallace is betrayed and murdered for one – while you, my lord of Annandale, gained a wife and all her lands.'

He paused, breathing heavily; he and Bruce locked eyes like rutting stag horns.

'Yet I would do it all again,' Red John added in a growl, 'for a rightful king of this realm. And neither you nor your threats nor your promises will keep me from it.'

There was silence for a moment, which was only because Bruce was fighting his own temper, beginning to realize that Red John was not about to be swayed and that revealing his compact with the bishops had been a step too far. Yet he was on the path and the only way was forward . . .

'There can be a rightful king of this realm,' he answered

carefully, 'though it requires your consideration, my lord, as leader of the Comyn. If I am crowned, with Comyn approval, I will not be slow with reward – Carrick and Annandale would be laurels to the Comyn.'

Red John's eyes narrowed; he knew Bruce's brother coveted those titles, so the bribe was daring, if not a little desperate.

'Do not oppose the bishops' choice, whatever it may be, at the very least,' Bruce added.

'The bishops' choice?'

It was hissed out, with all the venomous bile released by a knife in a dead sheep's belly.

'Yourself, of course,' Red John went on, his face ugly with sneer. 'You consider yourself a rightful king, chosen by God Himself.'

It was not a question and Bruce did not quite know how to reply, caught between his desire to shout it out and the shackles of prudence that had kept it secret for so long. In the end, he opened and closed his mouth a few times and said nothing.

Red John climbed up on to the tips of his toes and leaned a little, his scythe of red beard quivering as vibrantly as his voice.

'Even if John Balliol is a broken reed,' he declared, soft and vicious, 'he has a son. Even if the son fails, there is myself. Even if I fail, there are other Comyn more fitting to be rightful king of this realm than you, my lord of Annandale. This you must know, for even if Plantagenet, that Covetous King, took advantage of the moment, the conclave that decided you were not fit to rule was fair and legitimate even then.'

He flicked one hand, no more, on to the Bruce shoulder, a sneering dismissal.

'God has a plan for this realm,' he spat, 'but you do not feature in it as king, my lord. If you declare yourself openly as the usurping bastard you are in secret, you will find a Comyn opposing you at every turn.'

The flick tipped the pan of it, the arrogant sneer of it bringing the memory of when Red John had grabbed him by the throat – Jesu, actually laid hands on an Earl of Carrick. The rage filled Bruce, consumed him, for what he had failed to do then and what had burned him ever since when he thought of it.

He was aware of a bright, white light with a voice at the centre, which might have been God or Satan but was polite as a prelate's servant as it put the question to him. He felt the dagger hilt under his hand, had it out and slammed into the ribs of the posturing little popinjay who opposed him, all in the time it took to answer 'yes'.

Red John felt the blow, could scarcely believe that Bruce had dared to strike him and then, with a sudden, savage twist of fear, felt the tug and heard the suck of the dagger coming out. There was a burning sensation and his legs trembled.

Bruce stared at what he had done. The thunder of it was loud as a cataract in his head and he saw Badenoch teeter backwards on his high heels and start to bend and sag, so he dropped the dagger and reached out to support him, an instinctive gesture.

The blade clattered on to the stones, bounced and twisted, little drops of blood flying up like rubies, the sound ringing like a bell; every head came up.

Seton got to the centre of it first, with a bull roar to alert Hal and the Dog Boy, dragging his sword out with a grating hiss.

He was a step ahead of Red John's uncle Robert, whose bellow of outrage drowned Seton and rang round the Greyfriars stones. He sprang towards Bruce, his own blade clearing the scabbard and whirling above his head.

Seton grabbed Bruce by one arm, spilling the Earl backwards even as he cut viciously down on the springing Robert Comyn. Hal saw the blow slice into the flesh of the man's neck, heard the sinister hissing of it and the surprised little yelp Robert Comyn made as his head parted company with the rest of him, all save for a raggle of flesh.

'Get him away,' Hal yelled to the Dog Boy, who bundled

the flap-handed, stumbling Bruce away while Hal and Seton, panting like mad dogs, closed shoulder to shoulder, backing away from the fallen, bleeding figures; Robert Comyn's body writhed, his feet kicking furious splashes from the lake of his own blood.

Malise wanted no part of this. Cheyne of Straloch, equally paralysed, was starting to haul his blade out and Malise had no doubt that the thick-headed, barrel-bodied lout would plunge forward like a ravening wolf . . .

'Murder,' he yelled and sprinted for the back door of the chapel. 'Murder. A Comyn! Murder.'

Hal and Seton looked at each other and backed off towards the kirk's front door while Cheyne plunged towards them, stopped uncertainly, then knelt by the fallen Badenoch, unable to do much than flap a free hand while watching Hal and Dog Boy slither backwards out of the chapel.

Whatever happened now, Hal thought wildly, red war has returned to the Kingdom.

An hour later

The smoke was pall-black, thick as egret feathers and the English justiciars sat under it, miserable with surrender; Sir Richard Giraud wisely flung open the doors of the castle and Bruce men spilled into it, led by Edward, his great slab of a face grim as black rock. The English hovered uncertainly, fearful of what might be done to them and not even sure what had happened.

They were not alone in their confusion. In the hall of the fortress, the brothers Bruce and a few chosen straightened up overturned benches and sat, the Bruce himself a silent, floor-staring effigy.

'Has he spoke?' Edward demanded suddenly, rounding on Kirkpatrick, who pointed to the head-hung Bruce and didn't have to say anything more. Edward tore off his maille coif and scrubbed his head with frustration; he had learned that there had been a 'tulzie', that Badenoch and his uncle were down, probably dead and the perpetrator of it sat shivering and muttering about the 'curse of Malachy'.

Edward fought his own rising panic about that Bruce plague. He had sent riders to inform their supporters to gather their forces and had managed to take Dumfries from the quailing English by bluster and threat of burning. The Comyn, though, were still around and no doubt sending out for their own forces – the whole affair was as messy as dog vomit and his brother, the head of the family, was a gibbering uselessness.

'Innocent blood.'

The voice turned him round, into the anxious, raised face. Edward looked at his brother and thought he looked as he had when he was six and in trouble; it was not a look he cared to find on the Earl of Carrick and Annandale, the man who would be king.

'What happened, brother?' he demanded, for the umpteenth time. He had heard from Hal and Seton and the dark youth they called Dog Boy, but had not learned much about what his brother had actually done to Red John Comyn. Stabbed him, he had heard – but there was a pinking poke and there was a paunch-ripping thrust and Edward did not know which his brother had done.

Bruce's grip was sudden on Edward's wrist, a talon that pulled him close, into the anguish.

'God forgive me, Edward, for I have sinned. In a house of God, no less – the curse of Malachy . . .'

'In the name of Christ,' Edward thundered, snatching his hand back so vehemently that his brother was almost jerked from the bench, 'what did ye do to him?'

'No doubt I have killed him.'

The answer was low and hoarse and filled with pain and fear. Hal almost went to the man to lay the comfort of a hand

200

on his shoulder, but that was a step too far and he hovered on the brink of it.

'Ye doubt ye have killed him?'

The question was sharp and harsh, bringing all heads round to where Kirkpatrick, eyes feral and narrowed as a hunting cat, looked from the stricken Bruce to the brothers, one by one.

'By God, no,' Alexander said suddenly, seeing the way of it, while Niall and Thomas blinked and shuffled uncertainly. Without Robert, Hal realized suddenly, they are lost.

'You have a good heart, brother,' Edward said to Alexander, his French thick and hoarse, 'but one unacquainted with such work as this. Use your vaunted head, all the same – you are clever enough to see how this must be played out.'

There was silence for a heartbeat while this sank in; the timing was rotten as wormed oak, but the sense of it was clear – there was no going back from an attack on the Lord of Badenoch. The Bruce faction was now at war with both Comyn and English and, if they were to have a chance of winning, the head of it must be declared king of Scots. The eyes turned to the figure on the bench, still shaking and now gnawing his nails.

'No point to any of it,' Kirkpatrick growled, 'if Red John still lives.'

The truth of it hung over them, heavy as the smoke pall outside.

'Red John was the impediment to matters,' Kirkpatrick went on and would have said more, but Edward interrupted him.

'See to it,' he ordered. 'Then we must be away from here . . .'

'God in Heaven,' whispered Bruce. 'The curse of Malachy . . .'

Edward rounded savagely on him, almost unmanned himself by the summoning of that old Bruce plague.

'Enough, brother – get yer wit back. What's done is done and the path we ride now needs clear heads.'

'Will ye come?'

Hal stared at the grim-eyed Kirkpatrick, knowing with

sickening surety what was intended and that Kirkpatrick could not carry it out on his own.

'Mak' siccar,' Kirkpatrick added. Hal nodded.

They came out into the twilight streets, where the stone houses of the rich were the colour of old blood and the shutters barred. No-one walked abroad save themselves, prowling like a pack of wolves, all ruffed and snarling; Ill-Made and Mouse and Sore Davey followed Dog Boy and Kirkpatrick and Hal, turning this way and that, flexing anxious knuckles on drawn weapons, for there was little need of propriety now.

Somewhere lurked the Comyn and their supporters, who had been surprised and scattered, though it would not be long before they recovered themselves – at which point, it would be best to be elsewhere, Hal thought.

James Lyndsay of Donrod agreed, wiping his dry mouth with the back of one hand and shifting nervously from one foot to the other. He had been set to watch the front of Greyfriars with a parcel of his own men, equally hackled.

'Aye, he is in there yet,' he answered when Kirkpatrick asked about Red John. 'They have brought nobody out, though many have gone in – monks and the like, with clean linen and scurrying like squirrels. I have set men at the back and have had no word back o' any leaving by there.'

'So some of them live yet,' Sore Davey muttered, picking a scab.

'Not Sir Robert,' Hal replied, remembering the half-severed head of Red John's uncle, lolling in a spreading pool of thick blood.

'So,' Kirkpatrick said grimly. 'Red John it is who is alive yet.'

'Are ye for going after him, then, Kirkpatrick?' Lyndsay demanded and then eyed the chapel uncertainly. 'There are a wheen of men inside.'

'Then bring yerself an' yer *mesnie*,' Kirkpatrick declared, then looked round them all, his eyes lingering longest on Hal.

202

'Be set on it,' he warned hoarsely. 'There is one matter only here and that is the death of Red John. Everything else is thrall to it.'

He raked them all with one last glance, while the shadows dipped; somewhere a lonely dog barked, then howled.

'Are ye set?'

Not nearly, Hal thought to himself. Not nearly at all for dire murder in a chapel. But he nodded into the chorus of grim grunts of assent.

They hit the chapel door at a rush and stumbled in, falling over each other in a fury of desperate fear, fired to roaring anger at what they were having to do. A priest squealed and dropped a ewer of bloody water; a man with sword up and shield ready was swamped and bundled backwards by Ill-Made and Mouse, while Sore Davey cut the legs from underneath him.

There was a confused whirl of echoing screams and bell-clanging metal, which Hal plunged into blindly, Kirkpatrick at his heels. A figure loomed up, all leather jerkin and unfocused eyes – but the blade in his fist was sharper than his sight, so that Hal ducked, half-turned and scythed; there was a piercing shriek, almost high enough for only hounds to hear.

Kirkpatrick knelt by the prone figure, swathed in bloody linen, the budded mouth slack and the face pale as milk, so that even the neat little beard seemed to have faded to wheat-straw. He was aware of Hal above him, bull-breathing and dripping pats of slow blood from his blade; someone was screaming.

Hal stared in appalled disbelief at the foot he had severed, still in the raggles of a boot, which leaked blood in front of him. Strange, Hal thought with that detached madness that came on in the middle of carnage, to be lying there looking at your own foot where it should not be.

Kirkpatrick knew Red John was dying, that all the padded linen cloths, sodden with blood, were not choking the flow of life from him. His own fluted dagger seemed an irrelevance, but he slid it in anyway, so that Red John gave a little jerk, a final flicker.

'Da.'

The voice snapped heads up and they all saw the youth, half-sheltered behind a whey-faced Malise Bellejambe. Two panting men-at-arms stood to one side, blades bloody and faces desperate – Mouse was already closing on one.

The boy. Red John's boy, a gawky seventeen-year-old, brought to say his farewells . . . the realization of it hit Hal and Kirkpatrick at the same moment, but Lyndsay of Donrod was quicker still.

'Ach, no – would ye?' he gasped out, clutching Kirkpatrick's arm and half-hauling the man back to his knees as he rose, grim as a rolling boulder and the knife bloody. With a savage curse, Kirkpatrick swept his free hand like a closing door, slapping Lyndsay in the face and sending him arse over tip to the flagstones.

Malise saw him coming, his worst nightmare, blood-dripping blade and all and he shrieked, backing away, almost thrusting the boy at him. Hal saw it and, in a flicker of time, curled a sneer into the wide eyes of Bellejambe – then turned and slammed his fist into Kirkpatrick's face.

He was holding his sword when he did it, and it was only fate that made the flat of it slam Kirkpatrick forehead to chin, while the hilt-hardened fist knocked teeth from him and sent him spilling backwards to join Lyndsay.

The pair of them struggled like beetles until they righted themselves, Lyndsay scrabbling away from Kirkpatrick, who came up bellowing and blowing blood from his split lip.

'Would you?' demanded Hal, his blade held pointedly at Kirkpatrick. 'A boy, now. Why no' hunt out the mother and cousins, bring them to the altar and drown it in Comyn blood?'

Kirkpatrick saw, out of the corners of his eyes, the Herdmanston men moving subtly to defend their lord and realized he would make no headway here, though the anger and pain thundered in him. Dog Boy stepped closer to him, his face set as a quernstone and his foot on Kirkpatrick's spilled dagger. Kirkpatrick glared, then lashed it back to Hal.

'I will remember this, Herdmanston,' he spat. Dog Boy tipped the dagger towards him with the toe of one shoe, a tinkle of sound that was suddenly bell-loud in the silence. Kirkpatrick scooped it up, whirled like a black cloud and spun away.

Hal turned to the men-at-arms, half-crouched and wary; Malise had gone, but Red John's son still stood, pale and determined, his mouth a thin seam. The footless man had passed out or died, his final whimpers trailing echoes round the chapel.

'Take the boy an' run,' Hal told the men-at-arms, ''afore Kirkpatrick has mind to return.'

He stood while they hurried off, looking at the bloody bag that had been the Lord of Badenoch; he saw the boy's face again, grey with that shock of having your world reel and tip, of having the great tower and rock of someone you thought immortal vanish like haar. Hal knew that loss well and the needle of it was still sharp.

Lyndsay of Dornod let out his breath.

'Christ be praised,' he growled.

'For ever and ever,' everyone replied.

Hal's added laugh was a mirthless twist at this parody of piety in a place drenched with blood and sin.

Tibbers Castle, Dumfries
Feast of St Kevoca of Kyle, February, 1306

Thrushes and blackbirds and fluttering white doves spun the black smoke from the burning thatch of the outbuildings while a handful of grim, blackened men lounged against the remains of a stable wall and watched, chewing crusts.

Yet the hall of Tibbers had dogs gnawing bones and chickens scratching hopefully among the rushes; somewhere in the rafters baby sparrows were learning to fly, as if the world had not turned upside down.

Hal sat and watched Bruce and a huddle of others scatter vellum, plucked from the Rolls Chest with its brightly-painted coat-of-arms, a white trefoil-ended cross on black – *sable, a cross flory argent*, he said by rote to himself.

The owner sat at the far end of his own hall, face blank as scraped sheepskin, hands resting on his knees and flanked by two more of the Bruce men. Hal felt sorry for Sir Richard Siward, sitting there tasting the ashes of his outbuildings and the bitterness of defeat.

Tibbers had been added to Dalswinton and Caerlavrock, all castles swept up by the Bruce *mesnie*, as if desperate to stamp authority on what had happened – all but this one had been burned entirely, which would have made Tibbers singular enough.

More importantly, it was where Bruce woke up as if from a sleep, started issuing orders to his scowling brother, who had become used to independent command and now had to knuckle to it; he had been sent off with the other Bruce brothers to secure Ayr as a sop.

Now Bruce was feverishly explaining to a barely comprehending John Seton that Tibbers must be held by him, for it could not easily be slighted. The faces the desperate John Seton glanced at were less than helpful – the Lindsays, Bruce's taciturn nephew Thomas Randolph, Crawford of Ayr all presented the same stare, flat and iron as a shield. Even his own kin, Alexander and the grim Christopher Seton, seemed to grin ferally back at him, offering no help.

He is out of his depth, Hal thought, seeing John Seton's white face. We all are – burning out the Comyn stronghold of Dalswinton, capturing Tibbers and all the rest was simply thrashing about and achieving nothing. They could not afford to garrison other than Tibbers and had ruined the rest, which only annoyed the owners into the English camp.

Blinded by Comyn, Hal thought and did not realize he had muttered it aloud until the silence fell and he became aware of the eyes on him.

'You have something to say, my lord of Herdmanston?'

The voice was clenched as a fist, the hood-shrouded face glowering and both were the mark of the new Bruce, emerged like a foul phoenix from the aftermath of Red Comyn's murder.

'You are fixed on the Comyn,' Hal declared, realizing the mire he had walked himself into but plootering determinedly on, aware of Kirkpatrick's burst-lip sneer at the far end of the table. 'You are forgetting the English, who will simply come and take back everything here.'

Bruce needed Hal, so he was prepared to be patient, aware that his two hunting hounds had finally snarled and bit one another and well aware of why.

'*Fhad bhitheas craobh 'sa choill, bithidh foill 'sna Cuiminich,*' he said with a grim smile, then translated it for those who did not have the Gaelic. 'While in the wood there is a tree, a Comyn will deceitful be.'

Those surrounding him chuckled dutifully and Bruce let a parchment roll snap shut with a flutter of seals.

'You must never lose sight of the Comyn, my lord of Herdmanston,' he said, still smiling. 'They will come at you sideways, like a cock on a dungheap.'

He saw Hal jerk at that and knew why – Kirkpatrick had shared that confidence with him, a quote from Hal's father warning of how Buchan would strike in revenge for his wife. He heard Kirkpatrick's crow laugh harshing into the silence that followed.

'We lost sight of one Comyn, certes,' he growled bitterly, 'who should not have been allowed out of it.'

Bruce spoke quickly into Hal's rising hackles.

'The Comyn will require to be rooted out,' he said smoothly, 'the young son of Badenoch among them, so Kirkpatrick is right enough in that. Perhaps not there and then, all the same. There was enough blood spilled to affront the Lord in that wee chapel.'

'Christ be praised,' muttered John Seton uneasily.

'For ever and ever.'

It fluttered round the room like the fledgling sparrows and Bruce stood for a moment, what could be seen of his face etched with lines. Then he shook himself like a dog.

'We ride north,' he declared, 'to meet with Bishop Wishart and try for Dumbarton Castle as well.'

He strode brusquely across to the quiet dignity of Sir Richard Siward and stood over him until the man looked up, his gaze cold and level.

'You have backed the wrong side,' Bruce declared simply in French. 'I spare you, all the same, if only so you can take this to the Plantagenet.'

He thrust out one arm with a sealed packet in it and, after a pause, Siward took it and nodded. Bruce took a deep breath and plastered a forced, wan smile on his face as he turned to the others.

'Now, *gentilhommes*, look out your finest cloth – you are off to a coronation.'

Hal took the news into the yard, where the others were making some comfort in a portion of the stable that still had roof on it. They had started a careful fire, were heating pease brose and were less than enthused by Bruce's coronation plans.

'A bloody hard ride to Glesca,' Mouse mourned, stirring the pot and savouring what he could see, which was all he would get of the meal in it.

'Then to Scone, dinna forget,' Ill-Made answered bitterly, 'where kings are made.'

'In the wet,' muttered Sore Davey, looking up at the pewter sky through the raggles of remaining thatch.

'Afraid of a wee bit damp?'

The voice brought them all round, the recognition took knuckle to forehead; Mouse dropped to one knee, as if Bruce was already crowned king. Bruce moved in to the lee of the stable, a slight figure in clerical garb following after, pot hung round his neck and a quill and parchment ready.

'When yer lordship is ready,' Hal said diplomatically, 'there we will be, at your side. Rain or shine.'

'Since ye hold the purse,' added Dog Boy daringly and saw the eyes flicker with recognition when they turned on him, the raising eyebrows losing their annoyed arch.

'I know you,' Bruce said, at first only remembering the face from among those in Greyfriars – then it came to him. 'Dog Boy.'

'Aye, the verra same, yer grace,' Dog Boy responded cheerfully; the cleric scribbled and Bruce saw Dog Boy's quizzical look and smiled.

'Brother Bernard of Kilwinning is documenting matters,' he said, 'for a chronicle. This is part of what you put up with when you take a throne.'

'Aye, aye,' Dog Boy answered, smiling. 'Scribblings. Stappit with wee fa'sehoods and cheatry.'

Bernard bristled.

'This is for a true Chronicle of Events,' he blustered.

'Where black is not dirt,' Ill-Made Jock threw in, emboldened. Hal cleared his throat warningly.

'Ach, man, yer scrapings are as hintback as a creepin' fox with the truth,' Dog Boy ventured and waved a careless hand, while Hal watched Bruce to see if the amusement began to turn like soured milk. 'Like this – what have ye to say on this?'

Bernard harrumphed and made a show of consulting his notes.

'The fortalice at Tibbers was taken after a gallant struggle and Sir Richard Siward surrendered unto the mercy o' the king, who graciously spared his life.'

'Aye, aye,' Dog Boy said into the scoffs and jeers that

followed that. 'No mention o' the ones who were not spared I notice.'

'Some were put to death,' Brother Bernard responded cautiously. 'I could mention that, yes – in truth, I had thought to . . .'

'Put to death,' Dog Boy echoed and shook his grim, raggled head. 'There's nice for ye. Put to death. Much the better way to say how we had them kneeling an' bashed their skulls in. Eh? Blood everywhere and screaming, my wee priestie, like a herd o' freshly gelded nags.'

'Some matters,' Bruce said slowly, thoughtfully, 'are best left out, so as will not frighten bairns or women.'

He looked at Dog Boy, who agreed with a firm nod and the air of a man not about to let go the bone of it; Bruce remembered the last time he had spoken with the Dog Boy, though he could not remember when. About honour and vows, though – he remembered that and how it had made him feel, spilling out his revulsion at himself like vomit.

'What have ye to say about Red John's murder, then?' Dog Boy demanded of the priest and Hal almost leaped at him.

'Steady,' he began, stepping forward and not even daring to look at Bruce. Brother Bernard, however, was equally lost in the discourse of it.

'Naw, naw,' he answered, wagging a finger. 'Murder it was not, for there was no forethought felony in it, nae *praecognita malitia* of any sort. Rather it was a hot, sudden tulzie, a melletum that is called in law *"chaud-melle"*. Mind, in canon and common law baith, fighting is condemned – but God's creatures has a passion of nature as it were . . .'

He saw the looks, realized who stood at his back and went worm-limp.

'So it is argued, my lord,' he added weakly.

'I have heard,' he added faintly.

Bruce's head thundered at the memory of that slide of blade into Badenoch's body, as if there was only the thick wool of his clothing, as if there was nothing beneath at all.

'Gather your gear,' Hal harshed out, snapping them all from the painful silence. Bruce managed a shaky laugh.

'Bigod,' he said, 'I am seldom disappointed discoursing with Herdmanston men. Take good care of them, Sir Hal – and yourself. I have a singular task for you.'

Then he turned to the trembling cleric and clapped a hand on the man's shoulder with a jocularity that never quite reached the shroud of his face.

'*Chaud-melle*,' he repeated. 'Hot tulzie. I like the sound of that.'

Hal watched them go, Bernard of Kilwinning expounding his theory, Bruce appearing to listen. No forethought malice, Hal thought to himself – aye, that would sit better than what I suspect, though cannot quite bring myself to believe sufficiently.

That the entire event was planned, even down to the Bruce grief in it.

CHAPTER TEN

Herdmanston, Lothian
Feast of Saint Cuthbert of Dunbar, March, 1306

Even God rested on the seventh day, Hal thought, but Malenfaunt thinks himself greater than that – besides, he has the grim face of the Devil himself at his back, shaped for this occasion like the Earl of Buchan.

He and the young Patrick, heir to the earldom of March – here to legitimize the affair – had arrived at Herdmanston's tower in a smoke of righteous power, ostensibly to assert the rights of Malenfaunt to Herdmanston and capture one of the foul slayers of the Lord of Badenoch – though the truth, as everyone on the besieging side was careful to step round, was more to do with Buchan's wife and her lover.

There was a rustle and scrape as Sim scuttled to his elbow and both cautiously peered out between the roof merlons, the rain steady as sifting flour.

'Is that the young Patrick there?' Sim demanded and Hal raised himself a little to look. There was a dull thump of sound, a faint tremble up through the soles of their feet and both men instinctively ducked.

'Mind yer head,' muttered Sim, his badger-beard face

dripping with sweat, rain and scowl. Hal slithered his back to the merlon, face to the wet-black sky; he did not think the springald bolts would be a danger to his head at this height, for they were aimed where they had been pointed since the arrival of the besiegers – at the Keep entrance.

The stout oak door, studded and banded with iron, had cost the enemy four dead and twice as many wounded to drench with oil and fire down to cinders and twisted hinge metal. Now the springald was trying to shoot through the archway to the metal grill of the yett, but had succeeded only in scabbing stone from round the entrance and putting everyone's nerves on edge.

Sim promised himself that he would shoot one of the springald bolts up the arse of the wee hired mannie who had brought the bits and pieces of it to Herdmanston for the Earl of Buchan's revenge.

He would like to have put a bolt from his own crossbow in him, but the range was too great – peering out cautiously he could see the timber-box shape of the springald, three clever wee Flemings painstakingly rewinding the contraption, checking the chucked tilt of it to raise it by another quim hair. Near it, proud on a prancing *destrier* draped with dripping heraldry, Patrick of Dunbar waved his arms and made suggestions which the Flemish *ingeniators* ignored.

Sim slithered round to sit, shoulder to shoulder with Hal in the wet misery of the roof.

'The Earl o' March's boy himself, the wee speugh o' Dunbar, sent to puff out his chest feathers on our fortalice,' he voiced bitterly and left the rest hanging, thick as aloes in the wet air. Patrick of Dunbar was here because his da, the Earl of March, was too old for the business – and his mother Marjorie was a Comyn, sister to Buchan himself.

'So – the Earl of March's boy and Himself the Earl o' Buchan. If a man is made great because of his enemies, then ye are the finest knight in Christendom, lord Hal. I hear Longshanks is comin' here, too,' Sim growled.

'I hear he is in Berwick,' Hal countered wryly. 'And at Lochmaben, Stirling and Perth. And that he has grown horns to match his English tail.'

'Still,' growled Sim, 'a brace of the Kingdom's high *nobiles* is more than enow and a pair too many. D'ye think they have come for the Coontess – or the other?'

The very question that haunted Hal and the reason he had not fled and would stubbornly defend to the last. Below in the hall was Isabel and alongside her was a covered slab of sandstone – the 'other' Sim spoke of.

It seemed an age since Bruce had called him into the arched shadows of St Mungo's, where the stretched shapes of Wishart and Bernard of Kilwinning argued with Lamberton, recently fled from Berwick and full of reports of stunned English unable, it seemed, to agree on what to do.

Bruce, full of fresh resolve and newly absolved of any Red Comyn murder by the old mastiff Bishop Wishart himself, was wry and sanguine about the supposed inability of the English.

'Edward's wrath may be slow, but it will be scorching when it comes. I have sent him a letter by the Lord of Tibbers, asking his forgiveness for certain matters and warning him that I will defend myself with the longest stick I have if he comes after me. I am not expecting forgiveness.'

None of which was what the bishops needed to hear while Wishart, all purpling indignation, was preparing sermons excusing Bruce's actions and justifying his imminent coronation.

'It is essential that the King is divorced from these actions. A king of this realm is not involved in low acts and red murder,' he had pontificated at one of the many meetings and Kirkpatrick, with a bitter bravery that took even Hal by surprise, gave a bark of mirthless laughter.

'No indeed – he has me for that.'

It was a truth no-one wanted to admit and the faces round the table blanked, then pretended it had not been said at all;

214

Hal felt a sudden rush of sympathy for Kirkpatrick, saw the *mesnie* of new lords look sneeringly at his back and call him the 'auld dug' when they were sure he could not hear, because no-one was as feared as Black Kirkpatrick, or as close to the Bruce.

Yet Hal saw that the closer Bruce got to climbing on the throne, the more he distanced himself from his 'auld dug'.

Hal, useless in the maelstrom of all this and more aware of Kirkpatrick's smoulder than anything, was almost relieved when Bruce finally called him aside.

'I have a service,' he said and explained it. Wishart had rescued the rich royal vestements and even the royal banner and one of the crowns – but they lacked the meat of the matter. They even had, miraculously, the Rood which had been returned to Lamberton in Berwick by a stranger the bishop was certain was a Templar, a man called de Bissot, who had brought the relic 'in the peace of Christ and for the return of the relic to its home in God'.

But one of Wishart's notaries had been arrested, which had persuaded Lamberton to quit Berwick; he had no doubt the poor man would be put to the Question and did not want to be around when he told all he knew.

Hal and Kirkpatrick locked eyes at this revelation, knowing the chip of dark wood had been ripped from Lamprecht's neck and when and where; for a moment there was a shared, intimate ghost of old friendship, which just as suddenly shredded away.

'I have the Rood and a decent crown,' Bruce said to Hal when he had drawn him aside. 'But I need the Stone. And the Crowner, which should be a MacDuff. Because the MacDuff himself is a boy held by the English, there is only one candidate left.'

Isabel, Countess of Buchan. Bad enough that she was hunted by her husband because she had run off, Hal thought bitterly – now Bruce wishes her put beyond any mercy by having her actually place the crown on his head, legitimizing the entire affair as much as the Stone and the Rood and the blessings of bishops. There was not much left for Isabel to affront her husband with, Hal thought – but that would do it.

He had gone to Roslin with the Herdmanston men, riding hard for the place and welcomed by his kin and namesake Sir Henry, thirsting for news, raising men and preparing his castle. Once Hal had been fussed by Henry's wife and assaulted by delighted bairns, Sir Henry and he and Ill-Made had descended to the dark, chill undercroft and the secret niche built in the floor. There, nestling, glowing red-gold in the torchlight, lay the smuggled Stone of Scone, not having seen daylight for a decade at least. Red murder and treachery had helped bury it from the English – now it was lugged up, wrapped in sacking and loaded on a cart.

Wiping sweat that was not all from his labours, Sir Henry of Roslin took Hal's wrist in a firm, almost desperate clasp.

'I am glad, mind you, to be rid of the burden of keeping that,' he said, nodding towards the cart. 'I don't envy you the task of it now. I will come to Scone myself, all the same, bringing men for the King.'

The King. King Robert. The sound of it was strange as a death knell and, seeing the pale, stricken face of Henry's wife, bairns half-grown clutched to her, Hal finally realized the full measure of snell wind blowing through the Kingdom. Another rebellion – Hal cursed Bruce for it, and for wanting Isabel dragged into his maelstrom.

He said as much to Isabel, heating himself by the big hall fire in Herdmanston after labouring the cart and Stone from Roslin with Dog Boy, Ill-Made, Mouse and the others, buffeted by a howling gale and driving rain so that they had been grateful to roll the wretched affair into the garth and be done with it for a day at least.

She had smiled at him then, all russet hair and green gown and gentian eyes.

'There was always going to be a moment when this would be thrust on us,' she replied, with more surety and bravery

216

than she felt. Trembling, she added more to the sickle of her smile.

'How often is it that a wee Lord of Herdmanston holds two of the three adornments to the coronation of a king?'

For a moment the kings and princes, the great and good, loomed over them, golden, invincible, filling the room like a drone of chanting with the hidden haar of their power. Then, with the defiant tilt of her head, they smoked away and were gone; Hal knew that if he raked the earth and searched through the bright hair of every star he would not find a greater love than the one he felt for her now.

The warmth of it had vanished in the chill, drookit dawn, when Scabbit Wull tumbled down the ladder from the roof, shivering and damp and full of news.

The enemy was almost at the gates.

Hal shook himself from the memory and the wet from his face, while the rain lisped on the stones; in Scone, Bruce was impatient to be crowned king and Hal wondered how long he would wait for the Stone and the Crowner before going ahead anyway. He might desire all the trappings of the Old Style as he could garner – but, in the end, he would prefer the crown alone on his head.

Even now Hal could not be sure if the secret of the hidden Stone was what had brought Buchan and Dunbar to his door, or revenge for Isabel. The one surety was that it had nothing to do with Malenfaunt's spurious claims and that he was the string-worked mommet in this.

Not that it mattered much, since the cursed slab of sandstone, painfully and frantically manhandled up the stairs, across the plank bridge and into the keep, now lay in the Yett Hall, covered with a linen cloth and used as a table for Isabel's accoutrements for treating the wounded. Both it and she would be paraded in triumph if Herdmanston fell, Hal was sure – as sure as he was that the only part of himself that would be paraded would be his head.

Hal followed Sim's wet-black backside to the hatchway and down the steep stairwell to his own bedroom, stood there for a moment, dripping rain and staring at the shuttered folly of a window with its niched stone seats.

Out there somewhere, Buchan would be waiting, impatient as a wet cat to see his gloating revenge on his wife's lover. Malenfaunt brooded vengeance on all things Bruce, but Dunbar and the rest were here in a flush of righteous wrath for the killing of Badenoch – and that was yet another reason Hal would never make it from this place alive if it fell.

A shape shifted, dragging him back to the present, where the Dog Boy sat with a bow in one hand, peering out between the shutters to make sure no-one was thinking of scaling up to this great weakness in the wall. He turned and grinned, his face dark with new beard, his forearms muscled from working with the big deerhounds.

'Aye til the fore, my lord,' he said and Sim grunted acknowledgement of still being alive over his shoulder as he clattered down the stairs to the hall.

Hal paused a moment and forced a grin in return; the Dog Boy, as dark and saturnine as the day he had come from Douglas when he was twelve, still reminded Hal of the son who lay dead under the stone cross nearby, together with his wife and his father.

A stone cross, he recalled bitterly, about forty paces from the bloody springald, the graves trampled and spoiled by the boots of the *ingeniator* and his minions, who stored their gear in the stone chapel.

Down in the dim of the Big Hall Alehouse Maggie and a handful of mothers – a Jane here and a Bess and a Muriel there, all from nearby cottar huts – cluttered round the meagre fire in the large hearth, singing quiet songs to calm the fretting weans. Isabel was at a nearby truckle bed, checking on the occupant and turned as Hal clacked across the sparsely-rushed flagstones.

'No worse,' she declared and then bent and sniffed. 'Still smells like a privy hole, mark you.'

The figure on the bed chuckled weakly and Hal stepped to where he could see him, dark hair wild and ruffled, lopsided face pale as poor hope and a stain still leaking into the clean wrappings Isabel had only just bound him with.

'After three days,' said Ill-Made weakly, 'twa things stink – fish and an unwanted guest.'

Hal said nothing. Ill-Made had been hit three days ago by a crossbow bolt, a half-spent ricochet, the shaft shattered and the head ragged, which was why he had not died at once. Digging it out of his armpit had cost him more blood than he could afford, all the same and Hal knew, with sick certainty, that he would go to join the four others who had died in the seven days of siege.

There were at least a dozen less of the besieging hundreds who surrounded the tower, most of them casualties of the first day, storming up the stair to where the six foot gap had to be spanned to a lip at the foot of the oak door.

Splintering that door with axe and fire had cost them most of the dozen and others were picked off by Sim and Dog Boy from the roof, until the springald had appeared and the besiegers had drawn back.

It had taken most of a day to assemble the confection of sticks and metal – but after that it had started plunking great, long, fat-headed bolts at the ruined doorway entrance, hoping to smash the grilled yett beyond. Scabbed stonework showed they had not hit it yet, but the tireless whirr and bang of it, the creakingly painful reloading, grated on everyone.

Isobel came up to him, hair tendrilling out from under her headcover, her fingers bloody from ministering to Ill-Made; the springald bolt cracked again, though it was only the noise that jangled everyone for the walls of Herdmanston, at this level, were thick enough for rooms to have been scabbed out of the inside and still leave a forearm's length of solidity.

'What will they do now?' she asked in French, so that his answer would not be understood by Maggie and the others and he could speak freely.

Hal thought of it. The tower was the height of ten tall men and stood on a mound that not only gave it more height but pushed out the approach of any siege tower to where a ramp could not cross from it to the top of Herdmanston, even if one could be built that tall.

There was nowhere for a ladder less than such a height to reach, and no hook-ended ropes could be flung up that far. The garth was plundered and every hut burned – though that usually only meant the thatched roof, for the wattle and daub simply hardened and the few entire stone buildings were left blackened and roofless.

The Herdmanston cellar had beef and barley and oats enough and, providing it kept raining, the stone butts in the undercroft would keep enough water in them. Still, there was only a handful of fighting men in Herdmanston and too many women and weans for a lengthy siege, so sensible enemies, Hal thought, would sit and wait.

Buchan, he knew, was not sensible. None of them out there were, too twisted with their own desires to consider sitting and waiting. So they would assault and the only way was under the arch where the oak door had been and then the iron yett. That was where they would come and only after they had destroyed the yett.

'At which point they will offer terms,' Hal told her with a wry smile, 'it being a breach and honour requiring it. Young Patrick will so insist, being a right wee Arthur for the chivalry.'

She nodded, then stared at him with eyes velvet and liquid as blue pools.

'I should go,' she began weakly and he placed a finger on her lips.

'You will not, lamb,' he said. 'The terms are only for the nicety in it and to put a polite face on it for Dunbar. There is no good outcome from our failure to hold here – whatever peace is offered will not be offered to me, nor you.'

She looked round at the bairns, now being shushed by Annie and herded cautiously to the steps winding to the undercroft, where it was safer but dark and dank even with torches, which they could ill afford.

'The bairns,' she said with a pleading crack in her voice that Hal had to steel himself against.

'The children and women might be offered leave,' he answered, 'but they would have to scamper far and wide, with nothing to their backs or bellies or over their heads, to be safe from soldiery like this.'

He scrubbed his head and she saw the weary lines of him.

'Besides,' he went on, waving a hand at the covered Stone, innocuous as a nun's shift, 'there is that. Not only will Buchan have it, to display against Bruce's kingship, he will have you to show likewise. Is that what you want?'

'I would die first.'

He felt the tremble in her as he took her, let her lay her head on his breast; he smelled of sweat and leather and woodsmoke, but there was strength in him that she sucked at greedily. Like a lamb at the teat, she thought with a soft smile. It faded when she thought of what would happen.

They would die here.

The sudden explosion of noise, as if someone had flung an entire tin cauldron down a flight steps, flung them apart. Bairns shrieked and there were frantic shouts – cursing, Sim and Hal sprang for the stairwell that led below, to the Yett Hall.

Men milled, armed and ready but Hal saw that no enemy had burst in on them. But the yett was open and flapping like an iron bird wing, part of it bent and twisted; in one corner was a bloody smear on the wall and, at the foot of it, a rag-bundle that slowly leaked darkly into a puddle.

'Wull the Yett,' Sim informed no-one in particular, scowling darkly as if Wull had committed some crime.

Hal felt the cold stone of it sink in him. Auld Wull the Yett had been gatekeeper since his father's time, a recalcitrant, shuffling old misery, never done complaining. Until now, Hal corrected.

It was not hard to work out that the springald had scored a hit, spearing a fat iron-headed shaft in through the ruined doorway and striking the yett somewhere above the lock, where the iron grill had bent but not broken.

The springald shaft had shattered, though, sharding into a lethal spray of wood and metal in whose path had been Wull the Yett, lopsided pot helm on his head, raddled hand clutching a filthy, notched sword whose hilt rattled when he shook it defiantly. The blast of metal and wood had torn him to bloody pats and burst the lock on the yett.

'Fetch hammers,' Hal ordered, seeing the ruin of it. 'And Leckie the Faber,' he added as men sprang to obey.

For a moment Sim and he stood, pillars of silent grim in the whirl of activity round them. The lock was a ruin and could not be fastened, though the iron yett could still be barricaded shut . . .

Then they looked at each other.

'They will have heard it,' Sim forced out and Hal nodded. He heard the weans being soothed from snot and tears, became aware of the lack of rushes for the floor, torches for the walls, food, arrows . . .

They would ask for terms now and Hal did not know whether to refuse them, bad or good.

'You are certain, Master *Ingeniator*?'

Gaultier nodded, while his two assistants, sacking draped over their filthy heads against the rain, bobbed like toys in agreement.

'Through the arch,' the Fleming said with smug satisfaction. 'There was a great bang as it hit the gate – we all heard it.'

And the two toys nodded at him, at each other and then

222

at the dark brooding Malenfaunt. Patrick of Dunbar, round, wisp-moustached face framed by the ringmetal coif, beamed at the Earl of Buchan.

'Well – a palpable hit, by God. Damaged at least. Something we can claim as a practical breach, eh?'

Buchan, his thinned hair plastered to his bared head, nodded scowling, pouch-eyed agreement; there had been too long spent on this enterprise in his opinion and the reason for it sat cloistered in that hall, no doubt trembling at what might be done to her now. Well might she shake, he thought savagely.

'A white peace,' Patrick added pointedly. 'As we agreed – I look to you, my lord, to hold to this, as agreed.'

Malenfaunt laughed sourly, but said nothing. He seldom spoke these days, the fork of his tongue rendering it almost unintelligible and that, coupled with the deep, banked smoulder in him kept everyone at a distance.

Malise, dripping patiently by the side of his earl, watched Malenfaunt and remembered how he had come off worst in a tourney duel with Bruce and that there had been some scandal over a nunnery in Berwick, which had had to have the occupants scoured out of it and questioned.

Depositions of Devil worship and worse were, even now, being taken and Malenfaunt's name had come up more than once. Now he was here, banished from the *mesnie* of de Valence, shunned by every *nobile* who at least professed a measure of honour and trying to ingratiate himself into the grace of the Earl of Buchan, whose wayward wife he had once held to ransom.

War, Malise realized, would be a joy to this one for it would put an end to all the legalities threatening to swamp him and might even raise his stature; all knights would be needed soon, when Longshanks rose up off his skinny arse and started to roar like the mangy pard he was.

This time, he knew, there was no question of which side the

Buchan and Balliol and Comyn chose – the one which had a Bruce on the opposite.

'I have my reasons for being here,' Buchan said sourly, peeling off a sodden gauntlet to wipe his streaming face. 'Make what white peace ye care – but neither the Countess nor Hal of Herdmanston is included in it. That pair are mine, by God.'

They assembled in the lisping mirr by the stone cross, holding up a shield covered in white linen, turning dark with rain. Two figures came to the arched, flame-blackened doorway, the bigger, badger-bearded one holding a monstrous crossbow. Those who knew Sim and the lord Hal – Dunbar men and those locals who hired out for pay – gave a few friendly shouts, swiftly muffled. Save for one.

'Holla, Sim Craw – aye til the fore I see.'

The irrepressible Davy Scott from Buccleuch made all the other Scotts laugh, then curl their lip at the glares from the Comyn retinue.

'Davy Scott – I have heard nothing of ye since . . . bigod, it would be Roslin Glen. How long since was that?'

'Three years,' Scott called back, heedless of the glowers.

'A rattlin' time,' Sim shouted. 'A rare victory, so I hear.'

'Aye, man,' Davy enthused, his beady black eyes bright. 'There were Kerrs every which where, skitin' like hares. Ah saw Kerrs frae Cessford an' Graden an' others frae ower Teviotdale. A right rout it was.'

'And the English,' Sim pointed out wryly. Davy Scott had the grace to look embarrassed for a moment, realizing not only his preoccupation with an old feud but that he was now, to all intents, with the English he had once scattered so delightedly up and down Roslin Glen.

'Oh aye – them as well.'

Then Sim swept his eyes round until he found the face he sought; still fox-sharp, the eyes as cold and dark as of old, though permanently narrowed now, as if the man squinted.

Losing his sight, Sim thought. Then added viciously to himself: God blind you, Malise Bellejambe.

Malise felt the eyes on him and flicked briefly to them, then away. He did not like the big, keg-shaped grim of Sim Craw, who made him aware of a man he'd red murdered years before, the one called Tod's Wattie. A friend of this one, Malise remembered, seeing the banked revenge in Sim Craw's stare and not caring much for it.

Ignoring all of this, Buchan and Hal locked gazes. Hal saw the gaunt of the man and wondered at it. He has ten years on me, he thought to himself, but that did not explain the yellow tinge, the unhealthy fever of the stretched cheeks, the bones of his face like oak galls. He felt the heat of the man's anger.

Buchan, in turn, saw the still figure, grizzled these days and limned with hard life, but he barely took in the look of the man; his belly turned, for here was his revenge, looking him in the face. It came to him, in a sudden, sick dizziness, that there was no triumph in it, only a reflection of his own mean rage.

Dunbar thought it best to grip the hilt of matters a little tighter.

'Your folk may depart with honour and their lives,' he said curtly to Hal. 'You must hand over the Countess and yourself to the mercy of myself and the Earl of Buchan. Your fortress will be slighted.'

There was a pause, an indrawing of breath and no more, while everyone waited to see if Herdmanston would capitulate.

Patrick hoped he would not; though the prospect of storming the place was bloody, he wanted it with all the eager, frantic fervour of his twenty-two years; he had never been at such a matter before and Malenfaunt saw that and sneered at it. The wee earl's son would find the truth out at cost – if he lived at all, Malenfaunt thought to himself.

He had avoided such engagements, for the prospect of dying at the hands of a grimy-handed cottar for some pointless heap of stones was not chivalrous enough – yet the high-chivalry tourney with Bruce, who could have killed him, brought back the sweating, shrieking moment when he had thought death would happen.

He knew he had babbled and pleaded for his life then and the yellow memory of it soured his life like vomit, while the sinuous wriggle and flap of his own forked tongue, the result of what Bruce had done instead, repulsed him.

The only two who mattered in this were horns-locked at the eyes, cold and unblinking as basilisks until, finally, Hal spoke into Buchan's unflinching glare, though it was Patrick of Dunbar he addressed.

'I am fine where I am,' he said softly. 'Besides – I have only just fixed matters from the last time I was raided. I would liefer have the place unsullied.'

'I am your liege lord,' Patrick declared loftily, then realized he actually was not and hastily corrected himself.

'My father is. You owe him fealty and explanation for your constant turncoating. I have offered you more honour and mercy than you deserve . . .'

'Save your words, he does not care – he is Bruce's man now.'

Buchan's voice was a whip that lashed Dunbar to silence.

'If you do not give in now,' he went on, never removing his eyes, 'it will be the end of you. I will nail your entrails to a post and walk you round them until your life unfolds. I will allow that wanton bitch to watch, then throw her to my men and, when they are done, to the dogs.'

Patrick shifted and bleated protest at this, but Hal finally snapped his gaze from Buchan and rested it on the Dunbar lordling.

'Dinnae fash, Patrick,' he said companionably. 'Ye have taken up with bad company, for if Christ Himself walked among ye, the Earl of Buchan would deceive Him.'

Malenfaunt stirred then and made a long series of gabbling sounds, increasing in fury because he realized no-one could understand him. He was wrong and the astonishment in it stunned him to silence.

'My lord Malenfaunt declares,' Malise Bellejambe said at the end of it all, seeing the blank faces, 'that he has a writ from King Edward giving Herdmanston to himself. He has come to take over his fortress and desires you quit-claim from the place immediately.'

The silence and stares made him frown and he turned into the equally incredulous face of Malenfaunt.

'What?' Malise demanded. 'That is what you said, is it not?'

Malenfaunt nodded, his eyes wide as a dog who has found someone without a whip.

'I hold Herdmanston,' Hal answered with a growl, 'and will do so. If ye wish me or mine, *nobiles*, then you must exert yerself and do yer utmost.'

'Come away in,' said a new voice, lilting and smooth and so instantly recognizable that Buchan visibly jerked.

She came to the back of Hal, russet head proud and eyes blazing on her husband's face.

'There is little point in speaking with a man who would throw his wife to all his dogs,' she added in French and laid a hand gently on Hal's shoulder. Up on the roof, the Dog Boy saw the shift in the saddle and even from there, the rush of blood to Buchan's jowled face turned it almost black.

Buchan saw Hal's sudden smile at her touch as a glittering curve of leering triumph against him and all his walls broke. With a sharp cry, almost the scream of a girl, he raked the sides of the great warhorse; taken by surprise, it reared and pawed, then surged forward. Buchan's blade was raised high and capable of striking Hal's ankles, bringing him tumbling off the steps.

A dark shape slammed his horse on one shoulder, sending it skittering sideways. Davy Scott saw Patrick of Dunbar's furious face as he balked Buchan's horse with his own and he brought up the spanned latchbow he'd held, quiet and hidden, down one side of his horse, away from the sharp eyes of Sim Craw; if he shot Hal of Herdmanston now, Buchan would reward him richly . . .

'Stay yer hand,' Patrick of Dunbar bellowed furiously at Buchan. 'This is a truce, by God.'

For a moment, it seemed the unthinkable would happen and that Buchan would strike the son of the Earl of March – then the arrow hissed, snaking over the heads of everyone, so that only a few saw it and fewer still cried out and reached for weapons. By the time hand was on hilt, though, the best shot the Dog Boy ever did struck Davy Scott on his top lip and drove straight through his head, slicing his brainstem in two.

As if someone had cut all the strings of him, he simply flopped, slid sideways and toppled off the horse, the latchbow falling free; it hit the ground and went off, so that the bolt wasped over ducking heads.

There was yelling and confusion; Hal slid Isabel backwards into the keep, covered by Sim's crossbow, while Patrick of Dunbar bellowed at Buchan and everyone around him to stay their hand.

With a final savage wrench that took Bradacus' head back with a protesting whine, the Earl of Buchan reined round and trotted off, the old warhorse stepping delicately over Davy Scott's body, which Buchan never once looked at.

They came on in a rush an hour later. The rain had stopped and enough sun came out to steam the ground and bring out a rash of insects, which caused the horses to fret and quiver at their tethers; they were useless in this event and could only stand fast and be bitten.

The grim-faced men assembled, knowing this would be a hard affair, even though they hugely outnumbered the defenders; there was only one way in and that was up the stair, two wide.

The first four would have shields up, to front and above.

The next two would lug the awkward man-length of wooden planking to span the gap between the top of the stair and the lip of the doorway. The others would come up with spears and axes, the first for forcing the defenders back from the yett, no doubt reinforced and barriered as best as could be managed, the second for the close in-fighting, where even a sword was too long.

Young Patrick, fired and eager, moved down the ranks, trying to behave as a knight should, his earnest face red where it could be seen in the framing of maille rings and bascinet. He clapped shoulders of men he would never dine with at home and prepared himself to lead the ones carrying the spanning plank.

Buchan stood and glowered, armed and armoured, a glory of gold wheatsheaves on blue, but patently not involved; it was not the place of earls to risk themselves in such a combat and if the silly sons of earls wished to be foolish that was their own affair.

He had said as much to Malise, while instructing him to join the affray. Malise, accoutred in uncomfortable maille, stumped bitterly towards the pack clutching an unfamiliar axe and shield, the whole panoply of it a crushing weight that made him wonder if he could even get up the steps.

Malenfaunt stopped him with a hand on one arm, muttering in his gabbled way. Malise could not work out why no-one else could understand the man; what he said was clear as day to him.

'Stay out of it until they are inside,' the knight warned, then grinned, thin-lipped and mirthless. 'See the smoke there?'

Malise saw it, a curling wisp from a hole to one side, above the doorway; he nodded, confused.

'They have a fire going. It is in a wee kitchen, but I do not think they are making a basket of chicken.'

They stood and watched as the attack went in, the shielding men huddled and crabbing as fast as they could go, the ones lugging the plank roaring in desperate fear and fury to keep themselves moving forward.

An arrow spanged off a shield, a bolt took one of the shieldmen in the thigh and he fell with a shriek of despair and a clattering thump. The spanning plank went down and Patrick of Dunbar led the rush, bellowing, into the maw of the doorway.

The yett had been barricaded and buttressed with the tower's original spanning plank, while Leckie the Faber, expert blacksmith that he was, had hammered a bar of iron into a circle, fastening the grilled door shut after a fashion. Behind it, as Patrick's eyes blinked from the sunlight to the dim, were shadowy figures, flicking out spear tips between the metal squares of the yett grill.

Men crushed forward, Patrick yelling for his own to hammer the bar off the gate. Spears clattered on shields – then, suddenly, inexplicably, the men behind the grill scampered away from it. There was a moment of confusion as the attackers, with nothing to stab at, milled round the yett door, getting in the way of the men bringing in hammers – then there was a hissing sound, like falling rain, and the screaming began as boiling water poured from the murder-holes above them.

Malenfaunt nodded with smug righteousness as men howled out of the door. Three of them missed their footing on the plank or were shoved aside by the pack of panicked to fall in a whirl of arms and legs and screams. The rest half-ran, half-stumbled back down the stairs; one was smacked on to his face by a bolt in his shoulderblades and Malise knew that came from Sim Craw, high on the roof and hidden by the merlons. He shivered at the idea of almost having been in all of that and glanced sideways at the smiling Malenfaunt, who had saved him.

Young Patrick came out, bawling and screaming, hauling off his coif in a frenzy, throwing bascinet to one side; squires and servants ran to assist and shield him while he stripped himself to his broiled, blistering face and head, finally falling, moaning.

'Blood of Christ,' Malise muttered. He crossed himself.

'Amen,' mouthed Malenfaunt wryly.

They carried Patrick of Dunbar off to be balmed with goose-grease and reflect on the reality of knightly conflict and the loss of his good looks, while Malenfaunt grinned and nudged Malise to look at the blazing fury that was Buchan's own face. Even though he did not like the idea of Malenfaunt mocking his lord, Malise had to admit that the Earl of Buchan did look like an ox's backside with a bee up it.

Hal had taken little or no part in any of this, for Ill-Made was dying and Mintie Laidlaw had worked herself into such a state over events that her birthing was early, a combination which made for a deal more pain and suffering than anything going on in Herdmanston's scabbed doorway.

'Fetch me warmed watter,' Alehouse Maggie demanded of Mouse. 'Not the boiling ye are dumping on our enemies, mind – softer than that. Likewise a sharp knife, to pare my nails.'

'A good midwife,' Isabel said with a smile, 'needs short clean nails and should be a stranger to drink.'

'Ah, weel, my lady,' Maggie answered with a wink, 'half right is all good – Mouse, fetch also a cup o' fat. I would usually use almond oil to grease the privities o' the likes of Araminta Laidlaw, but needs must.'

Those who knew Mintie and her cry of 'I am *nobiles* born, albeit a poor yin' laughed, but it was tempered by the crash and clatter and screaming not far from them.

'Make certain ye fetch a cup with no burned bits in it,' Maggie yelled at the flustered scampering back of Mouse. 'We are easing a wean into the world, no' frying bacon.'

Isabel knelt by Hal, who was wiping the sweat grease from Ill-Made's uneven face. You could fry bacon on his forehead, he thought.

'Get you gone,' Isabel said gently. 'You are needed elsewhere

231

and this is no place for a man. This poor man will go, as we all go, alone to meet his God.'

'Christ be praised,' Hal said, eyeing the sight of Alehouse Maggie, trimming her nails and laying out a collection of vicious iron more seeming for a forge than a birthing.

'For ever and ever – now go,' Isabel responded.

By the time Hal reached the yett the fighting was done and the last moaning man was stumbling out. Two more lay dead, burned and stabbed and Hal's wolf-grinning men panted and wiped wet mouths with the backs of their hands.

The hours crawled past in a drip of endless mirr. They used pike spears, twenty long feet of shaft and wicked point, to lever the dead out of the doorway without opening the yett.

Ill-Made died, sudden as a blown-out candle, so they put him and the blood-fretted remains of Wull the Yett down in the darkest, coldest part of the undercroft, which act was a banner-wave of hope – in order to decently bury them, everyone else had to survive.

Mintie's bairn was born safely – a girl she was calling Margaretha, promptly christened Grets by everyone else and cooed over.

The attackers came again four hours later, just as the dark closed in and made them harder to see. This time, they had netted bags of burning straw which they hurled in the doorway, causing a storm of flaming embers and reeking smoke, under cover of which the men piled in, armed with forge hammers and a ram to smash the yett door open.

Hal watched them come through the swirling smoke, grey shapes half-crouched and huddled with shields up – black pard on white, a red tree, a series of red and yellow stripes, none of which made any sense to him other than that they provided cover for the men behind, the ones carrying the four-foot wooden ram, an iron cap crudely hammered on the end.

Beside him, Chirnside Rowan and Hob o' the Merse loaded and shot the only two other latchbows they had besides the one Sim was using on the roof. The bolts flashed like kingfisher wings in the mirk, spanging and ricocheting wildly; a man cursed and reeled into another, clutching his ankle and hopping until someone barged him over. They trampled on him to get to the yett, crowding the narrow way while the flaming straw choked everyone.

Metal glinted and banged, men roared battle cries or just incoherent bellowings and Hal seemed to be underwater, where the noise seemed muffled and dull. He sweated inside the maille and padding, felt the powerful urge to run, to piss, to throw up, or all of them at once.

Then the yett broke open and sprang back under the piling weight of bodies, who surged through with fresh, exultant cries.

Hal and the others met them in a way their grandfathers would have nodded approval at – shoulder to shoulder in a shield wall. The shields were the wrong shape, but the wall of them was just as daunting as any who had sent the Norse scampering away at Largs nearly fifty years before.

A spear wobbled at him and Hal twisted to avoid it, landed a good hard chop with his axe on the shield of the man trying to wield it, while Sore Davey slashed a rent in the man's gambeson, so that he tried to back away, grunting. The press was too great and the man was crushed forward, arms trapped so that he could see the needle point of Hal's waraxe coming at his face but could no more avoid it than a cart rolling downhill can avoid the house. He squealed when it went in, shrieked when it came out and then vanished, sucked under the trampling feet.

There was a moment of swaying to and fro, where no-one seemed to do much more than curse and struggle, spluttering and choking in the reek – then, like a stone on a mirror, the attackers broke from the rear and stumbled away.

Feeling the pressure lift, those in front reeled away, blind and breathless with the smoke. For a moment, Hal saw the twisted smile and rat-desperate face of Malenfaunt, forced at last to take part and huddled behind his gashed, striped shield.

There was a moment when Malenfaunt was about to hurl himself at Hal, to end the business in the best heroic fashion – until he saw the axe. A blade with a pick on the other side curved like a bird beak and a point out of the top of the shaft, another at the foot. He blanched, remembering an axe just like it and how he failed to ruin Bruce with it during the tourney; he raised his shield against it and backed hastily away.

Coughing, spluttering, red-eyed and half blind, Hal and the others shouldered the yett door shut and held it while Leckie hammered round a new fastening – a sword this time, which was not only an expensive waste, but probably useless since the iron jamb was coming loose from the stone.

Leckie said all this like a chant to the accompaniment of hammer blows and no-one much cared who actually listened to it. By the time he was done, the air had cleared and women had brought water, to drink and wash faces in; it was as good as goose-grease balm, as Clem Graham announced.

The dark slithered over them like a merciful cloak. A man hailed them asking for truce to pick up those wounded and dead groaning at the foot of the steps and that was allowed, watched by a scowling Mouse holding a torch, backed up by Chirnside Rowan's crossbow.

In the Lord's Room with its folly window, the Dog Boy faced Sim Craw and Hal, while Isabel chewed a lip and looked on.

'It is the only way,' Dog Boy said again and Sim scrubbed his nit-cropped head, knowing the truth when he heard it and reluctant to admit it. He looked at the coiled mass on the floor, a *mesnie* of knotted bast, twisted linen and leather from belts and reins, one end looped and braided round the postered boxbed.

'It will come to pieces like a hoor's drawers,' he growled, then bobbed apology to Isabel, who waved it away.

'That's why I must go,' Dog Boy answered patiently, flashing a white grin in the dark, 'since I am the lightest. Out and away, like a lintie off a branch. Easy.'

Hal knew someone had to get out, to find out if aid was coming, to remind Bruce what was at stake if he did not relieve Herdmanston. He nodded.

'Go with God,' he growled brusquely and, grinning ferally, Dog Boy hefted the coil and, helped by Sim, levered it to the window and over. Then he was out of it with a quick, neat movement, paused with his head and shoulders showing, grinned a last flash of teeth and was gone.

The bed groaned a little, shifted with a squeal. Sim, Hal and Isabel moved swiftly to it, adding their combined weight; it stopped; the makeshift rope trembled with Dog Boy's unseen movement and the knots on it creaked.

'If any daur tell how Isabel MacDuff lay in bed with Hal and Sim from Herdmanston, both at the one time,' Isabel said grimly, 'I will make his cods into a purse.'

'Dinna tell Maggie,' answered Sim vehemently and with more than mock fear.

Dog Boy slithered down the rope, his shoes skittering on the wet, mossed stones, each skid and scuff sounding like the ringing of a bell to him. He went down past the dark loom of the door, catching his breath at the stink of char and blood, down into the black well between wall and stair, reached the end of the makeshift, softly creaking rope and took a breath.

Then he dropped, almost shrieking aloud at the plunge into the unknown dark – he fell a foot, hit the slope of the slicked mound and skidded on his arse through the wet and the blood and fluids until he fell and rolled into where the dead had lain.

He lay in the cold seep of it, waiting and trying to hear over the thunder of his own heart and harsh breathing; no-one came. He heard distant laughter, a burst on the breeze, saw the red-flower flutter of flames and shrank away from it, crabbing towards the wall of the garth until the stones nudged his back.

It was taller than himself by an inch or two, a wall to keep out maurauding beasts on four or two legs from lifting valuable livestock and no more. Inside it, the keep's buildings had been ransacked and part burned – until someone had wisely asked where the besiegers would stay; now the bakehouse and brewhouse glowed faintly from the fires lit within, the half-charred thatch of their roofs still a wet stink as Dog Boy climbed over the wall.

It was the quick way, cutting off a long, arse-puckering crawl round the wall and through the enemy camp – but it held dangers of its own.

The first was the dark, which struck Dog Boy almost blind and left him with only the glow of the fires to let him know what direction he moved.

Now he blessed the persistence of Hal in giving him the old sword and scabbard; Dog Boy had preferred his knife – but that would be no help in a stand-up fight, God save you, Hal had said. The awkward sword had been slung on his back for the climb down and was rendered useless, for he would have needed the arms of a babery beast to draw it from there.

Now, though, he took it off his back, drew it, took the scabbard and placed it on the very tip, holding the belt fastenings in his teeth. Now he had a wobbling curve near the length of a man in front of him and, by swinging gently from side to side, he moved it like the feeler of a giant beetle.

He fell only once, a stumble that spilled him his length and he lay, feeling the wet seep, clenching the sword in one hand and the leather scabbard ties in his teeth so that he would not lose either. He strained to hear; laughter in the near distance calmed him a little and he reached out his free hand to lever himself up – then recoiled at the sensation of rough wet hair.

It was the deerhound, the one he'd called Riach because it meant 'brindled'. The beast's throat had been cut and Dog Boy felt a great welling sadness – he had not brought the dogs in to the keep, for there was not much more useless a creature in a

236

siege than a dog, which ate meat people needed and provided, in the end, poor fare of its own.

Dog Boy was certain the other, Diamant, was also dead for neither of these hounds would have countenanced strangers in the garth without contesting it.

He cursed the siegers then, promised vileness on them for it and a deal of his anger was for himself; I am ill-named, he thought as he pinch-stepped away, for it seems I bring nothin' but doom on decent dugs.

The scabbard tapped the far garth wall gently and he flicked it away with the sword, then gathered it in and fastened it on his back; behind, the laughter rose enough for him to hear the drink in it and he smiled grimly. Be gaggling on the other side o' yer face when I return, he thought. I will hang the doddles o' yon dug-murderer from the kennel door.

It took him all night to reach the Auld Chiel's Chelleis, a long, dark slog through whin and bracken in a wet drabble of night until the milk-glow horizon brought a marriage of birds and their joy of song to the dawn.

The thick, clumped bushes and trees that fringed the Chelleis grabbed his clothes and he had gone no further than a fingerlength in when he heard the rustle and then the voice.

'Swef. Bide doucelike else ah'll arrow ye.'

'God be praised,' Dog Boy gasped out at once and, after a pause, had back the reply.

'For ever and ever.'

It was Scabbit Wull, easier in his mind that what he had in front of him was human and not Faerie – then delighted and relieved to see it was Dog Boy. All the cold, wet folk in the Chelleis were delighted, for they thought matters had been resolved and they could leave their crude, damp shelters and come home to warm fires – which they dare not light themselves – and decent food, which they were running out of.

There were fifteen of them, all women save for Wull, set to guard the hidden valuables of Herdmanston – the garrons of the men, the plough oxen and the milch kine of those cottars who had managed to drive them here in time.

The Auld Chiel's Chelleis was apt named, Dog Boy thought, even as he explained the reality to Wull and the women. It was a great bowl of close bush and stunted forest, cleared in the centre to take the livestock and the people. Unless you knew the way of it, you could be lost inside the place two steps from the edge and it was where Herdmanston always hid when the enemy came – the English name for it was Satan's Cup and they would not go there.

'God go wi' ye,' Wull said to him as Dog Boy left and he promised he would break himself and the garron he rode to bring help.

An hour from the Chelleis, he ran into the armed riders.

CHAPTER ELEVEN

Abbey of Scone
Feast of the Annunciation, March, 1306

Dog Boy had never seen food like it. When he had gone from
Douglas to Herdmanston he thought he had fallen into all the
blessings of Heaven when he found he could eat a white porray
of leeks with boiled bacon bits in it – but this, the crowning
feast for a king, was another level raised entirely.

As was he, feted for being in the company bringing Stone
and Isabel the Crowner to Scone, placed so high above the salt
he was dizzy with it. Or it could have been the metheglin and
ale, the Leche Lombard of pork and eggs, graced with pepper
more precious than gold, or mortrews of chicken, pork and
breadcrumbs, venison boiled in almonds and milk, seasoned
with *poudre douce*.

Hal, catching a glimpse of the sweat-sheened joy of a face,
the dags of hair like black knives stuck to his cheeks, thought
it was because the boy had found Jamie Douglas, the pair of
them grinning and chattering and eating and drinking as if
there was no chasm in rank between them at all.

Hal had watched Dog Boy arrive with the mounted men,
the youth clearly filled with the moment of it, sliding off his

garron and running, shouting, to where Hal and the others were poking about in the slorach of the garth.

'I have brought them,' Dog Boy had shouted, and flung one hand delightedly back to the mass of armed men behind him, led by a slim, dark-haired youth riding at the right hand of Sir Henry of Roslin.

'Look who I have brought,' he added with a bright laugh and Jamie Douglas, with his deceptive, languid looks and lisp, had bowed from the waist, then squinted at Sim Craw and rubbed his ear.

Hal saw Sim flush like a maid; Jamie Douglas, heir to the Douglas estates in Lanarkshire, had been in France all this time and was now returned, like a bright flame, to the side of the Bruce. The last time Hal and Sim had seen Jamie Douglas he had been twelve and Sim had cuffed him for his cheek and impudence, which he was now reminded of.

'I would not care to belt yer lug now,' he added grudgingly and Jamie Douglas, grown to the full of his youth, laughed.

Hal and the others had known someone was coming because of a frantic scamper and a furious chopping as the Flemings started to hack axes at the wet-shrunk rawhide which bound the springald cage together.

There was more than hurry in it, there was a feverish flurry that let everyone know, sent Hal and Sim and others flinging upwards to the roof, to peer out through the merlons to where the Flemings were dismantling their springald in a frenzy, for the screw and windlass and skeins of catapult hair were their livelihood and should not fall into enemy hands.

Which is why they had their own lookouts to warn of a relief force.

Hal remembered seeing Buchan, sitting like a millstone and staring at the stone keep which had thwarted him. Without a word or a sign, he had suddenly reined round and ridden off and, within an hour, there was no-one to be seen and only the ruin and litter. Not long after that the Dog Boy had ridden up with Jamie Douglas, Sir Henry from Roslin and a long hundred of riders.

'Timely,' Hal had declared, bright with the moment of it and Isabel in the crook of his arm. Then he had seen Henry's face and the stone sank back in his bowels.

'It can't be held as Roslin can,' Henry had explained, though the words fell like dull pewter into Hal's head. 'You can send yer household to the care of Roslin and I will collect the rents . . .'

'The King has ordered Herdmanston slighted,' Jamie declared, wiping the smile from Dog Boy's face.

'Is Bruce king then?' Sim had growled and Jamie, smiling and uncaring as a hunting pard, had nodded.

'This very day. I foreswore my chance to be knighted on this day to fulfil his wishes to come here. He will go through the entire blethers of it again when we return with Stone and the crowning Countess – but he is king as of now.'

He offered a polite bow to Isabel who acknowledged it, aware of her soot-streaked dress and face and the frosted roots of her untreated hair.

Now Hal sat in the abbey hall at Scone with the feast flowing round him and the music of shawm and sithole, harp and fiddle circling and swooping. *Douce Dame Debonaire*, the troubadour sang, while the monks, daring as swooping swallows in the risk of their souls, peeked from hiding and tried not to let their toes tap.

Their betters – five bishops, three abbots and a slew of other clergy – were clearly safe from God's wrath and could beat the tables in roaring time.

And yet, while the troubadour detailed the exchange between the horse Fauvel and Dame Fortune, Hal could only see the weeping women and the bairns being kissed farewell by their menfolk, while the black feathers of smoke spilled out of Herdmanston's shattered doorway. Roslin men, grim with what they were doing, methodically fired Herdmanston to a ruin the Earl of Buchan would have exulted over.

241

'I am benisoned, it seems, to be burned out by kin,' Hal had remarked bitterly and Henry of Roslin, sick with the shame and sadness of it, could not speak at all.

From the top table, resplendent in finery that was not even his, Bruce surveyed the joy and would have been surprised to find another at the feast whose mood was as bitter as his own.

He was king. He had been crowned by the right person, in the right place with all the correct procedure and regalia, so that all the years of careful plans had come to final fruit – yet he sat in Balliol's coronation robes, felt the strange weight of Toom Tabard's gold circlet on his head, all hidden away by Wishart for this very moment.

Borrowed finery was bad enough – but because of it, he had to forsake the hiding hood and now his face, with the livid cheek scar weeping still, was there for all to see and wonder at.

Beside him sat the Queen and the bitter gruel of that flavoured all the meat and drink that found a way to his mouth. It was bad enough that they had been so estranged – he could not go to her with what he suspected he had, with his very breath the kiss of death – but now she was smouldering resentment, with all the fire of her seventeen years, at what he had done to her household.

It had been necessary for an age and Bruce had put it off – until the coronation loomed. He had gone to her then, been welcomed stiffly by a girl bewildered why her husband seemed to have taken a dislike to her. Wondering why he hid his face from her, all but his eyes, behind a veil like some Saracen.

He had told her that the entire ceremony would be repeated, this time with the Stone of Scone and the hereditary Crowner, the Countess of Buchan; that name brought her head up and flared her cheeks, for she had heard the rumours of the old love and did not care for it.

But it was the Lady Bridget, that older, pinched twist of

scorn who had been Elizabeth's nurse when she had been a babe, who set the seal on matters with her snort.

'Bad enough my lady is made queen to your king of summer,' she had spat, 'without having to go through such mummery again, this time with yer old hoor.'

The silence had stretched an endless age, while Elizabeth's eyes went wide with horror and all the entourage, down to the huddled little priest at the back, waited to see what would happen.

When it did, the sudden crack of it made them all jump; one or two squealed – all of them shoaled away from the fallen Lady Bridget, who struggled like a beetle and sat up, bewildered, astonished and afraid. She touched her lip, saw the blood on it and moaned.

Bruce, his knuckles stinging from the backhand slap, looked at his queen, feeling sick at what he had done – had to do, he reminded himself. Yet another stain . . .

'I have been tolerant, lady,' he said to Elizabeth, ignoring the whey-face sprawl of Lady Bridget, 'and you have mistaken this for weakness. Say your farewells to all of these, for they return to your father in Ireland after the coronation. You will have new tirewomen from among my Scots subjects – and, if you need the comfort of God, there is the dean of the royal chapel.'

He raked them all with his eyes.

'What I put up with as an earl was one matter,' he added. 'Now I am a king and at war, so I cannot have all my doings sent back to Ireland and on to Plantagenet.'

Yet the frightened, bloody face of Bridget, braided hate though it had been, left him feeling that stain yet and the sight of the one called Dog Boy brought it back in a rush. He remembered the boy, all those years ago round a campfire. *Nivver violet a wummin*, he had intoned as one of the vows a knight should follow and, even allowing for the mis-speaking of it, the memory of the strength in the lad's voice made Bruce ashamed.

'*Hare, hare, hye,*' they were singing, furious, red-faced, beating tempo on the tables until the trenchers jumped. '*Goudalier ont fet ouan d'Arras Escoterie. Saint Andrie – hare hare, goudeman et hare druerie.*'

Hark, hear it now, Jamie translated for the Dog Boy, who marvelled at how his friend and new-dubbed knight had learned French in the years he had been in that country with Bishop Lamberton. *Those ale brewers are turning Arras into Scotland. By St Andrew hear it – good men and good times . . .*

Across the table from them sat Kirkpatrick, solitary in the crowd and counting the heads. The bishops of St Andrews, Glasgow, Dunkeld , Moray and Brechin. The abbot of Scone and another from Inchcolm. Three earls – John of Atholl, Malcolm of Lennox, Alan of Menteith, spilling alkanet-coloured gravy down their fine wool tunics.

And that was it, apart from a slew of lesser lights, some of them dubious – Randolph for one, Kirkpatrick thought, would bear watching. Not a single Comyn, nor a Balliol – it was hardly a rich vote of confidence in the new king of Scots.

They were bringing in brawn with mustard and starting in to toast the 'good men and good times', while Jamie was telling Dog Boy of how some woman called Agnes they had known as boys in Douglas had run off with Fergus the cook and they now had a pie shop in Perth. And how a falconer called Gutterbluid was still there, serving the Clifford folk who ruled now and how, one day, Jamie would scorch all of them out of Douglas Castle.

He said it loudly and often, flushed as much at having been made a knight by a king as the wine and there was no lisp in the boy when he did it; Kirkpatrick wondered if Edward, the Covetous King, knew what hatred he had created in the north out of the generation of Jamie Douglases.

He wondered if Edward knew what had happened here in Scone – though he already knew what Longshanks would do

244

about it and could feel the sullen, embered wrath of the English king through the dark and the miles.

This was the last feast – what followed would be a famine of good men and good times.

The Painted Chamber, Westminster, London
Pentecost, May, 1306

Seraphs, prophets and the fulminating Judas Maccabeus all glared painted disapproval down at the huddle round the table, whose black echoes were stretched and monstrous on the walls; a wind flickered the sconces and the shadows danced like mad imps in Hell.

I have never been warm in that bed, Edward thought moodily, as the hangings of the gilded, green-postered bed swung like banners. For all that, he looked at it longingly, perched invitingly on a dais at the far end of his private chambers; it had been a long, long day weighted with fur and cloth of gold, crown and jewels, touching stumbling youths on the shoulders, youths who knelt as tyros and rose as knights.

Three hundred, at least, Edward thought wearily and all of them equally exhausted from their night of chapel vigil, the Templar courtyard choked with their tents and the press so great on the day that he'd had to clear a passage in the abbey with armoured knights on horseback.

It had been worth it, though, for the ceremony, the timing – Whitsun, when Arthur himself had held his fabled plenary court at Caerleon – and the binding of so many young knights to this one day and to his son.

He glanced at the boy, seeing his whey face and violet-ringed eyes. He had stood up well to the ritual of spending all night alone in the palace chapel. At dawn, he had knighted the boy and then the pair of them crossed to the abbey and, together, dubbed all the others.

After that was the feast of it, complete with the masterstroke of gilded swans on which Edward himself had sworn vengeance on Bruce, promising that, once he had vanquished his enemy, he would proceed to the Holy Land.

It was pure Arthur and only a few doubted that the King would do it, for he was magnificently prinked and preened, coloured and oiled. Not to be outdone, the prince had risen, resplendent in the heraldry of Gascony, to which he had also been newly raised, and swore loudly not to rest two nights in the same place until the Scotch had been defeated.

There were those who knew it was an echo of Perceval's declaration from the Round Table, when Arthur's knights set out to find the Holy Grail – but that was part of it all. That and the minstrels and the food and the drink and the boasts.

One or two looked at the old king and wondered, all the same . . . De Lacy, for one. He had seen Edward on the day news had arrived of Bruce's murderous treachery, seen the grey cast that seemed to turn the King's face to stone, then the mad flush that darkened it.

'God rot him,' he had exploded. 'I will chain him like a mad dog. Let him and all those with him be cursed and their accomplices in evil with them. He is now ranked with the fratricide Cain, and with Judas the traitor, and with Core, Dathan and Abiron, who entered Hell while still living for their revolt against Moses . . .'

There had been more, until the King fell to the floor and caused a mad scramble of alarm. He had lain in a dead faint for half a day and spent the next two weeks being carried about in a litter, so that de Lacy had thought he would never recover.

He had, almost miraculously, growling for retribution and sending off Aymer de Valence to the north to commence red war. De Lacy was relieved that de Valence been handed the task – at fifty-six the Earl of Lincoln did not want to be the one raising the dragon banner in the north, with no quarter asked or given. De Lacy was the last of the old warriors from

Edward's early days – Aymer's father, William, was long dead, John de Warenne was dead these three years since, Roger Bigod was too ill . . . the list went on.

Six wars and eight years it had taken not to defeat the Scots – and here they were again, setting off with an army to burn and scourge the north.

What settled despair in Edward, like a chill winter mist, was not the expense and weariness of yet another campaign, but the realization that there seemed no end to it; he had thought the matter done, thought Bruce, at least, valued the firm hand. Yet the very day of that lord's spurious crowning was a slap with a metalled gauntlet – Lady Day, ten years to the very day Edward himself had declared war on the Scotch.

This would be the last of it, Edward thought. I will burn and scourge them as they have never been. I will give them the breath of the dragon . . .

But he also knew it had to be the last of it. His contemporaries were all gone and the new breed would need to step up to the ring from now on; he sat at the round table – the echo of Arthur yet again – and stared at his son – the new breed.

He had done his best to bind him to the young firebrand *nobiles*, but he was not sure if the boy understood what had been done or why; even now, invited to speak to his father in his private chambers, he had contrived to bring Gaveston.

The King glanced sourly at the man his son favoured over all others, grudgingly admitting that the youth had borne the vigil well enough, looked fresh still. He had been the first one his son had knighted and was, the King knew, a fearsome tourney fighter, which did not endear him any better to those who distrusted his particular favour, disliked his arrogance and did not care to be dumped on their arse in the mud.

Edward took him in, up and down in a moody glance, remembering bitterly that he had brought this one into his son's circle thinking he would be a good influence. Of all the mistakes I have made in my life, he thought, this was the worst. It might be possible still to be rid of the man. Replace him with someone my son also favours – like that youngster, Roger Mortimer.

Gaveston's gilded cap of hair was bright, his tunics blue and brown – and a red silk one over all, decorated with embroidered birds in gold. His shoes, Edward noted with distaste, had been shaped particular to each foot and were, God help us all, pointed at the toe.

'I summoned you, Caernarvon,' he growled. 'I do not recall anyone else on that list.'

Caernarvon. The very name was a slap to a son who wanted a father; not even a son's name, but a title.

'I understood the summons to be a discussion on matters pertaining to the Scotch disturbances,' his son replied, while Gaveston wisely stayed silent. 'My brother here is well versed in matters of battle.'

Edward met the cool, bland eyes of Gaveston, then flicked his gaze back to his son's whey face. Jesu, he thought to himself, feeling the deep sinkhole of despair open in him, I have to leave the Kingdom to this one. God help it.

He rallied; if he was to leave it to frivolity and, Christ preserve it, pointed shoes then he would leave it in the best condition he could manage; no-one would stand over the tomb of Edward Plantagenet and mourn about the state of the realm handed over to his son.

'Brother you may call him,' he replied, flat and cold, 'but I never sired it. Out.'

Gaveston hesitated for a heartbeat, enough to bring the blood flushing up to Edward's neck. Then the youth bowed languidly from the waist, backed away two steps, turned and was gone. The King regarded his son with a look that would have turned milk.

'A summons to this place,' he growled wearily, 'is a family matter. You should know this by now – Christ and all His Saints, boy, you have had it dinned into you for long enough.'

'I thought only to please you,' his son replied miserably. 'It was my intent to ask permission to bestow Ponthieu on my brother, Sir Piers.'

The words sank into Edward like slow knives, so slowly in fact that his son did not realize the cut of them until he saw the King suddenly rise, the chair behind him tumbling with a clatter. Then the droop-eyed horror, face a dark bag of blood, made him recoil, remembering all the other times he had been victim of this wrath.

'Ponthieu,' Edward roared. 'Ponthieu . . . you bastard son of a bitch. Ponthieu?'

He was suddenly there, towering over his son, who had shrunk on to a chair. Then, with utter terror, the prince felt his father's hands batter him, like the wings of some maddened bird.

'You would give home lands away to a turd in silk? You? Who never gained as much as a clod in your entire life?'

He gave up trying to beat with a strength he did not possess; the prince had lost his cap and his senses, could no more resist this terrible old man than he could fight the wind, so he sat, bowed and let the thunder roll on him.

Edward saw the prinked and rolled perfection of his son's hair, saw the attempts at gilding it in a vain parody of Gaveston's and, finally, found a way to hurt. He grabbed handfuls of it while the prince, stung by pain and fear at last, shrieked and tried to free himself. Raw knots came away; blood flew.

In another eyeblink, the prince felt the storm rush away, stared up at the panting, furious figure who looked at the bloody tufts in his fists and blinked owlishly.

'I only wished ever to please you,' the prince managed, a whimper that he heard in his own ears and felt shame at; Edward let the bloody horror feather from his fists and bent to pick his son up. Twenty and three, he thought, taking him close, close enough to feel the stickiness of blood on his own cheek. He patted him absently and murmured, as if in some distant dream where the boy was still only three, with all hope bright.

'I know, boy. I know.'

Then, suddenly, the prince had the weight in his arms and could not hold it, let his father slip to the rushed floor of the chamber and called for help.

Near Cupar Castle, Fife
Feast of St Baithen, Blessed Successor to Columba, June, 1306

Kirkpatrick knew he was done, that God had finally abandoned him. He had, in truth, known in the minute he had clacked his way across the flags of Scone's private chapel, summoned by the King and running the gauntlet of scowling envy from the accumulated court as he did so.

He had heard them in his head, whispering about the Auld Dug, the De'il's ain imp. The young *mesnie*, with their curled hair and matching lips, he thought sourly and then with satisfaction of how the Bruce, new kinged, still needed him.

At least that was some balm on his mood, which was all wolfsbane; he knew why and did not like to admit it, either – that the quarrel with the Herdmanston lord had left him feeling estranged and somehow lessened, which was a feeling he did not care for.

The new court officials watched him huffily; there was now an etiquette for being presented to King Robert, involving so many steps, so many bows, waiting until summoned, leaving backwards . . . but none of it involved Kirkpatrick and the chamberlains and doorwards resented this.

Not that the King was enthroned for receiving – exactly the opposite. The new king of Scots lay on the tiles, arms outstretched and his scarred cheek pressed to the embossed pattern of the one in front of the chapel altar. The tiles were all different, each one a coat of arms of *Les Neufs Preux*, the Nine

Worthies, and Kirkpatrick was not certain whether the King thought the pattern on that particular tile would have some holy benefit. Hector, he saw, the hero of Troy.

The King, a cruciform of repentance and thanksgiving, was naked save for the play of red and blue light streaming down from the stained windows to pool exactly where he lay. He stirred, looked sideways up at Kirkpatrick and smiled wanly.

'I am breathing in the smell of holiness,' he declared, half muffled by the press of his cheek. Holiness seemed a little like scented smoke to Kirkpatrick, though that might have been the remains of incense clinging to him from the Mass the King had recently attended with Abbot Thomas. Like wasps, priests droned somewhere in the distance.

Kirkpatrick watched Bruce raise himself and sit naked and crosslegged, his still-flat belly stained red and blue with light. He knew, more than anyone, what had sucked the juice from Bruce, all the same, after a flurry of activity that had seen the new king trail his weary *mesnie* north as far as Aberdeen to put the fear in those supporters of the Comyn.

Bruce had extorted money from east coast ports and flung merchants into prison as hostage for it, demanded military service from Perth and elsewhere, threatened the Earl of Strathearn with hanging if he did not swear to the new king. His supporters had captured Brechin, Cupar and Dundee.

Now, though, it was beginning to unravel. Percy and Clifford were methodically scouring the southwest. Dumfries had fallen to them, as well as Ayr – and Tibbers, where the luckless John Seton had been dangled by the neck like bad fruit.

None of that was what had driven the King to the altar of a private chapel. A simple roll of vellum had done that, brought by two Templars, one of them the same Rossal de Bissot who had snatched Kirkpatrick from the long drop to the floor of St Olave's, who had gifted the Rood for the coronation.

Kirkpatrick did not know exactly what it said, but the

rumour of it was flowing out, coupled to the feverish, gleeful cries of the Comyn supporters – the new king, usurper and murderer, was about to have the Holy Church's saving grace withdrawn from him and the Pope's writ of excommunication was due any day.

'Everyone else enters life unsullied,' Bruce murmured, half to himself while Kirkpatrick tried to ignore the raising hairs on his arms. 'I entered already cursed by a saint and now I am burdened with such a panoply of sin. The Devil stalks me, Kirkpatrick.'

There was not enough cynic in Kirkpatrick to ignore such a statement and he peered right and left, as if to see it lurking, even in such holy shadows. Last year, near the Tweed, a priest had come upon an imp which had a lamb held in sharp-toothed jaws and had beaten it with his holy staff until it had finally dropped the beast and run off.

The local abbot had confirmed all this and Kirkpatrick had no reason to doubt it, so that a king – and all those who supported him – left without holy aid in a world of Satan was a doom better not contemplated. It was hard to ignore it, all the same, with Bruce's peeling nose and raddled cheeks cause for fascinating concern that the Devil had already paid him a visit and smacked leprosy into him.

Suddenly, Bruce unreeled a list of instructions, hurried and hoarse, as if he wanted the taste of it out of his mouth; Kirkpatrick struggled to take it all in – the Cathar physicker had disappeared and Bruce feared the worst in it. Find the Cathar physicker and make sure he could never speak of the medical secrets he had been privy to. On the way, ride with two Templars, one of them Rossal de Bissot, the knight who had rescued him in St Olave's, and make sure the pair reach Berwick safely.

Kirkpatrick nodded, as if he had fully understood, which was a lie since he did not see the need to hunt down and kill the little physician – unless, as he thought later, the wee heretic knew more than Kirkpatrick himself regarding Bruce's condition.

The idea of that soured him, but he growled out a repeat of his instructions and said that it would be done, though he marvelled quietly at how God tests you even as you are planning your life and thinking it your own.

Once before he had dealt with Cathars and the stink of the burnings had so choked him that he had vowed then to have nothing more to do with such an unholy Holy War. Now his vows would have to be broken. *Deus lo vult*. He did not realize he had spoken aloud until the King replied.

'*Ave Maria gratia plena*,' Bruce said beatifically, smiling at the dubious Kirkpatrick, whose loose-jawed gape was only a mild irritant on the peace he now felt.

'Do not worry,' he added as a soothe to Kirkpatrick's face. 'God has a Plan.'

Kirkpatrick, mindful of the new protocols even with a naked king, had bowed and backed out, his heart thundering, his body in flames and his mind like a fish in a cauldron about to come to the boil. He only hoped God's Plan included reminding the new king to put on some clothes before he stepped from his private chapel.

He could not shake the sight from him all the way down to Cupar with the two disguised Templars – the King with his skelpt-arse face and his naked body of parti-coloured light and, above all, that gentle, sure smile as if it was the most natural thing to be holding court with his pintle hanging like a dog and his soul hovering on the brink of eternal damnation.

The Templars did not help Kirkpatrick's cat-ruffle; for all their attempts at discreet, they rode like knights dressed like poor merchants, while they prayed and crossed themselves so often that a blind man could see they belonged to the Order. It was, Kirkpatrick thought moodily, head sunk into his shoulders against the summer mirr and the flies, more than likely that the

Bruce Curse of Malachy had finally been translated, like the red pox, to himself.

Which is why it came as no surprise when they ended up in the middle of the Welsh archers. Round a bend, down a straight portion of ruts, round another, with the peewits' call descending like a mourn at the end of the day and all their thoughts misted as breath on glass.

None of the three had anything in his head but a desire for hot food and a decent bed –and did not realize they were taken until the men were round them, grinning and jabbering.

Then the Templar called Jehan had whipped out his sword from under his cloak and launched himself with a hoarse cry of *'Deus lo vult'* which did not help. Kirkpatrick grabbed de Bissot's bridle, dragged his horse away as the knight fought his own weapon out.

'Leave him – he is giving you a chance,' he roared and Rossal de Bissot saw it, even as Jehan cut down two archers, the palfrey circling and baiting. It was no warhorse, all the same and Kirkpatrick saw the Welsh, cursing and scattering, were recovering themselves and dragging big arrows on to their warbows.

Rossal wrenched the head of his horse round just as Kirkpatrick's attention was locked on the desperately fighting Jehan and his hand on Bissot's bridle – the jerk wrenched it from his fist and himself from the back of his own horse, the whirling tumble of it a momentary confusion, the thump that bellowed the air from him a harsh pain.

None of it drove out the leaden sound of hooves drumming off into the distance – and the harsh irony of how he had saved de Bissot at the cost of himself.

There was the sudden scuffle of feet, a spray of muddy grit into his face, a sauce for it of Welsh curses, harsh as a spitting fire. Then he was hauled up into the square block of face belonging to an archer wearing a studded jack and a dark scowl; behind him, he saw Jehan's horse struggle to its feet, limping. The knight lay face down in the mud.

The dark scowl, clearly the leader, did not have much time for anything other than to make sure Kirkpatrick was disarmed before de Valence appeared, bareheaded but armoured and accoutred – Kirkpatrick knew him at once, the blue and white striped magnificence trailing a *mesnie* of *serjeants* behind him.

Then a figure shoved from behind the proud hawk of de Valence and Kirkpatrick felt the spear twist inside him at the sight of that battered, stained face.

'Kirkpatrick,' Malise Bellejambe said, his voice juiced with the relish of it. He sat back in his saddle while de Valence and the Welsh scowl exchanged information and, for a moment, there were only two men, Malise and Kirkpatrick, alone in the whole of splendid creation and horn-locked at the eyes.

'God is good,' Malise said and twisted his bruise of a face into a long, brown smear of smile, then turned as de Valence dismounted.

'Make sure he has no daggers hidden about him, Your Grace,' Malise informed de Valence viciously, fawningly climbing off his own horse so he would not be looking down on his betters.

De Valence did not like Bellejambe, the spy of the Earl of Buchan – but the Comyn earl was now England's friend and so had to be appeased and his creatures treated with some courtesy.

De Valence had drawn the line at Malenfaunt, all the same, a knight who had foresworn himself before God in a tourney *à l'outrance* with Bruce himself. Well beaten, he had been thrown out of all respectable company, tongue-split in a just and fitting punishment. De Valence, who thought Malenfaunt should have been properly killed in the duel, did the foresworn knight the courtesy of treating him as if he were actually dead; he would not permit Malenfaunt anywhere near him.

The twist in that was that he had to accept this Bellejambe instead, though he did his best to ignore the man where possible. Like now, as he turned his back on Malise and looked at the muddied, dark apparition held firmly by two of his armoured *serjeants*. Swarthy, a secretive, sly-looking scum, he thought to himself. Just the sort to be up to no good.

'You were with these Templars?' De Valence demanded and Kirkpatrick saw Jehan being hauled upright and away, his toes furrowing the mud; senseless, but alive, he thought to himself. There's a blessing at least.

'Peaceful travellers,' he began in French, which was designed to show his breeding but was brought up short when Malise snorted with derision, leaning forward with all the vengeance of the past welling like pus from his twisted soul.

'Liar,' he said and de Valence turned, his handsome face puckered in a frown of censure, for it was clear Kirkpatrick was something well-bred, if not a knight, and demanded some deference of rank. Malise wrenched all that from Kirkpatrick with his sneering hiss.

'This is the red murderer of the Lord of Badenoch.'

Near Cupar Castle, Fife
Next day – the English Feast of St Margaret of Scotland,
June, 1306

The monk's face was inflamed, even over the wind-chilled redness that had chapped his cheeks and his dark olive eyes were brilliant with outrage. De Valence sighed and shifted in the saddle; his buttocks ached and the damp that was not quite rain, not quite mist seeped straight through the layers of leather and linen, maille and padding to gnaw his very bones.

He wanted a fire and hot food and something warm and spiced. He did not want an outraged Italian abbot.

'In God's holy name,' this annoyance persisted stubbornly. 'You must put a stop to this. It is against Heaven.'

Aymer de Valence agreed. He was also aware that this figure, trembling more with outrage and cold in his white wool swaddling, was Abbot Alberto of Milan, sent from York to ensure that the holy presences of Bishops Lamberton and Wishart were not harmed by their rebellion.

Before that, the shivering, sallow little priest had been sent from Rome to investigate the increasingly disturbing reports of outrage among the Templar knights in England – and the wilds of war-ravaged Scotland. He was finding more than he had expected, de Valence noted grimly, on that matter.

What outraged the good abbot was a murmur among the rain-darkened trees, trunks and twisted branches so black it seemed they had absorbed their own shadows. It was, in truth, a stark, eldritch horror which, under other circumstances, de Valence would have ridden down, shouting for God's help and swinging a cleansing blade.

Not now, all the same. Now the dragon had been raised and the Order of the Poor Knights of Christ were caught in the vice of it – Aymer thought that was rather good. The vice of it; he had little sympathy nowadays with the Templars, whose arrogance and faked poverty had been annoying and whose blasphemies, if reports were to be believed, were vile – did his own men not say, grinning and nudging each other, that they were 'going to the Temple' each time they visited a brothel?

Still, what was being done was not exactly chivalrous, but that was the nature of matters when the dragon was raised by an angry king – it would breathe its fire on all, even an Order Knight who had contrived to entangle himself in a war he should have avoided.

Breathing fire was what the dragon was doing, if the Welsh could ever stir it to life. De Valence needed those dark, vengeful half-pagan little Welsh dwarves happy and, most of all, not focusing any resentment on himself. If that meant turning them loose to do what they pleased on a hated enemy, so be it.

Yet the abbot wore a ring on one finger which had the *biscione* engraved on it, a marvellous depiction of a coiled serpent seemingly eating a man but, in actual fact, giving birth to him – de Valence was sorely tempted to point out the heathen origins of that symbol.

He did not, for the symbol was the coat-of-arms of the Viscontis of Milan, one of the most powerful families in Lombardy and the conduit to papal sanction. Alberto may have been the least scion of it, but he was still a member and he had a slew of Inquisition priests at his back, the sinister black Hounds of God, the Dominicans.

'My dear Abbot Alberto,' he said through a smile like a sewer grating, 'you must see that I cannot put a stop to it. This Templar has put himself beyond the pale and contrived to slay some of the Welsh in his attempts to evade capture. I have influence, no more – and it seems that my influence does not stretch to interfering with their . . . singular observances.'

'Singular,' shrilled the abbot, lifting the word out of himself so that de Valence fancied he saw the monk step out of his own shoes. 'Observances.'

The little Italian opened and closed his mouth, the words so crowding his mouth, like gulls falling on abandoned fish, that he could not get a single one out. Taking advantage, Aymer waved one metal-gloved hand.

'Indeed,' he said. 'These are Welsh, from the distant mountains of my lord's kingdom and only recently gathered unto God's blessing, for all that priests like yourself have waved censors and crosses and prayers over their peaks and forests for centuries. It is hardly surprising that they have . . . odd practices.'

'Odd!'

It was a shriek now, so loud that it brought the heads of the Welsh round and de Valence closed his eyes and hoped they would not be offended. He felt the wolf stare of the one called Addaf fall on him and offered a prayer; if that one started in to be outraged, there would be a blood-bath and, though he had no doubt he and his handful of knights would kill them, it would certainly mean an end to the service of all his Welsh.

258

The smoke of the badly-burning fire cloaked over them like a vile benediction.

Mark you, Aymer said to himself, 'odd' was perhaps the wrong choice of words for what was happening in the clearing a little way away.

In it was a piled heap of damp faggots that the Welsh were trying to fan into life. In the centre of it, staked fore and aft, was a mercifully dead horse – a fine *destrier*, Aymer noted wistfully, that had deserved a better fate than to be throat-slit and then staked upright, as if still alive. And one, he added viciously to himself, that a supposed Poor Knight should never have been riding.

The Poor Knight was riding it still, lashed to the dead animal in his armour, bucket helmet on, broken arms fitted with shield and a lance bound to his shattered fingers. Fully armed and mailled, the Templar sat the horse, his mouth gagged under the helmet, still alive and waiting to burn.

If the Welsh could ever get the fire lit.

A stocky, cadaverous man wearing a studded jack and a green hood shouted instructions and the Welsh obeyed Addaf, fetching more wood, more lit torches, fanning the flames while the pyre sputtered and smoked; the edifice rocked a little as the desperate knight struggled.

The Welshman and the abbot from Rome had bristled and scowled at each other when they had met, one making warding signs as well as the cross with string-calloused fingers, the other crossing himself and offering a clasp-handed prayer. Like barely leashed mastiffs, de Valence thought wearily; my money is still on Addaf, the Welsh archer they called Mydr ap Mydvydd – Aim the Aimer.

'Madness,' Abbot Alberto spat. 'This is madness. The Pope shall hear of it.'

'The Pope shall hear of the mischief of the Order,' de Valence retorted, irritated now. 'Besides – if you find the evidence you seek, what will become of those Templars Holy Mother Church finds guilty?'

There was silence, no-one wanting to admit, of course, that they would burn, no differently from what the Welsh were doing now.

'You may have the other one when we capture him,' de Valence added in a conciliatory fashion. 'One Rossal de Bissot by name. Once the King's justice has finished with him.'

'They should not be party to secular justice,' the abbot persisted. 'They are of the Church and only the Pope may punish them. He will hear of this.'

'You have mentioned that once already,' de Valence spat back, then leaned forward a little in the saddle. 'Be assured, dear Abbot, that the Pope may be deafened to complaints by all the accusations against the Order. That and the sound of victory over his excommunicated enemies, which forgives all sins.'

'The end does not always justify the means,' intoned the abbot, drawing himself up. Behind him, a coterie of monks and clerics nodded and clasped pious hands.

Go home, Aymer wanted to say. Go home and help Galeazzo and all the other Viscontis dominate Milan and the Pope. Leave the serious business of the day to fighting men, who can see the madness in this and in everything to do with war yet persist in it, like a peasant ploughing a stony field.

The madness was necessary, too. Lamberton had given in at Scotland as well – but not before he had sent off all the men he could to Bruce – while the siege of Cupar had secured that arch-priest of dissent, Lucifer's Own secretary Bishop Wishart.

Resplendent in maille and helm, the recalcitrant old dog had dared plead the safety of his Holy Vestements, in an irony that would not be missed by anyone there, especially those who knew that the siege engines he had used to capture Cupar in the first place had been made by timbers sent by King Edward himself for the repair of Glasgow's cathedral.

There was no time for the qualms of an abbot, whether he be a Visconti, papal spy or Christ's Own Right Hand, for it was doubtful if King Edward would allow that to interfere with his own form of burning vengeance. Let the little Visconti pick the irony out of that, Aymer thought savagely.

A sudden high yell slashed through the stream of his thoughts, followed by cheers; the coterie of clerics crossed themselves and muttered prayers as de Valence stared into the furious eyes of the abbot, as burning as the sudden leap of flame from the pyre.

'Justified or not,' he said with a twisted smile. 'We have, it seems, reached the end.'

He closed the visor of his new-style bascinet and hauled the surprised horse round, then set off at a frantic pace, almost blind and only eager to move, to course blood into him and all thoughts out.

Up on a hill, belly flat and peering through wet fronds, Hal, Sim and Jamie Douglas looked at the smoke-stained wood and the figures round it. De Valence was easily seen, in his blue and white striped mantle decorated with a ring of red birds – *barry of twelve argent and azure, an orle of ten martlets gules* Hal translated to himself.

The others were less easy to work out – a lot of arguing prelates, a host of ill-dressed Welsh rabble trying to light a huge fire and a wary knot of *serjeants*, who galloped off after de Valence. Hal had no idea what was going on.

'I could have shot yon aff his fancy stot,' Sim muttered, moody at having been told to hold his fire by Hal, who gave him a sour sidelong glance.

'Which would have had us all looking like hedgepigs,' he grunted. 'Yon are Welsh bowmen – they have stacked their bagged weapons in shelter while they hunt dry wood for their fire.'

Sim's eyebrows went up and he looked, then nodded admiringly.

'Full price to ye – I missed that. Bigod, it is lucky for us they are so frowning over makin' a heat for themselves. Not that it is chill, as anyone can tell . . .'

'We should take a look,' Jamie Douglas declared eagerly. 'There are only a brace o' them left – see there.'

He was right – the Welsh were straggling off after de Valence and their leader, the tall one in the jack fitted with little metal-leaf plates, had barked at two of them to stay behind. Hal could not understand why and said so.

'Guarding their meal,' Sim said with firm conviction based on nothing at all. Jamie and Hal looked at each other and did not have to put voice to it – it was a gey muckle fire for a meal, even for as many Welsh as that.

'An entire coo at least,' Sim agreed cheerfully and licked meaningful lips. It was a point fairly made – Hal and his men, with Jamie Douglas in tow 'for the learnin g in it', had been sent by Bruce to scout Cupar, last known position of the English. It had been a long, hard, meandering ride in the warm damp of summer, plagued by a host of flies and a lack of decent food.

Yet, for all the promise of beef, Hal was uneasy and sour at the coiled strike that was Jamie Douglas, envying his youth and how all was adventure to him, while annoyed that he was prepared to put everything at risk for it.

He and Dog Boy were a pair, he noted, padding round as if leashed to each other – even now, Dog Boy held the garrons no more than a hidden score of yards away. As Sim had remarked, the pair of them were like the brace of deerhounds Hal had once owned, with Jamie the fawning one with a streak of vicious savagery you did not want to unleash and Dog Boy as the solid, relentless, reliable partner at the hinter end.

Hal did not like remembering those dogs, the pride of their handler, Tod's Wattie. Malise Bellejambe had poisoned the dogs and, not long after, red murdered Wattie in the back with a knife. What was worse, nothing had been done about that in the half score of years since.

'Well?'

The challenge was in French and Hal turned into the cocked head and grin of Jamie Douglas. He wants to be a leader this one, Hal noted.

'We can capture at least one,' Jamie went on. 'Valuable information for the King.'

'Ach weel,' interrupted Sim in a quiet whisper as he peered through the fronds, 'where is that wee mannie headed now?'

They looked; one of the Welsh had started off into the trees, away from the other.

'Bigod,' said Sim, with a beam of realization, 'he is away to do his business. Now's oor chance . . .'

They were out and away before Hal could decide, Sim half-crouched like a lumbering bear, Jamie moving like a gazehound. They came circling round, to where they could just see the figure, unlacing his braies and studying the ground for stinging nettles.

'Now,' Jamie hissed and felt the clamp of Sim's hand, turning into the quiet shake of the shaggy grey head.

'Wait.'

The Welshman squatted, grunted, let loose a long, sonorous fart.

'Now, while he is engaged,' Jamie hissed, excitement making him break into French, forgetting Sim did not understand it – but Sim understood enough.

'Wait.'

The man strained and fretted, then let loose a long sigh. He sought out a handful of leaves, reaching round to wipe himself; Jamie was in agonies of trying to contain himself, but Sim was a rock, grim and silent and implacable.

'He will be gone in another wipe,' Jamie whispered bitterly, but Sim merely smiled. The man stood, hauling up his braies to his knees – and turned.

Jamie saw it at last. The thing every man would do – he had done it himself – was to look at what he had created, a slow, almost proud examination. Now, with his back to them and braies half-way to his knees was the time, as Sim said with a hard nudge in Jamie's ribs.

The youth was out and across the distance between them in the time it took the man to nod, as if happy with the steaming pile – then something smacked him hard in the back, an arm snaked round his neck and cut off his breathing and shouts.

They fell, as Sim knew they would, Jamie on top and driving the breath from the Welsh archer so that, when Sim lumbered up, the man was already weak and flopping; a swift dunt with the hilt of his dagger settled the matter and now Jamie became aware of the learning in this.

'Christ's Bones, Sim,' he spat, looking at the smears, evil-smelling and fetid, on his clothes and hands, where they had rolled in the fresh pile. Sim Craw, who had known exactly what would happen, only smiled.

'It is in yer hair a wee bittie,' he pointed out helpfully. 'Since ye are already besmeared, ye may as well take the shittiest end for cartin' him back. Speedy now and we'll be away, sleekit and brawlie.'

It was then that they became aware of a new smell cutting through the stench of shit, a rich, sweet smell of cooking meat that Sim knew well. From where he crouched he could see the pyre, shifting and shedding sparks as it collapsed and, revealing clear in it, the horror of a blackened horse and the man on it; even allowing for the soot and scorch, the shield fastened to one arm still bore the crude slash, a mocking red cross of the Templars smeared in blood.

'Christ be praised,' he whispered and Jamie, looking up in time to see it, crossed himself.

'For ever and ever.'

They scampered from the place, half-dragging the man while

his comrade sat on, oblivious, in the reek from the burning knight.

When they had reached their own camp, dumped the Welshman and told their tale, there were dark looks flung at the archer; as Gib's Peggie said, even if it was a Templar steeped in sin it was not the Welsh who should be burning him but the Holy Mother Church and after guilt had been established.

Few, Hal noted, had ever liked the Templars, the supposed Poor Knights who arrogantly flaunted their wealth and power. No-one now questioned that these same knights were steeped in sin and he wondered how long it would be before the Inquisition writ stretched to *nobiles* who bore any semblance of the Templar cross, or had connection to them. The shivering blue cross of his own shield glowed like an accusation when he glanced at it.

The Auld Templar of Roslin, he added to himself, was well out of it these days but he had foreseen the ruin the Order had brought on itself the day they charged down Wallace at Falkirk, led by a brace of venal Masters who thought more of Longshanks' favour than their vows.

Most disturbing of all, of course, was the fact that it threw a harsh light on all men of God – for if the Templars, who were priests when all said and done, could be so condemned, what of the wee friar? The bishop, the cardinal and – God forgive the thought – the Pope?

More pressing problems drove such thoughts away with the flies. The English, it had been noted, were on the move, north and east towards Perth. Hal wanted away from here, to where the Scots army was assembling; the archer would be missed soon enough and Hal did not want to be near when the searching commenced – but there was time for a swallow of small beer and a bite of bread.

Good bread, but not as good as the stuff in France, as Jamie loftily pointed out.

'They make it with cheese in. Shaped in a ring and mair

265

pastry than dough. *Gougere*, they call it an' it is a recipe from angels themselves, you would swear.'

The others nudged each other and Sore Davey cleared his throat.

'Is that the way of it right enough, Sir Jamie?' he asked, bland and innocent as a nun at prayer. 'Bigod, you are the one for style in France. Is it there you learned to comb shite in yer hair?'

The laughter was long and loud, so that Jamie, dark and bristling, looked on the point of exploding – until he saw Dog Boy's grin and subsided with a rueful one of his own.

'Lesson learned,' he said to Sim, who nodded and handed him a leather flask of water, then helped him clean his curling hair, though a deal of lovelock had to be roughly hacked off with a knife, with much expression of disgust, which added to the chuckles.

Hal watched the Welshman, bound and afraid and miserably smeared with his own shite, which no-one offered to clean. Not that it would have mattered – after an hour, everyone mounted and moved off, the prisoner half-trotting, half-dragged behind Wynking Wull; each time Hal looked guiltily at the Welshman's bruised face and bloody flayed elbows and knees, the smell of the burning knight came back to him, driving all mercy out.

They followed the English army for an hour or more, tracking them by cart ruts and the ordure, horse and human, which slimed their trail. There were sick and runaways, too, most of whom fled at the approach of a band of riders; those who were too weak or stupid were ridden down and killed by men with the stink of burned flesh still cloyed in their nostrils.

It was a fair-sized force of several long hundreds, Hal thought – but no King Edward in it. *Satan has sent his lesser imp, de Valence to pitchfork us back to order.*

Another hour convinced Hal the English were headed for

Perth and he decided to break off following them, cut away with their prisoner to Scone, where he hoped the Scots were still assembling. He was growing wary with the approach of night, sure that the English would have heard of their dogged presence and be taking steps against it with their own light horse, the prickers and hobilars Hal did not want to meet.

They came up over a small rise, with the last of the day breathing itself out into a muggy dusk of insect whine and zip and halted, the garrons fretting, flicking tails and tossing their heads against the vicious bites.

Dirleton Will, scouting ahead, suddenly appeared, flogging his garron in a dead run into the pack of them, pointing behind him.

'Horse . . . three prickers chasing a lone man,' he panted. 'They will be on us in an eyeblink.'

There was a flurry of panic and scowls, brandished weapons and a few shouts but they had barely sorted themselves when the lone rider bounded up over the brackened lip of the rise, checked a little at the sight of them, then plunged down like a grateful bird to a nest.

The three hobilars who rode after him, closing in like harrying wolves, suddenly found they had charged into a pack of hunting dogs. Jamie Douglas, Dirleton Will and Mouse led the rush on them and there was a moment of squealing, flailing and blood which Hal tried to ignore as he faced the lone rider.

Browns and muted greens made the man a shadow in the shadows, the worn patch of him at odds with the way he carried himself and the voice he used to greet them; the way he moved was as slow and careful as a strange dog.

'God be praised,' he said.

'For ever and ever.'

The tension slackened a little because men had weapons ready and Sim's big latchbow, spanned and quarrelled, was level, though it weaved and wavered with the irritated movement of his horse.

'Unsmart that monster,' the stranger said with a foreign lilt to his voice that Hal knew was French, 'for if it goes off now, the dance of it is as likely to hit yourself as me.'

Sim scowled, though he lowered it and the stranger brought his arms carefully in, resting both hands lightly on the front of his saddle. Jamie Douglas plunged up on his excited, bouncing garron, grinning and waving a bloody sword.

'All dead,' he declared in French. 'English hobilars . . . is this who they were chasing?'

Hal was suddenly irritated by the young lord of Douglas, but he managed a smile.

'My lord James of Douglas,' he said to the saturnine rider, trying to be elegant in French himself. 'I am . . .'

'Sir Hal, the lord of Herdmanston and friend of the King,' the man declared with a twist of smile.

'I know you. My name is Rossal de Bissot,' he added and Hal's eyebrows went up at that, for he knew the name well, suddenly saw the face more clearly.

'You brought the Rood,' he answered, breaking into English, seeing now the carriage of the man, a Templar travelling in secret; the one broiled alive on his horse leaped to his mind and his throat so that, before he could stop, the mention of it burst past his lips.

De Bissot nodded, his eyes hard in a blank face and his accented English was terse and clipped.

'You saw the abomination?'

'I smelled it,' he answered and Sim Craw growled that he had seen it. Hal's eyes told de Bissot all that was needed and he sighed.

'It is a heathen thing from Outremer,' he said, flat as a blade. 'Crusaders brought tales of it back and the Welsh took to it when their lands were invaded. A Cantref Roast they call it there and they did it against every English knight they could ambush during the wars. Left them like markers to put the fear in, like a gaff on a fish.'

268

'Aye, weel,' grunted Sim, squinting to understand the man's way of speaking, 'they had reason, no doubt.'

De Bissot turned glassed eyes on him and nodded.

'In the name of God,' he said, 'I have ridden down fleeing women, burst the heads of children, thrown old men on the pyres of their own homes, committed more bloody ruin on the unarmed and innocent than any priest can stand to hear in confession.'

'In the name of God and against the heathen,' Hal attempted, but the fish stare swung blankly on to him.

'I did it against the Welsh, who were not considered Christian enough for mercy. This is one reason the Order is cursed by God.'

Folk shifted uneasily at this confession; it was one thing to hear the gleeful, whispered rumours, another to have one of God's own soiled angels admit his heresy.

'No man, cursed or other, deserves to be cooked like a haunch.'

The Dog Boy's voice was firm and sure, cutting through them all to place a ghost of smile on the shadowed face of de Bissot.

'The one they did it to here was called Jehan de Chaumont, a brave knight of the Order, who sacrificed himself so I might escape.'

'Escape?'

Rossal de Bissot nodded, broke back into swift French.

'My task is to try and preserve as much of the Order as I can from the ruin it has brought on itself. The Comyn are working against me and are now friends of the English – so their enemies are my friends. The Comyn would prefer me removed from the world, so your king sought to see myself and young Jehan – may God wrap him in His Arms – safe to France, but a certain Malise Bellejambe had different ideas. He is the . . .'

'I know who he is,' Hal interrupted, feeling the sinking

stone drag down to his bowels. 'Malise Bellejambe fell out of Satan's arse at birth and has been trying to find his way back ever since. He snared the wrong man – not the first time he has made such a mistake, but ruin for your friend, de Chaumont. Do you need help on your journey?'

'I do not,' de Bissot replied levelly, rising heavily to his feet. 'I thought you might care to know – the man your king sent with us was taken and is now a prisoner. Bellejambe and some Comyn riders are taking the man to Berwick. If you wish to save him, you must move swiftly.'

Hal knew the name as if God had whispered it in his ear, but he asked anyway.

'Kirkpatrick,' de Bissot answered and the shadows of his face writhed in a wry smile. 'I saved his life once before, in London. I cannot, this time, afford to try alone.'

The name, even allowing for the French knight's way with it, brought all the heads up and a silence which stretched to wrap the sound of the Templar's mount chewing the bit and shaking its head against the flies.

Hal finally turned into the grim, inquiring faces and laid the matter out like a length of poor cloth. It was received in silence for a moment, then men shifted and spoke.

'Kirkpatrick? Are you wit-struck?'

Sim's face was dark and truculent, a scowl which rasped Hal for no reason he could pin.

'Aye,' he answered. 'The De'il o' red murder hissel' – in need o' our aid.'

'Have you taken leave of your sense?' Mouse demanded and there were murmurs of agreement. Then Mouse saw Hal's face and added, hastily: 'Lord.'

'A hard task, right enough,' Clem Graham added sombrely. 'Your man is in fetters for sure and surrounded by Comyn, thick as fleas on an auld dug.'

'You are after wanting us to pluck him out, lord,' Dirleton Will summarized, inspecting hard cheese for the worst of the mould. 'From the teeth of the row we have already caused snatching away a Welsh archer, with folk out on the search for us.'

He popped a piece of de-moulded cheese in the middle of his beard where his mouth should be and chewed once or twice.

'And this Kirkpatrick is the same wee mannie who promised ye a bad turn, first chance he could take,' he added pointedly, so that those around him growled agreement as to the man having put himself beyond all aid by his own foul actions.

'Working for Templars,' added Fingerless Tam, nodding his point to those who looked his way. 'Who worship Baphomet.'

Rossal de Bissot heard that and shifted slightly in his saddle.

'They say,' he murmured, 'that God and all His angels have turned their backs on the Order of Poor Knights. Yet some of us hold to the vows.'

There was silence while folk turned that round in their heads, then Chirnside Rowan waved midges away from his face and snorted derision.

'Away wi' ye Tam Scott,' he jeered. 'Ye would not ken a Baphomet if it came up and beshat ye.'

There was laughter and Nebless Sandie, with a sly look at Jamie, took his chance.

'Ask Sir Jamie,' he declared, 'for it seems some Baphomet loited on his lovelocks only recent.'

'If he did,' Jamie Douglas answered, whip-smart, 'then Baphomet is a Welshman. If you have the belly for it, lads, there are a wheen of wee Baphomets over by, waiting for you to take a closer look.'

There were mutters at this dig on their courage, but Hal knew his men well; courage they had in plenty, but there was a deal of practical in it.

'It is fey, this plan,' Bull rumbled and, since he seldom said anything at all, the astonishment provided silence for him. He looked surprised himself and grew uneasy under the stares until he stared at his stirrups and grew red in the face. But Sim had spotted the grim jut of Hal's beard.

'You are set on this, then?' he demanded.

'I am a dubbed knight,' Hal said, feeling the closing jaws of it even as he spoke. 'I might only be a wee one from the Lothians, but the obligation is on me for it. Besides – Malise Bellejambe is overdue his reward.'

Those who remembered the murder of Tod's Wattie nodded and the others had heard enough of it to want to be part of a vengeance.

'Well said,' Jamie declared cheerfully. 'Count me with this *mesnie*, for I am a knight with no less honour than any here.'

'No knight me,' Sim Craw rumbled, 'but my honour is as fine.'

Dirleton Will stirred at that and shook his head.

'Away, Sim – ye are ower auld for chargin' into folk as if in a tourney fight. Better ye leave that to *nobiles* and folk who dinna need to roll out o' their beds in the middle of the night to take a pish.'

'Ye slaverin' wee lume. I will show ye auld – ye will reflect on it when I take ye by the clap of the hass and rip the harigails from ye . . .'

'Easy,' Hal said warningly and Sim subsided while Dirleton Will, unfazed by a threat to grab him by the throat and tear out his entrails, held up placatory palms to the scowling Sim and ruined it with a wicked sickle of smile.

Hal listened to the dry laughter, hoarse as a wind through stubble and knew it for the whistle in the dark that it was. Even this fearful, the Herdmanston men would still ride to war and Hal was sure much of it had to do with what the Welsh had done to the Templar knight in the pyre; he now had a name and that added to the horror for those who had seen and smelled him.

'If you will give me a brace of good men,' de Bissot declared,

'I will strike at their rear while you strike at their head. If, in the middle of this, someone can pluck Kirkpatrick free, we will have done God's work this day. Speed and surprise.'

'Och aye,' Jamie Douglas declared, his grin wild, the Dog Boy a feral mirror on his right. 'God's work. We are the braw lads for that, mark me.'

CHAPTER TWELVE

The Abbey of Scone
The same day . . .

He made a face and twisted the scar into a snake writhe.

'Christ's Bones, that's foul.'

Isabel's glance at the King was fouler still as she collected the bowl.

'Yon Cathar never fed me anything so sour,' Bruce persisted, smacking his mouth in a grimace of disgust.

'He never fed you anything worthwhile,' Isabel answered tartly, 'and has run off besides. A wee proscribed French Cathar Perfect, heart-afraid for his life now that he has shackled himself to a usurping king declared red murderer and about to be cast loose from Holy Mother Church. Now you have only me.'

'Aye, speak plain why don't you? Never bother sweetening it, woman.'

'You are a king and supposed to be stronger than others. Besides, I sweetened the brew I gave you with honey and spices and it seems to have made little difference to the taste.'

'What was in it?' he asked suddenly, his voice quiet; she heard the fear threnody in it.

'Rue, valerian, fox's clote, lady's bedstraw and laurel among others. This is an ointment of radish – do not swallow it, rub it on.'

'Will it work?'

She looked at him and smiled.

'It is not a cure for lepry,' she said, 'if that is indeed what you have. For that, any blessed water will be as good.'

'Then why am I poisoning myself with it?' he demanded, truculent as a babe.

'Because it will help with the skin complaint you do have, which is common enough and nothing to do with the lepry,' she answered. 'At worst the lady's bedstraw might dye your beard yellow, while the radish ointment, if you spread it on Lady Day, will keep you in funds all year if Hildegard of Bingen is to be believed.'

He heard her tone and lost his irritation in an instant. She had always dabbled in herbs and potions, he knew, but he thought it was merely a mild woman's interest, like they had in wool thread or good needles. He said as much, while managing to marvel at her expertise enough to rob the patronising sting of it.

'Better still,' she answered, 'is that you can trust me with the secret. That scar is a worry, certes, but there is nothing here that makes me believe in lepry, Robert.'

'The signs are slow,' Bruce replied and it was clear he had found out all he could. 'They take years to manifest.'

That was true, but Isabel refrained from pointing out that the usual first signs were when the appendages started to rot – the end of the nose and fingers. And the prick.

'I would stop hiding it,' she said. 'Once the skin clears, you can let the air and sun to that scar, which will do more than your hodden hoods. Besides – the mark of a great tourney knight is to have at least one scar on the face, to make women swoon and men cower.'

'Christ, Izz,' Bruce said, shaking his head and smiling. 'I should have married you.'

'Instead, you cast me back to my husband and married an earl's daughter. That will learn you.'

'I am a king now,' he growled, eyeing her sideways. 'You are not supposed to speak so.'

'You are a great bairn,' she answered lightly, 'who cannot sup a wee grue without making a face. Besides – we have both made our respected beds and now must lie in them.'

Bruce relaxed, tried not to pick skin from his cheeks.

'Aye – how is the master of Herdmanston?'

'More bitter these days than the brew you swallowed,' she replied brutally. 'His lands are scorched, his castle slighted, his folk scattered – and that done by those he has sworn fealty to. God help him when his enemies get to work.'

'I hope he knows the necessity of it,' Bruce answered suspiciously, then sighed wearily. 'I do not need to lose more good men. There are few enough as it is.'

Faintly through the thick walls, they both heard the sound of the few good men, drilling frantically in pike squares while their women stitched and sewed thick gambeson coats, the quilted flutes stuffed with straw.

'He will stick,' she said firmly, then gathered up her jars and packets. 'Now I must attend your wife in the role you gave me – lady to a queen.'

'An honour well earned,' he answered and she smiled wryly.

The last time she had seen the Queen she had been riding a palfrey using a *sambue*, a sidesaddle so elegant and so useless that the horse had to be led because the rider had no control of it. She and her new coterie were discussing the chansons of Guilhem and pointedly fell silent when Isabel approached; it annoyed Isabel, but only because all the other women were local wives and daughters who should know better – but the court, she knew, had a way of corrupting.

'An honour that does not sit well with Her Grace,' she answered, 'which you might have known. Bad enough I placed the crown on her head without constantly attending her as a reminder of how I was once her husband's hoor.'

'God in Heaven, Izzie – moderate yer tongue.'

He rose and paced for a moment, then rounded on her.

'Is she aggrieved?'

Her look was enough and he shook his head.

'I do not know what . . .' he began, then stopped and let his hands drop to his side.

'Start mending that fence,' she answered. 'Dine with her. Spend time with her. Else you will find the chasm too broad to leap.'

He straightened, breathed deeply, then nodded and turned to her with a smile.

'Good advice and good treatment. God keep you, Isabel – and your Herdmanston lord.'

'I trust he is safe,' she said and felt the deep, welling panic that he was not.

When she was gone, he went to a scrip on the table and pulled out the small, stoppered bottle, opened it and put a finger in. It came out bloody and he sniffed it suspiciously. Was that rot?

He sighed. Probably. He should have known better, even if the bottle was gilded and the cap jewelled, to have bought it from his confessed heretic Cathar physicker, even if it came wrapped in vellum and sealed with the Order's double-mounted knights as provenance. Yon wee pardoner, Lamprecht, would probably have sold me the same, he thought wryly.

He glanced at the crumpled parchment, knowing the Latin on it by heart – *Hoc quicumque stolam sanguine proluit, absergit maculas; et roseum decus, quo fiat similis protinus Angelis.*

Whomsoever bathes in the divine blood cleanses his sins and acquires the beauty of angels.

He looked at the beautiful little bottle which had done nothing at all for him. What had he expected? That the blood which flowed from His Hands and Feet had been collected in this, then translated across the centuries, miraculously, to arrive at Bruce's moment of need?

Perhaps it was. Perhaps it really was His Divine Blood and not the escape fund of a cunning, desperate physician. He felt a chill at the idea – better it was chicken or pig, for if even the Blood of Christ Himself had failed, where did that leave King Robert Bruce?

Yet, he thought, can Christ still save the world? All the signs are against it, Lord, and there are so few righteous left in a kingdom ravaged by endless strife, where Your flock is reduced to individuals and petty tribes suffering and killing one another.

But there was a Plan. If I am not here then barbarism and madness become law, the weak have their throats cut or become slaves and the future is a terrible nightmare of cruelty and bloodletting.

I am the leash, he thought. The leash and the lash and even tormented by the Curse of Malachy I will never give in. He thought of Wallace, saw the twist of his bloody face on the day they gralloched him like a caught stag. He thought of his part in it.

I think, he said aloud, that the wee Cathar was right – this world is, in fact, Hell.

And there is no other.

Near Cupar, Fife
That same moment . . .

Hell vomited over the ridge. Malise saw it, falling like some huge wave of horses that seemed to snarl, ridden by open-mouthed men desperate with fear and an anger that was as good as courage.

He had been watching Kirkpatrick, stumbling along behind

Malenfaunt's horse, falling now and then to be dragged when Malenfaunt, vicious and laughing, spurred it a little to make it too fast for Kirkpatrick to keep up.

'Walk faster,' he would yell, 'else you will be dragged to Carlisle.'

No-one but Malise understood the gabble of him, but all understood what he was doing. A few of the other *serjeants* laughed, harsh as old crows, but most did not and the leader of them frowned disapprovingly, for it was his charge to get this prisoner alive to Carlisle and then to the King himself.

What happened then, Sir Godard Heron thought, is none of my concern – but one of the red murderers of the Comyn leader would not be treated lightly. Still, he did not care for this Malenfaunt, a foresworn knight who should have lost his right hand, at the very least, for losing a joust before God.

Malise was thinking that he would have to begin to persuade Malenfaunt to find a horse for Kirkpatrick, not least because they were ambling along as if on a ride through a deer park, too slow for anyone's liking. Mostly because Kirkpatrick looked the worse for being dragged by a thin rope fastened round Malenfaunt's waist and he knew the Earl of Buchan wanted this one alive to face the King's questioners; it was essential Kirkpatrick admit his witness to the usurper Robert Bruce's murder of Badenoch.

He was on the point of saying so when the riders sprang up over the ridge and poured down on them, shrieking like the *bean-shìdh*.

Hal saw that the *mesnie* were well-armed and armoured, *serjeants* mounted on decent horses, though he thanked the good God that there were no warhorses among them, not even under the knight with the herons on jupon and shield.

He saw all this in the eyeblink it took to cover the twenty or so strides down the gentle slope, the garrons half-stumbling through the gripping-beast bracken, to plough into the centre of the milling mass of riders, a stone in the confused pool of it.

Hal rode close, almost belly to belly with the taller palfrey, which was wild-eyed and pawing the air. Hal backhanded the rider with a sweep of his shivering-crossed shield, cut across himself and missed, then was plunged on by the squealing, half-panicked garron he rode.

He reined it in viciously, trying to turn, saw Chirnside Rowan hook a *serjeant* out of the saddle while Nebless Sandie half-trampled, half-stabbed the luckless man with a furious flurry of blows. The knight with silver herons on his blue shield cut hard and savage and Nebless arched, howled and went off the garron like a half-filled sack of grain. Hal lost them in the sudden whirl of bodies, saw Jamie Douglas charge down on the head of the column, his face wild with mad delight – and then his world reeled.

The man who did it wore a new blue cloak and a feral snarl under a bristle of moustache, battering Hal's bascinet with the wheel pommel of his sword while fighting to keep his horse facing front. Hal got his sword in the way of another cut, the bell clang of it loud even in the shriek and scream of the fight; the snarling-dog whirl of it broke them apart, then Blue Cloak surged back.

What did I ever do to him, Hal thought wildly, as the blows thundered on his shield, that he seeks me out?

Because he sees you as leader, he answered himself in the calm centre of the maelstrom within him. If you are downed, they win.

He flailed with the sword, stabbed, felt it hit, saw the grimace of pain that twisted the black moustache and felt a surge of triumph at that. He took a blow on his shield, another that whipped the ailettes off one shoulder, a third that cut a deep groove in the cantle of the saddle. The sweat rolled in his eyes, he slashed hard, saw the edge dent the arming cap and rattle Blue Cloak's head sideways, saw the sudden limpness of the man as he fell away into the storm of hooves and mud.

'*Deus lo vult.*'

The cry brought Hal's head up briefly, as he fought for control of the garron, which just wanted to be away from this horror and was fighting the bit so hard he had to use both hands, awkward with sword and shield, to hold it steady. With the clear part of his blood-flushed head, he saw that Rossal de Bissot had timed it perfectly, waiting until the rear of the column had started to spur forward into the fight before launching his attack, bellowing the Templar warcry.

It was that which broke them – that and Malise. He had watched, stunned, as the riders fell on them, saw the shivering blue cross and knew who it was at once. There had been a long, long time of sitting, it seemed to him, watching the men on their little horses dart in with their long, vicious spears which seemed to include a hook and an axe as well. It was no longer than a few breaths, but he would have sat there forever, like a huddled rabbit, watching the slow curl and snarl of it – save for the cry.

Deus lo vult. It snapped him from the moment like a bell in a sleeping man's ear. He heard himself whimper, his head full of all the vengeance that could be visited on him from the owners of both the shivering cross and the warcry – then he reined the palfrey round so that it screamed with the pain of the bit and spur and sped away like a gazehound on a scent.

Some *serjeants* saw him, which took their panic to the winking brim, then spilled it over; they hauled their own mounts round and spurred away after him; Hal saw them go, felt the sheer exultant relief, the shock of it. We have actually won this, he thought to himself.

Kirkpatrick loomed up at the plunging feathered feet of Hal's garron. He had turned his back on a rider, seemed to be hauling on a rope like a man pulling on a heavy cart and he glanced up at Hal and grinned through the bloody bruise of his face.

Malenfaunt, fighting the horse, cutting furiously at speeding figures on little horses who would not stand still, suddenly felt himself flying backwards as the animal surged forward, hitting the ground so hard it drove the air from him. He knew, with a sudden stab of fear, thin and cold as a blade, that Kirkpatrick had hauled him from the saddle by the rope that bound them both.

'Kirkpatrick,' Hal yelled, grabbing the horse's bridle. A maddened rouncey plunged, bucking, from a knotted tangle of war and the rider, shield and sword both gone, hung on with both hands until a vicious backhand swipe took him in the ribs and swept him from the saddle.

Sim Craw, his face like a wineskin of blood and streaming sweat, whirled a sword in one hand to flick the gore from it and forced his garron to Hal's side scowling down at Kirkpatrick like a father on an awkward son.

'Move yersel',' he growled.

Kirkpatrick hirpled up and into the saddle of Malenfaunt's horse, an agonizingly slow process to Hal, bouncing on the back of his own maddened garron. He could not believe his eyes when he saw Kirkpatrick pause, take the cord that fastened his lacerated wrists and loop it carefully round the cantle of the saddle.

'In the name o' God, Kirkpatrick,' he bellowed, 'ride, ye sow's arse – we do not have all this day.'

They rode, breaking from the fray while Dirleton Will, Sore Davey, Mouse and others closed round them protectively. In another minute they were forging back up the slope, riders joining them in dribs and drabs as they broke off from the fight.

It took Hal another minute to realize that Kirkpatrick's horse was ploughing harder than the others because he was towing something behind him, heavy as a log, rolling backwards and forward and shrieking.

Malenfaunt.

They rode on at a flogging canter for a few more minutes, then Hal brought them to a panting, sweating halt, the garrons splay-legged. Men dropped from the saddle on buckling legs; Hob o' the Merse puked, bent over, hands on knees and Sore Davey was weeping like a bairn, his pustuled face twisted.

'Find how many are missing,' Hal ordered Sim and he nodded grimly.

'We dinna have long,' he warned. 'They are good *serjeants*, who will be black affronted to have been bested by hobby horse like us. They will be after us when they have collected their wits.'

Hal nodded, crossed to where Kirkpatrick wobbled by the side of the horse; he cut the man's wrists free with a swift gesture.

'Ye are hurt?'

Kirkpatrick's head echoed and he felt sick, while he only knew he was standing because he was upright, for his legs felt like wood, but he waved one hand and managed a grin. He could not understand why Hal had done what he had done and said so.

'I am wondering the same,' Hal answered grimly. 'When I ken the cost, I will give ye an answer.'

'Regardless,' Kirkpatrick answered in French, 'I am in your debt. I rescind our quarrel and am grateful to do so.'

That was something at least, Hal thought, stepping through the bracken to where the moaning figure writhed at the end of the cord. Malenfaunt looked up through a mist of blood and fire and saw the face.

'Aeel,' he said mournfully. 'Aeel.'

'What's he say?' demanded Chirnside Rowan, all bland curiosity.

'He yields,' Hal answered, then frowned. 'I think.'

He was distracted by a knot of men riding in, including Rossal de Bissot and Jamie Douglas, still grinning from his sweating face and reliving the fight with the Dog Boy, the pair of them laughing as they did so.

'Fower are gone,' Sim muttered in Hal's earshot. 'Nebless

Sandie, Andra, Roslin Rob an' Blue Tam. Nebless an' Andra are corpses, certes an' the others will no' survive the Heron's hatred.'

Which accounted for Sore Davey's snot and tears – Andra was his brother.

Kirkpatrick heard it, looked up and into the grey haar of Hal's eyes. Four lost to save him; it was a harsh price for the Herdmanston lord and Kirkpatrick knew it. He heard de Bissot murmur '*Ave Maria, gratia plena*' and found the Templar's eyes with his own.

'My thanks for your part in my rescue,' he said in French. 'I am afraid I am hardly suitable escort now.'

De Bissot looked at the figure, tattered and bloodied, his hands lacerated and his face lashed and scarred. There was a rib or two suffering in there, too, he thought and nodded.

'I will make my own way, with the help of God,' he said and turned to Hal.

'You have the thanks of the Order,' he said. 'We will meet again, you and I.'

Then he rode away, leaving Hal staring at his back and wondering, chilled, if that had been some blasphemous Templar prophecy. Malenfaunt's moans broke him from it and Sim's voice, urging movement, was sharp.

Kirkpatrick lumbered stiffly over to Malenfaunt, bent and searched, then came up with a smile and his fluted dagger.

'My knife – I thought so,' he declared, blood welling from his lips with his burst grin. 'Murderer and weapon both, to be presented in triumph to English Edward.'

He glanced at the misery that was Malenfaunt, now climbed to his knees and swaying.

'How the world turns, Malenfaunt,' he sibilated in blood-spitted French. Then, before anyone could move, the dagger flashed. Hal heard a hiss, like the puncture of a bloated sheep and Malenfaunt cried out, wide-eyed and staring, one hand clamped to the side of his punctured neck and blood spuming through his fingers. No-one else made a move, Hal saw.

'I have ruined that part of you called "the heart in the throat",' Kirkpatrick said softly, almost dreamily as men stared, horrified, at the whimpering Malenfaunt, his mouth opening and closing like a gasping fish.

'You will die and only God can halt it, though I doubt He will. They say you experience visions o' great wonder an' beauty, dyin' in this slow, peaceful fashion.'

Malenfaunt tried to struggle to his feet, but he was already too weak and sank back, a strange, blissful look on his face as the blood poured like a cataract. Kirkpatrick's face turned hard as a rolling millstone.

'I would not give ye the gift,' he added and took the dagger low and hard into Malenfaunt's eye, straight through to the brain, so that the man's last astounded look was open-mouthed with the horror and shrieking agony of it, the snake-fork of his ruined tongue flickering.

Folk turned aside as the knight collapsed and bled.

'Christ,' Jamie Douglas said, half in disgust and half admiration, 'you are a hard man, Kirkpatrick.'

Kirkpatrick said nothing, simply looked at Hal with the wasteland of his face and hirpled back to his horse.

'I have met corpse-strippin' hoors with softer hearts,' Sim called after him, ripe with disapproval. 'Away home and nurse yer injuries – keep out of the road of decent folk for a while.'

Kirkpatrick turned, bleak as a long roll of winter moorland.

'Like yersel',' he answered bitterly, 'I have no home. Unlike yersel', I have never owned to such a thing, so it is no loss.'

He crawled up on to the horse, the blood squeezing from between his ruined fingers as he took up the reins and cast away the rope that tied himself to a corpse.

'Never fear, Sim Craw,' he said, his voice thick with new weariness, 'I will be back among ye afore long. Mark me.'

'Ride,' Hal ordered brusquely, wondering if anyone would have a home when all this was done. He climbed wearily on to the trembling, sweated garron and paused to look down at the raggled remains of Malenfaunt, lying in a slow-spreading viscous tarn of his own blood.

This was red war, he thought, a war of the dragon unleashed and chivalry, even for the yielded, was now as lost as the Grail itself.

CHAPTER THIRTEEN

Methven
Vigil of the Translation of the Relics of St Margaret, June, 1306

In the murmuring night, spiced with woodsmoke and heavy as musk in the summer heat, the delegation came up between the lamplit panoplies, a series of shifting shadows flitting past the fumes of cooking fish and turnip, threading through the warm, fetid horse lines. They moved like ghosts in their dark robes to where the great pavilion stood with the yellow banner, the red lion on it limp.

The warleader's tent, Abbot Alberto saw, was dressed as Brother Jacobus had told him to expect – studied, with all the treasured care lavished on a concubine. There were swinging lanterns with mica panels, clean planked flooring strewn with fresh grasses and wildflowers, small tables with bowls of expensive *pistacia*, sugared almonds and *gingibar*.

The faces that met him from under the fine, ribbon-sewn hangings were not hostile, simply those of men with work to do, impatient, confident and competent. Somewhere behind a curtained recess he heard the low murmur of women's voices.

Bruce considered the little Italian Abbot carefully. Not much to look at, he thought, so all the more dangerous. A Visconti

287

with the ear of the Pope and so doubly so, yet he had not come, as Bruce had feared, bringing the *ferendae sententia* – the sentence of the ecclesiastic court – and ready to remove Bruce from Holy Church with bell, Book and candle.

That was something, at least, thought Bruce, though that Papal Bull is charging on its way. It only remained to find out why this Visconti was here and if it was as he claimed – he bore a message from Aymer de Valence, currently crouched like a wary dog in Perth and challenged by Bruce to come out fighting.

'I trust,' he said, smooth and guarded, 'your visit to our kingdom has been successful so far.'

The abbot ignored the 'our kingdom' and glanced at the one they called the Bruce. Tall, hard-faced – as they all were – with a bad scar on one cheek and a surprisingly neat beard. The one to his right was a squatter version, a dancing bear of a man with a bush of beard and he was sure this was the brother called Edward. The others were all the same to the abbot – warriors who followed.

'So far,' he answered urbanely, 'though King Edward would dispute the claim that it is your kingdom. Even if you are prepared to defend it – what was it you wrote to him, my lord? With the longest stick you have.'

'Your Grace,' corrected a stern voice. 'He is king.'

The abbot fluttered apologetic fingers.

'Do you come from the Covetous King?' asked Bruce coldly, forcing through the abbot's breach of royal etiquette which, he knew, had been no mistake.

'I come from the Holy Father, my son,' the abbot replied smoothly, 'to examine the commanderies of his Order of Poor Knights in the kingdoms of his brother in Christ, King Edward.'

'Found any good heresies?' interrupted the dancing bear; the abbot saw the flicker of irritation that crossed the elder Bruce's face at it.

'None of any note,' he answered and heard Brother Jacobus grunt and shift. He almost smiled at it; at least this usurper king and I share that in common – irritating minions. None was more rasping than Brother Jacobus, one of those dogs the Holy See found useful to let off the leash now and then, but whose constant whine and bark on their singleminded nosing was annoying.

The abbot knew that Brother Jacobus was clerk to Geoffrey D'Ablis, the Inquisitor in Carcassonne, and would return there in the spring. He also knew the man's real name was Jean de Beaune, because he had reverted to it on the treatises he had begun to write detailing the proper way to carry out inquisitions; it seemed this sin of pride had been ignored in general admiration for this rising star.

'Brother Jacobus thinks differently,' the abbot replied smoothly, without looking at the Hound of God. 'We have scoured the Poor Knights of the Order in . . . what is it called? Balan . . . something.'

'Balantrodoch,' growled the dancing bear. The abbot smiled. 'Yes. Outlandish name.'

'You found no heresies, you say,' Bruce offered, steering the conversation back to the path.

'Indeed. A few writings of no account . . .'

'Heathen heresy,' Brother Jacobus interrupted and Bruce saw the abbot close his eyes briefly, as if that triggered some damping of his temper. The abbot, opening them again, saw Bruce's benign curiosity and shrugged.

'Brother Jacobus believes that a treatise concerning how the earth revolves around the sun is a dangerous wickedness, so that all who own such should be burned. But there – I have voiced it aloud and now put all our souls in mortal peril. Brother Jacobus' pyre will need to be large.'

His scathing clamped the Hound of God's lips in a tight line. Bruce knew this Jacobus well enough, for he had been hag-haunting the Kingdom for a decade at least, flitting between York, Berwick and Edinburgh in pursuit of God knew what.

Before that, he had been told, the Hound of God had been in the entourage of Cressingham at Stirling Brig and had come there fresh from scourging Carcassone's Cathars. Bruce had learned all this from Kirkpatrick and his missing physicker – he wondered where the latter now was and what he was revealing. And to whom . . .

'I thought the earth was the centre of things,' said Edward Bruce, frowning and the abbot indulged him with another smile, his withered cheeks knobbed as winter apples.

'Just so. This . . . heresy, as the good brother would have it . . . is a heathen affair, as he says. Moorish, though it was Saracen before that and, in fact, Persian before that. They were all Godless worshippers of fire then and the Sun, being the largest of fires, was a deity to them; thus they placed it at the centre of things.'

He laced his fingers.

'In fact, it is no heresy. If I state that a galloping horse does not move forward, but rather the ground goes backwards – is that heresy? Or simple stupidity?'

'If enough believe it . . .' Brother Jacobus muttered and the abbot ignored him.

'So the Poor Knights of the Order are innocent of the charges against them?' Bruce asked.

'What charges are these?' countered the abbot. 'No charges have been made. The Order is guilty of arrogance, idleness, outlandish secrets and excessive wealth. What I have are copious sworn statements by come-lately initiates who allege that they refused to spit on the Cross, or kiss an idol of Baphomet. So far, I have seen no evidence of either.'

'Yet heresy exists,' Bruce declared grimly and waved a hand. 'Ask any of these *nobiles* and they will tell you of the sin of the Order.'

The abbot frowned, not understanding.

'Most of them had kin, or were themselves with Wallace at Callendar Woods,' Bruce explained stonily. 'Where the Order rode in the retinue of King Edward and slaughtered our people. Christians, Abbot Alberto, descending like wolves on Christians. Is that not a heresy worthy of the Holy Father's sanction?'

Now the abbot understood and nodded slowly, like a man falling asleep.

'Not heresy. More of that arrogance I mentioned and certainly a sin – that and the other sins they have fallen into are reason enough for them to merge with the Order of St John. Perhaps then these warriors can turn their sights back to God and the relief of his Holy Places.'

'The Order of St John wishes nothing to do with them,' Bruce replied. 'Wisely.'

The abbot tutted.

'We should be wary of casting the first stone,' he said gently. 'The sin of envy is in great part responsible for the problems of the Order – too wealthy by far, as I have said, even to the whispered rumour of usury. Brother Jacobus would have them scorching for that alone, but he and others of his calling have forgotten the teachings of Saint Bernard – "Persecution shows who is a hireling and who a true pastor".'

He paused, his sentiment genuine if only because of the vision of the Templar, strapped to his horse and burning . . .

'Amen,' Bruce answered and a muttered chorus followed it. Jacobus stirred a little, his hands shoved into his sleeves, but remained silent, a cowled mastiff leashed for the moment.

'But you are less interested in this and more in what the English commander in Perth has to say,' the abbot went on. 'He agrees to meet you on the field – but not on the morrow. It is the Sabbath and the Feast of St Gervase, the Martyr.'

'Of Margaret, saintly queen of Scotland and the translation of her relics,' Bruce corrected, that strange lopsided twist of a smile on his face. To avoid stretching the scar on the other, the

291

abbot realized suddenly, which meant it was not healed, even after all this time . . .

'So – we have a truce until the morn's morn?' Edward Bruce persisted.

The abbot hesitated, a heartbeat only that he would not have got away with in the cowled politicking of Rome. What caused it was – yet again – the vision of the burning Templar. That, coupled with the uncaring stone face of de Valence as he excused it, sure in his writ from pope and king, sanctioned by the fluttering of as pagan a symbol as anyone might find – a dragon banner which permitted men to risk any sin.

Yet the heartbeat went unnoticed here and the abbot nodded, for a truce was what he had been told and chivalry dictated the truth of it, even from the thinned, dubious lips of the lordly Aymer de Valence.

There was nothing else to be said; Bruce watched them ghost their way out again and waited for the clamour that would swamp him when they were out of earshot. It was not held back for long and the charge was led, as ever, by Edward.

They throw 'chivalry' at me like an accusation of heresy, Bruce thought, turning into their concern and outrage. There would now be an argument which would, in the end, come to eat itself because there was no way out of the circle.

They all knew it, too, even if they jerked and strained – de Valence was locked securely in Perth with an army roughly the size of the one Bruce had scraped together. The English lords, Percy and Clifford, were scouring the west with another and, somewhere to the south, like a distant stain of thundercloud, the Covetous King himself gathered yet another force with his son.

'If we do not force a fight here and win, my lords,' Bruce declared to their scowls and frowns, 'then we will gain no further support and will be too weak to face Longshanks when he comes. We must defeat de Valence here and to do that, we must persuade him to come out of his fastness and fight.'

If they did not, then my kingship is ended, he thought. Fleetingly, he saw the purse-lipped moue of his wife, preparing the 'I-told-you-so'. King and queen of summer only, she had once said. Unspoken had been the other part of that old pagan custom, where the King of Summer was ritually sacrificed, his blood making the Kingdom and all in it fecund.

Well, that would not be. Winning here, at Methven, would bring some solidity to his throne and, to do that, he needed someone to beat in an honest tourney. He needed to force *apokalupsis*.

He said as much, but only the scholarly Alexander understood that it did not mean the catastrophe it implied, simply a revelation, a new light. A new world.

Chivalry would bring de Valence out for a fair fight, he thought. The joust *à l'outrance*, writ large, would do it.

Because God is always watching at the edge of extremity.

Hal watched the train of priests and their escort coil between the fires, heading out of the camp and the road back to Perth. He heard one mutter '*Te deum*' but they passed in a wraith of silence for the most part, sinister as darkness. He did not care for these *Dominie Canes* much and remembered the ones who had brought Cressingham's ultimatum to Wallace and Moray at Stirling . . . God's Wounds, almost ten years to the day.

Ten years. It weighed on him, sudden and heavy as an anvil and he sighed under it, so that Sim Craw glanced up from under his own shaggy brows – then surprised Hal with his own thoughts.

'I remember thon chiels,' he muttered. 'At Abbey Craig. Christ, Sir Hal, that was a wheen o' years ago.'

'Aye, ye were sprightly then,' chaffered Chirnside, grinning.

'Sprightly still,' Dog Boy replied. 'If you keep charkin' your gums on such, you will find how he can stop your yatter.'

Sim stirred a little, fed a stick and some dried grass to the fire.

'My thanks for yer care, Dog Boy,' he answered, slow and serious, 'but Chirnside is not wrong. A man gets to feel the years pile up an' I am not so spry sometimes in the morn, while I have to roll out at night to let out watter and my bones are mostly ache.'

Men stared, amazed and Hal felt a flicker of uncertain fear, seeing the lines on Sim and the grizzle that was more grey than black these days. He was old, Hal thought suddenly – Christ, he is a handful of years more than me and I am old myself. If he was starting to fail, then the world was trembling . . .

Then he saw the sly look peeping out from under the shag of eyebrow and almost leaped to his feet with the delighted relief of it.

'But I can still maul the sod with the likes o' a cuntbitten hoorslip such as yersel', Chirnside Rowan.'

The hoots and laughter flamed the face of Rowan, while the nudges from his neighbours threatened to topple him off his log seat. He eventually acknowledged Sim's mastery of the moment with a flap of one hand, which turned into a slap against a nipping midge.

'Christ,' he growled. 'We must be the blissin' o' Beelzebub on his Lowland midgies, and if their dinner would only cease slapping them it would be a midgie paradise.'

'These are wee yins,' growled Sim Craw. 'Where Black MacRuiraidh is from they are bigger and thicker, with a stinger like a tourney lance.'

The Lothian men laughed and the butt of the joke joined in. In months past all the Lowlanders would have stared at the Islesman, Black MacRuiraidh, his tangle of jet hair and his big axe, as if he had landed from the Moon itself, but already they were used to him and the others of his kin who had come to join King Robert. Christina of Garmoran had sent them and there were nudges and winks about what their new king had done to this Isles queen to have had such richesse lavished on him.

Scots all, Hal noted, from Chirnside Rowan of the Border, busy feeding a twist of dried bracken into the fire, to the near-unintelligible men of Dingwall beyond The Mounth, who had come, freely enough, defying the Earl of Ross who was not a declared supporter of the Bruce.

Not yet – tomorrow would decide all things.

The galloping horse that was Jamie Douglas burst on them, stirring them like a wind shifting embers from the fire. He stuck bread at the Dog Boy, had shared meat in return and, within minutes, the pair of them were off, restless as hounds into a dusk like smoke and the faint music and screeches of women's laughter.

Life was all in the way a man thought of it, Hal had decided. The way a young man thought of it, in fact, for when the blood was strong and hot the whole earth was new, like a calf waiting to be licked dry.

When he got some years on him, all the same, it was different. Down deep, bone-deep, Hal knew the world was old, so old he wondered sometimes what chiels and lords had been on it before civilized people came to it, before even the dark, fey Faerie.

Jamie Douglas made a man feel old with the knowing that the younger ones believe the world was new and that they alone were discovering it, as if no-one else ever had.

The squeals and shrills of women – God alone knew where they came from, or how they survived – brought grins and the backs of hands to dry mouths from men considering their luck or their siller.

Sim Craw did not think of thighs and quim. He thought of the shrieks of the Welshman, the shit-smeared archer brought in as prisoner and put to the Question; not hard, Sim recalled and, in fact, not hard enough for Sim's liking, for he was sure the man had more he might have told.

Let off light, Sim had thought – until Edward Bruce's retinue men had held the man down, cut off the first two fingers of his right hand, the drawing hand, and seared the wound shut with pitch, for mercy.

'You will never shoot another Scot,' one of them had declared, hands on hips and straddle-legged as the Welshman was set free, hugging his pain to his breast and hirpling off scarce able to see through tears and snot, yet blessing his luck that he was alive. Sim had seen Edward Bruce's scowl at it.

'You should have cut the tongue from him as well,' he had growled, 'so he could not tell what he saw here.'

Hal, on the other hand, was glorious with thoughts of Isabel, somewhere in the rich panoply behind the King's own tent attending to the Queen. In a while he would go off and find her, when he was sure the Queen had been bedded down for the night and that he could claim Isabel for his own.

For now he lay back and looked at the darkening sky, already shot with sharp, bright stars like fresh-struck tinder, listening to the men slap and complain about the whirling moths and midgies.

'If ye listen close,' Bull rumbled, 'ye can hear their war cries. If they were as big as we, no army would stand agin them.'

'Aye, weel,' answered Erchie Scott, 'we needs offer a soul to some wee imp o' Bellies-bub, Lord of Flies, in return for such an army. Then we leave them to fight the English and we can all ride home.'

'God be praised,' declared his brother, Fingerless Tam as he crossed himself. 'To speak it is to summon it – clap yer gums on that, brother.'

'Besides,' yawned Chirnside, 'it is clear there will be no fight on the morn. Yon wee priests will have come to beg King Robert not to break the Sabbath.'

'Away,' scoffed Sim Craw. 'The Sabbath is it? When has that made a difference? When God handed Wallace yon fat Treacherer Cressingham on a silver platter, we fought wee fights with them from one Holy Sabbath Day to the other at

Stirling Brig – and the big battle itself was fought on the Ferial Day after Finian's feast, which is also holy.'

He beamed into their chuckles.

'Holy Days, my wee rievin' ribald,' he added, 'is when we fight best – in the sight o' God.'

Those who remembered the tale of Wallace's triumph nodded into the soft chorus of 'amens', then sat, smeared with the honey memory of that glorious day.

It came to Hal that there were few who had actually been there at the time, kneeling on the wet grass to receive the Sabbath pyx from the monks of Cambuskenneth Abbey. The promise of that day had vanished in hunger and death and defeat so that here they all were, too many years later, still fighting and no closer to victory.

A figure loomed, turning all eyes. He was a middling man in all respects, from height to years, dangled about with maille that seemed more collected than worn and with a battered shield on his back, deviced with something almost too faded to read.

'God be praised,' he said from a weary threadbare face, bushed with grizzled beard.

'For ever and ever,' came the rote reply, then Hal rose up and grasped the man, wrist to wrist. There was a brief exchange of greetings, a request answered at once and the man skliffed off through the trampled grass with a peck of oats for his warhorse.

'Christ betimes,' grumbled Wynking Wull, his tic working furiously with annoyance. 'Bad enough that the likes of the landless Douglas boy can steal our meat. We will all have buckles clappit to backbones if we give out hard-gotten fodder to any raggy chiel who asks.'

'No raggy chiel, but Sir John Lauder of the Bass,' said Sim Craw and proceeded to put them right on the matter while Hal lay back and thought on the likes of Sir John Lauder of the Bass, the least scion of the Lauders who held Bass Rock from Patrick of Dunbar.

Sir John had a wee manor at Whitekirke, a half-stone affair where his 'baists' were quartered below and his family above, a holding barely raised above the level of a villein, though he was a *nobile*.

Yet he had sacrificed even this for the Bruce, slaughtering his beasts, burning his crops and hall, sending his family off to their kin and marching to Methven with the raggles of his father's armour and his grandda's sword.

He had no servants and certainly no warhorse – the peck of oats was for himself and the only food, mixed with a little water, he would eat unless he could beg better without losing the last ragged cloak of his dignity.

In the morning – if there was to be a fight at all – he would take station with a solid square of pikes, shoulder to shoulder with barefoot sokemen and others of lesser rank, closing files and keeping the unwieldy phalanx together until they won or died.

Beside him somewhere would be young Jamie Douglas, a powerful *nobile* of Scotland in his own right, yet no richer now than Lauder of the Bass because the English sat in his castle and took rent from his lands.

Hal thought of Herdmanston under a blue sky, blue as the paint they used on the Virgin's mantle on a church wall, with the good brown earth rolling beneath it and himself between. He put himself in the tower that was his own, with a great feeling that threatened to burst his chest. But for all he tried, squeezing his eyelids tight shut, he could not rid himself of the last rotten-tooth black vision of its stones and the crow-feather smoke staining the sky like a thundercloud.

Gone and gone, like the wee house of Lauder of the Bass by now. All gone, save for the great feeling in his chest and the reason for that lay in the gathered dark, tending to a queen. He got up then, urgent with the need to see her, hold her.

He found her spreading bracken in a bower of bent hawthorn

at the back of the proud tents and she straightened from the task as he approached; he saw the weariness in her.

'How is Her Grace?' he asked and had a Look for it, even as he drew her into the cage of his arms.

'Stoic,' Isabel told him, muffled against his chest, then surfaced for breath.

'Behold, a wee love nest.'

'Brawlie,' he admired, trying to keep the smirk from his face and failing. She struck him lightly on the chest.

'Less to do with your voracious appetite than not wanting to spend another minute in that wee cloister o' weemin,' she informed him and he nodded, sinking on to the soft bracken and feeling her stretch out the length of him.

'Bad is it?'

'Enough to make me consider passing time in the company of any of the men round a fire,' she snorted and he laughed.

'Best not, love,' he advised. 'I would then spend the evening fighting them all, one by one.'

'Ah, gallant knight,' she replied in a strained falsetto. 'Hold me not so tight, you are crushing the rose blossom of me.'

'There will be a few round those fires who would desire to nip your rosy buds,' Hal answered wryly. 'Little they know of the thorns they risk.'

'I need all my thorns for the Queen and her women, so it is hard to put them away easily at the end of day.'

'You need them still?'

Isabel made a 'tsschk' of annoyance.

'The Queen is stoic, as I say. Like some auld beldame faced with fire, flood and famine, for all she is a girl yet. She does not care for it much, but she will dutifully follow her man, to Hell if that is where he is headed. I am sure she believes it lies beyond the next hill.'

'The King's sister is not so bad – Lady Mary is of an age not to have her head turned by events. It is the others,' she went on sourly. 'Good dames o' the court whom I have to remind that I am a countess, even if they sneer at the title these days. An' Marjorie . . .'

She broke off to shake a sorrowful head.

'She is a recent elevation to princess, yet still enough of a bairn to pout about the lack of ermine and pearls, or warm hall being feted by all the young men.'

'Which she would be,' Hal noted, knowing the attraction rank added to a woman, 'for all her chin.'

They grinned at each other, sharing the sly spite on the chin of Bruce's daughter, a heavy inheritance for such a flower. 'You have an interest there?' Isabel demanded archly. 'If you can suffer the chin you will have a princely reward.'

'And leave you to pine in some hawthorn arbour?' he countered. 'Alone and weeping?'

'I am told that has attractions for some.'

'Ach weel – pray for luck that kills me then. Men love to comfort a mourning lover.'

The game ended with her sudden, fierce clutch.

'Weesht on that,' she said, her eyes big and round. 'I am not so stoic a matron that I can listen to that sort of talk.'

'Swef, swef,' he soothed. 'Lamb. Shall I comfort you with the poetry of the Court of Love? Demand you turn the moon of your countenance on the misery of my night?'

'God forbid,' she answered and lay back, suddenly loose and lush. 'I would concentrate on unlacing instead.'

He began, then paused.

'The King will send his queen away in the morn, for safety,' he said into the moonlit pools glowing in her face. 'This may be the last time we see each other for some time.'

'I know it,' she said and buried her face in the curve of his neck and shoulder – then dropped back on to the bracken.

'Are you having trouble with the knots?' she demanded. 'I have dirk if ye need to cut them.'

Afterwards, lying in the strewn bracken bed, he listened to the soft laughter and the sudden chords as Humfy Johnnie struck up a harp tune, his crooked back as bent as his gaping grin.

There was still the wild, strange feeling in Hal as he listened to her breathe softly beside him and, when he fell asleep, he dreamed that the blue sky and the brown earth were tilting him away from her altogether.

He woke in the dark, afraid.

Methven
Translation of the Relics of St Margaret, June, 1306

In the lush of morning, the summer lay on the ground, delicate and soft as a cat's paw. The sun drifted lazily in a sky like deep water, soaking the spread of fields round Methven so that it seemed to Hal that the land lost the pinched skin of itself, softening and rolling under the hooves of the horses. Larks sang, hovering.

They were coming round in a wide sweep, out north and west from the raggle of poverty that was Methven vill, swinging round in a forage that had found nothing but horse fodder and beans.

Half the army, Hal knew, was trying to glean something from the empty basket of this place. He was glad that the household was to be packed up and sent north with two of the Bruce brothers, for it meant Isabel might get a decent meal. He would miss the music of her, all the same.

Sore Davey, scouting ahead, came back at a fast lick, flinging one hand back behind him as he gasped up.

'Men,' he said and, by the time Hal had established where, how many and whether they were on foot or horsed, the rest of the riders had tightened their straps and loosened their weapons.

A column of foot, three wide and deep enough to contain a good hundred, even allowing for Sore Davey's poor tallying and seeing double, was moving at a steady pace up over the fields, having come out of a copse at one side.

Such a column moving without straggling or stravaigin' was certainly not Scots, for none of them were this far out on foot and none were as disciplined on a march. They were no foragers either, who would be in handfuls like thrown gravel, just strong enough to overcome a few peasants and steal their livelihood.

'English,' savoured Chirnside, 'plootering aboot the countryside spierin' out chickens.'

In threes, neat as a hem? Hal voiced the doubt aloud and those with heads agreed, nodding soberly. Still – there was nothing to be done with his twenty riders but take a look, so they rode forward, steady and careful, to where the column scarred across the green grain, cutting a careless swathe through it. Some snatched ears, even though it was unripe and had been left unburned because of it.

Lightly armoured, Hal saw, in leather and bits of maille with hardly a helmet between them and those no more than light leather caps. The one who led them, stepping out and pausing now and then to watch his men go past, was dark-haired and had a studded leather jack; all of them seemed to have short spears for throwing or stabbing and were bundled about with scrip and cloak and pack.

Then, sudden as a shock of iced water, Hal saw the black columns behind, first two, then four, then five, all footmen, moving in loose blocks. A swift tally gave him three, perhaps four hundred.

'Christ betimes, they have broke the truce.'

It was a fact as harsh as a stab in the eye. The English had come out of Perth, hard and fast and Hal knew that he saw the foot only because he had already missed the horse, riding eagerly ahead.

He called Dog Boy, whey faced from his night with Jamie Douglas, yet grimly determined.

'Ride to Bruce, hard as ye can,' Hal said. 'Charge into his fancy tentage if needs be but warn him that the English have broke the truce and the horse are upon him, wi' the foot comin' up hard.'

He did not add what he was doing, for he knew Bruce would work it out. The others had already done so, looked at the vanishing back of Dog Boy with envy while the warm summer's morning turned cold as blade; yet their hands sweated on the shafts of the Jeddarts as they wheeled out like a flock of sparrows, into the view of the worming column.

Addaf saw the horsemen at once across the far side of the field and threw up a hand to bring his men to a halt; they stood in the sea of calf-height green stalks, watching the faint morning breeze ruffle it in slow ripples, like waves.

Light horse, Addaf saw without even narrowing his eyes much. Prickers, but Scotch ones and he had seen these kind before – more mounted foot than horsemen, though they could manage the latter at a pinch. Glancing quickly behind, he was pleased to see his men, quiet and calm in their ranks, standing hipshot and still as if paused on a pleasant stroll.

Good men, mostly with around twenty summers on them, a few older – and one, Hwyel, colt-young and eager. It struck him, suddenly and for no reason, that he was the oldest one and that none of them had been with him more than a five-year.

It would be the Scotch, he thought, bringing on such memories, for he had been leading men in the French wars for long enough and the last time he had been this far north had been the King's campaign of '97 against Wallace. Christ – near ten years since, he realized.

Not one of the men he had been with then were around now and most of them were dead of sickness and disease, the others gone home. He alone had survived and the Welsh band who had fought for Edward then had become a company hired out to the highest bidder and he, though he hated to think of it, had become that most reviled of men, a contract captain.

Contracted, in this case, to de Valence, a retinue Addaf did not care to be in because he remembered de Valence riding down Welsh archers in that same campaign against Wallace. Drunk and quarrelsome Welsh, he admitted, but none that deserved death at the hands of English knights; King Edward had been fortunate that any of the Welsh archers had fought at all on the day and most had not out of spite, leaving most of the work to the Gascon crossbows.

That was when Addaf had seen Scots like this, whirling in and out on their little, fast-gaited horses, hauling proud knights out of their saddles with hooks, stabbing and slashing them as they scrabbled on the ground.

That was then and this was now; none of the ones he barked orders at cared who de Valence was, only that he paid on time and let them plunder. Obedient to Addaf's instructions, the column turned smartly to the right, to become a loose-ranked block three-deep, facing the horsemen; there was a birdwing rustle as the bows came out of their bags.

'Smart your sticks,' Addaf called and his bowmen strung the weapons with swift, easy movements.

Hal led his riders out at a fast walk, all spread out to look more threatening towards the flanks of the column. His plan was to keep just beyond the hurling range of these spear throwers and harass them with shouts and waving, pinning them in place with the idea that, if they turned to move off, the riders would fall on them. He saw another fat column, coming to an uncertain halt to one side and tried to watch it as well as the one in front. Slow them all down, he thought. Give Bruce time to fight the English heavy horse.

The flicker in the middle of the three-deep column of spear throwers disturbed him a little, as did the determined, cool way it moved – unlike the second one, who were now waving spears like beetle-feelers and milling in an ungainly, uncertain mob.

Closer still and his unease turned to a deeper chill; not one of these little javelinmen had a shield. Not one . . . the cold plunge in his belly coincided with the pungent curse from Sim Craw.

'Virgin's erse-cheeks – they are Welsh bowmen.'

Bowmen. Welsh. The two words struck a gibbering panic into everyone and Hal had to fight himself for control. It wasn't that they had better bows or more skill than the archers Hal knew from Selkirk and elsewhere – it was because the Welsh delivered death in steel sleet, all loosed together rather than the ragged shooting Hal was used to seeing, even from the vaunted Gascon crossbows.

It was a rain of arrows that swept men down like sudden storm did summer wheat, flattening them to ruined stooks.

'Turn. Away,' he yelled and took his own advice, hearing the giant barndoor creak of drawing strings, then the Devil's-breath rush of feathers in flight.

Too late. Hal knew it even as he flogged the garron into a mad race for the far side of the field, half-stumbling through the fetlock-clinging barley. Too late. He heard the evil breath of it the way a night mouse hears the owl's wing, an eyeblink before the talons close.

There was a rising hiss and then the rain fell on them. He saw Jemmie o' The Nook arch, heard the drumming thumps and the scream from him as his back turned to a hedgepig; the garron, stuck in rump and haunch, squealed, veered off and he was gone.

Another garron went over its own nose, but the man on it was pinned to the saddle through the thigh and backbone and was plunged to the bloody greenery whether he cared or not.

Hal's horse leaped in the air, came down half on and half off the ragged bundle of him, then stumbled on for a stride or two until it stopped, head down, legs splayed. A great gout of blood and a groan came from it, then it started to fold and Hal kicked free of it, only seeing the strange sprout of feathered twig in one side. Into the lungs, he thought wildly; it missed my knee by a hair.

Addaf was satisfied with the one shoot, for he would have to send men out to recover what arrows they could; they were in short supply and too crafted to waste. He watched the riders vanish into the treeline on the far side of the field, saw the riderless little horses, some running in mad circles, most limping painfully.

A single man staggered and Addaf, tempted, started to nock an arrow – a long shot, but no longer than ones where he had put a big battle-arrow through a willow-wand . . .

The sudden shouts distracted him and he turned to see the second column, now no more than a crowd, waving weapons and cheering.

'An audience appreciates you,' he said, nodding to them, and his men laughed.

'We make them jig, we make them kick,' yelled out the irrepressible Hywel, 'with a feather shaft and a crooked stick.'

All of them laughed aloud and, when Addaf remembered the limping man and looked for him, there was nothing to see. He frowned, unsmarted the bow and sent men out to fetch the arrows back, or dig out the valuable points for re-shafting.

In the treeline, Hal sank down, sweating and panting, while others retched, spat and then examined each other and their mounts for unseen wounds.

'How many?'

'Six,' Sim Craw told him. 'Five are gone down the brae, certes, and Hob o' the Merse has a barb in his back and says he cannae feel his legs. Eight garrons down. God be praised.'

'For ever and ever,' Hal answered, then struggled up. 'But not this day, I think. Mount and ride, double if you need – Sore Davey, I will climb ahint you, since you are lighter. Throw Hob over a saddle an' bring him. There is a battle yet to be won.'

He was wrong. There was no battle left to be won and they discovered the heart-sick lurch of truth when they came up on their old camp, into a confused, whirling affray of men in knots and struggling knuckles, fighting like dog-packs with no order or command.

There were men on foot, formed in little rings half-armed and defiant, while others ran like fox-struck chooks in a coop, pursued by vengeful men in maille mounted on warhorses. Glancing over the shoulder of Sore Davey, to the left of where they had come up, Hal saw a huddle of riders, the bright blue and white stripes and red martlets of Aymer de Valence blazing from the horse barding of himself and his retinue.

'The King . . .' Sim Craw bellowed and pointed to the fist of riders surrounding a figure. He had no jupon, but the golden lion rampant shield was clear and he wore maille and a coif, but only a bascinet, the gold circlet on it gleaming in the sun. Beyond, half-sunk like some sugarloaf in the rain, the striped confection of the royal panoply sagged and round the tangle of it came Dog Boy, his tired garron staggering after his flat-out run to warn the King.

Isabel, Hal thought and slapped Sore Davey on one shoulder, even as he bawled out to the others to go right, towards the tents, away from de Valence. The Dog Boy saw them and turned the garron obediently to meet them, though he was thinking of Jamie Douglas somewhere in the chaos of blade and blood.

They rode past three men, two of them on foot, the rider holding horses; Hal's heart missed several beats at the sight of the woman struggling between them, but it was one he did not know and was grateful for it.

Dog Boy did. He hauled the garron up short, which balked Sore Davey and Hal cursed him for it, sliding over the rump as he saw the armed men turn in shocked surprise; he shrugged his shield off his back to his arm and hauled out a blade, while Dog Boy, his face ugly with anger, forced the garron at the rider, roaring incoherently and striking out with the big Jeddart staff.

Sim Craw saw the weave of it and brought his own mount to its haunches; two or three others followed and they whirled, flogging back to help; the rest rode on, oblivious so that the shrieks of the slung Hob, woken to a world of terror and agony, faded into the distance.

Dog Boy rode the Jeddart at the *serjeant,* who cursed and ducked, letting the horses loose as he did so; the shaft slithered over his mailled shoulder, the hook caught in his jupon and Dog Boy, slamming briefly into one of the shocked and plunging horses, rode on, dragging the man out of the saddle. Whooping and roaring, Sim Craw and the handful of men with him rode over him, stabbing downwards.

The woman went flying, discarded and forgotten in an instant while the men dragged out their weapons and turned with the desperate air of cornered rats. One of them saw Sim and the others and bolted away while the other stood in a half-crouch, head moving from Sim to Dog Boy and back to Hal.

He glanced briefly at the shield, discarded in pursuit of the woman, then he made his mind up and charged at Hal, sword held in both hands.

He was a wet-mouthed raver and Hal offered no finesse after the first blow scarred a new ruin on the shivering blue cross of his shield, the shock wave rattling his teeth; he put his shoulder down and launched himself forward, snarling. With a last mighty heave he took the shield in a swinging door slam that made the man grunt, yelp and stagger backwards to fall on his arse, legs and arms waving like an upturned beetle, the sword spilled from his grasp.

In the next second, he found himself staring at a new world, shrunk down to the wicked point of Dog Boy's Jeddart, which hovered over his face; behind, the abandoned garron snorted at the stink of blood and moved to join the riderless rounceys.

'I yield,' squeaked the man and there was a moment when

he thought this snarling youth would kill him anyway, a shocking, bowel-loosening moment.

Chirnside Rowan, still mounted, gave a grunt of derision.

'Christ betimes,' he growled. 'No content wi' dreaming of a rank ye can never have, ye think of being Roland at Roncesvalles, or Sir Galahad chasing the Grail.'

'Aye,' Sim Craw declared, coming up behind him, 'our wee Dog Boy is a *gentle parfait* for sure. He holds the knightly vow that ye should nivver violet a lady.'

Dog Boy turned to see the woman he'd rescued squatting by the *serjeant*'s corpse, rifling it expertly, and Hal was standing over her.

'The Queen and her women?' Hal was asking her urgently. 'Where are they?'

The woman hauled off a boot, turned it up and shook it, frowning when nothing fell out.

'Rode away,' she answered. She grinned up at Dog Boy.

'Marthe,' he said. 'Are ye weel?'

Marthe tore off the other boot and up-ended it; a double-edged dagger fell out and she took it, frowning when nothing followed it, then beamed back at Dog Boy.

'Weel enow, thanks to yersel' an' yer freends,' she declared and then winked lewdly at him. 'I owe ye – whin it is convenient, I will rattle the teeth out of yer head.'

Dog Boy's face flamed as he looked at Hal.

'Creishie Marthe,' he explained. 'Her man is a woodcutter from Selkirk . . .'

'The Coontess,' Hal growled and Creishie Marthe's head came up, eyes narrowed in recognition.

'Och – it is yersel', yer honour.'

She scambled up, bobbed a curtsey.

'The blissin' o' Heaven on ye, yer honour,' she went on calmly, 'but the Coontess went aff some time since, wi' loaded ponies an' yon nice wee brother o' the King, Niall.'

Hal sagged with relief. Escaped – he almost laughed aloud,

then Dog Boy brought him to his senses by growling and pointing to the ruin of blue and white tents nearby; in the depths of them, something stirred and cursed.

In a moment, all the men were off their horses and closing in. Sore Davey slashed expertly and the sail canvas parted like ripe fruitskin – a figure rose out of it, flailing and cursing. There was a moment of raised blades and snarls – then they all recognized the figure and subsided like empty wineskins.

'Kirkpatrick,' Hal declared weakly. 'In the name o' God, man – what are ye up to now?'

Kirkpatrick, his bruised face sweating red, hirpling still with his hurts, clutched a casket tight to him and managed a smile as he tapped it with a free hand.

'Saving secrets,' he announced. 'The royal Rolls.'

Hal knew it at once and raised an eyebrow – everyone had fled in such haste that they had left the list of those in service to the King, what they had brought as retinue and how much they were owed. In the hands of de Valence, it would provide all the evidence needed as to who the Bruce supporters were.

'Not that they deserve it, mind,' Kirkpatrick added bitterly. 'Half our brave community of the realm stuffed their jupons under their saddles, covered their shields so as not to be recognized and ran like hunted roe.'

Creishie Marthe had turned her attention to the yielded *serjeant*, and drawn a swift second smile under his chin with a dagger she'd taken. Ignoring the blood and the kicking, she was rifling under the hem of his maille for hidden wealth.

'Bigod,' said Chirnside admiringly to Dog Boy, 'your choice in weemin' is growin' dangerous, my lad.'

Kirkpatrick saw the ring when Marthe peeled back the man's maille mittens; the knife flashed and the bloody finger was already vanishing inside her considerable bosom when Kirkpatrick caught her wrist.

'Dinna even think o' it,' he hissed into her savage glare and flourished dirk and she saw the eyes on him, knew instantly

310

who it was and whimpered, giving up the grisly prize and the ring on it.

Hal saw it all and shot a quick look at Dog Boy to see if he had noticed that Creishie Marthe had been 'violeted' – but Dog Boy was staring blankly back at the whirling battle. Men sprinted past; a horseman galloped furiously further down and it was clear to everyone that the fighting was closing in on the royal tents. Creishie Marthe knew it and was already gathering her skirts and running off.

'Jamie,' Dog Boy muttered, gathering the reins of his garron, and Hal, half-way into the saddle of one of the patient rounceys, looked back to the black thundercloud of struggling men.

'The King,' he said, though he knew there was nothing that would make him drag the remains of his *mesnie* into that mess.

The King was in trouble and he knew it. Truth was he had known it from the moment the messenger rode up, the one he recognized as Dog Boy. It had given him and the others enough time to struggle into maille hauberk, though he had thrown the awkward leggings to one side. He had a coif attached to the hauberk and long sleeves with mittens, and now blessed the one-piece garment he had roundly cursed in the past for its weight while trying to get it on.

Dog Boy's arrival had given him time to issue orders sending the Queen to safety, to have a palfrey saddled – his warhorses all went with the Queen, having just been fed and now useless for battle – and take up the bascinet with the golden circlet.

Balliol's, of course, as was so much of his royal finery, though that king had never worn it. Truth was, it was a little loose for Bruce but he gave up on comfort for the advantage of being seen easily by his own side, who would take heart from their battling king.

The other side of that spun coin, he thought to himself in the sweating, belly-clenching moments before the English knights closed on them, was that being tumbled off would rip the heart out of them.

He thought of that in the eyeblink before the charging figure came down on him, featureless in his bucket helm, waving a battleaxe and trying to rein in the over-eager warhorse. Bruce danced to one side, slashed out with his sword and spun the palfrey as the warhorse went plunging mad, half its tail sheared off and all of its rump bloody and fired with agony; the knight sailed off and hit the ground with a clatter. The German Method . . .

Bruce had little time to exult and none at all to see if the knight got up, for others were on him and his own *mesnie* closed in protectively. He realized at once that this was no battle and was lost whatever you called it – there was only a *mêlée* now and Bruce was master of that.

He ducked a swinging blade, banged the man out of the saddle with his shield, cut right, cut left, took a blow that made him grunt and hope his maille was good and the sword blunt. A man plunged out, on foot, to grab the bridle of his horse, helmetless and roaring with triumph that he had taken the King.

Bruce slashed down and the man shrieked and fell away, while the rouncey threw up its head and panicked at the grisly ornament of hand and wrist that dangled, clenched and bloody in the bridle. Bruce lost a foot from one stirrup and sat deep while the rouncey plunged itself to a trembling halt.

The knight who had first attacked suddenly lurched from the other side, having thrown away his bucket helm and dragged out a sword. He was bleeding from a broken nose and snoring in desperate breaths, but he reached out a free hand and tried to grab Bruce by his leg, missed and grasped the free stirrup.

'He is mine,' he bellowed in a spray of blood. 'Yield yerself sirra –aaaaah.'

His triumph ended in a shriek when Bruce rammed his booted foot back in the stirrup, grinding fingers into the metal

312

and trapping the hand; when he spun the rouncey the knight was dragged off his feet and whirled sideways, screaming, until he bowled into a knuckle of men, scattering them and tearing his fingers free.

Then a blow seemed to stave in the whole side of Bruce's face, a crash as if the world had fallen on him and he reeled at the edge of consciousness, hanging on to the palfrey by some last reserve of tourney skill.

'I have him,' yelled a voice. 'I have him.'

He saw a silver lion on a red shield and thought it might be Mowbray – but he was dimly aware that everything was red on the left side, felt the sudden strange coldness there. God help me, he thought wildly, I am blinded . . .

He felt himself dragged off the horse, saw hands frantic to grasp him – then there was a roaring sound which he thought was his own blood in his ears and he lay, staring blindly up at the red-misted sky, watching the flurry of legs. Mailed, hooved, booted, they stamped and circled –there was a rushing crash and someone fell full length, so that when Bruce turned – oh, so laborious and slow – he saw the twisted agony that was Mowbray falling from a vicious blow, blood washing down over unfocused eyes.

Hands gripped him, hauled him up.

'Into the saddle, Your Grace, ' said an urgent voice and Bruce felt himself hefted up, found a reflex that cocked a leg and dropped him into the cantled security of a fresh horse. He looked dazedly down through the blood, saw the black figure of Simon Frazier grinning back at him.

'Seton – tak' the King to safety. He is sore hurt.'

Sore hurt. Bruce did not want to know how sore his hurt was; he could feel it like a great numbing on the side of his face and was sure he had lost it, eye, cheek and all.

Lost. All was lost on this Malachy-cursed day . . .

Methven
Late evening, the same day

The priests droned like flies in the growing dim and de Valence thought of the abbot, somewhere back in Perth, carefully out of the way of matters, so he could not see what sins were being done here under the dragon banner.

There were a lot of sins, de Valence knew, as many as there were flies, and the flattened fields of rye and barley around Methven were as good as a pewter plate smeared with meat juice to them. Flies and shadows flitted in the dark, both of them stripping the corpses.

De Valence sat on his warhorse, surrounded by grim-iron men and sweating in the heavy drape of his heraldry, wishing the last dregs of this mummery were done with and he could climb off the beast and out of the war gear.

It was as well he had won here, he thought, otherwise he would have to face the wrath of Longshanks for failing to capture Bruce – or anyone else who mattered – and losing Badenoch's murderer en route to Berwick.

The bitter sauce of it all was having to sit here and smilingly acknowledge and reward all the galloping fools who came up clutching a pennon, or hauling in some luckless lordling of no account until it became dark enough to admit that the battle was over.

Sourly, he watched the lone figure come up on foot, the torch he held bobbing as he strode in a curious, long-limbed way. He knew the walk, though the face of the Welshman, Addaf, was made no easier on the eye in the dancing shadows from the torch. Christ's Bones, he thought, now even the contract captains are behaving like chivalry.

'Your Grace,' the man said, offering as little a head nod as he thought he could get away with and de Valence smiled wryly to himself. The Welshman was still of use, him and his mountain dwarves, even if he used the 'Your Grace' like a spit in the eye, so de Valence gave the man his due.

'Mydr ap Mydvydd,' he said, the title given by admiring Welsh archers to someone they trusted to lead them.

'Found this, Your Grace,' Addaf said in his sing-song English and handed the object up. De Valence examined the bascinet and Robert Tuke leaned over, squinting for a better look, then gave a short bark of laughter at the sight of the battered helmet with its twisted circlet of gold, only half of it still remaining.

'We have his usurper's crown,' he crowed over his shoulder to the others. 'Soon we'll have his head to match it.'

The laughter rolled out into the night, over the scatter of darkened corpses and the wounded, desperate for relief, yet trying not to groan because it would bring the throat-cutting scavengers.

De Valence looked at the ruin of the helmet and did not need to wonder where the missing half of the crown was, though he would not pursue Addaf on the matter. More to the point was the damage done to it, a hard sword blow.

A man who had worn that had taken a harsh face cut, he thought. It will be a ruined head when we eventually find it.

Bruce woke from a nightmare where his loving daughter's kisses had turned to sucking wolf bites, ripping his skin, grinding into the bones. He woke to pain and mad, flickering torchlight, a sickening tugging and pulling on the left side of his face, which he tried to dash away with one hand.

'Hold him,' growled a voice.

'Howk the torch higher, yer honour,' said a woman. 'Else I will sew up his bloody neb.'

Get off me, Bruce said. Get away – I am the King . ...

He was appalled at his own weakness and heard only gug-gug sounds coming from his mouth; a face swam into view, big and sheened with sweat with a grin like a sickle moon. The light danced mad, lurid shadows of blood on it, but he knew it all the same. Edward, he thought. Brother Edward. He said it, feeling his mouth strange on one side, almost sick with the relief of hearing something approaching sense from himself.

'Swef, Rob,' said Edward. 'Ye ken me – that's good. At least yer wits are still in yer head, though it's a miracle – God's Holy Arse, wummin, do not pull his face to bits.'

'A wee bit bone – it fell oot,' Bruce heard the woman answer, indignantly shrill. Dear God, he thought, what has been done to me? What is being done to me?

There was sharp pain, one fierce sliver after another and he tried to cry out but could only make incoherent sounds, tried to thrash the pain away then found he was gripped by strong hands. Eventually, his face seamed with fire, the hands relaxed.

'Done, yer honour,' the woman's voice said and he saw her briefly in the torchlight, sallow skinned, a tangle of hair which she brushed back from her face with bloodied hands; there was a needle held in the thin clench of her lips. Edward loomed into view again, peering.

'Not bad, Creishie Marthe. Neat as a hem.'

'A wish my ma were here to see,' the woman answered with a shrill cackle. 'She swore at my stitchin' betimes – now it is part o' a king's face forever.'

'Aye, weel – now there are two things ye are good at,' someone said and the woman huffed indignantly at this affront to her honour.

Edward grinned cheerfully at Bruce and nodded.

'Rest. We must be away from here, brother, and swiftly.'

'What happened to me?' Bruce managed to ask, coherent at least. Edward dismissed it with a casual wave.

'Lost a wee tourney fight with the English,' he answered, 'and took a dunt. Your eye is fine, mark you – the cut is above and below it. It will leave a fine scar – you have a naming face now, brother.'

A naming face. Bruce heard the others laugh, daringly suggest names their king would be remembered by – Robert

316

the Scarred, Dinged Rob, King Hob the Screed . . . the voices faded and Edward, frowning, patted his shoulder.

'We left your fancy war hat behind, mark you,' he said. 'The crown is lost.'

The crown is lost. Bruce struggled and Edward looked alarmed as his brother sat up.

'I have not lost the crown,' he shouted, before pain wrenched his face and sank his swimming head down on the pallet again.

I have not lost, he thought through the swirling agony. By God, I have not.

CHAPTER FOURTEEN

Lanercost Priory
Ferial day following the Feast of the Exaltation of the Holy
Cross, September, 1306

It was white-knuckle cold in the Priory, a place of high, shadowed walls, chill fluted stone and wide floors of glacial flags. The room held a meagre fire which only accentuated the damp and the only decoration was a bleak-eyed statue of Mary Magdalene, staring from a niche with one hand raised.

Asking, no doubt, for another log on the fire, Edward thought to himself as he approached the man seated at the table, his back to the King. A priory servant, hunkered by the flicker of flame in the huge fireplace, leaped to his feet and bowed, so that the seated man immediately knew who was behind him.

He stood, scraping back the bench and turned, bowing.

'Your Grace,' he said, then wiped gravy from his moustaches.

'Sit, sit,' growled Edward, flapping one hand and shuffling up to perch opposite, his back to the fire. He hunched himself a little, then rounded on the servant.

'Fetch some logs and build that blaze, damn your eyes.'

Marmaduke Thweng thought the King and a two-day old

318

corpse had much in common, but the rouge and prinking made Edward look worse.

'Eat, eat,' Edward declared expansively. 'You have come a long way to deliver your charges, Sir Marmaduke, and deserve a decent pie, by God. Tell me everything.'

Thweng looked with sadness at the half-eaten bacon and beef pie, which was delicious, aware that he could not follow both commands at the same time.

'The women follow on slowly, Your Grace, in carts as befits their station. Your son decided to send the Earl and the Bruce brother ahead with me, on horseback. He knew you would wish to see them at your soonest convenience.'

'No doubt to ingratiate himself. Bastard boy,' Edward scowled, eyeing the pie and feeling his belly gripe. No more food like that for me if the physickers are to be followed, he thought to himself bitterly. Crowfoot powder for the belly gripe and fare that loosens the bowels, so the act of losing a turd did not bring excruciating agony – damned black biled humours of the arse would not even allow him to sit in comfort.

His malady was well known and Thweng thought back to the moment the King had quit Scotland after stripping Balliol, the moment he had sneered that 'a man does good business when he rids himself of such a turd'. Like the ones he strained to pass now, that one, too, had been painful and costly.

Thweng knew better than to speak on that, or about why the King scowled over his son; Sir Giles D'Argentan and a whole slew of knights, who were supposed to be scouring the north in the host commanded by the prince, had all decided to go to France. For an Important Tourney. The prince, of course, had permitted them and it was only a Holy Miracle that he had seen sense enough not to go himself.

The memory of it clearly rankled stilll. Twenty-two arrest warrants had been spewed out from the King's wrath – even for his son-in-law, the elegant fop Humphrey de Bohun. The others were all the gilded youth, the new breed Edward had so painstakingly fastened to his son at the Feast of Swans.

Even that he contrives to subvert and ruin, Edward thought. Even that . . .

Thweng watched him reach out and scoop up the meat of the pie and stuff it in his mouth, gravy dripping down his curled beard and off his fingers.

'Have they found Bruce?'

Thweng shook his head.

'Not at Kildrummy, nor Dunaverty,' he answered and the king hunched and brooded, sucking the delicious gravy over his teeth. Gone, like the mists of those damnable hills, he thought. Vanished. Dunaverty and Kildrummy – bloody barbaric names they had there – were the last strongholds where the usurper could possibly have lurked.

It meant he was hiding in the woods and hills, with places that translated to 'loch of the ambush', 'wolf's burn' and 'murder hole'.

'You could find him,' Edward declared, sucking his fingers. 'You are a thief-taker in your own Yorkshire lands, are you not? For the bounty?'

Thweng's eyes narrowed, for he did not like the thrust of this; he would not be thief-taking at all if he did not need the money it brought, for decades of service to the King had been less than lucrative.

'Trailbaston and outlaws, Your Grace,' he replied flatly. 'In a country I know with my eyes closed and one which seeks to help me. A different matter to hunt down one man in a strange land whose folk offer every resistance.'

'He must be found,' the King persisted, helping himself to more of the pie. Thweng nodded, trying not to show the inward weary sigh he felt. It would, he thought, be best if Bruce were found and dealt with if only to stop the welter of dragon-banner blood that had already claimed so many. There were a score or more and the gutters had stank with blood for

320

two days, according to the reports. Thweng had known most of the noble dead.

'Will you speak with the Earl of Atholl, my lord?' he asked.

'I will not,' the King declared savagely. 'He will try to plead his case, no doubt, tell me he is a kinsman of mine through his mother, who is some king's bastard. He is for the axe, by God.'

Now Thweng was alarmed; no earl had been executed in England for two hundred years and more and he said as much. The King regarded him sourly, the drooping eye flickering with a tic, gravy sliding down his fingers.

'The Bruce brother – Niall, is it? Yes, him. I will axe him, certes and send his head to Berwick for spiking. Atholl must also suffer, earl or no. He can hang instead. If he is higher in rank than any of the others, then we can add thirty feet to his gallows drop, for benefit of his station.'

He smiled greasily. 'As for the Bruce women – well, I have an Italies punishment for them.'

He saw Thweng's bewilderment.

'After Fossalta – you recall the battle? The Bolognese imprisoned Henry of Sardinia in an iron cage. It took him twenty-two years to die.'

'In the name of Christ's Mercy,' Thweng blurted before he could stop himself and saw the storm gather on the royal brow, reined round and came up on another attack.

'You can scarcely do that to his wife, Your Grace. A De Burgh of Ulster? And the Bruce daughter, Marjorie, is a slip of a girl yet.'

Edward frowned, then shrugged.

'True. I shall send them to a convent. But the others – his sister and that harlot of Buchan's who crowned him – them I shall have in cages, by God.'

He sucked his fingers again, then winced and shifted as his stomach flickered with pain – anger flooded him at his own betraying body.

'If any of those bastards dare return from their French

tourney,' he added, 'I shall find more cages for them . . .'

He broke off as a tendril of chill circled his feet like an anklet and he rounded on the hapless servant.

'God's Holy Arse, you sludge – will you get that fire going or I will burn YOU in it.'

Baleful as a wet cat, he turned savagely to Thweng.

'I want Bruce. Go back to my son and make him hunt the usurper out.'

Thweng smiled wanly, looked at the finger-ruined pie, then pushed it away.

Near Dunaverty Castle, Kintyre
Feast of St Malachy, November, 1306

The fires were small, but a welcome warmth to the men huddled in heavy wool cloaks in the bowl-shaped depression. The snow had been driven back by the flames, but it still fell in soft, slow drifts, so that the men were warm at the front and felt the cold bite their backs, even through the layers they wore. The surrounding trees sighed and creaked under a rising wind.

There were ponies, too, stamping nearby as they kicked hopefully at the ground to try to dig up a little to eat and Dog Boy wanted to leave the men and go to his with a handful of oats he still had in his pack. He dared not, for it would mean admitting he had a peck of oats in the first place and he was sure these wild men of the north would have something to say on it.

He and Sim Craw, Hal and Chirnside were all that was left of the Herdmanston men, who had been running and fighting since Methven, driven north and dependent now on the good graces of these Campbells and MacDonalds and even wilder tribal trolls from beyond The Mounth. He did not want to seem to be getting above himself.

Hal caught Dog Boy out of the corner of one eye, watched him fret and saw his eyes move to where his horse was, saw him shift, but not dare move. He did not like to think of the boy . . . God save us, hardly that these days . . . fretted by the presence of these Kintyre growlers. They were fighters, these men of Neil and Donald Campbell, Angus Og of the Isles and others, loyal still to King Robert, where the earls of Ross and Sutherland had turned.

Ross especially, who had broken into the sanctuary shrine at Tain and dragged out the Queen and all her women. Isabel . . . Hal felt the rising heat of it, was almost driven to his feet by it and fought to sit still, though it trembled him to do it.

All anyone else saw, if they looked, was a lean, grim man, all planes and shadows, made darker by the greasy black wolf cap he had taken from a dead man and the thick cloak he had filched at knife-point. His maille and hardened leather were hung about him, wrecked and rusted by weather and hard use; with his gaunt, unsmiling face he looked like a cadaver, newly surfaced from the forest mulch.

Neil Campbell appeared and men stirred. He wore simple clothes and a furred cloak, affected a fox hat – ears and all – while his own hair was as red as the hat and he wore gold in a thick braid round his neck, like one of the Old Norse.

Hal and his men – a dozen when they had set out weeks ago – had been making for Dunaverty in Kintyre, where it was said King Robert had taken refuge, but the English were already sieging it when they arrived.

They had then fought running battles in and around the steep glens and forests until, cut to shreds by disease and half-starved, they had fallen in with men barely clothed never mind armoured, with slings and short spears and long knives.

A lot of Herdmanston men had thrown up their hands then and Hal had sent them away, back to whatever life they could make round the ruin of his old tower, or at Roslin. There was no such possibility for him – and, besides, he needed to find

323

out if Isabel had escaped the Earl of Ross' wrath, or had been taken with the Queen; in the sinking stone that was his heart these days, he was sure he knew the truth.

Now himself, the ague-trembling Sim, Dog Boy and the grim Chirnside Rowan were what was left, living more and more like animals with these hillmen, who spoke in their own way and knew little or no other tongue. It wasn't until Neil Campbell turned up, with as much easy command of French as he did the Gaelic, that Hal caught up with the news.

It was grim enough – the King had escaped from Dunaverty and was gone, almost certes out of the Kingdom and probably for good. Isabel was taken. The King's brother, Niall, was dead. Even the Earl of Atholl was dead.

Yet the Campbells and MacDonalds, as much fighting against old enemies the MacDougalls as the Invaders, had at least a thousand bare-footed, bare-arsed fighting men, which was a feat considering the time of year and the fact that they had been at war since the summer. No harvest had been gathered and the families of these men hungered – though that seemed the lot of these people, Hal saw.

Here, though, there were barely a hundred, the leaders and what passed for a *mesnie*, met to try and sort out what to do now that their king seemed to have vanished, as if taken by Faerie. They gathered in a circle round the fires, the flames dangerously close and unheeded at their own cloaks, passing a jug of something harsh as burned wine and glaring at each other, for old tribal grievances lurked just under the surface of them all.

Not that it mattered much to Hal, now that his worst fears were confirmed; all he wanted was to find the King and plead for whatever help he could raise on Isabel's behalf.

Neil Campbell, big and splendid and grinning, raised the jug, drank deep, smacked his lips and began the matter by raising the oak branch he held in one hand. At once someone rose and took it from him and the others subsided, growling and waiting for him to finish having his say.

The man spoke Gaelic and Neil Campbell waited, then translated it for the benefit of Hal and his handful of men; the wild men glowered impatiently and the speaker curled a hairy lip. He had braided hair and missing teeth, a Lennox man Hal recalled vaguely, from some wild cleft above Loch Lomond.

'I have heard,' the translation said, 'that the siege at Dunaverty has failed to locate our King Robert. Yet the Invaders are still there and so we must be after deciding – do we fight them, or go home.'

No-one spoke. No-one passed the jug to Hal, whose grin turned feral and snarling at this rudeness. This was a farce, he thought. These men had no choice but to fight, since anything else returned the English raids to their pathetic little lives. He almost said so, but chewed on it, thinking of Sim Craw lying, sweating and groaning in a thick fever and needing their care.

'The power of hills and isles will destroy them in the end,' Neil Campbell translated, as a man took the stick and spoke. It was Grann, a MacDonald islesman Hal had been fighting with for several weeks, a black-avowed killer with a tangle of hair and beard who gralloched captives like stags in case they had swallowed their coin and trinkets.

According to Neil Campbell, Grann came from some island to the north and west and thought himself something because of that and the fact that he had a fine weapon, a sword, taken from some old Viking pirate, with a tarnished and worn-smooth silver cross set in a fat pommel. It did not make Grann any less of a heathen.

'Only the power of the arm will halt them,' Hal growled, unable to stop himself. 'Our arm, with steel in it.'

There was a silence, for some were chilled by the teeth-grinding delivery and others embarrassed that Hal had dared to speak without the stick, or dared to at all, for he was a southerner with so few men that he was of no account.

Neil Campbell translated for those who had no Southron, glancing at the dark scowl of this Lord of Herdmanston, but showing nothing in his face as he did so.

He saw the corded sinews and old scars on the back of the man's hands, the tangle of grizzling hair and beard, the whole of him hung about with tattered links and old leather. Somewhere in these hills, he thought to himself, this Lothian lord has become like darker, older folk, even older than the one in *Ma-ruibhe*'s sacred oak grove, like the ones who had blood-sacrificed to gods. He reached for the oak stick and held it up.

'The Lord of Herdmanston is correct,' he said, in English and Gaelic, and that brought heads up.

'We scattered the Invaders at the Old Glen,' he went on, 'while Angus Og and his men killed many good warriors and took a deal of their provender as plunder.'

He broke off and looked round at them all.

'But the Invaders are like lice. If you do not kill them all, they will simply return.'

There were nods and grunted agreement at this – then a man stood up and held out his hand. Dog Boy knew him as Gillespie a small chief from somewhere that was barely in the Kingdom at all. He did not like the man, the way he did not like strange dogs.

'I am Gillespie, known as Erkinbald of the True People of Auld Burn in Cawdor,' he said, sibilant slow. 'I have listened to His Honour and seen the Lothian lord who stands with him. It is all very fine that this Lothian lord has come to defend the birthright of the True People of Auld Burn and very fine that we are gathered here to do the same.'

He stopped and looked round at the others while Neil Campbell muttered the meanings to Hal and the wind flared into the silence, flurrying snow and flattening the flames.

'I did not see anyone here defending the birthright of the Auld Burn folk when the Irishers raided, even though they had to cross some of your lands to get to us. Nor do I hear the Lothian man telling me how he and his wee handful will kill all the lice.'

Again he paused and folk stirred, some eager to reply but bound by the conventions of the oak branch. Others had their hands out, but were silent still.

'My father's father,' Gillespie went on with maddening slowness, 'fought against your people, Grann. Seventy-four different battles. My father never passed a day without shedding the blood of either Grann's folk, or of less than kindly neighbours to us. I myself have fought the Invaders fourteen times. You claim we are all of one blood, but if the Invaders had not come to these lands, we would be fighting each other, or even the lowland men from Lothian, who send priests to turn us to their way of God and away from the old way of our own saints and Christ priests.'

There was a flurry, like a shadow of wind and, suddenly, Grann had the stick and was almost nose to nose with Gillespie, who took a surprised step away from the man snarling at him. He spat out the words like the sparking of wet wood, looking round the fire-blooded faces.

When he had finished, he waited, standing stern as an old tree, while Neil Campbell spoke the English of it to the Lothian lord. Then he went on, with the same bitter rage as if he had not stopped.

'There is Gillespie, whose father's father fought mine and lost as much as he won. Whose father fought all his neighbours and gained neither land nor honour from it. Who himself fought the Invaders – who still burned him out. Until he came here with all the rest of us, he has never won.'

He broke off and slashed them with his feral stare while Neil Campbell bent to murmur the translation only in Hal's ear, glancing uneasily at Grann, for he felt the tension coiling in the snow wind.

'I know my father's deeds and his father before him,' Grann

spat, the Gaelic liquid as flowing fire, 'but I also know what I myself have done. I have fought these English and everyone who supports them, be it MacDougall or MacDonald, every day of my waking life since good king Alexander died.'

There was a half-angered, half-shamed shifting among the MacDonalds at that, for there had been a birling of politics beyond The Mounth since Bruce had taken the throne.

Before it, the MacDougalls had been patriots and the MacDonalds pro-English; now the reverse held true, though Hal was black in his thoughts that it could all change, just as easily. No matter which of them supported Bruce, Hal knew, the other would take the opposite stance, for old feuds would not suffer a MacDougall and a MacDonald to stand shoulder to shoulder.

'There has never been a day I did not take a head to preserve in oil,' Grann went on and folk shifted uneasily at that, which was altogether too heathen for Christian men to hear.

'But Gillespie is right in one thing,' Grann went on, ignoring them. 'Not all blood is the same. These English have blood that is black, like the belly-blood of slaughtered hogs, fat with the best of our own land. The blood of the Lothian lord's people is red, but flows thick and slow. The blood of the Auld Burn people is thin and clear – like water.'

There was a howl at that and Gillespie hauled out his only weapon, an eating knife. There were yells and growls and, eventually, Neil Campbell signalled to his own men and they waded in, dragging people apart.

Neil himself took Grann by the arm and led him out of the circle, taking the stick from him as he did so. He handed it to Hal and then called for silence; the Dog Boy saw the Lord of Herdmanston, slightly embarrassed, turning the stick round and round in one grimy hand.

Hal did not know what to say or what he thought Neil Campbell wanted him to say. He no longer cared whether King Robert ruled or ran away, only that he had enough power left to help him free Isabel and could be persuaded to use it.

Hal could not believe how bestial these trolls were and did not envy anyone trying to rule them. These were the ones left to defend the Kingdom? He wanted desperately to gather his men and ride back to the Lothians, to ferret out the whereabouts of Isabel and leave all this dog-puke rebellion alone – but Sim Craw was raving sick and he had two men left to him in all the world.

He needed food and shelter. He needed news on Isabel and where she was. So he smiled at them and nodded to Neil to translate his words.

'The gathering in . . . this place,' he announced, forgetting what these skin-wearers called the bowl-shape in the wilderness, 'is so that you can all settle your differences . . .'

'This new king,' said a voice, sing-song sibilant and speaking English the way a man walked in new shoes, 'is he a Wallace or an Empty Cote?'

The man was white-haired, bland-faced as oatmeal – at least what could be seen of his expressions under the great smoke-puff of hair and beard. Hal knew he was a rebel MacKenny chieftain from the true wildlands which belonged to the Earl of Ross and had a holding on the shores of a loch Neil Campbell called *Ma-ruibhe* in the Gaelic. Even in a land as strange as a two-headed goat, this Alaxandair Oigh caused his neighbours to blink.

'There is an island in his loch,' Campbell had told Hal, 'where Saint *Mael Ruaba* has a shrine and where many folk are buried. There is a tree there, an oak and on it are nailed many bull's heads, for they sacrifice there in the old way. To get to this island you have to brave the loch's monster, the *muc-sheilch*. Truly, these folk are not like us.'

Coming from the likes of Neil Campbell, that was almost laughable, but Hal was chilled to the marrow by the tale of Alexander the Elder and had no mirth left in him. For all his lightness, Neil himself was careful around the old chief.

'You should have demanded the stick, Alaxandair Oigh,' Neil Campbell said sternly, though Hal heard the deferential politeness in his voice. The old man waved a hand.

'Aye, aye. A Campbell puts me right, so he does – yet the question remains, wee stick or no wee stick.'

The silence fell like the sift of snow. A Wallace or a Toom Tabard – a fighter or a kneeler? Hal marvelled at how far and fast the legend of Sir Will had gone – and how the future of the King himself depended on it. Trolls or not, these were the only forces left.

'He is the King,' Hal replied carefully. 'Wallace was Wallace, Balliol is his own man still. King Robert is also his own man – but if you want to know if he will fight, then let me say that his knees do not bend and the only way his cote will be stripped is from his dead body.'

There were approving growls when Neil translated that and Alaxandair Oigh nodded thoughtfully; amazed at himself, Hal realized that he actually believed what he had told them and the rest of it spilled from him, unbidden.

'Your folk are gathering for this,' Hal went on to his face. 'It will be a foolish leader who, in years to come, has to tell his children that he missed out on the saving of the Kingdom and its king because he was cold and did not like his neighbours.'

That brought laughter and Hal handed the stick back to Neil Campbell and stepped away, glad to be rid of the whole matter. He went swiftly to Sim Craw's sickbed, followed by the padding faithful of Dog Boy and Chirnside Rowan; they all looked down at Sim, seeing the pale of him and the fat sweat drops popping out on his forehead like apple pips.

Then they looked at each other, these last three and could find nothing to say. Hal tucked the blankets tighter round Sim, hoping that what he felt on them was cold and not damp, though it was hard to tell with his numbed fingers.

He glanced up at the rough canvas and branch roof of the bower, praying the snow did not turn wet, or even to rain and that the wind did not rise enough to blow this mean roof away. Dog Boy fed sticks to flare their fire to warmer life.

'Bigod,' said a growl of voice. 'Ye turn a fair pretty speech – His Grace the King will be pleased to hear that his esteem is being lauded in these wild hills.'

They all whirled to see the familiar, dark, gaunt figure hirple out of the shadows, a lopsided grin on his face.

'Kirkpatrick,' Hal managed weakly.

'The same,' Kirkpatrick declared, hunkering stiffly by their fire and peering briefly at Sim Craw. He tutted and sucked his teeth.

'He is looking poorly, certes,' he said. 'Jesu – the snaw is early this year. Another bad blissin' frae Saint Malachy, whose day this is.'

Hal stared blankly back at Kirkpatrick's revelation of what day it was, as numbed by his appearance as by cold.

'What brings ye here?' demanded Chirnside truculently and Kirkpatrick held out his hands to the flames and rubbed them, unconcerned by Chirnside's scowls or the frank amazement of the others.

'I am here telling these chieftains that His Grace is alive and well and will return in the spring,' Kirkpatrick said. 'This will be greeted with smiles by these sorry chiels, since it means they can go home for the winter.'

He rubbed his hands more vigorously, as if the mention of the word had brought more cold, though it might have been the sudden swirl of snell wind.

'Then I am headed south on a mission for . . . someone else,' he said mysteriously.

'So he is alive and well,' Hal declared. 'Himself, the King.'

'A wee bit battered and bruised,' Kirkpatrick admitted, 'after taking a dunt at Methven. He and others have been scrambling ower these hills since, runnin' an' fightin' like hunted wolves.'

'Where is he?' demanded Chirnside Rowan roughly and Kirkpatrick placed a shushing finger on his lips.

331

'Safe. Last I saw of him he was smiling like a biled haddie at Christina Macruarie of Garmoran and his dunted face seemed no hindrance to her liking of it. He is in the care of a wheen of Islesmen of that rare wummin's *mesnie*, including a fair fleet of galleys. Mind you, I suppose he will be on his knees most of this day, begging the forgiveness of Malachy in the hope of better advancement.'

'Christ's Bones,' Chirnside breathed admiringly. 'He is sparkin' a new wummin? Yin with galleys?'

Hal poured a scowl on him.

'With his queen fresh taken by his enemies,' he pointed out scathingly. 'And us sitting chittering oor teeth in the cold and wet. Others are even worse, with necks in a kinch or on a spike.'

'Ach, you're a bowl o' sour gruel, man,' Kirkpatrick scoffed. 'At least the King is safe.'

'Unless he dies from labouring at the tirlie-mirlie,' Chirnside laughed. Dog Boy offered his own scowl at this shocking vision of the King swiving Christina Macruarie to terminal exhaustion. Then he looked at Kirkpatrick like an eager dog.

'Jamie?' he asked and grinned delightedly when Kirkpatrick nodded.

'Safe with His Grace. It was young Jamie Douglas who found the only wee boat for miles that let us row away from Dunaverty afore the English arrived.'

Hal wondered if there was a boat still waiting for Kirkpatrick after his mission and whether it would take four more; Sim Craw, he thought bitterly, would benefit from some of this Macruarie hospitality, if only the bed and her lovenest blanket. Distantly he heard the murmur of Neil Campbell's sibilant voice, telling the others the news Kirkpatrick had brought.

It was over, he thought dully. Another failed rebellion. More blood and ashes – and where did that leave him and the others in his care? That brought memory on him and he turned to

332

Kirkpatrick, who was exchanging more of his news with Chirnside and Dog Boy.

'Where are ye headed?' he demanded and Kirkpatrick smiled soft and slow, for he had not arrived here by accident and he now gathered in the Herdmanston lord, gentle as tickling trout.

'Ah – I wondered when ye would recall that. South. To where a certain countess is being held.'

Hal stared and Kirkpatrick tried not to be irritated at the blankness of it; Christ's Bones, the man was mainly for sense save ower this wummin.

'Isabel,' he persisted, as he would to a child. 'I ken where she is being held. I thought you and I might go there.'

CHAPTER FIFTEEN

Closeburn Castle, Annandale
Ferial Day following the celebration of the Sancti Quatuor
Coronati (Four Crowned Martyrs) November, 1306

Cheese and sobbing. Not the best of the world, Isabel thought, to take into Eternity but fitting enough for this prison which might see the end of me.

She tossed the half-round of hard cheese away and laboriously heaved at the sack it had lain on until she had struggled it across the floor in arcs, leaving little trails of barley from the gnawed holes. Mildewed, she thought, which is why it was left when they emptied this place to use as a prison. Now it will be a pillow, at least. She blew a tendril of hair from her face and fretted at the untreated grey in the russet.

'In the name of God, girl, shut up.'

Mary Bruce was stern as a stone Virgin, but her French was pitch perfect and precise; Marjorie was past all that, the fear rippling her body with weeping.

'Auntie, they will kill us all,' she wailed and Mary slapped her shoulder, then gathered her into her bosom in the next moment.

'Swef, swef,' she soothed. 'They will not kill us – and speak

French. You are the daughter of a king, girl, not some Lothians cottar.'

Isabel, who knew some fine Lothians cottars, thought of Sim Craw and Dog Boy and what they would do if imprisoned in the undercroft of Closeburn among the remains of old stores. Would think themselves well off, Isabel was sure, being warm and dry and finding old cheese rind and mildewed barley with which to make a meal.

Marjorie subsided to hiccups, for which Isabel was glad at least. Mark you, you could scarcely fault the girl, a child on the edge of womanhood, from being a gibber of fear after what had happened at Tain.

It had been a bad idea, as far as Isabel was concerned, to head north of Inverness and the chance of a boat to Orkney, where Norway held sway – and another Bruce sister was queen. That sanctuary led through Buchan and Ross lands, both those earls on the hunt for rebels; it came as no surprise to Isabel when wild-bearded men snarled out of the wet, foggy bracken of the hills and stampeded the column into flight.

They had reached St Duthac's shrine, with its four weathered pillars marking the sanctuary of the garth and, by that time, four men had already been lost. The Duthac garth had been an illusion, for the Earl of Ross himself had curled a lip and strode into it, his men overwhelming the last resistance in a welter of blood; it was then Marjorie had started into screaming and sobbing and was only now subsiding.

Mary Bruce had drawn herself up to her full height, which was taller than the cateran who approached her, licking lascivious lips; she had stared down her nose at him, then dared him, in good Gaelic, to lay a finger on the sister of Scotland's king.

Whether the cateran was impressed or not would remain a mystery, since the Earl of Ross had beaten his liegeman to a bloody pulp with a flute-headed mace and hanged the remains from a pillar at St Duthac's shrine to remind the rest of his prowling wolves that he meant what he said when he told them to leave off the women.

The setting for this slaughter only emphasized that the Earl of Ross did not even consider God held power greater than himself.

'Take a good look,' Mary Bruce had said to Ross when the bloody remains were hauled up. 'That is your fate for having violated this shrine and laid hands on a queen.'

The Earl of Ross had merely shrugged and smiled; his deference was all kept for the Queen herself, strangely aloof from all this and Isabel knew then that she would go one way and all the other women another – that the Queen would not be harmed because she was the daughter of Ulster.

Which was exactly what happened; without a backward glance, Elizabeth de Burgh had gone off, bundled up warmly and ridden away, while Mary, Marjorie, Isabel and the tirewomen had been huckled into carts to be transported south.

Isabel had seen Niall Bruce and Atholl, with chains at wrist and ankles, being dragged along in the wake of the carts, but only once, and when they arrived at a nunnery in the dark, the pair of them were gone. With grim irony, the nunnery was Elcho, though the prioress and all the nuns she had known had been replaced.

Now they were here in Closeburn and Isabel was no wiser as to their fate. South, probably – Carlisle or further still, away from any possible rescue.

She heard the familiar jingle, then the grate of a huge key in a fat lock: Dixon, their shuffling old gaoler, his great blued lips pursed.

'Ye have a veesitor,' he said, and nodded his fleshy head towards Isabel. 'The Maister entertains him with wine and sends me to allow time to be presentable.'

Isabel snorted.

'And how, pray, am I to achieve that?' she demanded. 'Empty

336

this barley sack and wear it? Certainly that is more presentable than the dress I have on.'

'Aye, aye, betimes,' muttered Dixon, mournfully.

'Suitable for this guest room, mark you,' Isabel scathed.

'Aye, aye,' Dixon replied and turned one glaucous eye on her, the other shut as if considering.

'The reason ye have this room is not because we cleared it out,' he mourned, 'but because it has been ate oot, rind an all, by the chiels we have crowding in. It will be a hard winter for us, ladies, when ye have passed on from here, since you and all those with ye have ruined us from hoose and hame.'

'Then it seems clear I should hang on to the sack with the barley in it,' Isabel replied tartly. 'Bring on my "veesitor", gaoler.'

'Who could it be?' Marjorie asked when the man was gone, and Isabel heard the hope of rescue or ransom in her voice; she looked at Mary Bruce and they shared the unspoken knowledge that it was unlikely to be either.

It was, as Isabel suspected, her husband.

He came in fur-wrapped against a chill that the women had grown used to but clearly bothered him and followed by the loathsome shadow of Malise Bellejambe. Her husband stood straight, Isabel saw, with a squared hint of the powerful shoulders left, his dirty grey grizzle of beard cocked haughtily.

Yet he was yellowed and gaunt, the hair on his head lank and the fur wrapping made him look like he had been caught in the embrace of a mangy, winter-woken bear and was struggling to break free.

She felt a leap of pity then, and an echo of feeling at his eyes, pouched and rheumed and unutterably weary – but it was an old statue, that feeling, the marble glory of it worn and weathered, clogged and smothered with the moss of neglect and anger.

Yet the death of Badenoch must have hit him hard, she thought, not to mention the forced alliance with the English he had always struggled against, because the Bruce stood on the other side.

Their endless feud was killing them both, she thought.

'*Ma Dame*,' he said icily. 'You are fair caught. I am vindicated at last.'

She heard the cold in him and felt only sadness at it.

'A great nation of vindicated corpses, that's us,' Mary Bruce answered and he turned his wet fish eyes to her, raking over the trembling Marjorie on the way.

'Quiet you,' he said with a stunning calm and a chilling dismissal of any deference to her rank. 'You are bound for Roxburgh, lady, while the child is bound for a nunnery somewhere south. Count yourself fortunate to be alive – though you will not think it when you find the plan Longshanks has for you.'

Marjorie started to wail at the thought of being parted and Buchan grimaced with distaste, then turned his gaze back on Isabel.

'You are bound for Berwick, where you will share the same fate, but on my own terms,' he said, which was sinister but left Isabel none the wiser. He jerked his head and, obedient as a belly-fawning mastiff, Malise moved to her, his grin feral in the dark ruin of his face.

'Malise will see to it. I commend you to his care, *ma Dame*. I commend you to God, for this is the last time you will see me. Never ask to do so, for it will be refused.'

He saw her, still lush and ripe – yet her face was haggard and there was snow in the autumn russet of her hair. She was, Buchan thought, a woman in the same way that a lion could be called a cat.

The memory hit him of the power he had had over her, the punishments he had inflicted for her transgressions, when he had gloried in her being stripped to 'twa beads, yin o them sweat'. Her transgressions . . .

'The last gift I shall give you will be the head of your lover when we find him, which you may care to look on before it is put on a spike.'

Which at least let her know that Hal was alive and free – and that she would live herself, though the triumphant sickle on Malise's face made her wonder if that was preferable. When she turned to her husband again, there was only a hole in the air where he had been.

'Come, lady.'

It was not a request and the hand Malise held out was not an invitation. With a chilling stone sinking in her belly, she looked into his too-bright eyes and realized she had been handed to her worst nightmare.

Closeburn Vill, Annandale
Vigil of St Athernaise of Fife, December, 1306

They came down to the English-dominated lands of the Bruce in a mourn of snow and sleet, stumbling from abbey to priory through brutal, metalled days of silvered frost and skies of iron and pewter. They were deferential and pious or garrulously merry when circumstances demanded it and no-one spared a single suspicious glance for two packmen, sweating south like snails with their lives on their backs.

Kirkpatrick had purchased the cheapjack wares from two delighted mongers paid more than they could earn in a year; one of them announced that he was quitting the travelling life for good and now Hal knew why, even as he applauded the disguise in it.

'It is perfect,' Kirkpatrick enthused, watching Hal eye up the hide packs, black with old grease against the weather. 'We are travelling at the right time, coming up to the Christ's Mass.'

He had that right, too, for they were in great demand for ribbons and silk thread and needles from folk who could ill afford the cost. It had become the fashion for burghers, cottars and serfs to give gifts to the manor 'for the glory of Christ's Mass' and, though an acorn tied with bright ribbon, or a sacking purse sewed up with silk thread seemed nothing, it was a sacrifice to folk who had little to begin with. And was done, Hal saw, out of only the hope of future favour.

So they tramped, horseless, down the days towards Closeburn, where Kirkpatrick had said Isabel lay.

'Three women,' he had told Hal. 'Taken to my kinsman's holding, together with Niall Bruce and the Earl of Atholl.'

'The women might be gone,' Hal had answered morose and hopeful at the same time. The 'or worse' was left unsaid, for he could not be sure, in his sinking cold belly, that a vengeful King Edward could kill Niall and an earl of the realm and yet spare the women.

'Aye, right enough,' Kirkpatrick had declared, 'but I am charged to seek out the King's sister and wee daughter, so that is what I will do. Will you come?'

There was no refusing it and he had made what provision he could for those he left behind. He remembered the thrashing Sim Craw, soaking his pallet branches with sweat and steaming in the cold air, while Dog Boy and Chirnside Rowan looked on.

'Take him to the King,' he had said. 'Neil Campbell will help. When that is done, go where ye will.'

Chirnside Rowan, who wanted home, nodded agreement, but Hal could hardly find the courage to look Dog Boy in the face and, when he did so, his heart creaked like a laden bridge.

'I ken,' he said softly, 'that there is little left at Herdmanston, less at my kinsman's Roslin. I may never return to it, even if this venture is a success, for I am outlaw and there is nothing for me there.'

Dog Boy felt stunned by it, could not move nor speak.

'I took you from Douglas,' Hal went on, speaking faster now, as if to rid himself of the words, 'at the behest of Jamie's stepma and never regretted it for an eyeblink. Now I release you. Find Jamie and tell him this – he will take you into his care and, Heaven willing, you will both be back at Douglas when God and all His Saints wake up in this kingdom.'

The youth's face was with him now, as he stood in the snow-humped riggs of a backcourt, feeling the wet cold seep up through his ruined soles. Pale and stricken at the thought of never seeing Hal again, the Dog Boy had brimmed his tears over and they had clutched briefly; the ache of it now was sharper than the keening snow wind.

Kirkpatrick tapped on a door, then again, then stood away from the faint light that would be spilled when someone came to answer it. He was grinning to himself when he saw it was her, her hand raised with a smoking crusie in it, the other clutching the wrap of warm wool to her as she stood, peering uncertainly.

'Who is it there?'

He stepped forward, into the falling faintness of the crusie's glow.

'Annie,' he said. 'Bigod, yer as lovely as ever ye were.'

Hal was astounded at the sharp yelp and the plunge of darkness as the crusie fell to sizzle in the snow. There was a pause and all their eyes adjusted.

'You . . .' she said and Kirkpatrick, still grinning, nodded. The blow took him by surprise, a calloused round-house slap that whipped his head sideways. Then Hal heard her burst into tears and Kirkpatrick felt the soft warmth of her, flung into his arms.

'Annie,' he said, working the jaw to see if any teeth had been loosened.

'Ye cantrip, recking dungheap,' she replied and sprang from him, hands on hips and the wrap flowing free so that Hal saw the considerable matronly curves of her through a dress too thin for the biting wind. She will catch chill, he thought wildly, then looked right and left to see if any of the nearest of her neighbours had come to spy.

341

'I will return, ye said,' she accused. 'And so ye have – a dozen years later.'

'Fifteen,' Kirkpatrick corrected and then wished he had not piled the truth on it.

'I was a lad,' he added weakly. 'With scarce any chin-hair.'

Her voice lowered too, with a swift backward glance – o-ho, thought Hal, there is a husband in this mix.

'And I scarce had quim fluff,' Annie hissed, 'neither of which stopped ye.'

'Ye were not unwilling,' Kirkpatrick replied desperately, for this was not entirely on the track he had planned. But he and Hal saw her face soften. It was plumped and blurred a little from the heart-stopper Kirkpatrick remembered, but still brought a stirring in him. First love, he thought with a sudden ache of loss and a leap of envy at what the hidden man in the house behind her had achieved over him.

'Weesht on that,' she said, with another quick, birdlike flick over one shoulder. 'I have a man noo – a good man who makes a fair livin' from shoemaking and merchanting in charcoal and I am Mistress Annie Toller. I dinnae want to present him with an auld love on his threshold.'

'Then do not,' Kirkpatrick declared with a rueful smile. 'Present me as Rab o' Shaws, a cheapjack in need of shelter. This is Hal o' Herdmanston likewise. Tell him we will give fair pay in ribbons and geegaws for warmth and whatever food he can spare.'

She shivered and not entirely from the cold.

'Black Roger,' she said softly and Kirkpatrick jerked at the name while Hal cocked his head with interest; this name was new.

'We hear of ye from time to time,' Annie went on. 'And that is the name that comes with it. If ye are back here on dark business, Roger, ye can go your way.'

'Nothin' o' the kind,' Kirkpatrick lied. 'I need ye to find Duncan, all the same. I need his help on a matter.'

'What matter?'

Kirkpatrick bridled.

'Annie, it is freezin' cold – yer turnin' blue on the step here.'

'What matter?'

Kirkpatrick turned and indicated for Hal to come forward.

'This is Hal o' Herdmanston,' he said. 'Sir Hal, no less. He and I are here after his light o' love, the Coontess o' Buchan.'

She had heard the tale of it, which raised eyebrows on Hal, for he had not realized. My love life is a bliddy *geste*, he thought savagely, for all to gawp at.

Kirkpatrick knew Annie would have sucked up the story of it and now she stared at the troubadour tale turned reality, standing with his soaked boots and mournful face on her doorstep. She bobbed a curtsey as one hand went to her mouth to keep her heart from surging out of it.

'Oh,' she said. 'The poor man. The lady. Oh. Come away in. In, afore ye freeze.'

Hal glanced sideways at Kirkpatrick and caught the sly grin and wink as he ducked through the door.

Her husband, Nichol, was a bluff-faced barrel of a man, at once suspicious of two strangers within his house and eager for their news and the payment promised, which would sweeten his wife for weeks to come.

'Ye can sleep in the coal shed,' he declared and shot a sharp glance to silence the start of protest from his wife. 'And eat separate an' what ye are given.'

Yet, while he pressed them for news of the roads and whether carts laden with coal could go up and down from Glasgow, he took Hal's boots and worked on them, almost as if his hands were separate from his nature.

In the end, of course, he gave more than he got in news and Hal marvelled at the subtle cunning of Kirkpatrick that unveiled the presence of too many English soldiery in Closeburn and that it had to do with the prisoners within.

'The Maister o' Closeburn is seldom seen,' Nicholl informed

them, stitching quietly and speaking with an awl in one corner of his mouth, 'at table or elsewhere. He plays chess and has found himself a clever opponent he is reluctant to give up, it is said, even though the others who came there at the same time have moved on.'

'A wummin?' asked Hal before Kirkpatrick could stop him; Nichol glanced up, beetling his brows.

'I never said so,' he replied, then lost the frown and shrugged.

'There were wummin arrived,' he admitted. 'The sister of King . . .'

He stopped, looked at them and carried on working needle through leather; Hal knew he was in a fury of worry about having started to mention Bruce and the word 'king' in the same breath among strangers who might report him. Kirkpatrick chuckled reassuringly.

'Dinna fash,' he soothed. 'No tattle-tongues here. It is to be hoped the sister does not share the fate o' her wee brother, God wrap him safe from further harm.'

There was a flurry of hands crossing on breasts, but Nichol grew taciturn from then on and, eventually, the conversation died; Hal and Kirkpatrick went off to the dubious comfort of the coal shed – which, Hal pointed out, was mercifully emptied, save for old dust.

'Aye,' Kirkpatrick mused. 'Poor commons, it seems. Too many to heat in Closeburn these days. To feed, too, for certes.'

'Which means it is stappit full of folk we need avoid,' Hal replied uneasily, knowing that the task they had set themselves was made harder.

'It can be done,' Kirkpatrick said out of the coal dark of the place. 'We need Duncan.'

Hal had been told of Duncan of Torthorwald, another Kirkpatrick but one who had followed Wallace and now suffered for it; he was outlawed and Torthorwald held now by the Master of Closeburn.

'He is prospering, is my namesake,' Kirkpatrick had declared.

'Closeburn and Auchencas and now Torthorwald, with Lochmaben handed to him to hold, on behalf of the Bohuns.'

And Hal had heard the bitterness there.

'Will this Duncan help?' Hal asked, wondering if a man who had fought in support of a Balliol king – and so a Comyn – would offer assistance to a Bruce. There was no reply and, eventually, Hal fell asleep.

He woke to the sound of rustle and grunt, a throaty sound bordered between shriek and hoarseness, so that he lay quiet in the velvet dark, unlatching the dirk from inside his tunic. The rhythm of it ended in the rasp of mutual breathing and then a faint, whispered voice.

'Did we wake him?'

'Naw. He dreams of his lost love and what he will do when he gets her back.'

Kirkpatrick slid out of the warm depth of Annie and silently blessed Hal and his countess for it had been that honeyed tale, as much as his hand at her fork, which had persuaded her to part with her old charms while they waited at the coal-shed door for Duncan.

He did not know of her desperate need to find a little of what had been lost between then and now, in the compromise of poverty and the grief of bairns lost in birthing, but he felt a little of it touch him, a tendril of something sharp and sweet.

It brought the knowledge, complete and out of the casket, of what he had given up all those years ago, sacrificed to the lure of the wider world and all its possibilities. His hand idled back to her wetness and she slapped his arm.

'Enough,' she hissed. 'We have been fortunate that my man sleeps like an auld log. I will risk no more. Never again, Roger – that was for sweet memory and auld times.'

Yet the fierce kiss she gave revealed the lie in it and choked his throat with all he wanted to say. The sudden arrival of a shadowed figure relieved him of the moment.

'Mistress,' said the shape, nodding to Annie.

'Duncan,' Kirkpatrick said.

'Black Roger,' the shadow acknowledged.

'Good,' said Hal, emerging from the black of the coal shed into the clear night, brilliant with stars and moon. 'I am Hal of Herdmanston, knight. Now we're all introduced, perjink and proper.'

Duncan nodded at Hal, stepping forward so that he was silvered by moonlight, a ghost in the dark. He was tall and broad, with a great bush of black beard grown against the cold and a cloak wrapped round him – as much to hide the weapons, Hal thought, as for heat.

'Ye had best go back, Mistress,' he said to Annie. 'Lest yer man miss ye.'

She bobbed a curtsey and half-paused as if to say something to Kirkpatrick, then ducked away; Hal could feel the heat of her emotions as her face disappeared into the dark.

'Ye are a muckhoond,' Duncan said, soft enough so that only Hal and Kirkpatrick could hear it; Kirkpatrick wondered how long Duncan had been waiting in the cold shadows, listening to him and Annie and said as much, adding, viciously, that he was sorry if he had strayed on to Torthorwald territory.

Duncan was suddenly close enough for Kirkpatrick to have the warm smoke of his breath on his face.

'Nichol Toller is a good man and, until ye arrived, Annie was a well-conducted wife,' he said. 'They dinna deserve the likes of you.'

'You will back off a step,' Hal said gently, though his voice held a rasp and Duncan felt the nudge in his ribs and looked down at the moon-silvered wink of steel.

'We are off to a bad start,' he declared and Hal nodded.

'Let us begin again, then,' he said. 'I am Sir Hal of Herdmanston. You address me as "my lord" an' you ask what you can do to assist us both and His Grace, the King.'

'What king is that, then?' Duncan demanded with a sneer.

'The one ye will wish as a friend in the future,' Kirkpatrick answered, recovering himself. 'The one who is not in France with his empty cote and no wish to return to these shores, having been pit aside by the *nobiles* o' this kingdom. Nor is it the covetous English one, whose death heralds the freedom of our realm – if ye believe the prophecies of Merlin. Have ye tallied it up yet, Duncan?'

'Whit why are ye here?'

Kirkpatrick smiled and laid out the meat of it and what he needed – good horses and supplies enough for five, for they hoped to have three women in tow when they came out of the castle of Closeburn. Duncan was no fool; he had heard of the prisoners and said so, rubbing his beard with the idea of such a blow being struck.

'That was weeks since. They may not be there still,' he added warningly. 'There has been a deal of skirrivaigin' by folk since then and a deal of it in secret, to foil such attempts.'

'Yet the Master of Closeburn plays chess with a prisoner,' Hal pointed out and Duncan's eyes narrowed.

'Ye have good intelligencing,' he answered, nodding. 'He is the man for that game, right enough, and complains of havin' no good players here. Until recently.'

'Isabel plays chess,' Hal answered, fixing Duncan with a grapple of eyes. 'So does Lady Mary Bruce.'

Duncan stroked his beard, frosting with his own breath in the night chill. Then he nodded.

'Five horses. Garrons only, nothin' fancy – those days are long gone,' he said, the last added with a grue of bitter ice.

'How will ye get in?'

Kirkpatrick smiled and winked.

Berwick Castle
At the same time

Isabel tallied up the number of years a body spent in growing, then in dying. Then she thought how long a person spent in bed,

347

asleep or awake, sick or well, fevered with lust or bad dreams. In her real world, only sickness or love justified daylight hours in a bed – yet this was not the real world and she knew that.

Snow-white sheets, a sable-fur covering, a red-velvet waterfall of privacy hangings, her head on down and linen – she dreamed of Balmullo and lay on filthy straw as if nailed. She had the imperative to move, knew she could not make her limbs work and felt like a laired toad, a salamander caught by the tail.

The room was hazily outlined and she knew people came and went, but she could not speak or even move her eyes and the panic this had first created in her – oh, what a lurch of heart, of shrieking terror that had been – was gone, replaced only by the calm slant of faint light on the stinking floor.

She could hear the sound of hammering. The cage. Malise had taken delight in telling her of it all the long journey across from Closeburn and she was not surprised, that first night they had stopped at Devorguilla's abbey in Dumfries, when he had come to her.

Sweetheart Abbey, they called it and the irony was not lost on her. She had fought and he had beaten her almost senseless, then forced his way into her. It had been mercifully short that first time, but he had done it since and more than once in the same night; she knew it was as much to do with the power he had now as with the act itself.

Malise would have been surprised at this, for he thought he was secret with his thoughts. The first time – Lord, that first time; after all the fervid dreams he'd had, he thought he would die of pleasure, especially when she fought and he had her, as he had always imagined it, naked and helpless and trembling at his feet.

She would have been surprised, too, that the foulness he spilled on her, thought and deed, was not from vicious hate but the opposite – Malise had found his love at last. She was his and his alone. At last, he could share all his thoughts and dreams with her, for she was not shared with anyone, saw no-one else.

So she had it all from him, all the things he could not tell anyone else, the cruel and obscene things he had kept to himself and now emptied on her like spilled seed.

Tortures of men and women, killings of them and children, too, in the name of her husband and for the greater furtherance of the Comyn and Badenoch and Balliol – and for his own pleasure and interest.

He knew bodies as well as any Bologna surgeon, she realized in that part of her mind which was turning as feverish as her body. He spoke of nerves laid bare, muscles racked or slashed, breasts torn off, the monstrosity of forced couplings.

Once, musing on whether he would fare better than his master and get her with child, he revealed how such a creature did not amount to very much.

'If you have it in your belly,' he marvelled, 'everyone lauds you for it, but the truth is that it is hardly anything of interest. I cut such a lady open once and it was such a frog of a thing with a big head, all curled and sticky. I threw it to the dugs.'

By the time they were crossing the Tweed into Berwick, she was littered up and barely conscious; the castellan, Robert de Blakebourne, took one look at her and savaged Malise away, cursing him.

Malise, concerned that he had gone too far, took to gnawing his nails and making his mind to be more circumspect while the castellan, a good man, tried to prise the lady loose from him entirely – and failed, with orders from an earl and King Edward himself.

A girl, Agnes, fed Isabel bread soaked in watered wine and she had been grateful for that because of the thirst – then watched the girl steal her last jewel, a locket with his hair; she hoped Malise did not catch the quine, for there would be blood.

She wondered where Malise was. There had been too much

349

blood already and she knew now that what had happened to her was the punishment of God for all her sins. She tried to call out her own name, but could not speak and all that came into her head was '*Ave Maria, gratia plena*' and then '*panem nostrum quotidianum da nobis hodie*'.

She lay in the tower room while they took away the shutters and made the window into a door leading to the cage they were fixing on the wall. When she was better – and the weather warmer, the castellan had insisted – she would be forced into the cage, in full view for most of the day, though she could retire 'for purpose of her privies' by asking her gaoler, Malise.

Blakebourne had also, for mercy, insisted that the cage be on the inside wall of the Hog Tower, so only the castle would see and not all the gawpers who chose to come up from the town itself.

Apart from the workmen, no-one came. When they had gone for the night, leaving her in the chill dark with the cold swooping talons through the open door-window, she breathed softly, easily, regularly. Started to count them – one, two. Out, in. Measuring her life.

She knew the dark was closing in. She liked the dark. In the dark she could dream up the sun of Hal and bask in it.

Closeburn Vill, Annandale
The day after . . .

They walked the market on a day of blue and gold and cheesecloth clouds, where breath still smoked and people bundled themselves up and stamped their feet. Closeburn was too small for a decent market and seemed to consist mainly of deals being done for the staples, the fleece skins of sheep slaughtered at Martinmas. Hal, who knew the business well, reckoned the clip would fetch a good price when it, in turn, was sold in the spring.

Kirkpatrick, chaffering and huckstering, dispensed good cheer and sold well, while Hal scowled and tried to keep his new-soled boots out of the worst of the mud. He felt guilty that Nichol had waterproofed them with pig fat while Kirkpatrick had been swiving his wife.

By the middle of the afternoon the glory of the day was gone back to iron and pewter, the dark closing in – but the deed, as Kirkpatrick said with satisfaction, was done; two cheapjacks had been seen plying their trade in the market and would now, unremarked, seek the hospitality of the castle, in the name of Christ and for a consideration to the Steward.

The Steward was a fat, harassed wobble and looked them up and down with some distaste. They had smeared fat on their faces against the cold and the charcoal dust had blackened it, while the rags wrapped round their hands against the freeze were grimy, the nails half moons of black.

'For God's Grace I cannot turn ye away,' he grumbled, 'but ye will eat at the end of the table and will share each other's platters – I cannot see another wanting yer mucky fingers in his gruel.'

Hal knew that it was more the gift of silver than God's Grace that had landed them at the Master of Closeburn's table, while Kirkpatrick hoped the reference to gruel was a jest and not a reality in this place of poor commons.

The hall was well lit and Kirkpatrick slid in, mouse quiet and head down, keeping his pack close to him when he sat and taking it all in. Hal dumped his in a corner and joined Kirkpatrick at a bench, where they exchanged wordless information on what they saw.

The top table was dominated by empty high seats – the Master of Closeburn was absent again and Hal drew attention to it with a sharp nudge in Kirkpatrick's ribs.

'Chess,' he whispered.

Kirkpatrick was scanning faces, relieved to see a few he knew slightly and who would know him only when he was not dressed so badly, or blackened of face. He had been more worried about the Closeburn women, but had suspected – correctly – that Closeburn's fortalice was too dominated by soldiery for their taste; they would be in Auchencas, peaceful and unmolested.

Most of those at the low table, above and below the salt, were soldiery of some sort, or travellers like themselves. There were a peck of wool dealers from the Italies, a friar and a deal of rough-faced men that Kirkpatrick thought to be garrisoned here rather than passing through.

The top table held three only, one of them a knight of St John, dark and sinister in his black surcote with its white cross. Kirkpatrick did not know any of them and nudged Hal in turn.

'The thin one with the fancy beard,' Hal whispered. '*Or, a fesse between two chevrons, gules.* That's Fitzwalter's arms – the crescent on it makes him a second son.'

'There is a John, I believe, who did not go to the Church,' mused Kirkpatrick softly. 'All the Fitzwalters are retinued to King Edward's son, the Caernarvon, so that explains them being here. How about the other – the younger one?'

Hal squinted while the noise washed the hall; a servant brought them dishes and slapped them down with poor grace, no doubt considering himself a cut above the ones he catered to.

'*Or, three bougets sable,*' Hal said with a frown. 'Again with a crescent. I know the device, but it should be three silver water butts on red, not black on gold – the arms of Ross.'

'Ah,' said Kirkpatrick, spooning pottage – surprisingly good – into his mouth. 'The Wark end of the Ross family, not the Tain end. But the end is the same – where a Ross is, there are his captives.'

Hal felt a leap inside him – yes, of course. The Ross had holdings in England, at Wark on the Tyne, so perhaps this sprig of the family tree was here to escort Isabel and the others further south. The idea gripped him, almost sprang him to his feet to rush off and search – the wet nose of a questing hound brought him sharply out of the moment and he looked down.

It was a rough-coated talbot and the feel of it, the smell of the pennyroyal rubbed in its coat against fleas, brought the Dog Boy so harshly back to Hal that he had to bow his head to hide the unmanning of his eyes. He would never see the boy, or Herdmanston again, that much he was sure of. Once Isabel was rescued, he and she were gone from this God-forsaken realm . . .

There was a ripple down the length of the hall; the high table had called for entertainment and declared that all the lower orders must provide some form of it for their supper. The friar had started to sing in a surprisingly good, if unsteady voice and folk beat the tables appreciatively. One by one the wool dealers started in, with songs and capers and jests of varying success; Hal started to shrink his neck into his shoulders as the wave of it washed towards them.

Then the young Ross was peering the length of the table and pointing his eating knife.

'You. You there – the babery at the foot.'

Folk laughed and Kirkpatrick immediately sprang to his feet and bowed, then capered with his arms long and his jaw thrust out, exactly like the baboon he had been compared to. There was a raucous roar of laughter and Kirkpatrick, from the corner of his mouth, hissed at Hal.

'Jakes. Search.'

Hal slithered away, clutching his stomach and those that bothered to see him at all jeered. Kirkpatrick watched him go, then capered further, picking up plate, eating knife and, finally, the priest's wooden spoon, juggled them briefly, then bowed again as people thumped the table.

The priest took back his spoon, staring at the imagined grime on it with distaste; Kirkpatrick bowed like a pretty courtier and apologized.

'You should think before you act, my son,' the friar sniffed piously.

'As to that, Father, I have to say that it is God's fault,' Kirkpatrick answered. 'For he gave Adam the means to think and a stout pizzle – but the ability only to work one at a time.'

The laughter was loud and long, inflamed by the rash of the friar's outraged face.

'Good,' declared the knight of St John in French. 'Do you perform other magicks? You are as black as any *saracin*.'

'Not as skilled as any of those you have just called "robber" in their own tongue,' Kirkpatrick replied in good English and saw the eyes of the Fitzwalter narrow. Good, he thought bitterly, let him know I understand French and the paynim tongue and am not the cheapjack I seem – well planned, Kirkpatrick.

In the same moment, he had heeled round on to the new road and spurred up it with a fresh plan.

'I can, however, reveal where you have lately come from,' he went on and the Hospitaller frowned a little at that, then shrugged.

'Well – speak on.'

'Let me know when I am wrang-wise,' Kirkpatrick said. 'From . . . Carlisle.'

Folk jeered, for that was hardly a feat given that anyone passing through Closeburn was either coming from or headed to that place.

'Before that – York,' Kirkpatrick added and had a murmur when the Hospitaller stayed silent. 'Before that . . .'

He paused and folk strained expectantly.

'London.'

Folk laughed. If York had been correct then London was less of a struggle for anyone to work out.

'Afore that,' Kirkpatrick went on. 'Bruges.'

The knight's forearms, straight on either side of his trencher, flexed under the tunic and his knuckles went white;

folk murmured at it, but most – who could not see that far – applauded this feat.

'Before that . . . Genoa,' Kirkpatrick went on smoothly and now the knight was leaning forward, snarling like a dog on a leash.

'Before that,' Kirkpatrick declared with a flourish, 'Cyprus.'

The knight rose with a scrape of chair, his face thunderous. He crossed himself.

'Heathen magicks,' he bellowed. 'Heresy . . .'

'Christ's bones, Sir Oristin – sit.'

It was the Fitzwalter, waving a languid hand and shaking his head. The Hospitaller sat, glowering into the easy smile of Fitzwalter, who turned appreciatively to Kirkpatrick, narrowing his eyes.

'Well done,' he said. 'Now explain the trick of it. I hope you do it well, for this brother in Christ has burning faggots in his eyes.'

There was silence now at how this had transpired and even the drunks were dry-mouthed – though Kirkpatrick would have wagered all his day's profits that one or two would count a burning heretic as fair entertainment to end with.

'No magic,' he said easily, spreading his hands. 'Carlisle is simple enough – no great spell needed to thasm up that. A one in two chance that the lord was coming and not going.'

His confidence unlatched the tension a little; a soldier, drunker than the rest, sniggered and was then cut off by a neighbour.

'Once Carlisle was sure, it is easy to pin York, because there is a commanderie of St John there,' Kirkpatrick went on and nodded deferentially to the knight. 'A good and pious knight of the Order would wish to have himself excused for spending too many nights away from any commanderie, to commend his soul to God before travelling onward.'

Now the knight was mollified and eased, Kirkpatrick saw; Fitzwalter was nodding and stroking his thinly razored beard.

'London is obvious, because it is where all travellers come from the ports of the south,' Kirkpatrick went on and paused, which was partly the showman in him, partly because this was the tricky part.

'Bruges,' he said slowly, knowing this was the tricky part, 'because it avoids Paris and a deal of France, which is an unhappy place thanks to King Philip the Fair. Or unfair, if you are a Templar or a Jew.'

Folk laughed at this – the Italies wool dealers mostly, who knew of the French king's plots against the Templars and of his banning all Jews so that he could seize their holdings and goods. No-one made much comment on the latter, all the same, since the king of France was simply copying the king of England and for the same reason.

'Indeed,' Fitzwalter mused. 'So far, so reasoned – Sir Oristin wishes to avoid the . . . awkwardness . . . of association with the Poor Knights in a country already fired with crusading fervour for proscribing heathen Jews.'

He turned to the Hospitaller. '

'Does he have the right of it so far?'

The Hospitaller, who was not proud of his avoidances, admitted it with a grudging nod.

'How did he know I have come from abroad at all,' he said in a sepulchral voice, 'let alone Genoa.'

Kirkpatrick shrugged.

'You were never born as dark,' he said with a laugh to take the sting from it, 'so acquired such a slap from a sun you do not find in these lands.'

'And Genoa is first and most common port for anyone coming from Cyprus,' he added with a lofty flourish, 'where the Knights of St John have had their largest commanderies since they left the Holy Land.'

Now there was laughter, from relief Kirkpatrick thought. The young Ross of Wark shifted in his seat as though cocking a buttock to fart and scowled at Kirkpatrick.

'You are well informed for a cheapjack,' he pointed out suspiciously and Kirkpatrick beamed back at him.

'I make as much from news and the reasoning of it as from ribbons and needles,' he answered and those who knew business well enough nodded agreement and grinned. Kirkpatrick, buying time for Hal, nudged the stallion of this up into a canter.

'It is such reasoning that lets me reveal, if the bold knight of St John allows, why he is here in Closeburn.'

Fitzwalter's eyebrows went up and the Hospitaller shifted uneasily.

'Well,' Fitzwalter declared slyly, 'this is better entertainment – what say you, Sir Oristin? Can he magick out your secrets?'

'Reason, not magic,' Kirkpatrick corrected hastily and Fitzwalter acknowledged it with a mocking bow while the heads of all the others swung to and fro between them; some had even worked out the danger of the game being played.

The Hospitaller was clearly unhappy at the prospect, but he could not admit it under Fitzwalter's eye and eventually nodded. Silence fell and people waited eagerly.

'Your commanderie in this kingdom is Torphichen,' Kirkpatrick declared, 'which is far from here – yet you would be there now if you had travelled from the one in York. You did not and will pay penance for it – so your reason for being here is pressing.'

The Hospitaller stiffened.

'A lady?' the drunken soldier called out and the celibate knight was halfway out of his seat seeking the culprit with glaring eyes; young Ross wisely soothed him sitting again.

'Not lady, nor pursuit of personal gain,' Kirkpatrick went on, as if thinking it out – though he had done that long since. 'So a quest then. The Holy Grail perhaps.'

The Hospitaller relaxed in his seat a little and some of the audience applauded, thinking he had got it right. One or two called out 'God be praised' and the rote reply sibilated round the table.

357

'Yet,' Kirkpatrick declared like a knell and let it hang there for a moment.

'The Grail has remained hidden for many hundreds of years,' he went on. 'They say the Templars have it and that Order does not deny it, so knights seldom quest for it these days – and knights of St John are forbidden to do it, out of the sin of pride.'

'True enough,' Fitzwalter confirmed. 'So – no Grail discovered in Closeburn then.'

Kirkpatrick held up one grimy, wrapped hand and brought the laughter to a halt.

'There are other reasons for a knight of St John to be abroad from his commanderie,' he continued, 'but almost all of them are because he is on the business of the Order.'

'Which should remain the business of the Order,' the knight growled warningly.

'As it will,' Kirkpatrick answered smoothly. 'Though this is not the business of the Order.'

'You dare . . .'

'Let him speak,' Fitzwalter declared and there was enough steel in his voice for the Hospitaller to glance at him with a threat of his own.

'The business you have with the Order is at Torphichen,' Kirkpatrick went on while the two knights locked glances; he saw it was the Hospitaller who looked away, 'and you are a confirmed and pious and loyal knight of St John.'

'I am,' growled the knight. 'You would do well to remember that.'

'You are also Sir Oristin Del Ard,' Kirkpatrick went on, 'and have retained the arms of your house on the hilt of that fine eating knife. Not permitted by your Order, of course, for the sin of pride and avarice and a few others no doubt. But excusable – you are not alone in it.'

The knight was all coil now, like a snake waiting to pounce.

'The Del Ards are in the retinue of the Earl of Ross in the

north,' Kirkpatrick went on and then waved one hand to the young scowl on the other side of the Hospitaller.

'And here is your liege lord's kin, from Wark. No doubt he will be pleased with the news you bring to him first, before you take it to Torphichen.'

Now both the knights were on their feet and snarling demands for this to end. Fitzwalter thumped the table until the noise of that beat down the cries and shouts; the young Ross and the Hospitaller subsided, scowling.

'Well,' said Fitzwalter with a thin smile. 'That was more entertainment than any imagined. I am sure these two *nobiles* are pleased that it is over, before the curiosity of their very heads is brought out for our amusement.'

There was laughter and the talk flowed back, soft as honey; Kirkpatrick was not surprised when Fitzwalter sent a man down with coin – more than was necessary for the amusement provided. He wants to know the news the Hospitaller brings to Ross, he thought to himself, and will be disappointed, for I am not about to reveal it.

Kirkpatrick was almost sure – and revealing it would unveil his own standing in places too high for his disguised station – that the knights of St John were planning an attack on heathen-held Rhodes. That had been the talk in the quiet of the Bruce night, between brothers and those as trusted. Partly, they had worked out, because the Hospitallers needed a new base, not dependent on the good graces of the Lusignan who owned Cyprus, and because such an attack would show the Pope and others that they, unlike the Templars, were still capable of striking a blow against the infidel.

Knowledge of the when and where of all that would be financially advantageous to the Ross, who had trading concerns in Cyprus.

'What does your companion do?' demanded the young Ross loudly, cutting through the chatter. 'Is he as gifted with reason?'

'Almost the opposite, my lord,' Kirkpatrick said, standing and bowing deferentially, 'since he has not the sense to avoid drinking water from streams, which accounts for the state of his belly. Never drink water in preference to small beer, my ma said to me.'

There was laughter at that, but Kirkpatrick was sweating at the attention drawn to the absent Hal. Yet he had his own plan and started to put it out.

'In truth, I hardly know the man. I met him on the road two days since and we travelled for the safety in it.'

'You say?' murmured Fitzwalter thoughtfully, but Ross of Wark had the recent bitterness of plots revealed still stuck in his craw and wanted to bring this mountebank cheapjack down.

'I reason,' he said triumphantly, 'that you are a lute player, since you wrap those grimy rags round each individual finger, so allowing you to strum.'

'A good bowman does the same,' Kirkpatrick pointed out and Ross dismissed it with a scornful wave.

'You never drew one well,' he sneered.

'A lockpick does the same,' Fitzwalter offered. 'Or a light-fingered dip.'

'Heaven forfend,' Kirkpatrick answered, crossing himself piously and hoping that no-one worked out that a good man with a dirk needed his fingers nimble, too. Then he smiled.

'Or a wee chiel who sells fiddly needles and thin thread and needs pick them out o' a pack,' he added and Fitzwalter acknowledged it with a thin smile, while the rest of the table laughed.

'Your reason is flawed,' Fitzwalter said to the sulking young Ross. 'Your monger here wraps his fingers to preserve his fortune. Pity – I would have welcomed a good lute player.'

'Reason and Fortune were ever rivals,' Kirkpatrick declared, while the food wafted in and out of his nostrils, clenching his belly with desire. 'I have tale on it, if your lordship pleases –

and is disposed to make a wee bit meat come my way, by way of recompense.'

'A tale? Good enow. Steward, I daresay you have mutton, hung for the right amount of time and now cooked – hung since Martinmas if these wool dealers are any mark. I am expecting it on my own trencher and am sure you can find a bone or three for this man.'

The steward managed a smile and a deferential bow. The hall silenced, looking at Kirkpatrick, who took a breath.

'Once,' he began, 'Reason and Fortune argued over who had rank on the other. Fortune declared that the one who managed to do more would be the better. "See that ploughboy there?" he said to Reason. "Get inside him and if he is better with you than with me, I will stand aside for you anywhere we meet." So Reason got inside the boy's head.

'When the boy felt Reason in his head, he began to think: "Why should I plough field all my life? I could be happy somewhere else, too." He went hame then and telt his da, who promptly beat him for his impudence and ignorance, since serfs bound to the land cannot just do as they wish.'

'And with good reason,' the friar announced, then realized what he had said and subsided, face flaming, amid a welter of laughter.

Good, good, Kirkpatrick thought as he waited for it to die. Now they have forgotten the wee Lord o' Herdmanston; I hope he takes due advantage.

Hal had gone out and up the spiral of worn stairs, for all jakes were up and there was a servant nearby who could see him on the stairtop. He wanted to go down, for captives were more likely to be down – but there was the chance that the chess-playing lord of Closeburn would not be pushing rooks and pawns in the cellar, but in his own comfortable solar. With Isabel.

He went up, reached the next floor. Left or right – he went

right, along a flagged corridor, narrow enough to make him weave along it to avoid the sconces. Well lit, he thought, feeling for the hidden dagger – then recoiling from the hilt as if it stung.

Foolishness. Try anything with a blade in it and they were lost . . .

He stepped cautiously round a corner – this was the keep at Closeburn, square and solid as a stone block – and came face to face with an astonished servant, his hands full of bowls and a brass ewer. Food and wine, Hal noted swiftly, for those who were behind the door, open enough to spill out yellow light – expensive yellow light, Hal noted, from beeswax candles, which turned the helmet of the guard to gold.

'Who . . . whit why in the name o' God are ye up here?'

The servant was astounded and truculent, his round face indignant. Hal clutched his belly and whimpered.

'That way, ye jurrocks,' the servant declared, pointing with his chin back the way Hal had come. 'An' dinna you mess the floors afore ye get to it.'

Hal, obedient and scurrying, whipped round and left, his mind racing with the certainty that he had found the Master's refuge. Behind him, he heard the servant berating the guard to follow Hal and make sure of him; in turn, the guard stolidly defended his remaining where he was, as ordered.

He reached the spiral stair and went down, back to the level of the hall, paused to make sure the servant could no longer see him and darted downwards. Incongruously, he heard only one voice and knew it was Kirkpatrick's but did not know why – if he had heard it right – the man would be discoursing about ploughboys.

'The ploughboy,' Kirkpatrick declared to his rapt audience, 'whose name was Tam, then ran off, never thinking of what ruin this brought on his da and his brithers, left to pay the price to their liege lord. Tam ran to the nearest toon, for it is kent that if ye can stay hidden in a toon for a year and a day, ye escape the punishment o' yer rash disregard for God's plan for the world.'

Kirkpatrick paused, to allow for the head-shaking and tutting of noble and friar.

'He sleekit himself into work at the castle, though it was of the meanest kind – he became a gong farmer, covered in shite crown to toe every day. But paid well for it – as much as a good latch bowman.'

The crossbow soldiery took the jeers of their comrades well enough, though some sharp words from the top table had to stop the drunken worst from rabbling there and then. Kirkpatrick waited patiently, ticking off the seconds and hoping Hal made the most of them; the sweat was trickling icy trails down his back and pooling where his tunic belt cinched.

'The castle never smelled as sweet wi' Tam at the cesspits, so that the Earl declared it a pleasure to turd and it was to be hoped that this sweet-smelling addition to life would please his daughter. She was a ripe beauty, right enow, with a chest o' treasures in more ways than just the one – but had stopped speaking entire when she was nine and had not peeped once since then. Not a single person kent the why of it, neither.'

The soldiery perked up at this – beautiful damsels with large chests of treasure made for a good tale in their eyes and Kirkpatrick, who had known this – and even tailored his speech from the neat southern English to the rawer north, where most of the men-at-arms came from – saw Fitzwalter had also noted this, was stroking his beard, thoughtful and considered.

He is a creishie wee fox, that yin, Kirkpatrick thought, hoping he did not go dry-mouthed, hoping – Christ save us – that Hal remembered his place. One slip and we are spiked on some city gate.

Hal had no idea of his place save that it was in the dim of the undercroft, a maze of cellars, most of them emptied. He knew the kitchen was on the other side of the hall and surmised that

363

these cellars had been emptied to take captives, but the doors of most of them were locked tight.

Then, in the grey gloom, he heard a door rattle open, the jingle of keys and a burst of red-gold light. He froze, trapped, then fell into the belly-curled whimper he had been adopting all along, so that Dixon stared, amazed, his blue bottom lip wobbling with the surprise of it.

'Jakes,' Hal groaned and Dixon stirred and frowned.

'A garderobe in an undercroft?' he growled. 'Are ye slack-wittit? Go up, ye daftie. Get ye gone . . .'

He lashed out with his only weapon, the heavy keys and Hal took it on a shoulder, wincing as he backed away and scuttled back up the stairs, to where a troubled earl wanted his daughter to speak.

'The Earl declared that whoever teased his daughter to speak would be married on to her,' Kirkpatrick declared. 'Many tried – clivver *nobiles* from all the airts and pairts – but the lovely quine stayed silent.'

'Now there's a blissin',' called out one of the soldiers. 'A perfect wummin . . .'

The laughter allowed Hal to scurry into the hall again, but Kirkpatrick saw Fitzwalter staring past him and, when Hal arrived back at the table, knew the knight had been marking the return.

'So Tam was busy digging out the cess this day when the Earl's daughter passed, walking eechsie-ochsie with her wee pet dug, which was a four-legged clevery and seemed to ken what his mistress wanted without her speakin'.

'So Tam began to talk to the dog: "I heard that you are very smart and I want advice from you. We were three travellers – a carver, a tailor and me, who journeyed on as yin. At camp that night, the carver took first watch and, because he had not much to do, he took a piece of wood and made a nice wee girl of it.

'"Then he woke the tailor. The tailor saw the wooden girl

and took scissors, needle and thread and began to sew a dress, which he put it on the girl. Then it was my turn to watch – and I taught her to speak, so that she came into life. In the morning, when they woke up, everybody wanted to have the girl. The carver said: 'I made her.' The tailor said: 'I dressed her.' I also wanted to have the girl. Tell me, wee smart dug, who should have the girl?" And Tam waited, cocking his head as if expecting a real reply from the wee dug.'

There was silence in the hall as everyone mulled the problem; Kirkpatrick could hear Hal's ragged breathing, glanced quickly down to see him nurse his shoulder and did not like what that revealed or the unease it crawled into him.

'Well?' demanded the young Ross truculently and Kirkpatrick was jerked back to the moment.

'Well,' he declared, spreading his hands, 'of course the wee dug did not speak – but the Earl's daughter did. "Who else than you should have her?" she says, tart as you please. "What is a carver's wooden girl? What is tailor's dress without speech? You gave her the best gift – life and speech – so you should have the girl."'

There was laughter at that, for they all knew Tam the *gongfermor* had won.

'That put fox in the henhoose,' Kirkpatrick declared, sweating now. '"So you have decided for yourself," Tam said to the Earl's daughter. "I gave you speech and life, so you should be mine." Needless to say, the Earl had other ideas about his precious quine getting married on to a shit-covered chiel. He offered another good reward, but Tam had Reason in him, telling him that an earl's word was law in his own domain and if the Earl wanted people to behave according to law, he must behave in that way too. The Earl must give up his daughter.'

'This will not turn out well,' the friar mourned and folk shushed him. Kirkpatrick acknowledged the priest with a wave.

'You are right,' he said, 'for the Earl announced that Tam

would lose his head for his impudence and the poor boy was bound and led to the block. The best axeman turned up and spat on his palms, then raised his weapon high.'

Kirkpatrick paused for the effect and had gratifying silence.

'Fortune stepped in. "Get well out of him," Fortune declares to Reason. "See what a pass ye have brought the lad to." So Fortune got in the boy, the axe swung – and the shaft snapped. Before he could fetch another weapon, the daughter had prevailed on her da to relent, that she would marry the lad.

'So there was a grand wedding,' Kirkpatrick declared with a flourish, 'to which all were invited, Reason included, and most came. But seeing he would meet Fortune, he ran away – and, since that time, when Reason meets Fortune, Reason stands aside so Fortune can pass.'

There was applause and laughter; with an airy wave, Fitzwalter had the steward deliver meat to the two packmen and the hall washed with new chatter and arguments over Fortune and Reason.

'What was all that?' Hal hissed, head down as if concentrating on his trencher.

'Smoke and mirrors,' Kirkpatrick answered grimly. 'I hope it was worth the work – did you find anything?'

Hal was suddenly ravenous, turned his black, greased, beaming face on Kirkpatrick as he reached for bread and meat.

'I ken where your named kinsman is,' he said between mouthfuls. 'So there she will be also.'

Kirkpatrick nodded, chewing and thinking of the fulfilment of his mission to his king – and the revenge he would take at the same time.

He thought of the ring, the one he had taken from Creishie Marthe at Methven, the one she had cut from the hand of a throat-slit man-at-arms.

The ring now snugged up in a purse under his armpit. Such a wee bauble, he marvelled, to bring such ruin to lives.

CHAPTER SIXTEEN

Closeburn Castle, Annandale
Later that night . . .

They went up, creeping from the snoring hall, stepping
carefully over the sleepers; the friar stirred and yelped like a
bairn in some deep dream and Hal stopped like a deer with a
scent, one foot half-poised in his felted socks.

He had his boots round his neck because Nichol's cobbling
had resulted in new, thick leather slats for grip, which now
clacked like nails, loud as a bell in a rimed silence such as this
cold hall.

The sleepers here were all of Closeburn's least – the servants,
the dogs and the ill-considered guests; Kirkpatrick wondered
if the friar was dreaming some idea of what the future held,
when daylight revealed all that had happened.

Hal stepped on, his breath grey-blue smoke; they wreathed
out and up, Kirkpatrick's soft, deer-soled boots making no
sound. Hal envied him as the cold seeped chill through the
wool and into his feet.

They went along the corridor, the sconces burned to dark
ash now, crept to the corner and poised, trying not to breathe,
harsh with the tension. This was where the guard had been –

Kirkpatrick, his mouth dry, risked a look, drew back and put his lips close enough for Hal to feel his hot breath on his ear.

'The servant only – across the door. We will needs deal with him.'

Hal locked eyes with him, knowing what Kirkpatrick meant. He shook his head, mimed a blow and Kirkpatrick, after a pause, shrugged. He moved close to the sleeping bundle across the threshold, knelt and put the fluted dagger in the man's heart at the same time as he smothered his mouth. There was only a brief whimper and then stillness, so that when Hal came up, all bristling with silent outrage, Kirkpatrick straightened, wiped the dagger and shrugged.

'Always best to *mak' siccar*,' he hissed and opened the door.

The room was warm, the brazier on a slab still glowing like a fierce red eye. There were three beeswax candles in tall holders streaked with old meltings and the light was a glow on the two men, heads almost touching, bent over the chess set; they looked up with astonishment as Hal and Kirkpatrick stepped in, the latter dragging the body of the servant and closing the door.

'Who in the name of God are you?' demanded one, starting to rise, but Kirkpatrick was round on him like a stoat on a rabbit, the long dirk winking like gold in his fist.

'Easy, kinsman,' he said with a vicious grin and Sir Roger, the Master of Closeburn, sat down heavily, one hand at his throat.

'Black Roger,' he said faintly.

'The same.'

'Where is Isabel?' demanded Hal, looking round in bewilderment and then at the other player. 'Who are . . . wait. I ken your face.'

'So ye should,' Kirkpatrick declared and moved swiftly to disarm his namesake of his dagger. 'Yon is the wee man who treated us both at times, for injuries gained in the service of his liege lord.'

'The physicker,' Hal said uncertainly. 'Bruce's doctor.'

'What do you want here?' demanded the Master of Closeburn, recovering enough to try and reassert himself; Hal saw him clearly for the first time and was struck how like Kirkpatrick he was. You could not miss the kinship, Hal said to himself, though the Master was older, heavier of face and body.

It was a marvel Kirkpatrick had not been spotted the minute he stuck his face inside the castle – but then the face had been black as a Moor's and no-one would have given a wee cheapjack a second glance. Still – Hal now knew why Kirkpatrick had looked so sweated, having to stand with all eyes on him and the possibility of his likeness to his namesake kinsman imminent.

Kirkpatrick nudged him impatiently out of this, indicating for him to search the physician for arms and, when that was done, turned back to his namesake, now sitting upright and tensed as if to spring.

'I would unlatch that look,' Kirkpatrick said, 'if I were you, kinsman. A word or deed misplaced will see you trying to stuff yer blood back in yer throat with both hands.'

'Whit why are ye here?' Sir Roger demanded again, though he unclenched a little.

'He is here for me,' said the physician quietly and Kirkpatrick chuckled and nodded. Hal looked from one to the other, then back to Kirkpatrick.

'What is this? Where is Isabel?'

'Isabel?' repeated Sir Roger. 'Isabel who?'

'Coontess o' Buchan,' Kirkpatrick answered smoothly, then threw something on the desk, where it tinkled and spun slightly; a ring, Hal saw. The physician reached out one hand and lifted it as though his fingers had suddenly become fat sausages that did not belong to him.

'I took it from Creishie Marthe at Methven,' Kirkpatrick said, 'who had fresh cut it aff the finger o' a wee man-at-arms whose shield told his allegiance – Closeburn.'

'Robert Haws,' Sir Roger said, almost wearily. 'He never returned. We never found trace of him at all.'

'Aye, weel, he is dead, certes, since I saw Creishie Marthe slit his throat wide. Ye are goodly shot of him,' Kirkpatrick answered, 'for he was the thieving wee rat who stole James of Montaillou's most precious possession. Being a prisoner, poor wee James could hardly protest and you would not have cared much then, kinsman – until ye discovered what secrets this physicker had to tell. Secrets to bring a rich reward from Edward of England.'

He nodded at the doctor, sitting stunned and holding the ring.

'A singular ring,' he went on, 'which I noticed more than once when ye were tightening wraps on my ribs and slapping stinging ointment on my bruises.'

He stopped and grinned savagely at Hal, who stood like an ox, as stunned as the physician and the Master of Closeburn by all this.

'If ye look closely at it,' Kirkpatrick went on, speaking rapidly now, 'ye will see it has a hand, a heart, a bag of gold, a death's head and some fine wee writing in Langue D'Oc that says: "These three I give to thee, Till the fourth set me free." I surmise the fourth has set the wummin free.'

'She was my wife . . .' the doctor said, then stopped and bowed his head.

'Until ye became a Cathar. Did ye renounce the world as a Perfect? Or did she?'

James of Montaillou groaned and turned his anguished face on Kirkpatrick.

'You know. You have seen. You were there.'

Kirkpatrick nodded grimly.

'I was there. With Fournier and D'Albis during the *risorgimento*.'

Hal heard the bitter venom in his voice, knew it for the shame it was and was surprised. He knew the names of

Jacques Fournier and Geoffrey D'Albis, resolute prosecutors of the Inquisition; so that had been Kirkpatrick's crusade – against the Cathars in Carcassone. Small wonder he knew the lands of Oc, songs and all – and the *lingua franca* of the likes of Lamprecht.

'Was she a "Bonne Femme", my wee runaway?' Kirkpatrick went on, vicious and soft. 'Yin of these women who have achieved complete denial of the flesh you folk say is the province of the Devil? Yin who would no longer suffer resurrection back into it and so could die happy?'

The physician bowed his head and sobbed; Hal shook himself and growled. He did not know what Kirkpatrick was talking about, but the 'bonne femme' brought back why he was here and what Kirkpatrick was doing to the wee Bruce physicker. He might just as well have stuffed embers under the man's fingernails.

'Enough of this – the Coontess o' Buchan,' he spat. 'Lady Mary Bruce and the child, Marjorie. Where are they kept?'

Sir Roger opened and closed his mouth a few times, then saw Kirkpatrick's face and laughed, a sharp, nervous bark.

'Is that why you are here?' he demanded and laughed again so that Hal lifted his own dagger a fraction in warning.

'They are gone, weeks since,' the Master of Closeburn said. 'Mary Bruce is in a cage at Roxburgh by now – the Coontess o' Buchan similarly prisoned at Berwick. The wee lassie went south to a convent – Christ's Bones, a man who had jaloused I had a Cathar here would have kent that the wummin were long gone.'

He smiled, a lopsided sneer, looking at Kirkpatrick's stone face, then at Hal's stricken one.

'Ye have been cozened, sirra – and ye will hang with this one, mark me. A word from me . . .'

'And ye die,' Kirkpatrick declared, then turned into Hal's stare.

Hal knew the truth of it; Kirkpatrick had known Isabel

371

was long gone from here, had used him to help in this task – whatever it was. He did not know what business Kirkpatrick had with his kinsman or Bruce's physicker, but the sick certainty in it was red murder, of which he had been made a part. Again.

Kirkpatrick saw the sea-haar grey cloud Hal's eyes, knew it well and grew alarmed.

'Hal, there are matters here beyond ye . . .' Kirkpatrick began and then reeled as he was struck. With a cry he stumbled back and fell – Sir Roger immediately leaped up, heading for the baldric hanging in the shadows and the sword sheathed up in it.

'Ach – no. Hal – have sense . . .'

Hal saw Sir Roger's rabbit bolt and, by sheer instinct, went after him. James of Montaillou saw his chance and sprang for the door – caught a foot in the bundle of the dead servant and fell headlong, clattering loudly into the door.

Cursing, Kirkpatrick spidered his way upright, scrabbled across to where James of Montaillou lay, moaning; there was blood coming from his head and Kirkpatrick found the frantic trapped-bird beat of his heart beneath his tunic, felt for the right spot with his fingers – individually wrapped, he thought with a vicious triumph – and slid the dagger in.

The physician bucked and kicked. Behind him, Kirkpatrick heard clattering and cursing.

Hal caught Sir Roger round the waist an instant before the man's hand reached the sword hilt, dragging him back and on to the floor. A candle holder toppled; the chess set scattered with a patter like rain and they wrestled, panting and growling like pit dogs, amid the sputtering wax.

Sir Roger was stronger, almost hurled Hal off, managed to get to his feet and was gripped again, so that they strained like locked stags; Hal felt the sinews pop, felt the burn of overworked muscles and knew he could not win by strength.

He had come up with a desperate strategy when his opponent suddenly coughed and all resistance went from him.

Then he vanished from in front of Hal, who stood and blinked at the curled snarl of Kirkpatrick, dagger in one hand and the dragging weight of his namesake in the other.

Kirkpatrick let the last of the Master of Closeburn sink to the bloody litter of the floor and he and Hal stood facing each other, half crouched and panting raggedly.

'Done and done,' Kirkpatrick said hoarsely and was wrenched forward into Hal's face by a fisted hand.

'Ye cantrip,' Hal hissed. 'No Isabel – ye cozened me, Kirkpatrick . . .'

'Afore someone comes to find out the bangin' in the solar,' Kirkpatrick answered with a hiss of his own. 'It would be better for us to be gone and argue this later.'

Hal burned with the rage of it, the sheer injustice of it – and the fact that Isabel was further away than before. In a cage, yet. A cage!

'I hope this was worth it,' he snarled at Kirkpatrick, who offered a shaky smile. Well, both men were dead and the secret of Bruce's lepry, if that was what it was, was safe from the ears of his enemies. Mind you, Kirkpatrick thought, the wee physician did not deserve it – but the Master of Closeburn did. All the same, Kirkpatrick would have done in his kinsman namesake for the pleasure of personal revenge for old slights and the fact that he was an enemy of the Bruce was as good an excuse as any.

He said nothing all the same, only indicated for Hal to fetch the dead Sir Roger's sword.

It was a fine weapon, with the Master's arms emblazoned within the pommel circle – the blue cross of Bruce's Annandale, surmounted by a blue bar with three glowing gold grain sacks, arrogant symbol of the source of Closeburn's wealth; Hal offered it pointedly to Kirkpatrick, who grinned and shook his head.

'You are handier with a sword than me,' he declared. 'I have little use for it.'

Then he was out, wraithing as silently as he had arrived on his deer-hide soles, leaving Hal to turn and look at the ruin they left, stinking with the fresh-iron of spilled blood, littered with the raggle of bodies. A slaughter, he thought bitterly, the wake Kirkpatrick always left.

He stuffed it into the great locked and iron-banded chest inside his head which was already creaking under all the sins put away in it. Pandora never had such a box, he thought.

Then he followed Kirkpatrick, sword in hand, felted sock-soles sticky with congealing blood, leaving only the gore and the bodies and the job done for a king. He had gone a dozen steps, back to the top of the spiralling stairs before he caught up with Kirkpatrick and they glided down together, back to the hall entrance, where they stopped and listened.

Breathing and snoring . . . and a shuffle below them, growing stronger. A jangle that Hal knew well enough, for the bruise it had left ached to the bone on his shoulder and he mimed the turning of a key for Kirkpatrick's benefit, saw the man nod and felt the wind of him leaving.

There was a grunt and soft slap of sound and, a moment later Kirkpatrick was back, wiping the dagger on his sleeve; he gave Hal a feral grin and then moved quietly into the hall.

Jesu, Hal thought, that is four he has killed in less time than it would take to drink a stoup. He felt his gorge rise at the thought and quelled it with vicious panic – fine thing, to be caught because he bokked over his socked feet in the middle of a sleepin' hall.

They got out of the hall because the small postern set in one of the big locked doors was unbarred and the servant sleeping near it could have been stepped on and never noticed, judging from the smell of pilfered drink seeping from him like heat.

They ran out of luck at the last. The main gate had its thick-grilled yett lowered, the great double doors heavily shut and barred, the guards awake and alert in the stamping cold – but this was Closeburn and Kirkpatrick knew it well; there was a postern sally-gate in a wall behind the stable and he led them to it unerringly.

Unguarded at every other time but this, he discovered, and cursed because he should have realized that the heightened alerts, the important captives, the swirl of English and the threat of Scottish raid would all have conspired to place two good men on this weak spot.

Hal and Kirkpatrick came up, sleekit as thieves and all unaware until the shapes materialized from the shadows and hailed them with growls.

It was the matter of them coming from inside that saved them, Hal thought, for the guards were looking for folk from outside trying to get in, so these were no threat. That changed when Hal swung up the sword and slashed one man's forearm with it, the blow hitting leather and mail, slicing through both in a spray of metal rings and breaking the bone with the force.

The man screamed like a girl, high and shrill, so that Hal, cursing, rammed the point in his mouth, snapping teeth and driving straight to the back of the man's skull and out the far side; the falling weight dragged Hal in a half-stumble and he wrenched and tore at the now trapped sword, while the dead man's head flopped and jerked.

Kirkpatrick went for the other one, the adder's tongue dagger flicking, only to hiss off the man's maille. Shocked, the guard staggered away, losing his spear and fumbling for a sword even as he brought his shield up. No chance now for fancy dagger work, Kirkpatrick realized and hurled himself bodily on the man, bowling the pair of them over; the guard bellowed.

Hal saw them rolling, the guard frantic to shove Kirkpatrick away and the shield now a liability as Kirkpatrick fought to grab the sword hand. Hal put his blood-soaked foot on the dead man's face, two hands on the hilt and hauled the sword out like Excalibur from the stone, the sudden release scattering a spray of bone and brain.

The second guard was wild and whimpering, flailing madly with the shield to keep Kirkpatrick at bay; a lucky blow whacked a knee and Kirkpatrick felt the white pain explode in him, the dazzling burst of it blinding. Scrabbling madly, he managed to get to his feet, the knee thundering with agony, saw the guard's triumphant snarl and the sword in his other hand like a long bar of deadly light.

Then there was a hiss and a thump, the guard's head bent sideways on his neck, a peculiar slew that was all wrong for his body; then he was gone and Hal stood over the fallen shadow, panting like a mad dog, the sword bloody in his fist.

'Aye til the fore,' he growled, his grin sharp in the clear moonlight. Kirkpatrick moved shakily, his knee buckling and lancing pain into him. There were shouts and lights – then the dread sound, like a knell, of someone beating an alarm-iron.

'Said ye were the man for that sword,' Kirkpatrick growled, limping to the postern and throwing up the bar on it. 'Now we had better make like a slung stone.'

Their progress was more of a slow-rolling pebble and Hal had to help the hirpling Kirkpatrick along most of it until, stumbling out of the riggs of a back court on to a rough track at the edge of Closeburn he stopped and sank down. Even allowing for moonlight, Hal thought as he glanced at him, that is a milk-pale face. Behind, bringing both their heads round, they heard the bark and bay of dogs.

'Hounds,' Kirkpatrick said, hoarse with pain. 'Go. Fetch the horses here. Hurry.'

It was as good a solution as could be found, so Hal did not argue and paused only to force his soaked, sticky feet into his boots, then moved off in a half-crouch to where Donald was supposed to be waiting, feeling the ooze of other people's blood between his toes.

The loom of the horse, like some dark nemesis from the shadows, almost made him scream and lash out, but he saw the figure leading it, caught a glimpse of her pale, anxious face

376

and stopped the blow with an effort that left him shaking and panting.

'Sir Hal.'

Annie was fretted and shivering and Hal knew something was badly wrong, so that when she laid the weird of it out, he was less stunned by it than he should have been.

Donald and Annie and her man had waited with the horses and even then Annie had known something was wrong. Then the alarm went and Donald announced he was leaving, though he could only manage the horse he rode and two others – the other two he left with Nichol and Annie 'for mercy'.

'Nichol is wild over Roger,' she went on in a panicked, shrill whisper. 'He waited only to tackle him – he heard us . . . exchanging auld whispers in the coal house. He cast loose the horse he held and has gone hunting Black Roger in the dark.'

She had brought this mount a little way, hoping to meet her old lover first, Hal thought and cursed them both.

'Oh, Christ's Mercy,' Annie declared, giving up the reins to him and sinking down in the slush. 'I did not want either of them harmed. In the name of God, I did not want any of this.'

Hal felt the rush of it – they were not so different, he and Annie, caught up in madness. He patted her awkwardly, as you would a sick dog, then left her there and went back to the road, trailing the one horse and looking for Kirkpatrick.

He was where Hal had left him, still hobbling desperately, but he stopped when he heard the hooves ring on the frozen ruts. Then his face got grim through the pain.

'One?'

Hal told him, swiftly and Kirkpatrick groaned and hauled himself to the stirrup leather.

'Aye. Well, there ye have it. Now ye can say that I am mainly for sense, save ower that wummin and have yer revenge.'

'Haul yourself up,' Hal declared. 'We can ride double. Get settled while I have a listen for the hounds.'

He moved off, cocking his head and straining to hear deep

into the dark, judging by the questing bell of the dogs whether they were on the scent or still looking. There was a sudden movement behind him and he turned, in time to see the dark figure spring out of the shadow between two howfs and run at Kirkpatrick's back.

Kirkpatrick, laboriously hauling himself into the saddle of the patient mount, heard the final boot scuff too late; the blow smacked him in the back, slammed him into the horse, which skittered away and let Kirkpatrick fall and roll in the slush.

He knew he had been attacked and by whom, knew he had been stabbed, too, and was astonished by it, for he had never been in all his life so far. So that is what it is like to have the knife in, he thought, that terrible feeling of steel violating a place it should not be, that sickening, sucking grip of his own flesh, as if reluctant to see the blade withdrawn. Then the burn hit him and he struggled to rise.

'Ye filthy boo,' Nichol was spitting, breathing hard and standing straddle-legged. 'Ye golach gowk-spit. I will learn ye to get on my wummin . . .'

He was cursing half in triumph, half in horror at what he had done, then turned and bellowed at the top of his voice.

'Here. Over here. I have Black Roger . . .'

Then he remembered the reputation of the man who was struggling back to his weaving legs and whirled to face him, uncertain of what to do and afraid to close and finish it. The sudden clack of boots behind him made him whirl again, in time to see Hal come running up, the great blade of the sword bright in one hand.

Nichol yelped and fled, shrieking; Hal let him and darted to where Kirkpatrick, down on his one good knee, was gasping.

'Christ and all His Saints,' he panted. 'That is sore.'

'You are alive yet,' Hal said, lifting him so that he grunted with pain.

The hounds were close, their baying loud. Hal forced

Kirkpatrick up into the saddle, then looked steadily into the man's pain-filled eyes.

'Get gone back to your king,' he said flatly. 'Tell Dog Boy what happened here.'

Kirkpatrick knew that the horse would not outrun the dogs with two, knew what Hal was going to do and almost railed against it, but the hand came down on the horse's rump and it sprang away into the night, leaving Kirkpatrick with all he could do to hang on as it went.

Hal was aware of what he had done, what was coming, with the small part of his mind not calculating the trajectory of the arrowing dogs. If he thought at all of whether Kirkpatrick deserved this, or whether this was some martyr's posturing in the Kingdom's Cause, it never registered more than a flicker.

He was here. He was a knight, defending the back of a weaker man who, for all his faults, had more to offer his king. It was enough . . .

The first dog darted out like a slim wraith and Hal stepped sideways, slashed once and left it tumbling behind him, yelping. The second he speared, but the wrench of it tore the sword from his grasp and then the rush of men came up, led by Fitzwalter and the Hospitaller, the fat young Ross lad peching up behind.

'Alive,' roared Fitzwalter. 'Alive . . .'

Hal fought with fists and boots and teeth, until something crashed on him, a world of pain and dark scarlet, as if he had dived into a bloody pool that grew black and old the deeper he fell.

Then there was darkness only.

EPILOGUE

Crossraguel Abbey, Ayrshire
Feast of St Drostan, July, 1307

The fields lolled, the forest was still, both breathing in the hot air of noon through leaves and grasses, sifted with dragonflies, green frogs and brown toads all looking to the relief of water. There were curlews and hares and squirrels – but most of all, there were flies.

They came to feast on the bloat of dead cattle and sheep, rising off the carcasses as thick as the smoke that curled from the abbey buildings. Folk moved with cloths over their mouths against the stink and even the hardiest of them winced at the smell.

'Bad cess to them,' Jamie Douglas said and the Dog Boy, looking at the bloodied, snarling muzzles of the abbot's dead hounds, could only agree. Bad cess to the English, who had viciously swiped one petulant claw at the defenceless, as if to reassure themselves that they were still in charge despite being beaten at Loudon Hill scant weeks before.

That had been the garland on a new spring. There had been a long hard winter of exile and then, as the thaw melted everything to drip and yellow, the news went out, leaping from head to head like wildfire.

The King was back.

Slowly, like a winter bear emerging from its cave, the Scots crawled out into the Kingdom and started to make their mark against the surprised English.

Kirkpatrick had been busy, too, with coin and promises, most of which came to ripeness – the last fruits had arrived only the night before, clutched in the brown mouth of a man who looked like a packman and had been taught as a priest.

There were a score or more of them, men and women both. Anonymous as dust and dark, they went where Kirkpatrick sent them and did as they were bid for revenge, the promise of advancement or – and Kirkpatrick's cynical nature was amazed by it – increasingly for belief in the King and the Kingdom.

This one brought news.

'He's dead,' the man said and, for a moment, Kirkpatrick felt the coursing shock of it plunge him to limpness – then the next words rushed him with relief.

'At Burgh on the Sands, a week or less. They have not told the army yet.'

Longshanks. The news should have raised Kirkpatrick up, but he was too relieved that it was not the other man he had set agents to watching. Not Hal, then – Kirkpatrick blew out his cheeks. He had found where Hal was held and did not understand why the man was still alive. But he was, though no closer to rescue than before.

Now Kirkpatrick waited impatiently while the abbot of the charred Crossraguel, grim and resigned, accepted the commiserations of his king – after all, the Bruces of Carrick had founded the place and it was donations from there that kept it going. So the abbot tried to ignore the ruin and war that had been brought to him, smiled and bowed and fervently agreed to keep perpetual Mass for the souls of the King's brothers, Thomas and Alexander, who had been slain at the start of the year.

The chapel was a miracle of beauty, left untouched even

381

by de Valence's rabble. It was a beautiful kingfisher of stone, small and perfect as a jewel, whose glowing painted walls were barely smoked by time, tallow and incense.

Bruce genuflected and then knelt, placing his hands on the eternal, untarnished altar as if to force it to prevail over the memory of those he mourned. He remained kneeling while all those half-in and half-out of the dimmed cool vault of it dared not come any closer, even though some were kin. Even the King's chaplain remained outside, hands clasped inside his sleeves and head bowed.

They looked at the disordered, bowed head, the long, scarred face and the hands laid flat on the cold stone and thought he looked the very image of a warrior king, bowing before his Maker to ask for mercy and peace for those lost and for help in returning to claim the Kingdom from the Plantagenet father and son. They lowered their own heads, for they were back in the Kingdom – and would need all of God's help to stay.

Bruce felt them like the rustle of moths in darkness, his mind full of the sins he had committed – and the ones yet to come – while the harsh taint of burning seemed to heighten the loss of two more of his brothers; Alexander, especially, was a crushing ache, for Bruce would miss the inciteful young mind.

Then there were the others, the defectors and waverers – Randolph, his own nephew, taken at Methven and pardoned into King Edward's good grace on condition that he fought for the English; that he had so readily agreed to it was what rankled. And young David Strathbogie, new Earl of Atholl, who had been panicked enough to run off and clamour for English mercy from the very king who had hanged his father.

He heard the sudden burst of wild laughter, angrily shushed, that marked where Jamie Douglas had arrived from yet another *herschip* raid; even he had wavered and sent a letter that seemed to beg King Edward's mercy. The success at Loudon Hill had forestalled him and both he and Bruce pretended no such letter had happened at all, yet it was an ache to Bruce that even Black Sir James, who so hated the English, had been brought low enough to offer a hand to them.

But young Alexander Bruce was the worst loss, the more so because all he had wanted was to be a scholar. Now only Kirkpatrick knew the secret he and Alexander had shared and Bruce was aware of the irony of events; I am returned and my forces swell daily, but even as my kingdom grows the circle of those I can trust shrinks.

As if in response, Kirkpatrick hirpled up, pushing through the throng, even shouldering past the scowl of the last brother, Edward.

Kirkpatrick felt as he knew he must look – grey-faced and sick. Nichol's knife had missed vitals by a fingerwidth and the recovery from it had been seven long, feverish and painful months; even now he was not fit for much – yet he was still invaluable to his king, more so now than ever.

In the dim of the chapel he waited until Bruce had raised himself up, crossed himself and turned back into the world. Then he said it, having thought of ways to present it all the limping way here and discarding them at the last.

'Longshanks is dead,' he said flatly. 'Has been for a week or more, but they will not announce it yet for fear of taking the heart out of the army. They wait for the son to arrive.'

There was a long pause and Kirkpatrick knew that others had heard him say it – the sudden shouts rippled out as the news leaped from head to head.

Bruce did not need to ask if Kirkpatrick was sure. Instead, he turned away, blinded by a sudden spring of tears and Kirkpatrick looked on, amazed; the Covetous King had slaughtered three of his brothers, imprisoned his queen, his sisters and daughter – yet Bruce wept for him.

Bruce was surprised himself, yet he knew the lie of it and knew, also, that everyone had seen the same and was marvelling at it. The tale would spread, of the saintly king who could weep for the death of his worst enemy, though the truth was something Bruce would never admit – that it was simple relief and release.

Longshanks was dead. This is the moment I should have waited for, he thought, the moment to claim the throne. If he had waited until now, if he had never gone to Greyfriars, so much might have been different – Thomas and Niall and Alexander . . .

He threw it from him with a violent shake of his head and turned into Kirkpatrick's worried frown, not helped by the sight of his king's face, the livid scar above and below the left eye and the still unhealed blight of his right cheek.

Yet the King was smiling and his eyes glittered as he looked at all the expectant faces.

'The pard is dead – now the lion can roar,' he said and they murmured their approval. The abbot began offering thanks to God, sonorous and fervent, while folk bowed, crossed themselves and knelt.

Bruce had a sudden vision of his grandfather's face, grim as a shroud. The Competitor had been the one who had dinned into him the justice and rights of the Bruce claims to kingship, pointedly ignoring the disapproving scowls of Bruce's own father, who seemed to have turned his back on all of that.

Until now, Bruce had reviled his father for his lack of spine, for not having the commitment that drove The Competitor and himself. Hag-ridden, he had thought, by the Curse of Malachy.

Now he knew the truth that his father had realized long before – there was no God in the right of the Bruces to rule. Brothers, friends, marriage, the grace of golden opinion, peace of mind, the very wine of life – even eating and sleeping – had all been subsumed and sold for a throne and what went with it. Smiling lies and mouthed honour, deceptions, delusions and the accusing whispers of Judas. Scorpions of the soul. The Curse of Malachy.

Ambition, he now knew, was the Devil.

The world had ended days ago, yet somehow people moved and spoke and acted as if it had not. The Royal clerk himself found that there were still matters to attend to, ones which always took him back to the room, laden with sweet-smelling flowers and herbs and burning incense that still failed to hide the stink.

He was here again, standing at the door of the room where the world had ended, with his head down so that all he saw were the clacking boots that arrived – green and red leather, fine heels and Cordoban workmanship, all muddied with hard travel.

'You are?'

He raised his head into the eyes of the Lord of Caernarvon, seeing the resemblance, like a blur in water, to his beloved king. He is as tall, he thought . . .

'Norbert the Notary,' said a voice at Caernarvon's elbow as the clerk hesitated. The Lord Monthermer, he noted, struggling to find his voice.

'You took my father's last words down?' demanded Edward and Norbert nodded, fumbling for the parchment; Edward waved impatiently, then indicated the closed door.

'In there?'

Norbert nodded again and Monthermer stepped forward and flung it open, then recoiled at the smell, cupping his nose and mouth with one hand.

'A week dead,' Edward said thinly, 'in this damp heat and having died of a bloody flux of the bowel. You should have expected that, my lord – what did he say, at the end?'

Norbert, taken by surprise at the last sharply-barked question, hummed and erred, then brought out the parchment of it, though the truth was that he knew it by heart.

'He wishes his heart removed to the minster in London,' he

croaked. 'His body is to be boiled and the bones casked up and placed at the head of the army, for he swore to invade Scotland and so he will.'

There was silence, for a moment, then Edward stirred.

'Did he now. Nothing else?'

Norbert cleared his throat nervously.

'*Pactum serva*,' he answered and saw the prince's drooping eye flicker a little. *Pactum Serva* – hold to the vow.

'Is there more?'

Like a father's love, thought Marmaduke Thweng, coming up in time to hear this. You will find none of that, new little king, only your da's reminder of what you swore at the Feast of Swans. Then he took to breathing through his mouth against the smell, noting the surreptitious attempts by all the others in the coterie to ward it off in some way.

Edward did not seem to notice them or the smell, but his next words gave the lie to it.

'Cask him up. Lead line it – strip the church roof here if you have to. We will take him south for burial.'

Norbert blinked.

'My lord,' he began. 'The King's command . . .'

'Is that you tomb up the dead man in the room,' Edward declared in a grim voice. 'And do something about the stink. Am I understood?'

He did not wait for a reply, but walked off, while Monthermer closed the door on Edward the First and turned to Norbert.

'You have annoyed your king, notary,' he said with a sharp smile. 'I would start running and catch up with events if I were you. That and look for a new position.'

Norbert swallowed hard and then looked at the lists clutched to wrinkled ruin in his sweaty fists, all the prisoners awaiting the King's pleasure in castles scattered all over the north. The most dangerous, those who had assisted in crowning the rebel king or colluded in the murder of the lord of Badenoch, had been granted the King's peace until he decided on their fate.

Three miles, three furlongs and three acre-breadths, nine feet, nine palms and three barley-corns, he thought, the mystical radius of the verge of the King's peace. Within it, no man was to come to harm. But the world had ended and that king was dead – did his peace still exist, in law or under God?

It was clear that the insouciant new king – Norbert still could not accept it completely – was in no mood to consider the matter. So let the captives languish, he thought, with a sudden, sharp rebellion of his own, until this new king is remembered of them and comes to me. Or someone like me, he added, recalling Monthermer's parting words.

Out in the air, folk breathed easier, benisoned by the persistent cold drizzle of rain which had suddenly relieved the oppressive heat in a thunderstorm the night before.

'What of the army?' asked Marmaduke Thweng. 'Do you join it, my lord? Or go south with your father?'

Edward sighed. The army waited under de Valence to lumber north on a pointless exercise that would add to the crippling debt that was his inheritance. Debt and boiled bones my father left, he thought bitterly, yet no loving final words for me.

He wanted to be in Langley, swimming. Digging a ditch. It came to him, in a sudden heady rush, that he could do that without worry now.

He looked round at the assembled lords, more suspicious of them than he was of the Scots; Monthermer arrived, smiling blandly and bowing and Edward bowed back. A mummery, he thought savagely – his sister, Joan, had just died and she had been Monthermer's wife, so that the lowborn former household knight had enjoyed the titles of Earl of Hartford and Gloucester, and added Earl of Atholl to them after Strathbogie had been hanged.

Now, of course, he had nothing – Joan's young son Gilbert had the first two titles restored to him on his mother's death and young David Strathbogie had been given his Atholl lands back, so that Monthermer had a pile of gold in lieu.

Half of it from the royal coffer, Edward realized with bitter anger, yet another debt my father left. From having three earldoms Monthermer now had no title at all – and Edward did not trust him; Gaveston had been sure the man had been too friendly with Bruce years before.

Gaveston. The ache for him was intolerable . . .

'Bruce is gathering strength, Your Grace,' added a voice, deep as a bear's. 'Since he kicked de Valence's arse at Loudon Hill, he and the raggle he commands have been strutting. Folk believe more and more in him and that cursed lie being preached by hedge-priests, that the death of your father is a prophecy from Merlin heralding liberty for Scots and Welsh, in concert against us.'

It was delivered firmly by Sir John Segrave, all grim in black and silver, and had obviously been rehearsed – though Edward knew the truth of it well enough already. Bruce, curse him.

'We must let them know differently,' Segrave added and Edward closed his eyes briefly against the beat of it.

The truth was that the army his father had so expensively and painstakingly gathered would never meet a Scots army stupid enough to face it. It would march up and down in a pointless *chevauchee* and then retreat south again, before it melted away. Everyone knew it, but the ritual dance of it would have to be followed one more time.

After, Edward thought viciously – the crown is on MY head . . .

'First, I will have to at least escort my father some of the way south,' Edward pointed out and no-one could argue with that. 'To York seems fitting enough. Then I will need to be crowned king, my lords, before I lead any army.'

In MY name, he thought triumphantly. Not my father's, nor led by his bloody boiled bones. His time is done – an exultant thought struck him like a thunderbolt.

'Send to France,' he ordered to anyone who was listening. 'Fetch my loving brother Lord Gaveston and the others who languish there. If we are to have a coronation and a war, we will need all the lords of the realm.'

Segrave looked darkly at Thweng, who merely drooped his moustache a little more and cocked a jaundiced eye at the rain. St Swithun's Day, he noted – there will be forty more days like this if the prophecy of the saint holds true.

Hopefully, by the time the King is ready for the army, neither it nor its commanders will be too damp or hungry to appreciate it. He looked at Segrave and saw the scowl that gave lie to hope.

Thweng hunched his shoulders, against the weather and the bad cess of the moment. Once more, he thought, we will scour the north and bring fire and sword to everyone in it, making a place where wolves survive while sheep go under. And all the fighting men of that land have wolves as godfathers; one day those beasts will bite us back . . .

Cold rain and Black John, he thought bleakly. Not the recipe for a happy war.

AUTHOR'S NOTE

The era portrayed here is one which defined both the Kingdom of Scotland and its people, large and small. The initial heady rush of rebellion, the successes – and disasters – of Wallace's tenure as Scotland's leader are long gone and only the iron will of the man himself remains, unbending and resolute.

It is easy to hold Wallace and Bruce up against one another and see the black and white of the former and the many shades of grey in the latter – but, as always, the world is more complex than that.

Wallace's adherence to the kingship of John Balliol is never fully explained in any account. It seems obsessive and stubborn to me, which is the stamp of the man in general. In the end it was also pointless and Bruce, who had realized this long before, could not fight for the return of a Comyn-backed king who not only represented the end of Bruce hopes for the throne, but a man who did not even want the crown.

Kept alive by Comyn desires, until it was clear there was no hope, exiled John Balliol had only one function left – to pass on the legacy to his son and so keep alive the claims and hopes of the Dispossessed, those Scots lords who had lost their lands in supporting King Edward.

By the opening of this book, the small battle at Happrew

– in Scotland most battles were between no more than a few hundred men a side – throws the whole of Scotland's grief into stark relief.

On this bleak moorland in the Borders, Bruce fought for the English and Wallace for the last dying echoes of the rebellion crushed at Falkirk years before. Whether they met in personal combat on that field is unknown, but given the small size of the forces, the delicious what-if of it is too good to pass up.

Wallace, last hold-out of a war-weary Scotland, is not only increasingly isolated but vilified by the commonality; the darling freedom-fighter of earlier years is now simply standing in the way of everyone else's peace to raise crops and family.

Did Bruce betray him? Probably not, but he was capable of it – and some Scot did, for the point of King Edward's cunning exercise was not only to capture this rebel figurehead, but have his own former supporters do it.

The Apostle rubies, of course, are fiction – though the Holy Rood of Scotland is not. Taken south with other coronation regalia, it would have been placed in the Minster Treasury, which was robbed in 1303 by Richard of Pudlicote and others. The equivalent of a year's tax revenues was removed and most of the thieves got away.

King Edward's wrath was considerable, so much so that he had Pudlicote flayed and his skin nailed to the door of Westminster Abbey. Yet the Longshanks character is such that it is perfectly possible for him to have pardoned Wallace if that man had shown the least remorse for his alleged crimes. The Bruce character is such that, knowing this, he might easily have taken steps to ensure that it could never happen, by planting evidence of Wallace involvement in the Minster burglaries. That King Edward would never forgive.

But this is primarily a story of relationships. Bruce with his perceived friends and known enemies – and himself. King Edward with his son, his barons – and himself. Hal, Isabel, the Earl of Buchan, Lamprecht and the secretive Kirkpatrick –

the complex weave of plot, counterplot and paranoia are the pillars of a kingdom at war with itself.

So, by the time of the murder in Greyfriars, when Bruce slays Red John Comyn, Hal cannot be convinced that the soul-searching agony of Bruce is entirely real – and that view has persisted. Did Bruce plan the murder of Red John, removing yet another impediment to the throne? Or was it a moment of madness, which resulted in a premature rebellion? Some 700 years later, I still cannot make my own mind up and neither can most scholars.

The end result, planned or not, was a disaster for Bruce – the small support he garnered was smashed apart by the rout at Methven, so that only his own loyal retainers stayed with him. Yet, just as all seemed lost, the Cause recovered and, falteringly, began the long return to strength.

As ever, treat this as an uncovered cache of monkish scribblings which, when read by a flickering tallow candle, reveal fragments of lives lost both in time and legend.

If any mistakes or omissions jar – blow out the light and accept my apologies.

LIST OF CHARACTERS

ADDAF the Welshman
Typical soldier of the period, raised from the lands only recently conquered by Edward I. The Welsh prowess with the bow and spear was already noted, but the true power of the former – the massed ranks of Crecy and Agincourt – was a strategy still forming during the early Scottish Wars. Like all the Welsh, Addaf's loyalty to the English is tenuous, especially since, in the years since his involvement in the craft of war, he has become a contract captain – a mercenary.

BADENOCH, Lord of
The Badenochs were of the Comyn family and known as Red Comyn, because they adopted the same wheatsheaf heraldry as the Buchan Comyns, but on a red shield instead of blue. Sir John, second Lord of Badenoch, died in 1302 – of what had happened to him while a prisoner in the Tower, it is alleged – leaving the title to his son. Despite being married to Joan de Valence – sister to Aymer de Valence, Earl of Pembroke – John the Red Comyn was a driving force in early resistance to Edward I – and truer to the Scots cause than Bruce at the time. Despite the fact that the Earl of Buchan was, in the hierarchy of the time, ranked higher in stature than the Lord of Badenoch,

it was the Red Comyn who held the bloodline claim of the Comyn to the throne. His murder by Bruce and his men in Greyfriars Church, Dumfries in February 1306 spurred the Bruce lunge for the throne – and all that followed.

BANGTAIL HOB
Fictional character. One of Hal of Herdmanston's retainers, a typical Scots retinue fighter of the period – Chirnside Rowan, Sore Davey, Ill-Made are names of others, the common men of Lothian and the Border regions, the March, who formed the bulk and backbone of the armies on both sides.

BELLEJAMBE, Malise
Fictional character, the Earl of Buchan's sinister henchman and arch-rival of Kirkpatrick.

BEVERLEY, Gilbert of
A real character, though I have maligned him here. Mentioned in the 15th century epic poem on William Wallace by Blind Harry – which is one of the main 'source' documents for this period – Gilbert is probably Gilbert de Grimsby, whom Wallace's men rechristened Jop. Described as a man 'of great stature' and already 'some part grey', he was a Riccarton man by birth and had travelled far in Edward's service as 'a pursuivant in war' – though Harry says he consistently refused to bear arms. No doubt he was the 'Gilbert de Grimmesby' who carried the sacred banner of St John of Beverley in Edward's progress through Scotland after Dunbar, a distinguished service for which Edward directed Warenne to find him a living worth about twenty marks or pounds a year. Whether he was a Wallace relation is unknown, though I have intimated that because of his stature, the fact that he came from Riccarton, a Wallace stronghold, and that he quit the army shortly after his twenty marks had been confirmed (on October 13 1296) and supposedly joined the rebels.

BISSOT, Rossal De
Fictional character, though I have made him a descendant of the family who helped found the Templar order. Aware of the secret machinations to undermine and destroy the Order, he is attempting to prevent this.

BRUCE, Edward
Eldest of the Bruce siblings and the most reckless, with ambitions of his own. Impatient and impulsive, he was the strongest and most loyal right hand Robert Bruce had, though his ambition was eventually his undoing. His other brothers – second oldest Niall and the youngest, scholarly Alexander – did not survive the struggle to put brother Robert on the throne and, of Bruce's sisters, only Mary and Christina make an appearance here. Edward Bruce was eventually given the task of invading Ireland in the year after Bannockburn, a task he succeeded in, becoming High King of Ireland. However, in true rash style, he overreached himself once too often and died in the Battle of Faughart, 1318.

BRUCE, Robert
Any one of three. Robert, Earl of Carrick, later became King Robert I and is now known as Robert the Bruce. His father, also Robert, was Earl of Annandale (he renounced the titles of Carrick to his son when they fell to him because, under a technicality, he would have had to swear fealty to the Comyn for them and would not do that). Finally, there is Bruce's grandfather, Robert, known as The Competitor from the way he assiduously pursued the Bruce rights to the throne of Scotland, passing the torch on to his grandson.

BUCHAN, Countess of
Isabel MacDuff, one of the powerful, though fragmented, ruling house of Fife. She acted as the official 'crowner' of Robert Bruce in 1306, a role always undertaken by a MacDuff

of Fife – but the only other one was her younger brother, held captive in England. In performing this, she not only defied her husband but the entire Comyn and Balliol families. Captured later, she was imprisoned, with the agreement of her husband, in a cage hung on the walls of Berwick Castle. Her character here is almost certainly maligned – most of the claims for her affair with Bruce were later Comyn propaganda – and the reality is that she probably never survived her imprisonment, since she vanishes from history after this point.

BUCHAN, Earl of
A powerful Comyn magnate, cousin to the Red Comyn Lord of Badenoch, he was the bitterest opponent of the Bruces. His wife, Isabel MacDuff, outraged her husband with her alleged affairs – and, worse still, betrayal of the Comyn cause in favour of the Bruce.

BURGH, Elizabeth de
Daughter of the powerful Red Earl of Ulster and Bruce's wife – and so Queen of Scotland. Captured by the treachery of the Earl of Ross, she was sent into captivity in the south of England for eight years, until ransomed following the Scottish victory at Bannockburn – where her father's forces fought for Edward II. She and Bruce subsequently had three children who reach adulthood, one of whom became David II, King of Scots.

CAMPBELL, Sir Neil
In Gaelic, his name is *Niall mac Cailein* – Neil, son of Colin – and historians originally tagged him as the eldest son of Sir Colin Campbell, the famed *Cailean Mór* (Black Colin) of Clan Campbell. Latterly, it is thought Colin Campbell's eldest was Neil's unsung brother Domnhall. Sir Neil was a trusted Bruce adherent from the earliest years – sent to Norway in 1293 with personal items for Robert the Bruce's sister, Isabella who

was queen there. By 1296, however, he had sworn fealty to Edward I and stayed that way until Bruce was crowned when he became one of the first adherents of the new king. Both Neil and Domnhall stayed loyal to Bruce in the depths of defeat and fought at Bannockburn. Sir Neil died in 1316.

CRAW, Sim
A real character – though Sim of Leadhouse is mentioned only once in history, as the inventor of the cunning scaling ladders with which James Douglas took Roxburgh by stealth in 1314. Here, he is Hal of Herdmanston's right-hand man, older than Hal, powerfully built and favouring a crossbow as a weapon.

DOG BOY
Fictional character, a peasant of age with the young James Douglas, with whom he was brought up in Douglas Castle. It is becoming clear to them both that the lowly Dog Boy is in fact a bastard son of Sir William Douglas and that Jamie is his half-brother. War has brought a sense of his own worth to the Dog Boy – and will elevate him further in the service of the Bruce.

DOUGLAS, James
Son of Sir William 'The Hardy' Douglas by his first wife, a Stewart whom he simply sent off to a convent in order to marry his second, Eleanor de Lovaigne. After the capture and death of his father, James went to Paris under the auspices of Lamberton, Bishop of St Andrews. He returned as a young man in the retinue of Lamberton, trying to persuade Edward I to restore his lands, now held by Clifford. Impatient, impassioned and angry, he joined Bruce's rebellion, rising to become one of Robert the Bruce's most trusted commanders. A slim, dark youth with a lisp, his courtly manner is at odds with the near-psychotic rage that possesses him in battle, fuelled by an undying hatred for the English.

DUNS, John

A Franciscan priest, known as Duns Scotus, he was one of the more important theologians and philosophers of the Middle Ages, nicknamed *Doctor Subtilis* for his penetrating thought. His involvement with the emergent Bruce and Church-fomented rebellion is pure fiction on my part – but he was expelled from the University of Paris for siding with then Pope Boniface in his feud with Philip the Fair of France over the taxation of church property. He died in 1308; the date of his death is traditionally given as November 8 and the same tradition has it that he was actually buried alive following a lapse into a coma. In the sixteenth century, his teachings were dismissed as 'sophistry' and gave rise to the word 'dunce', meaning someone incapable of scholarship. The typical dunce's hat came from his own conical monk's cap. See Bernard of Kilwinning, below.

EDWARD I

King of England and the oldest ruler with the longest reign so far. At the time of this novel he is facing the prospect of failure: failing to become ruler of a united Britain, and above all failing to achieve his true amibition, a Crusade to free the Holy Land. He is also aware that his son and eventual heir is terribly flawed. Yet there is still power and cunning in the old pard . . .

EDWARD II

A tragic figure in many ways, overshadowed by his father – whom he seems to have loved and hated in equal measure – and ignored by him save when it mattered. Probably as a direct result of that tortured relationship, his character was deeply flawed, the main fault being a tendency to become obsessively possessive with others, the favourites and promoting them at the expense of others. At this time, the favourite was Piers Gaveston.

KILWINNING, Bernard of

A Tironensian abbot in the time of the Scottish wars, he first appears as Abbot of Kilwinning in 1296, then vanishes for a decade before re-emerging as Bruce's Chancellor, then Abbot of Arbroath. There is no evidence that he was clerk to John Duns – but he is the one generally credited with drafting the Declaration of Arbroath and later became Bishop of the Isles. He died in 1331.

KIRKPATRICK, Roger

Fictional character, but based on the real Sir Roger Kirkpatrick of Closeburn, whom I have as kin to the fictional one. This is because my Kirkpatrick is a staunch Bruce supporter from the outset and the real Sir Roger was not – he even fought for Clifford in the English retinue at Falkirk. In later years, he adopted the words 'Mak' siccar' (make sure) as a motto and a bloody hand holding a dagger as his heraldic device.

LAMBERTON, Bishop

Bishop of St Andrews and now thought to be one William Cunningham from Kilmaurs, he owed his elevation to Wallace and supported both him and Robert the Bruce. Chosen as the third Guardian, to stand between Bruce and Red John Comyn in 1299, he was used as a diplomat and envoy, while diverting the funds from his vast diocese to help the Cause.

LAMPRECHT

Fictional character, a relic-seller and pardoner from Cologne, who speaks *lingua franca*, that mix of common Latin, French, Spanish and other Mediterranean languages originally used by crusaders to make themselves understood. Lamprecht pretends to be a pilgrim who has travelled to Jerusalem – but he has only ever been into Moorish Spain and has learned *lingua franca* while moving around the countries bordering the Mediterranean. A sometime spy and agent of those who pay most, he becomes involved in the Buchan plot against Hal of Herdmanston.

MALENFAUNT, Sir Robert

Real family, fictional character – a knight of dubious renown who is smarting over being duped by Bruce, Hal and others into releasing Isabel MacDuff, captured at Stirling Bridge, to what he assumes is her husband. This makes him a suitable tool for use by the Comyn and Buchan.

MONTAILLIOU, James of

Montailliou is a real place, but this is a fictional character – a physicker of dubious standard, who professes to be a doctor but is probably no better than a barber-surgeon. Nevertheless, he is Bruce's physician and seemingly loyal because he is a Cathar, a heretical Christian whose sect is being persecuted in Langue D'Oc, and owes his safety to his position. He is also party to the Bruce fears of leprosy, a dangerous secret to hold . . .

SEGRAVE, Sir John

Black John, appointed Governor of Scotland at one time and, with his son Stephen, much hated English commander who was responsible for taking Wallace back to London in chains.

SIENTCLER, Sir Henry of Herdmanston

Fictional character. Known as Hal, he is the son and heir to Herdmanston, a lowly tower owing fealty to their kin, the Sientclers of Roslin. He is typical of the many poor nobles of Lothian who became embroiled in the wars on both sides of the divide. Hal himself is torn by doubts as to who he can trust, even between Wallace and Bruce, in a kingdom riven by family rivalries and betrayals. The Sientclers of Herdmanston are a little known branch of that family, appearing prominently for one brief moment in 15th century history. Herdmanston is now an anonymous pile of stones in a corner of a ploughed field and any descriptions of it are pure conjecture on my part.

SIENTCLER, Sir Henry of Roslin
In reality, held as a hostage for ransom by the English, with his father also held in the Tower. Eventually ransomed he later fought in the Battle of Roslin Glen alongside Red John Comyn and Sir Simon Fraser and against the English of Segrave and others, a famous victory for the Scots in 1303, when victories were scarce.

THWENG, Sir Marmaduke
Lord of Kilton in Yorkshire, a noted knight and married to a Lucia de Brus, distant kin to Bruce himself, Sir Marmaduke is the accepted, sensible face of English knighthood. A noted thief-taker – bounty hunter – in his own realm, he was also part of the tourney circuit with the young Robert Bruce. Fought at Stirling Bridge and was one of few to battle his way back to Stirling Castle, where he was eventually taken prisoner. Took part in subsequent campaigns against the Scots including Bannockburn, where, in his 60s, he fought until he could surrender personally to Bruce and was subsequently released without ransom.

VALENCE, Aymer de
Eventual second Earl of Pembroke, de Valence was related to the French royal house and was one of the Lords Ordainers who attempted to curb the power of Edward II and Gaveston. At this time he was the young, thrusting commander (knighted only in 1297) and trusted by Edward I with control of the English army in Scotland.

WALLACE, William
The legend who led Scottish forces to victory at Stirling Bridge and defeat at Falkirk was forced to relinquish his Guardianship

and eventually betrayed to the English. Described as a 'chief of brigands' at the time of the rebellion, he was barely of the nobility of Scotland and accepted by them unwillingly and only while he was winning. He was, however, the only one of them all who never gave in, or changed sides. The arguments regarding his prowess continue – there is, even allowing for hero-worship, enough evidence to show his personal fighting skills, though historians disagree on his expertise with commanding large bodies of men, claiming Moray was the one with this (being a noble born and so trained to it). They offer as proof of this, the glorious victory of Stirling Bridge with Moray present, and the disaster at Falkirk, organized by Wallace alone. This seems dubious to me – if nothing else, what few documents we have reveal Wallace as a man who, if not skilled in diplomacy and dealing with foreign interests, had the wit to surround himself with those who did. Similarly, he would not be short of experts in the grand tactics of the age – but no battle ever goes to plan. If you look closely at the battle at Falkirk, it becomes clear that even the victor, King Edward 1, greatest warrior general in Christendom, badly mismanaged the affair himself and almost lost control of his knights. Ironically, of course, it was Wallace's own brigand tactics that became the norm for Scottish armies too small and weak to oppose their neighbour's forces – hit and run, almost all the way down to Bannockburn. However, the one glaring flaw in the Wallace character is also the one which made him great – the undying obsession with putting John Balliol back on the throne and a refusal to admit when that cause was lost.

WISHART, Robert, Bishop of Glasgow
One of the original Guardians of Scotland following the death of King Alexander III – and partly responsible for inviting Edward I to preside over subsequent proceedings – Bishop Wishart became the engine of rebellion and a staunch supporter of first Wallace, then Bruce. He and Lamberton, Bishop of St

Andrews, were instrumental in bringing support to Bruce. The bishops' reasons for rebelling were simple – the Scottish church was responsible only to the Pope, who appointed all their senior prelates; they did not want the English version, where the King performed that function, and could only maintain that difference if Scotland remained a distinct and separate realm.

GLOSSARY

ALAUNT
Large, short-coated hunting dog of the mastiff type, used for bringing down large game.

AVENTAIL
Neck guard on a helmet, usually made from MAILLE.

BABERY
Term for any ape, but applied to the carvings on the eaves of churches – which were wonderful confections of people, beasts and mythology – apes featured prominently, frequently wearing the garb of bishops and priests as a sly joke by masons.

BACHLE
Untidy, shabby or clumsy. Can be used to describe bad workmanship, a slouching walk, or simply to insult someone as useless and more. Still in use, though more usually spelled bauchle.

BARBETTE
Women's clothing – a cloth chin strap to hide the neck and chin, to which was attached a variety of headgear, most commonly the little round hat known then as a turret and nowadays as

a pillbox. Compulsory for married women in public and still seen on nuns today.

BASCINET
Open-faced steel helm, sometimes covering down to the ears. The medieval knight or man-at-arms usually wore, in order from inside out – a padded arming cap, a COIF of MAILLE, a bascinet and, finally, the full-faced metal helmet, or HEAUME.

BATTUE
A hunt organized as if it was a mêlée at a TOURNEY, usually involving indiscriminate slaughter of beasts driven into an ambush.

BLACK-AFFRONTED
Ashamed. A Scots term still in use today and probably derived from the act of covering your heraldic shield (affronty is a heraldic term) in order not to be recognized. Scots knights did this as they fled from Methven, in order not to be subsequently accused of being supporters of Bruce.

BLIAUT
An overtunic worn by noble women and men from the 11th to the 13th century, notable for the excessively long drape of sleeve from the elbow in women, from mid forearm on the male version.

BRAIES
Linen, knee-length drawers, as worn by every male in the Middle Ages. Women had no true undergarments, though 'small clothes' were sometimes worn by gentlewomen.

CAMILIS
The usually white, flowing overtunic worn by some knights. Despite military sense dictating the use of tight-fitting clothing

in close-combat, the urge for display frequently led to extravagant and impractical garments and headgear.

CATERAN
Originally a term to denote any fighting man from the Highlands, it became synonymous with any marauders or cattle thieves. See also KERN.

CHARE
A narrow, twisting medieval alleyway. See also VENNEL.

CHAUSSE
Legging, originally made like stockings until eventually joined in the middle to become trousers. MAILLE chausse were ring-metal leggings including the foot and with a leather sole.

CHIEL
Scottish term for a man. See also QUINE.

CHIRMYNG
Charming – most commonly used (as here) as the collective noun for finches or goldfinches.

CHITTERING
Scots for chattering.

CLOOTS
Scots word for clothing and still used today for any old rags. The term 'auld cloots and gruel' used in the story means 'of no account' or 'everyday'.

COIF
Any hood which covered the head and shoulders. Usually refers to one made of ring-metal and worn like a modern balaclava.

COMMUNITY OF THE REALM
Medieval Scotland being enlightened – this referred to the rule of law by all the Kingdom, not just the King. However, it *was* the Middle Ages, so the Community referred to was one either with land and title, or rich merchant burghers from the towns. The commonality – peasants – of the realm still had no say.

COTE/SURCOTE
Old English and French for men's and women's outergarment. The male cote was a tunic varying in length half-way between waist and knee, sometimes slit for riding if the wearer was noble and almost always 'deviced' (ie bearing the wearer's heraldry) if you're someone of account. The TABARD was a sleeveless version. King John Balliol, whose ceremonial tabard was ritually stripped of the heraldic device, became known as 'Toom Tabard' (Empty Cote) forever after.

COWPED
Scots word for tumbled.

COZEN
To trick or deceive.

CROCKARD
The stability of Edward I's coinage had the unfortunate side-effect of allowing merchants to take the silver penny abroad as currency. This enabled unscrupulous Low Country lords to mint a debased version, which became known as a crockard. See also POLLARD.

CROTEY
The dung of hare or coney (rabbit). See FIANTS.

DESTRIER
Not a breed, but a type of horse – the warhorse of the Middle Ages was powerful, trained and cosseted to the

point where it was to be used, at which point, depending on the importance of the affray, it was considered expendable. Destrier is from the Vulgar Latin *dextarius,* meaning right-handed, either from the horse's gait, or that it was mounted from the right side. Not as large, or heavy-footed as usually portrayed they were about the size of a good riding horse of today, though more muscled in the rear. They were all stallions and each one, in 1297, cost as much as seven ordinary riding horses.

DRIECH
Scots term to describe a dull, grey day where it never actually rains but you still get wet from an unseen drizzle.

EECHIE-OCHIE
Neither one thing nor another.

FASH
To worry. The phrase never fash means don't worry.

FIANTS
The dung of the fox, wolf, boar or badger.

FOOTERING
Fumbling.

GAMBESON
Knee-length tunic, sewn with quilted flutes stuffed with wool if you could afford it or straw if you could not. Designed to be worn over or under MAILLE to negate blunt trauma but frequently worn as the sole armour protection of the less well-off. A lighter version, brought back from the Crusades, was known as an aketon, from the Arabic *al qutn,* or cotton, with which it was stuffed.

GARDECORPS
A cape-like overtunic with a slit under the armpit so that you could wear it sleeveless, its shapelessness appealed to those of a larger size. As if to compensate, many such garments were given BLIAUT style sleeves, sometimes with long tippets, or dagged hems, while the collar and cuffs were trimmed with expensive fur.

GARRON
Small, hardy Highland pony used widely by the HOBILARS of both sides, though more favoured by Scottish foot. It enabled them to move fast, raid like cavalry and yet dismount to fight on foot if faced by the knight on his heavy horse – and no archers to hand.

GLAUR
Scots word for sticky mud.

GRALLOCH
The contents of a stag's stomach which has been 'unmade' after a kill. The gralloch, in medieval times, went to the hounds as a reward.

GUDDLE
Scots term which, as a verb, means to grope blindly. As a noun it means mix-up or confusion.

HAAR
One of the many Scots words for rain – this refers to a wet mist.

HEAUME
Another name for the large medieval helmet. More properly, it was given to the later TOURNEY helmet, which reached and was supported on the shoulders.

HERSCHIP
From hardship, a Scots term for vicious raids designed to lay waste and plunder a region to the detriment of the enemy.

HOBILAR
English word for light cavalry, recruited to counter the Scots raiders and so called because they were mounted on large ponies called hobyn. This gives us the modern child's toy, the hobby horse, as well as the generic name for horses everywhere – Dobbin.

HOOR
Scots pronunciation of whore.

HUMFY-BACKIT
Scots term for hunchback.

JACK
Origin of our word jacket, this was a variation on the aketon or GAMBESON and usually involved the addition of small metal plates sewn to the outside. Also known as *jazerant*.

JACOB'S PILLOW
The Stone of Scone was popularly believed in Scotland to be the same one consecrated to God by Jacob in the Book of Genesis, following a vision while he slept.

JALOUSE
The original Scots meaning was surmise. Some time in the 19th century, the English adopted it but, mysteriously, used it as jealous. It is used here in its original sense.

JEDDART STAFF
More properly known by this name in the 16th and 17th century Border country (the Jeddart refers to Jedburgh), the

weapon was essentially the same – a reinforced spear which also incorporated a thin cutting blade on one side and a hook on the other.

JUPON
A short, closely-tailored arming cote worn over MAILLE in action, to display your heraldry.

JURROCKS
Lowlife servant.

JUSTICIAR
An official appointed by the monarch, from the time of William Rufus, son of William the Conqueror, to ease the burden on overworked SHERIFFS.

KERN
Irish/Scots soldiery. Later, it came to refer to the Gallowglass warriors of Ireland.

KINE
Scots word for cattle.

KIST OF WHISTLES
Scots term for a covered, boiling cauldron or kettle, kist being any kind of container, from clothes chest to tomb.

LATCHBOW
Originally, a light crossbow with a simple latch release, it came to be a common term for all crossbows and arbalests.

LAW OF DEUTERONOMY
Specifically Deuteronomy 20, which states: *And when the LORD thy God hath delivered it into thine hands, thou shalt smite every male thereof with the edge of the sword: But the*

women, and the little ones, and the cattle, and all that is in the city, even all the spoil thereof, shalt thou take unto thyself; and thou shalt eat the spoil of thine enemies, which the LORD thy God hath given thee. Used by medieval Christian commanders to justify the sack and slaughter of any city which did not yield before a siege ram or ladder touched the walls.

LIMMER
A low, base fellow – also a prostitute.

MAILLE
The correct spelling of mail, which is also incorrectly referred to as chainmail and should be properly termed ring maille. The linked metal-ringed tunic worn by warriors since the early Roman period. By the 13th/14th century, these had evolved – for those who could afford it – into complete suits, with sleeves, mittens and integral COIF, or hood.

MAK' SICCAR
Make certain. A famous phrase uttered by Bruce's loyal follower Sir Roger Kirkpatrick of Closeburn shortly before he returned to Greyfriars Church to ensure the death of Bruce's rival, the Red Comyn. It became the motto of the Kirkpatrick family, under the crest of a bloody hand holding a dagger.

MESNIE
Can refer, loosely, to a medieval household, but more usually to the trusted group of knights who accompanied their lord to war and TOURNEY.

MILLINAR
Any knight or SERJEANT appointed to command a band on foot.

MOUDIEWART
Literally, a mole, but frequently used as an insult.

NEB
Scots word for nose.

NOTARY
Nowadays it is a person with legal training licensed by the state to perform certain legal acts, particularly witnessing signatures on legal documents. In the Middle Ages it was a man who could read, write, take notes and acted as clerk to a JUSTICIAR.

ORB
Scots word for young bird. See also SPEUGH.

OS
From the Latin, a mouth or opening – usually applied to the female parts, whether human or animal. In some cases, the os of hind was considered a delicacy.

PACHYDERM
Medieval classification usually applied to elephants, but which also included pigs and wild boar.

PAPINGO
The popinjay or parrot – any brightly coloured bird, or person who resembles one in dress or manner. Can also refer to an archery competition, where such a live bird was placed on a pole and used as a target. It still pertains to the present – there is an annual Papingo Shoot at Kilwinning Abbey – but the papingo target is no longer a bird, live or otherwise.

PAYNIM
Medieval term for heathen, particularly Muslims.

PLENARY INDULGENCE

The remittance of sins, granted by the Catholic church after confession and absolution. However, these could also be sold as a sort of cheque drawn on the Treasure House of Merit, an abuse which was widespread in the Middle Ages.

PLOOTERING

Scots word meaning to walk carelessly, with the added connotation of splashing, as through puddles or into marsh or mud.

POLLARD

A fake silver penny of Edward I's reign, so called either because of the miscast head (poll) of the monarch or because it had been clipped (pollarded) of some of its metal, making it smaller.

POW

Scots word which can either refer to the head (as in 'curly pow') or an expanse of water meadow cut up with small pools.

POWRIE

Scots Fairies which, as you might expect, are not ethereally-pretty winged creatures. They are short and wiry, with ragged pointed teeth and sharp claws like steel. They wear a red bonnet on their heads and are generally bearded with wrinkled aged faces. They kill by rolling boulders or tearing at people with their sharp claws. They then proceed to drink the blood of their victims and dip their hats in it, giving rise to their other name of Red Caps. In particular they haunt castles with a reputation for evil events in the past. Also known as Dunters.

PRIGG

Scots word meaning to beseech or plead.

QUINE
Scots word for a woman or a young girl. See CHIEL.

RIGG
Scots word for a strip of ploughed field.

SCAPULAR
Large length of cloth suspended from the shoulders – monastic scapulars originated as aprons worn by medieval monks, and were later extended to habits.

SCHILTRON
The first mention of the schiltron as a specific formation of spearmen appears to be at the Battle of Falkirk in 1297. There is, however, no reason to believe this is the first time such a formation was used and there are references to the Picts using blocks of spearmen in such a fashion. The name is thought to derive from the Middle English for shield troop.

SCRIEVING
Scots word – to move swiftly and smoothly.

SCRIVENER
Medieval term for anyone who could read and write.

SCULLION
Servant performing menial kitchen tasks.

SERJEANT
The armed 'middle class' of medieval England, only differing from a knight in that they had not been recognized as such. Equipment, training and skill were all more or less the same.

SERK
Scots word – originally Norse – for a shirt or undertunic.

SHERIFF
A contraction of the term 'shire reeve', he is the highest law officer in a county. A term and idea which has spread from England to many parts of the world, including the US and Canada. In Scotland, English sheriffs were particularly hated, none more so than Heselrigg, Sheriff of Lanark and the man Wallace famously killed to begin his part in the rebellion.

SKITE
Scots word meaning to slip or skate.

SLAISTER
Scots word meaning a dirty mess, or slovenly work.

SLEEKIT
Scots word for crafty or sly.

SLORACH
Scots word for a wet and disgusting mess of anything.

SNECK
Scots word for a bolt or latch on a door. Still in use today in the Borders and north of England in the term 'sneck lifter' – the last coin in a man's pocket, enough to let him open a pub door and buy a drink.

SONSIE
Scots word for a woman with a generous, hour-glass figure.

SPEUGH
Scots word for baby sparrow.

SPIER
Scots word meaning to inquire after, to question.

SPITAL
Medieval short-form of hospital, which was any place – usually in a monastery or abbey – which cared for the sick.

STAPPIT
Scots word for stuffed full.

STOOKS
Scots word for sheaves.

STRAMASH
Scots word for a noisy disturbance.

STRAVAIG
Scots word meaning to wander aimlessly.

STUSHIE
Scots word for being in a state of excitement. Also for a shouting argument.

SWEF
Medieval bastardized French for gently or softly.

TABARD
Medieval short tunic, sleeveless, or with shoulder pieces, designed to show a noble's heraldic device or arms – hence the term cote of arms. Still seen today on ceremonial heralds.

TAIT
Scots word for a little item or a small portion.

THOLE
Scots word meaning to suffer or to bear.

THRAWN
Scots word for twisted or misshapen, which can be applied equally to a tree, a face or a disposition.

TOLT
Medieval word for a tax, usually on wool.

TOURNEY
Simply put, this was the premier entertainment and sporting pursuit of the medieval gentleman. It involved, usually, the Mêlée, a mass of knights fighting each other. A Grand Mêlée could involve several hundred and be fought over a large distance – it was not a spectator sport. The object of the Mêlée was to unhorse your opponent and take him for ransom – as was expected in a real war – though the weapons were blunted for the tourney and no-one was expected to die or get hurt (though, of course, some did). Latterly, the one-on-one joust became more and more popular, simply because it *was* a spectator sport and everyone could see your skill.

TRAILBASTON
Medieval term for the itinerant judicial commission ordered by Edward I to combat outlaws and brigands, it became the name for the perpetrators themselves.

VENNEL
Scots word for alleyway.

WHEEN
Scots word for many, a lot.

YETT

Scots word for a door, originally applied to the grilled inner gate of a fortress.

ACKNOWLEDGEMENTS

As ever, the list of people who made this book possible is enough to form a rebel army – but, at the head of it stands Jock Simpson, unsung and long dead. He was my English teacher at St John's Grammar in Hamilton and the man who saw not only the flicker of a writer in the boy, but an interest in the history he was passionate about and which was not taught in any class I was in. If any man began my journey through 13th century Scotland and beyond, it was him.

As an uncaring youth, I failed to see what he had given me until much later and this is my way of saying a shameful sorry for never having acknowledged it while he lived. Hard on his heels, of course, has to come Nigel Tranter, whose books on Scotland's history, particularly the trilogy on Bruce, are hard acts to follow. I hope he is not birling in his grave too much.

I am also continually indebted to the members of Glasgow Vikings (www.glasgowvikings.co.uk) and the rest of the Vikings, national and international (www.vikingsonline.org.uk) who provide entertainment and education in several countries and have caused a beer drought in at least one small island. Although they are predominantly Viking, they are interested in all aspects of Scottish history and can gear up to fight at Bannockburn recreations at the drop of an iron hat. The upcoming 700th anniversary is keenly anticipated and I owe gratitude to the NTS and the Bannockburn Heritage Centre for their kind help in this and later volumes.

Katie Espiner, my editor at HarperCollins, has to be congratulated for taking no nonsense from this auld Scot and insisting, wee English beauty that she is, on not permitting me to descend into Scots-speak more than two or three times.

None of this would have been possible at all if my agent, James Gill of United Agents had not had vision to see the possibilities in my writing – I hoist my glass in his general direction.

The process of writing this has been encouraged by a firm band of fans, who have followed the Oathsworn and now want to carry on reading – my thanks especially to Warren Cummin, descendant of the very Comyn in the story, who takes a keen interest from the distant reaches of Canada.

More power to you all for your praise, criticism, comments and unfailing humour. I hope this one pleases you as much as the others seem to have done.